Making your Peace

Never Give Up : Book Six

by

Suzie Peters

GWL
PUBLISHING

First Published in 2022
by GWL Publishing
an imprint of Great War Literature Publishing LLP

Produced in United Kingdom

ISBN 978-1-910603-99-4 Paperback Edition

GWL Publishing
2 Little Breach
Chichester
PO19 5TX

www.gwlpublishing.co.uk

Dedication

For S.

Chapter One

Jemima

I park my Honda Accord at the front of the veterinary surgery, in one of the three spaces reserved for employees. I don't know why there are three, being as there are only two of us working here, but I guess that's one of life's mysteries. You know, like why the toast always lands butter side down, why there's never any ice cream in the deep freeze when I need it most… and why I had to fall for the most unattainable man in the world.

I'm talking about Doctor Oliver Gould. He takes unattainable to a whole new level. Not that he's unapproachable, or aloof. He's neither of those things. In fact, he's the opposite. He's kind, warm and helpful. Of course, there is the minor issue that he also happens to be my boss. That isn't the thing that makes him unattainable. It just makes falling for him a cliché… although there's not a lot I can do about it.

Because he's also gorgeous.

He's very tall, with broad shoulders, and his reddish-brown hair always looks like he just got out of bed. *If only…* As for his eyes, they're a kind of amber color, with tiny green flecks in them. If you're wondering how I know that, it's because I've looked. I do a lot of looking when it comes to Oliver… and not very much else.

It wasn't always like that. When Mom and I first moved here, at the beginning of last December, and I got the job as Oliver's receptionist,

I barely noticed him. That might sound crazy, considering I can't stop thinking about him now, but the only excuse I can give is that I was recovering from a broken heart – or at least a disappointed one. With hindsight, my heart can't have been broken. It never belonged to Donavan in the first place, so how could he break it?

Still, I'm not going to think about that now.

I need to get inside and start my working day. I know Oliver's first appointment is in twenty minutes, and sitting out here in my car won't get my computer turned on, or the coffee made.

I open the door, feeling a blast of icy wind, and pull my coat up around my chin as I get out, gazing at Oliver's Jeep, which is parked beside my car. I know he'll be inside already, preparing for the day, because he's like that. He's very diligent and good at his job… as well as being kind and helpful… and gorgeous.

But that's where the problem lies. Just about every woman in town seems to fall over herself to get to him. They're all the same… dragging their perfectly healthy pets into the surgery, just so they can spend thirty minutes with 'Doctor Gould'. He doesn't seem to object, and is universally pleasant to everyone… not just the pets, but their owners, too.

I can't really criticize them. After all, I enjoy spending time with him just as much as his clients. At least, I have since that day back in the summer, when I finally woke up from my disappointed heart, and noticed the perfect man leaning against the doorframe to his office. Somehow – and I really don't know how – he makes green scrubs look sexy, especially with his arms folded across his expansive chest. I stared at him, taking in the beauty of his face, and the way his muscles flexed when he breathed in and out, as he asked me to show in his next client. I don't know why I was staring. He didn't look any more handsome than usual, because that's not possible, and as far as I'm aware, he didn't sound any more sexy, either. He was just different.

That was when it happened.

Like a bolt of lightning.

I fell in love.

I don't suppose anyone can ever fully understand the reasons behind that. If they could, they'd bottle it, and make a fortune.

As it is, I just know from that day to this, I've been hopelessly in love with the man… and I mean hopelessly.

I walk to the glass door, pulling it open and take a quick glance down Main Street. Unlike Eastford, where I grew up, Sturbridge is much more of a sprawling town, its shops and facilities all spread out. Here by the veterinary surgery, we've got a sandwich shop, which I'm familiar with, because I go there every day, and a florist's, an attorney's office and a realtor. A little further down the street, there's a café and a restaurant, and Oliver's brother runs a counseling service from one of the buildings by the architect's office, I believe. The beauty salon is near there too.

Other than my hairdresser, who's called Cindy, I don't know any of the people who work in these places. I don't even know Oliver's brother. We've never met.

Why would we?

I duck inside, pulling the door closed, and shrug off my coat, hanging it up on the stand before going over to the corner of the room and turning on the Christmas tree lights. The tree is artificial, but enormous. It's so big that Oliver and I had to move the furniture around to fit it in. That's to say, Oliver moved the furniture, edging the chairs further apart and moving the coffee table so it's up against the far wall of the reception area, while I stood and admired him. Then I put up the Christmas tree, decorating it with red baubles and white lights. He seemed pleased with my efforts and thanked me profusely afterwards. I know he was only being friendly, though. If there's one thing I've learned about Oliver since I've been working for him, it's that he's friendly… with everyone. That's why falling for him was a dangerous move. Nothing can ever come of it.

I don't have space in my life for a man like that.

Friendly is great… obviously, and so is kind. Gorgeous is a distinct advantage, too, but more than anything, after all that's happened to me, I need reliable. I need trustworthy. And unfortunately, that means there's no hope for Oliver and me. There are simply too many other women trying to get their claws into him. I couldn't handle that… not again.

Besides, like I already said, he's simply unattainable.

"Is that you, Jemima?" His voice rings out from his office.

I'm not sure who else he thinks it's going to be, but rather than being facetious, I just say, "Yes," before I walk around behind my desk, which faces the main door, and switch on my computer. As I turn to go to the kitchen at the back of the building, I almost jump out of my skin at the sight of Oliver, leaning back against the wall by his door, with a slight smile on his lips. He's already dressed for work, in his green scrubs, although I know he'll have driven here wearing jeans and a shirt, usually with a jacket over the top. He always changes first thing in the morning, in the small, curtained-off area at the back of his surgery, and then changes back before he goes home. That smile is still twitching at his lips, and for a moment, I wonder if there's something wrong with my appearance. I even take a quick glance down at myself to make sure I'm not still wearing my pink slippers. I'm not… thank God. My feet are clad in the same high-heeled black pumps that I wear to work every other day of the week, and my gray skirt and white blouse are completely decent; no hems awry, no buttons undone, although a couple of them are gaping slightly. That can't be helped, though. I'm built that way.

I gaze up at Oliver again and he pushes himself off of the wall, and steps a little closer, making a clicking sound with his tongue at the same time. The noise is answered by the patter of feet on the linoleum floor and, within a second or two, Baxter appears from the surgery behind him.

He's the most adorable chocolate brown labrador, and he follows Oliver into the reception area, going around behind my desk and flopping down into his basket. He knows that's where he spends the day, and although he occasionally gets up and wanders around, he's no trouble at all.

"Did you have a good weekend?" Oliver asks, surprising me by perching on the corner of my desk.

"Yes, thanks."

He looks at me for a moment, like he expects me to elaborate, but there isn't much to tell. I did the laundry, I tidied the house, and cleaned the bathroom. I wrapped Christmas presents, and helped my mom with some baking for the holidays. Nothing earth shattering. Just an average weekend, with the addition of Christmas preparations thrown in for good measure.

"I—I think I owe you an apology," he says, surprising me even further, not just with the apology, but with the fact that he stammered over it.

"You do?"

He nods his head, folding his arms across his chest at the same time. "Yes."

"What for?"

"Because I forgot it's Christmas."

I glance at the Christmas tree twinkling in the corner of the room, my brow furrowing. "Um... how?"

He smiles, and I melt a little inside. "I didn't exactly forget," he says. "But the party completely slipped my mind."

"Party? What party?"

"The one I have here, every year, at Christmas."

That melting feeling subsides and my stomach churns slightly. "You have a party?"

"Yes." *And I'm only hearing about this now?* "Deanna used to organize the whole thing," he says. "I guess I got used to coming into work and finding it had all been arranged, so I didn't give it a second thought. Except I went to my brother's house yesterday for a big family dinner and his girlfriend – who's now his fiancée – had decorated the house and made it look really festive, and that's when I realized... it's Christmas."

"I see." I'm not sure I do. "So, you didn't notice the shop windows, and the town being decked out with Christmas lights, and the freezing cold weather, or the annoying festive music that seems to play everywhere you go?"

He chuckles with a deep, sexy laugh, which makes my insides tingle and turn molten again. "I noticed all of that," he says. "I was just kinda ignoring it, until I got to Mason's house, and saw the Christmas tree they'd put up in their living room. Isabel had made it look really pretty, and it reminded me."

"That it's Christmas?" I say, shaking my head at him.

"Yes."

"I assume Isabel is your brother's fiancée, or girlfriend, or whichever it is?" I'm not really sure why I asked that question… not when I ought to be focusing the bombshell of this party he's so far failed to mention. But I'm intrigued. I'm also reeling from the fact that this is the longest conversation we've ever had. I know that's my fault, not his. Falling for him is one thing, but letting him into my life is something else, and I decided a while ago that my best defense mechanism against losing my heart completely was to keep him at arm's length, while admiring him at close quarters… if that's physically possible.

"She's his fiancée now. Mason proposed to her after dinner last night. It was kinda unexpected."

"Why?"

"I guess because they haven't known each other for very long."

"Does that matter?" What's wrong with me? Why am I getting even deeper into this discussion with him? Aside from protecting my heart from him, I don't even know these people, and I doubt Oliver's interested in what I have to say.

"Of course not… if you've found the right person."

"And you don't think your brother has?"

"I'm damn sure he has. He's never been so happy." He's smiling, like this matters to him, which is kinda cute.

"Then why shouldn't they get married?"

His smile fades, and he shakes his head. "I didn't say they shouldn't get married. I just said his proposal was unexpected. Normally he tells me everything, including when he's been an idiot, but I knew nothing about this. I'm surprised… that's all."

"Sorry," I say and he frowns, standing up and coming around my desk.

"Why are you sorry?" he asks.

"Because it's nothing to do with me." I reach into my drawer for my notepad. "You were telling me about this party?"

He hesitates for a moment, like he wants to say something, and then steps back slightly. "Yeah. I was. It… It's not really a party, though."

"What is it then?"

"It's a kind of open house thing. I always hold it the day before Christmas Eve."

I frown, looking up into his whiskey-colored eyes, fighting the urge to lose myself in them. "This coming Thursday?"

"Yes. It's not a big deal." It sounds like it is, especially with so little notice. "We just make eggnog, and Deanna used to bake cookies, and people just drop in throughout the day."

He makes it sound so simple, but I've never even drunk eggnog. I don't have a clue how to make it. And as for Christmas cookies…

"I'm sorry," he says. "I should have told you."

"It's fine," I lie. It feels very far from fine. It feels like a nightmare. His clients will be popping in all day, fawning over him while I hand out cookies and eggnog. I can't think of anything worse.

"Thanks, Jemima. I don't know what I'd do without you."

I'm not 'with' him, so that seems like an odd thing to say, but I don't comment, and just smile up at him. "You should probably get ready," I say. "Mrs. Williamson is due in five minutes."

"Oh, great. That's just what I need… a yapping Chihuahua."

He rolls his eyes and then steps around my chair, kneeling in front of Baxter's basket and clasping his face between his hands.

"Be a good boy for Jemima," he says.

Baxter yawns, settling his head on the soft blanket in his basket, and Oliver stands again, walking into his office and closing the door.

I let out a sigh of relief and flop back into my chair, regretting almost all of that conversation. It might have been our first, but it'll probably be our last after that performance. I should've just stuck to work, and the party, and not raised the subject of his family. He talked about them first, I suppose, but that didn't mean he wanted me to question him, did it?

I'm still shaking my head when the front door opens and Mrs. Williamson comes in on a waft of expensive perfume, clutching her Chihuahua to her ample chest and almost smothering the poor thing.

"I know I'm early," she says as she gets to my desk, purring like a cat. "I'm sure Doctor Gould won't mind."

I smile at her as I offer her a seat, and as I make my way to Oliver's office, I wish today had never started. I wish I could still be at home, lying in bed, dreaming about Oliver, instead of facing the reality of a life spent working with him, watching other women drooling over him, and knowing he can never be mine.

Oliver

"What's wrong with her?" Mrs. Williamson looks up at me from across the examination table, her eyelashes fluttering, her lips slightly parted, and I smile back, trying to look reassuring.

Mrs. Williamson – who keeps insisting I should call her Nancy – is probably in her mid- to late-fifties. She dresses at least ten or fifteen years younger, and I'll admit, she's worn well. It's her hands that give away the secret of her passing years, and she has a habit of waving them around, or touching my arms, which makes them more noticeable.

I don't mind her flirting. I accept it as an occupational hazard, and my clients pay me very well for what I do; so if I have to tolerate a little flirting on the side, who am I to complain?

"I think Coco's going deaf," I say. "It's fairly common with Chihuahuas, I'm afraid, and the fact that she's ignoring you when you call her, and that her bark is getting louder, is fairly indicative."

"Oh, no." Her eyes widen, and I wonder for a moment if she might cry.

"It's not the end of the world." I soften my voice, and she manages a smile. "If I'm right, it just means you'll have to be more careful with her when you're out, and you'll have to adjust how you approach her. You'll need to make sure she can see you, rather than coming up to her from behind. Just little things like that will make a big difference to her."

"I see," she says, nodding her head and lifting Coco into her arms.

"I've got some exercises you can try with her." I wander over to the filing cabinet in the corner of my surgery, pulling open the second drawer down and retrieving a sheet of paper, before turning back to Mrs. Williamson. "These will help us find out whether I'm correct, and if I am, how severe her deafness is," I say, handing her the sheet of instructions. "Try them out for seven days, and I'll see you again next Monday."

"My husband and I are going away for the holidays." She looks up at me with those fluttering eyelashes again, and I'm almost tempted to frown or shake my head at her. Anything to remind her that, while she's flirting with me, she's also talking about her husband. "We're leaving on Christmas Eve and won't be coming back until Monday evening."

"Okay. I can see you on Tuesday, I think. We'll check with Jemima when we get outside."

She nods her head, putting Coco down for a moment while she folds the piece of paper, putting it into her purse, before she tucks the dog under her arm again, and I head for the door, holding it open as she passes through.

"I'm so grateful, Doctor Gould," she says, resting her hand on my upper arm.

"You don't need to be." I'm just doing my job, after all. "Oh, by the way," I say, as I follow her out into the reception area, "we're having our usual Christmas gathering on Thursday. I hope you'll be able to drop by at some point?"

"Of course," she simpers, gazing up at me. "That's so kind of you."

She's acting like I've issued a royal summons, but I don't disillusion her. Instead I just smile and go around behind Jemima's desk, relishing the opportunity of being close to her.

"Can we fit Coco in for a thirty-minute appointment next Tuesday?" I ask her, trying not to get too close, despite the temptation.

"The twenty-eighth?" she says, looking up at me, her pale blue eyes fixed on mine for a breathtaking moment.

"Yes." My voice sounds croaky and I cough.

Jemima looks away again, staring at her computer screen, and bringing up the online booking system I started using about two years ago, scrolling through to December twenty-eighth, before she turns her gaze on Mrs. Williamson.

"I can offer you ten-thirty in the morning, or two-fifteen in the afternoon."

I hope she goes for the ten-thirty. Two-fifteen is the first appointment after lunch, and I don't relish it being with Mrs. Williamson.

"I'll take the ten-thirty," Mrs. Williamson says, and I breathe out, hoping she doesn't notice that as a sigh of relief.

Jemima taps on her keyboard, her fingers moving like lightning, and then she looks up at Mrs. Williamson again.

"You'll get a confirmation email," she says. "Would you like me to write the appointment down on a card for you as well?"

"Yes, please," Mrs. Williamson replies, staring at me again, although I'm preoccupied with Jemima, watching her write out the appointment on one of our calling cards in her neat handwriting.

I have to admit, I'm still feeling a little stunned after our conversation this morning. It wasn't that there was anything exceptional about what we were discussing; it was the fact that we had a conversation at all. I've been trying to talk to Jemima for such a long time, and this morning, it just kinda happened. I remembered Mason saying that his first proper conversation with Isabel came out of the blue, and mine with Jemima seemed to be the same.

Of course, it started off being all about work – or at least, all about the party – but she turned it around and asked about my brother and Isabel. I'd rather she'd asked about me, but we weren't talking about me. We were talking about the fact that I went over to Mason's house last night for dinner with his girlfriend, Isabel, Dad, my sister Destiny and her new husband, Ronan, and Isabel's sisters, Ashley and Reagan. We were getting together as a kind of pre-Christmas thing, because we missed out on having a family gathering at Thanksgiving. It won't be possible for us to see each other at Christmas either, because Destiny and Ronan are spending the holidays with his sister in Lexington. So, we met up at Mason's place yesterday. As I said to Jemima, that was when I noticed the beautiful Christmas tree Isabel had decorated – which reminded me about the party. It was also when Mason proposed. Jemima picked up on that and asked me about it, although she reacted weirdly when I said Mason's proposal had been unexpected. It had. That was what I was trying to explain to her. Mason hadn't mentioned it, and that surprised me. I thought I knew just about everything that had gone on between him and Isabel; from his lame idea about getting her to be his fake girlfriend at his college reunion, to him forgetting to use a condom when they first slept together. When Isabel found out about the fake girlfriend part of that, she walked out on him and went home to her sisters in Vermont. But then, I had warned my brother it was a really dumb idea. He went after her, of course, and won her back, and it transpired that although his error of judgement with the condom didn't have any consequences, they're actually trying for a baby now, *and* they're engaged.

I didn't tell Jemima about the fact that they're trying for a baby. She seemed surprised enough by my reaction to their engagement, which she completely misunderstood. I wasn't being critical, even if she took it that way. I was just commenting on my surprise… that was all. But looking at her now, as she shows Mrs. Williamson to the door, I'll admit her response has made me wonder whether there might be something in her past that made her respond like that.

If only she'd opened up to me…

She didn't. She apologized, although God knows why. What did she have to apologize for? She said it was because it had nothing to do with her, and while I wanted to tell her it did, she seemed keen to keep things professional after that.

I could hardly argue, could I?

After all, we'd just had our first real conversation, and although it hadn't gone to plan, I didn't want to spoil things completely by arguing with her.

"You've got just over ten minutes until Mrs. North is due," Jemima says, breaking into my thoughts as she closes the front door and turns around. She doesn't come back over to her desk, where I'm still standing, but remains where she is, looking across at me... or rather, straight past me. Once again, I feel dismissed.

"Oh. Okay. I guess I'd better clear up and get ready."

I move away from her desk, my heart sinking as I notice she goes back there the moment I've vacated her space.

Could she be any more subtle?

I make my way into my surgery, closing the door behind me and leaning against it for a moment.

I'm so in love with Jemima, I can almost taste it. She clearly feels absolutely nothing for me, though, and being around her so much is torture. Not that I'm thinking of letting her go. I'd rather torture myself, punish my heart, body, and mind on an hourly basis, than risk never seeing her again. I'll always be grateful she's here, no matter how much it hurts.

I can still remember the moment I first saw her, just over a year ago, when she walked in the door for her interview, answering the ad I'd placed in the local newspaper for a new receptionist.

I'd been dreading the whole process of finding a replacement for Deanna. She'd been with me for years, and with my predecessor before me. She was great at her job, but her husband had just taken early retirement, and she wanted to spend more time with him. I understood her reasons for leaving; I just didn't need the hassle of finding someone else who could do the job as well as she did.

Deanna told me her plans at the beginning of last December, giving me a month to find her replacement. I thought it would be easy.

If only I'd known...

I set up the interviews over three days, having had a lot of responses, but by lunchtime on the third day, and I was wondering whether it was a lost cause. None of them had been even remotely suitable. Then, at three o'clock on that Friday afternoon, Jemima walked in and took my breath away.

She was tiny. I estimated her to be no more than five foot four, but she wore high heels to compensate, adding probably three inches to her height. She still had to crane her neck to look up at me, though, as I stood and walked around my desk to greet her. I hadn't done that with any of the other candidates, but there was something about Jemima that made me want to be as close as possible to her. I think it was the slightly scared expression on her face, and the way she was biting her lip.

It made me want to bite it too.

I shook her hand, which was small and soft, and then offered her a seat, before resuming my own and gazing across my desk at her, finding myself tongue-tied.

That's not normal for me. But I couldn't think of anything to say, and for a while, we just sat there.

She was shy; that much was obvious, just from her demeanor, from the way she wouldn't make eye contact and fiddled with the hem of her jacket, and I wondered if we were destined to remain that way forever. I wouldn't have complained. I had the most perfect view in the world. But then Baxter wandered over and nuzzled in to me, wanting some attention, and while I stroked his head, Jemima studied him and said, "He's beautiful. What's his name?"

"Baxter." I silently thanked him, because he'd helped break the ice between us, and then I asked Jemima what experience she had in working with animals.

She replied, "Absolutely none," which made me laugh.

"At least that's honest," I said, and she smiled.

"There's no point in lying." She shrugged her shoulders. "I didn't realize experience with animals was necessary."

"It's not." And even if it had been, I'd have waived the requirement for her. "I just wondered if you'd done any work like this before."

She tilted her head then, betraying her confusion, which wasn't that surprising. I had her resume in front of me, after all. It told me she'd had a couple of part-time jobs in her hometown of Eastford, Connecticut, one working at a bakery, and the other for a company offering hot-air balloon rides to tourists. That last job was quite seasonal, I imagined, and while I probably should have asked her what she did with the rest of her time, I didn't really care.

"I've done administrative work," she said, my silence clearly bothering her. "I had to organize the schedules for the balloon rides."

"Did you ever take one yourself?" I asked.

"No. I'm scared of heights."

I chuckled, and she smiled as I glanced down at her resume again, noting her age, which was only twenty-one. I guessed that explained some of her shyness and her lack of experience. It also meant she was twelve years younger than me. I wasn't sure why that thought came into my head. After all, what did it matter what the age gap was? It certainly shouldn't have done. And yet it did… because I'd fallen for her.

Love wasn't something I'd ever experienced before, but I knew, without any doubt, that I was in love. It was hard not to be, when she had the softest voice I'd ever heard, and the lightest blue eyes. Her makeup was natural, her skin smooth and flawless. Her blonde hair was tied up in ponytail, although a couple of strands had broken free and were framing her perfect face, and as I gazed at her across my desk, I knew there would never be anyone else for me.

"When can you start?" I asked her.

"Y—You're offering me the job?" We'd spent less than fifteen minutes in each other's company and I'd asked her almost nothing. Her confusion was understandable.

"Yes," I said, and while it may not have been the most sensible thing I've ever done, I've got no regrets. She's great at what she does. She's fantastic with the clients, and their pets, and their children, when they have them… and she clearly adores Baxter, who sits with her during surgery hours, and who I've noticed is often reluctant to come back to me. Her love for my dog would have been route one into my heart, if it hadn't already been hers. I just wish I knew how to tell her that. I wish I knew how to tell her anything, really. Because, even though she accepted my offer and started working for me the first week of January,

I still know nothing about her, other than the meager details she included on her resume.

That means I've spent nearly a year trying to get to know her, and getting nowhere.

I've spoken to Mason about the situation, because as well as being my brother, he's also a psychologist, and even he thinks it's kinda odd that I still know so little about her. It's just not normal to spend so much time together and have so little understanding of each other.

I guess that's why I got so excited earlier, when she asked about Mason and Isabel. I thought she was taking an interest. She wasn't... clearly. Because if she'd been interested, she wouldn't have dismissed me and changed the subject like she did. She was just querying the way I'd phrased my sentence, I think.

I push myself off of the door, realizing time's running out and I need to wipe down the examining table, which only takes a few minutes.

Of course, they're a few minutes during which I keep thinking about Jemima. But why wouldn't I? She's all I think about these days.

I feel guilty for springing the Christmas party on her like I just did. As I explained to her, it's not a party at all. It's a lot harder work than that. It goes on for the whole day, and sometimes into the evening too, because the surgery doesn't close until six pm... although I forgot to mention that to Jemima. We have to plaster a smile on our faces for the entire time, too... and dish out drinks and cookies to everyone who walks through the door. Of course, it's Christmas, so everyone is in good cheer, but that doesn't make it any easier, and I wonder now if I should've warned her.

I know I should've given her more notice, but I genuinely forgot. If that sounds pathetic, then there's not a lot I can do about it. I've been so wrapped up in Jemima for the last few months, trying to work out how to break down the barriers between us, I haven't been able to think straight at all. I've been trying to work out whether I should forget about conversation and getting to know her and just show my hand, and ask her to have dinner with me.

It's strange... I'm not usually a shy man. Mason is. At least, he's more shy than I am. But I'm not sure shyness is the cause of my reticence with Jemima. I've contemplated asking her to dinner more times than I can think about. I've even acted out the scene in my head, and I don't think it's shyness that's getting in my way. To be honest, I think my main issue is, I'm scared. And what scares me most is that if I really showed her my hand, Jemima might leave. Because I think she'd see right through me and realize that dinner isn't all I want.

That's why I haven't asked her yet… because I'm scared. I'm a coward.

No, I'm not. Not really. I know that being scared of something isn't a reason to give up on it. I don't intend to, either.

I just need to work out how to go about this without breaking my heart… or losing her.

I sit and gaze out across the lake, ignoring the icy chill and staring at the reflection of the moon on the still water. It's freezing… so cold that even Baxter has abandoned me and gone to sit indoors by the fire.

I don't care about the cold.

I just wish I could sit here with Jemima, holding her close to me, keeping her warm, feeling her soft body beside my own, and having her share this perfect piece of paradise that I call home.

I love living here in my cabin by the lake. I love the quiet and the seclusion, especially on nights like this, when I just want to think. Thinking isn't getting me anywhere, of course. It hasn't helped me work things out with Jemima. It hasn't helped me to understand why she practically ignored me for most of the day, and then ran out of the office when it was time to go home, barely acknowledging my "Goodbye."

It also hasn't helped me come to terms with the fact that, while my sister just got married, and Mason got engaged yesterday, I'm sitting here by myself. As I gaze out on the silvery shadows and dark mists lying across the lake, it all starts to blur and I let my head fall into my hands, whispering her name and letting the loneliness wash over me in waves.

Chapter Two

∞

Jemima

I'm a bundle of nerves and mixed emotions this morning, which I guess isn't surprising. Today is the day of Oliver's party… not that it's a party as such. In fact, I'm not really sure what it is, other than hard work. Oliver made a point of telling me that Deanna used to organize the whole thing, and even though he's given me almost no time at all, I still feel like I have to make a success of it. That alone would be enough to make me anxious, but on top of that I've been lying here, wide awake, since five-thirty, dreading the thought of getting up, because I know the fawning and flirting is going to be even worse than usual today.

Okay, so I know it would be impractical and inadvisable, and downright stupid to get involved with Oliver, but that doesn't mean I want to watch half the women of the town throwing themselves at him.

That thought has been bothering me, ever since he first mentioned the party, which is why I've been shutting him down over the last couple of days. It's easier than facing the reality that he's my boss, not my boyfriend, and that I need to stop daydreaming about things that can never be.

My alarm beeps, telling me it's six-thirty, and I reach out and switch it off, then throw back the covers, and sit up on the edge of the bed, glancing over at the bags of Christmas presents in the corner of my room. They're all wrapped, ready to be put under the tree, and I'm glad now that I got myself organized in advance, because the last few evenings have been spent looking up recipes and cooking... with Mom's help, of course. Because when I realized I was going to have to provide the food for this party, I'll admit I was kinda lost.

Oliver said Deanna used to make eggnog and cookies, but as I drove home on Monday night, I decided I'd try something different. The reason for that was simple; I couldn't help recalling my first day at work, when he showed me around, explaining how Deanna did this, and Deanna did that, like she was some kind of secretarial goddess. I'm sure there was nothing wrong with the woman, but his constant praise of her made me feel even more nervous about working for him than I already was – and that was saying something. This is the first proper job I've ever had, and I didn't want to screw up. I couldn't afford to. I still can't. Equally, I'm not Deanna, and I'd like to prove to Oliver that I'm capable of doing things... my way. So it's probably a good idea if I get a move on and get showered.

"I've put out some large plates for you to take with you," Mom says as I walk into the kitchen, my stomach churning. She's over by the stove, boiling the kettle to make her morning tea, as usual, and she's already dressed, in tight-fitting jeans and a sweater, her blonde hair loose around her shoulders. My mom is forty-six, and while she looks a lot younger, she doesn't have to try hard to achieve that effect, unlike a lot of the women who come to see Doctor Gould.

"Thanks. That's great." I glance over at the serving platters she's put on the countertop, next to the boxes of cakes and tarts we baked together yesterday evening. "I think I'm gonna load everything into my car and head off."

"What about your breakfast?"

"I'll skip it." She frowns. "I can't be late today, Mom. I've got a lot to do when I get to work."

She hesitates for a moment and then nods her head. "Do you want me to help you carry things out?"

"No. I'll be fine."

"Will you be late home?" she asks, with a slight tension in her voice.

"I don't know. I'll try not to be."

She nods her head again and at that moment the kettle boils and she sets about making her tea, while I start loading up my car with boxes of cakes and bottles.

I can't blame Mom for being moody with me. She works just as hard as I do, if not harder, and I very much doubt she wanted to spend the last few evenings helping me get everything ready for a party she won't even be attending. Although parties aren't really her scene, and she hasn't complained about helping me; she's not that kind of person. In fact, we've quite enjoyed cooking together. It's not something we get to do very often, and we've had fun finding the recipes, adapting them to suit the ingredients we could get hold of, and then making a huge mess in the kitchen.

Even so, I'm sure she'd rather have put her feet up at the end of the day, just as I know she'd prefer me to stay for breakfast.

"I'll be going then." I come back into the house, having wedged the last of the boxes into the trunk of my car. Mom's standing in the doorway to the kitchen, leaning against the frame.

"Okay." She smiles, her mood clearly forgotten. "I hope it goes well."

"So do I."

I give her a quick hug, and when I pull back, she looks me in the eye. "Try and have some fun," she says.

"It's work, Mom."

She shakes her head. "Maybe, but you need to have some fun too."

Fun? I've forgotten what that feels like, and for a moment I just want to cry. I'm twenty-two and I feel like any chance of fun passed me by a long time ago.

The drive to work takes less than ten minutes, although I take it easy and don't brake too sharply. I'm carrying a precious cargo, and the last thing I need after all our efforts, is to get to work and find it's all ruined.

I park up safely though and am just about to get out when Oliver pulls up in his Jeep. I'm a good hour early, and I suppose I'd expected to have the place to myself while I got everything ready, so that churning in my stomach becomes a little more tidal at the prospect of having Oliver for company.

Still, I can't sit here and expect to get anything done, so I climb out of the car, going around to the trunk and opening it.

"Good morning," he says, coming up beside me. "You're early."

I look up into those perfect amber eyes, struggling to breathe, as I take in the sight of him in his dark blue jeans, white button-down shirt and black leather jacket. I've seen him dressed like this hundreds of times, but not for very long. He's usually rushing to get changed into his scrubs, or following me out the door at the end of a busy day. To have him standing here beside me, looking as sexy as hell, is more than I can take, and I suck in a deliberately long breath to try and regain some control. "Yes," I say eventually. "There's a lot to do."

He tilts his head and then glances down into my trunk, doing an almost comedic double-take as he notices the contents.

"W—What's all this?" he says.

"It's the things we need for the party." I would have thought that was obvious.

His brow furrows, and he turns back to me, confusion clouding his eyes. "I didn't expect you to do all this. I thought you understood… I only told you about the party so you'd realize today isn't gonna be routine."

Why is it we're always talking at crossed purposes?

"I assumed, when you said Deanna made cookies and eggnog…"

"That I'd expect you to do the same?" He finishes my sentence, saving me the trouble.

"Yes. Except I didn't make cookies and eggnog. I made brownies, and orange and lemon cupcakes, and some white chocolate and cranberry tarts. And I bought the ingredients to make punch – with and without alcohol – because I didn't know where to start with eggnog."

He smiles, his eyes lighting up. "You sure know how to make a guy feel inadequate."

"I do?"

"Yeah."

He takes my hand and although I'm breathless again at the physical contact, I let him guide me over to his Jeep, where he opens the rear door, revealing a cool bag and a box which contains packets and packets of store-bought cookies. "The eggnog is in the cool bag," he explains and I look up at him, trying not to smile, just as he bursts out laughing, and I do the same.

"We don't have to make the punch." I'm feeling guilty now.

"Oh, yes, we do… I don't even like eggnog."

I laugh again and he stares down at me for a moment before we both seem to snap back to our senses. "Do you think we should start taking everything inside?" I suggest.

"Yeah. It's freezing out here, and Baxter's dying to get indoors. But, more importantly, I can't wait to taste all these things you've made."

I smile up at him, biting my bottom lip, which seems to catch his attention for a moment, and then I walk back to my car. "Can you take these boxes?" I say, as I hand him the first two, containing the brownies.

"Sure."

I grab a couple more boxes while he calls to Baxter, who jumps out of his car and follows us into the surgery, Oliver balancing the boxes while he unlocks the door.

"We'll take these through to the kitchen," he says, flicking on the lights. "Then you can perform the vital task of putting the coffee on, and start setting things out, while I bring in everything else. Okay?"

"Absolutely."

He seems to have forgotten, he's my boss. He doesn't need to ask, but I like that he did, and I follow him through to the kitchen, where we stack up the containers on the small countertop beside the sink, and he goes back out again.

Baxter has come with us, but has stayed with me, rather than pursuing Oliver, and he's sitting, looking at the boxes, clearly sensing there's food inside them.

"You're being optimistic," I say, patting his head, before I fill up the coffee machine with water, and go back out to the reception, to drop off my purse, my keys and my coat. Back in the kitchen, I take the lids from the boxes, while Baxter remains, staring up at me, which makes me chuckle.

On his third trip, Oliver brings in his cool bag and the serving platters, balancing them carefully.

"That just leaves the bottles," he says. "Can you give me your keys and I'll lock your car?"

"They're on my desk." I take the plates from him, glancing around. "Aren't you gonna bring the cookies in?"

He smiles. "No. There's only so much humiliation a guy can take."

I bite my bottom lip again, struggling not to smile at his comment, and tilt my head. "What are you gonna do with them all?"

"Eat them, I guess."

"That's a lot of cookies."

"I wasn't gonna eat them all at once." He grins, and then disappears again, and I start laying out the cakes on the platters, arranging them neatly. In the process, I drop a few crumbs onto the floor, and Baxter's there within seconds, licking them up.

"No, Baxter," I say, crouching down and pulling at his collar, even though he pays me no attention, and continues to forage at the floor, snuffling out whatever he can find.

"I've left your keys on your desk again," Oliver says from behind me, and I stand, turning to face him, as he frowns. "Is something wrong?"

"I don't know. I—I just dropped a few brownie crumbs on the floor by accident and Baxter started eating them, but I wasn't sure if he was allowed…" I let my voice fade as he dumps the boxes of bottles onto the floor and crouches down himself, clasping Baxter's face in his hands and leaning right in to him. The dog's tail wags furiously as he laps up the attention from his master, just as voraciously as he did those few crumbs.

"You're incorrigible," Oliver says, while the dog licks his nose. "You know you're not supposed to go looking for scraps, but the moment my back's turned…" He shakes his head, and then glances up at me. "Don't look so worried," he says, releasing Baxter and standing up. "He won't have come to any harm."

"You're sure? I didn't know…"

"I'm sure." He moves forward, standing right in front of me. "Chocolate isn't recommended for dogs, but the odd crumb won't hurt." He stares down at me for a second and then glances over at the plate of brownies I was just arranging. "For humans, on the other hand," he says, reaching over and picking up a piece, "chocolate is actively encouraged." And with that, he pops the brownie into his mouth, closing his eyes as he savors the rich, gooey treat. "Wow. They're good." He finishes chewing and reaches for a second one, and without thinking, I slap the back of his hand. He pulls back and turns to me, the corners of his lips twisting upwards.

"There won't be any left," I say, although I feel I should also apologize for slapping my boss. How can I though, when he's smiling at me like that? My inside are even more gooey than the brownies, and it's very distracting.

"Would you like me to behave myself?" he says, and I'm tempted to say 'no', just to see what it might be like to misbehave with him.

Except I can't say that, so instead I just shake my head and say, "I'd like you to reach that big pitcher down from the top shelf of the cabinet."

"Sure." He opens the door, grabbing the glass pitcher and handing it to me.

"Thanks. If I'd been at home, I'd have had to get a chair."

"Well, you've got me now," he says, and my breath catches in my throat. I know he doesn't mean that in the way I want him to, and even if he did, it could never work, but… oh, what a perfect thought.

To distract myself from thinking about it, I put down the pitcher and then bend to grab the one I brought from home, which is in the box with all the bottles.

"Why did you make me get the one from the cabinet if you've already got one?" Oliver asks, tilting his head slightly.

"Because we're serving two kinds of punch… one with alcohol and one without."

"Oh, yeah."

"I only have one pitcher, but I remembered there was one here, so I didn't worry about buying another one."

"I'm glad to hear it," he says, just as I remember something vital, which for some reason hadn't occurred to me until now.

"Do we have glasses?" I ask him.

"No. But we have paper cups. Deanna bought several hundred of the things last Christmas, so we're not exactly gonna run out anytime soon."

"Do you know where they are?"

He frowns, glancing around the tiny space and then scratching his head. "Give me a minute," he says, and then disappears from the room.

I can't help smiling as I put down my mom's pitcher beside the other one, and get back to my original task of laying out the food, putting something of everything onto each of the platters.

"Found them," Oliver says, coming back into the room, carrying yet another box.

"I don't know where we're gonna put them." I look around at the crowded countertop and floor and he smiles.

"I'll leave them out in the hallway for now."

"Probably wise."

He goes and then comes straight back in, empty-handed this time. "What can I do?" he says.

"Make the coffee?" I suggest. "I only got around to putting the water in the machine."

He rolls his eyes, grinning. "Honestly. Call yourself a secretary."

I chuckle as he reaches over, our arms touching briefly, before he pulls the machine a little closer to him, and fills it with coffee grounds.

I like being this close to him. I like the heat from his body seeping into mine, and the way it feels when he touches me like that. It's a struggle to remember that I'm his secretary… and that while I might want to be so much more, it won't end well. He's not the man for me, even if I love him so much my body aches.

He turns the machine on and, as I'm delving into the box to retrieve a cupcake, he grabs one from the plate. I'm too slow to stop him this time, and he takes a bite as I shake my head at him.

"You must work out a lot, if you can keep eating like this, and still look like you do." The enormity of my statement hits me like a wrecking ball, even as the words leave my lips. I can hardly retract them, though. Apart from the fact I meant everything I just said, to go back on it would be an insult... and that would be even worse.

"I don't," he says, as he finishes his mouthful.

"You don't what? Work out, or keep eating like this?" It seems best to carry on the conversation as though I didn't just make a fool of myself. At least for now.

"I don't work out," he says, surprising me and I turn to face him.

"Really?"

"Yeah. I don't have time, and I'm not a great fan of gyms."

I look him up and down, my eyes raking over his toned abs and broad, muscular chest. "Then how...?" I say, without thinking... again.

"I live in a cabin, by a lake," he says, his voice really quiet and soothing, which ought to help calm my nerves. It probably would, if my heart wasn't pounding in my chest.

"And?"

"Baxter likes to walk."

"Oh, I see."

"And I like to swim."

"In the lake?"

"Yeah. Not when it's freezing, like it is now. I'm not completely insane. But when it's warm enough, there's nothing better than stripping off and diving into the cool water."

"S—Stripping off?" I whisper.

"Yeah. There's no-one for miles. It's very invigorating." He stares down at me, and I don't doubt him. I'm invigorated just thinking about it.

"D—Do you think we should make the punch?" I say with a stutter, my mind still preoccupied with the thought of him skinny-dipping, even though I know time is moving on.

"Okay." I'm almost certain I see something that looks like disappointment in his eyes. Except that doesn't make sense. What on earth has he got to be disappointed about?

*

I'm not sure how, but it's lunchtime already. We won't be getting any lunch today, though… we're just too busy. People have been coming in throughout the morning, and they're showing no signs of stopping. Still, both Oliver and I have nibbled at snacks all morning, and I know I'm not hungry. I doubt he is either. We've both stuck to the non-alcoholic punch too, just so we can keep our heads clear.

I've struggled, though, with the way every single female who's come into this place has been pawing him like they own him. I keep wanting to shout out, "He's mine." Except he's not. I don't think he's anyone's actually. He's not married. I know that because several of his female clients refer to him as Sturbridge's most eligible bachelor. And thinking about it, I'm wondering if there's anyone in his life other than Baxter. He certainly never mentions any women, other than members of his family, and no-one calls for him, either by phone or in person. No-one drops by to take Baxter for a walk, or even just to say 'Hi'.

Which I guess must mean he's single.

That fact ought to make me happy, but it doesn't. Despite our conversation this morning, he's not interested. I might want to join him for a naked, moonlit swim, but the thought won't even have crossed his mind. I might want to mess up his hair, just a little more, while he kisses me… hard. I might yearn for him to pin me against the wall, with that perfect body of his, and to feel his hands wandering… everywhere. But to him, I'm just the receptionist. Or the secretary, as he called me earlier. Either way, I'm not girlfriend material.

And, despite everything my heart and body might want, my head knows that's probably for the best… especially when I'm watching Mrs. Ellis flirt with him, like she has been for the last ten minutes.

I can't have a man like that in my life, no matter how much I want him… and the sooner I wake up to that, the better.

Oliver

Today is going so much better than I'd hoped. In fact, so far, it's been beyond my wildest expectations.

For a start, I never expected Jemima to cater the entire party. I never expected her to do anything at all. I only told her about the event so she'd know how it worked, like I explained to her earlier. But this morning, she arrived with a car full of Christmas cheer and a beautiful smile on her face, looking sexier than ever. I don't know why that was, because she was dressed exactly the same as she always is, in a dark gray skirt and white blouse, but there seemed to my eyes to be something different about her. As usual, her skirt fitted to her hips, like it was glued to her, and her blouse gaped, just slightly, which is something I've always liked about her. It's sexy that her clothes hint at what lies beneath, without actually screaming about it.

I didn't bother to change, which I normally do when I get in to work. But I only had two appointments, which I'd made by accident, before I remembered the party, and I knew I'd get through those without changing into my scrubs. I wanted to feel more like myself today… more 'normal'.

And it seemed to work.

I felt especially normal this morning, in the kitchen, when Jemima and I were getting everything ready. There was plenty to do, but we had time, and no interruptions, and that gave us the opportunity to talk. And we did. We even made each other laugh a few times, and while I was touched by her concern for Baxter, and by how much work she'd put into the preparations for the party, the best moment of all was when she paid me that not-so-veiled compliment. I wasn't expecting it. All I did was to steal a cake. Only, unlike that time before, when she slapped my hand so playfully she took my breath away, this time she asked me if I needed to work out to stay in shape. I didn't comment on the compliment itself, because I could see the blush creeping up her cheeks, and I knew she was embarrassed. But I liked the fact that she'd been looking, and I decided not to hide behind a change of subject and told her I like skinny dipping in the lake. Every word I said to her was completely true. It is very invigorating on a warm evening to strip off my clothes and dive under the cool water, but I'll admit, when I said that, I was thinking about having her with me; her naked body beside mine, and I was finding it hard to focus. I saw her reaction, though. Her eyes widened and her mouth opened slightly as she gazed at me, and then she bit on her bottom lip, which is something she does quite a lot. It turns me on enormously, and if we hadn't been running out of time, I'd have kissed her, there and then… and to hell with her shyness. To hell with the fact that I know so little about her, I don't even have a clue whether she's in a relationship already. I wanted her lips to be mine.

I still do.

I think I always will.

Who am I kidding? There's no 'think' about it.

I love her. I need her. Nothing's ever gonna change about that.

I think most of my clients have been here today, some with gifts, but most with smiles and fluttering eyelashes, and as the day draws to a close, I'm relieved it's nearly over. One of the things I was dreading most about today was the flirting, because while I accept it as an occupational hazard, and I know it's not unusual, I can normally hide behind my job. I can pretend to be busy and put them off. Today was all about socializing, rather than working, and that meant there was nowhere to hide. I hated it. All the while I was smiling and nodding, and pretending to enjoy myself, the only person I wanted to be with was Jemima.

She's been busy all day though, handing out food and drinks, smiling at my clients and looking after Baxter, so we haven't had the chance to pick up where we left off this morning, or even to exchange a few words.

It's gone six-thirty now, and I've just got rid of Mrs. Welch, who's been here for over an hour, the last fifteen minutes of which she's spent trying to persuade me to attend a drinks party she's having on New

Year's Eve. I found a way out of it, telling her I'm spending the evening with my family, which I'm not, but the last thing I need is to have to see in the New Year with a client.

"Thank God that's over," I breathe, shutting the door and leaning back against it.

Baxter looks up from his basket, but doesn't get up. It's like he knows we're not going home yet. We've got to clear up first.

"I think it went well, don't you?" Jemima says, picking up a couple of paper cups and stacking them together.

"Yes. Mainly thanks to you."

She blushes. "I didn't do anything."

"No, of course you didn't. You just catered the whole thing, and acted like a glorified waitress all day."

She shrugs her shoulders, not giving me an answer and instead, goes over to the other side of the room, picking up more cups and tidying the table top. It looks like she's in a hurry to get home, and while I don't particularly want to think about the reason for that, I have to be fair; she's been here for nearly twelve hours now.

"You should go," I say and she turns to look at me, frowning.

"I wouldn't dream of it… I'll stay and help clear up."

She carries on with what she's doing, cutting off our conversation, which seems a shame after we were getting along so well this morning. If she's going to stay, I'd rather we could at least talk to each other.

"You'll have to let me know how much I owe you." I'm struggling for things to say, and while I'd rather talk about her – or even me – any conversation is better than none.

"What for?" She doesn't even bother to turn and look at me this time.

"For all the food and drink."

Now she stops what she's doing and turns, gazing up at me. "Don't worry about it."

Is she serious? "You're not paying for all this," I say, with a firm voice, and she blinks at me a couple of times.

"Okay." Her voice is a whisper, but I can still hear it. I'm fine tuned to hear her voice, I think. "But I don't know exactly how much it was… not without checking."

"You can let me know in the morning, or after the weekend, and I'll transfer the money into your account."

She nods her head and then bites her lip, and it's like something flips inside me. I don't know whether it's the festive atmosphere, the fact that I'm so desperate for her I can't think straight, or just that she looks so damn sexy when she does that, but suddenly I forget all my fears about her rejecting me, or there being someone else in her life. I forget any doubts I might have had about her and me, and us, and I walk right up to her, looking down into her upturned face.

"I wish you wouldn't do that," I murmur, struggling for breath.

"Do what?"

"Bite your lip."

Her brow furrows, which has the effect of making her look cute as well as sexy. It's a deadly combination, and I almost groan out loud. "Why shouldn't I?" she says. "It's my lip."

"I know." I take a half step closer and she blinks rapidly, biting that damn lip again. "But I want it to be mine."

She releases her lip as her mouth drops open and she stares up at me, the words, "Oh God," falling from her mouth in a hushed breath. And then, as she swallows, she shakes her head and ducks away from me, glancing over at the door. I think I know she's going to run before she does, but I'm powerless to stop her. She's nearer to her desk than I am and she dashes over, grabbing her purse and then bolts to the door, muttering, "I'm sorry, I—I can't…" as she flees from the office.

"Jemima!" I call after her, but she's already gone, and as I run to the door, I hear her car starting and the squeal of tires as she pulls out of the parking lot.

I don't think I could have screwed that up any more if I'd tried, and while I know I should probably stay away from her, I can't. Besides which, she's left her coat here. She'll need it in the morning… assuming she wants to come back to work here ever again.

That thought fills me with fear. The idea of never seeing her again is more than I can handle, and I go into the surgery, and over to the filing cabinet, pulling open the bottom drawer, where I keep all my insurance documents. The one I'm looking for is in the front folder. It's the health insurance I arranged for Jemima when she started working here. Her contact details are on the policy, and I quickly note her address and cell number onto my phone before I shrug on my jacket, check I've got my keys, flick off all the lights, and then return to the reception area.

"Here, boy." I call to Baxter, and he gets up immediately, his ears twitching. He trots over to me and looks up as I take Jemima's coat from the stand by the door. "Let's go see if I can undo this," I murmur, and he follows me out through the door, waiting while I lock it, and then walks by my side as I head for my car, letting him onto the back seat, then getting in the front.

Placing Jemima's coat on the passenger seat, I start the engine, and then tap her address into my Sat/Nav, waiting for a moment or two while it makes the calculation and then the female voice instructs me to turn left onto Main Street. I do as I'm told, taking the time to work out what just went wrong. It's clear I mis-read the situation, and that I need to apologize and make it right again... somehow. I guess this is the proof – if I needed it – that she must have someone in her life. I can't think of any other reason she'd suddenly run out on me like that. Unless she finds me physically repulsive, of course. Either way, I need to explain to her I made a mistake, and this was all my fault. I'm not harassing her, and I'll never do anything to make her feel uncomfortable again. I just can't bear the thought of having hurt her...

I've been driving for about six or seven minutes when the Sat/Nav tells me to turn right onto Willard Road. I do so, slowing down because it's dark, and then, when instructed, I pull up outside a stone built, single-story property, set a little way back from the road. It's lit up with a light by the front door, and two more on the pathway that leads up to it, as well as a couple of Christmas trees with sparkling white lights, so I can see the building fairly well. I can also see that Jemima's car is parked at an angle across the driveway, and I wonder if she drove here feeling upset... or worse still, angry. I feel like even more of a loser now, at the thought that she could have come to harm, driving without taking care of herself, just because I decided to hit on her.

God, what an idiot.

Sitting in my car feeling like an idiot won't make things right again, though, so I grab her coat and turn off the engine.

"Stay here, Baxter," I mutter, as I get out. He doesn't make a sound. He doesn't even raise his head and look out the window as I start up the path, Jemima's coat clutched in my hand, wondering how on earth I'm going to face her and apologize.

My nerves are in pieces by the time I get to the door, but I ring the bell anyway, and step back slightly, examining the knotted wood on the surface of the door, and taking a few deep breaths, until it opens and my heart stops beating.

"Jem…" I say, taking in the sight before me, as I fail to even utter her name properly, because she's standing before me, still in her skirt and blouse, but without her high heels, clutching a baby in her arms. He's got slightly darker hair than Jemima's and is wearing navy blue pajamas with dinosaurs printed on them. He looks to be about a year old, or maybe a little more, and he turns his head, gazing at me, with a kinda shy smile, before burying it again, and throwing this arms around Jemima's neck. I raise my eyes and look at Jemima now, noting the tears on her cheeks, and although I want more than anything to hold her, I can't. Not now. Not ever.

She's got a family. Not just a boyfriend, or a husband. She's got a damn family. And I don't know what to say to her. So, for a moment or two, we just stare at each other, neither of us uttering a sound, until I remember what I've got in my hand and hold it out to her.

"You forgot your coat," I murmur, and she takes it, balancing her child on her hip. She looks good like that, I have to say, but I banish the thought.

She belongs to someone else. She'll never be mine.

"This is my son," she says, in a whisper.

"Yeah. I kinda guessed that."

What else does she expect me to say? I just came on to her. I just told her I wanted her lips to be mine, and all the while she knew they were someone else's. She knew *she* was someone else's, and rather than just telling me that, she ran out on me.

I'm confused.

I'm beyond confused.

I don't know what to think… except I can't stay here anymore.

"Goodnight," I murmur, and I turn, making my way back down the path. I don't dare to look back. I'm not that brave.

It's strange, but as much as I've hated to think of Jemima with another man, I've often wondered whether she's married… or at least attached. I've talked it through with Mason, too, discussing with him whether that's why she's so quiet and secretive… why she never talks about herself. It makes even more sense now, although why she's kept it all a secret from me, I don't know. But then I guess I've never told her about my life either. Why would I? It's not like she's interested in me. She's got a family of her own, for Christ's sake. In any case, I don't have much to tell these days. The last time I had a woman in my life, or my bed, was over a year ago. Her name was Mandy Tucker, and I ended my brief relationship with her on the day I met Jemima. I know that might seem like a rash decision, but it didn't seem fair to keep seeing Mandy when I knew I was in love with Jemima. The thought crossed my mind that I should try to fight my feelings for Jemima, but it was too late by then… my heart was already hers. So, I met up with Mandy and told her we were over. We weren't that serious, or I didn't think we were, and she seemed to take it well. But as she drove away, I thought I saw her wiping a tear from her eye, and I felt bad about that. I know I'd have felt worse, though, and so would she, if I'd kept seeing her, when nothing could ever come of it.

I've been home for a couple of hours now, although I have no memory of getting here. I have no memory of anything other than the look on Jemima's face. She'd been crying, although I don't know why… unless she'd told her husband, or her boyfriend, that I'd hit on her. Maybe she did, and he was mad at her. He had no right to be, if he was. It was my fault, not hers. Should I go back there and straighten things out? Or would that just make it worse?

I don't know what to do, but I hope I haven't caused any problems for her. I feel bad enough already…

I feel as though I've lost her, which is ridiculous, considering she wasn't mine to lose, but the pain is more than I would have thought possible. It hurts more than anything I've ever experienced in my life… even when my mom died. I had Mason and my dad then, to help me and give me hope and comfort. Now, I feel so alone.

I pick up my phone, ignoring the fact that the screen is a blur, and I call Mason, because he's the only person I can think of who'll understand, but my call goes straight to voicemail, and while I could leave a message, with hindsight, I can't see the point. He might understand, but what could he do? He could tell me I was crazy not to have found out more about Jemima before I told her wanted ownership of her lips… both of them; not just the one she keeps biting. I drop the phone again and let my head fall into my hands, thinking about how stupid I was to think I stood a chance. Of course, someone as beautiful as Jemima was going to already be taken… and probably by some young, fit, handsome guy, much nearer her own age. It makes perfect sense. Who was I kidding that she'd be available to someone like me?

Myself, of course.

But the idea that she's got a family is beyond my comprehension. It's so much worse than anything I'd imagined, even in my worst nightmares.

My thoughts return for a moment to her tears and I wonder again if I ought to do something about that. I could tell her husband, or boyfriend, that she never came on to me. It would be the truth, because she didn't. I was the one making the moves, not Jemima. Okay, so she paid me that compliment this morning, but that was just a joke. I was the one over-thinking things. I was the one reading more into it than there was. Because I was the one who wanted her. She didn't put a foot wrong, and assuming she comes to work tomorrow, the very least I can do is offer to explain things to her partner… if she wants me to.

If she even comes to work, that is.

If I ever see her again.

I sit back on the couch and, because I can't fight it anymore, I let the pain consume me.

Chapter Three

Jemima

I watch Oliver walk away, and although I'm tempted to call after him, I can't. So I close the door, clutching Adam to me and trying not to cry anymore.

I cried all the way back here, struggling to even steer the car.

When I got back, I made the excuse of needing the bathroom, so I could run in there and try to clean my face of the evidence of my tears. I didn't want Mom asking questions. But once I felt reasonably respectable, I came out again, and she handed Adam to me.

To be honest, I was surprised he was still awake. Surprised, but pleased. I needed one of his special hugs, and I was feeling guilty that I hadn't been able to stay behind this morning and wait for him to wake up. His hug cheered me up, and although she didn't ask questions, I think Mom sensed I wasn't feeling too great, and she told me I could sit with Adam while she finished getting the dinner ready. I wasn't about to say 'no' to that offer, and I'd just got him settled on my lap when the doorbell rang.

"I'll get it," I called to Mom, getting up again and bringing Adam with me. I didn't want to let him go, not after today, and I went out into the hallway and opened the door to find Oliver standing there, staring down at me.

I think my heart actually stopped beating then. Just like it had at the office, when he'd stood in front of me and told me he wanted my lip to be his. I think he meant both lips, not just the one, but I was too stunned to ask. Stunned, and flattered, and hopeful... and scared. Rather than telling him that, though, or asking him what he meant, or just telling him to put me out of my misery and kiss me, I ran.

I don't know why I did that, and staring at Oliver, standing on the doorstep, looking down at me, I couldn't think of a single reason why I would have run from him.

Maybe it was because I'd spent the whole day watching other women fawning over him. That had made me think – yet again – that he wasn't right for me. And yet, having seen that intense gaze in his eyes, having felt his body so close to mine, I honestly felt he might be. After all, it's not his fault all those women flirt with him, is it? I've never seen him flirt back... not once. So that doesn't seem like a sound reason for running from a man who gives the word 'love' a whole new meaning.

Was it a fear of getting hurt again? Or was it the way he looked at me, like he wanted a lot more than my lips? Was it a kind of dread that if he took my lips, and wanted more, he'd be disappointed? I've seen myself naked. Or, to be more precise, I've tried to avoid seeing myself naked ever since Adam was born. I know pregnancy and childbirth have taken their toll. I might have lost most of my pregnancy weight, but my shape has changed. My hips are wider, my breasts are definitely larger, and they're not as firm as they were before I had Adam.

So was that it? Was it fear?

I've got no idea, but staring at Oliver wasn't getting me anywhere, and I was about to apologize to him when he held out my coat, telling me I'd forgotten it.

Was that all he came here for? To give me back my coat?

Did that even make sense? The look in his eyes when he said he wanted my lips to be his spoke of something deep, even dark, and passionate. It had nothing to do with forgotten coats.

"Dinner's ready," Mom calls out and I pull myself together, hooking my coat up behind the door and squaring my shoulders as I carry Adam down the hallway and through into the kitchen.

Mom's dishing up the pasta, and she turns to look at me. "I don't know how he's still awake," she says, smiling at him. "I fed him over an hour ago, and he's had his bath."

"Did he have a long sleep this afternoon?" I ask.

"No." She looks over at me, rolling her eyes. "He managed an hour, and then he decided sleep is for wimps, not for big, grown-up boys."

"Poor you," I say, and she smiles. "How did you get anything done?"

"Oh, he's been good all day. I did some ironing, and he's played with his bricks most of the time."

Somehow, that doesn't surprise me. Building bricks are his favorite thing at the moment. He's progressed from needing someone to build them up so he can knock them down, to actually being able to create towers of his own… right before he destroys them again. It's a boy thing, I think.

"He doesn't look like he wants to go to bed yet," I say, putting him in his highchair at the end of the kitchen table. "So he may as well sit with us. At least I'll get to spend some time with him."

I hand him a piece of cucumber from the salad bowl and he munches on it, while I pour two small glasses of wine for Mom and me, and she brings over the pasta, sitting opposite me.

"How did the party go?" she asks, helping herself to salad from the bowl and giving Adam some more cucumber.

"Fine," I reply, being as noncommittal as possible. I don't particularly want to talk about it. I certainly don't want to tell her that my boss just hit on me, and that I liked it… but that I also ruined it by running away, for some reason that I still can't fathom.

"Was that your boss at the door just now?" she asks.

"Yes."

"What was he doing here?"

"He just came to return my coat," I say. It's the truth, after all. He didn't give any other reason for coming over.

"Did you leave it behind then?" she asks.

"Yes." I fumble for an explanation. "I was in such a rush to get back to see Adam, I ran out of there and totally forgot about it."

"You needn't have worried. This one seems to have decided not to bother with sleeping." She tweaks Adam's cheek, and he grins over at her. My heart is still aching, but I have to smile. My little boy is such an angel, I can't help it.

By the time we've finished eating, Adam actually seems to be getting tired. I put him to bed, reading him a story, which makes him fall asleep after the first couple of pages, and while I'd like to sit in here and watch him sleeping, I feel guilty about leaving Mom to do all the clearing up. So I kiss Adam on the forehead, and tiptoe out of the room, closing the door quietly behind me, before going back into the kitchen.

"Let me finish this," I say to Mom. She's stacking the dishwasher, and she turns to face me.

"I've got a better idea... Why don't I finish this while you make us a coffee? They're showing the first *Die Hard* movie tonight, and you know how much I love Alan Rickman, even when he's playing a particularly mean baddie."

I shake my head at her while filling up the coffeepot with water. "You're the only woman I know who watches that movie for Alan Rickman, rather than Bruce Willis."

"I admire the man's acting," she says. "Nothing more, nothing less."

She goes back to stacking the plates and I get on with making the coffee, wondering – not for the first time – whether they broke the mold when they made my dad. I never met him. I've never even seen a photograph of him. But I've never known my mom to even look at another man, either.

I guess she must've loved him very much; even though he abandoned her.

As I fill the coffee machine with grounds and switch it on, watching the dark liquid filter through, I wonder whether my fear goes that far back; whether it's so deep-rooted, it's an instinct in me, rather than a rational thought. It wouldn't be surprising, I guess.

My dad abandoned my mom before I was born, just like Adam's father abandoned me. I guess it's only natural that I'd be scared of the same thing happening again.

I'm still not sure whether that's why I ran from Oliver, but as I pour the coffee and add a splash of milk, I know I'm going to have to explain it to him. No matter how hard it is.

If he hears me out and he decides he wants nothing more to do with me, then I guess I'll be looking for a new job after the holidays... and I'll be trying to fix my broken heart too.

"At least you've only got to work until lunchtime," Mom says as she hands me the toast and I set it down on the table, my stomach churning even more than it did yesterday. I daren't skip breakfast again, even though Adam's still sleeping, and I doubt he'll be awake before I have to leave. Not that it matters so much today, because, as Mom just said, I'll be home at lunchtime.

"Yeah," I reply, spreading a thin layer of jam onto my toast, and taking a bite. Mom gets homemade jams from somewhere... a friend of hers, I think. This one is strawberry, and it's delicious. It's almost enough to calm my churning stomach, except it isn't quite, because I still have to face Oliver.

I check my watch, knowing I can't be late; not if I'm going to have time to talk to Oliver before his first appointment of the day, which is at nine-fifteen.

"I'd better go," I say, finishing the last of my toast and gulping down some coffee. "We didn't get through all the clearing up last night, so I'll have to do it this morning."

Mom nods her head. "What time to you think you'll be home?"

"Around one, I guess."

"Okay."

"Why?"

She smiles. "It's just that I have to go out this afternoon, but not until around three."

"That'll be fine then. Are you gonna be back for dinner tonight?"

"Yes, of course. It's Christmas Eve. Where else would I be? I've just got a few errands to run, that's all."

"Okay. Well, I'll definitely be home by just after one, so you'll have plenty of time."

She nods her head, smiling as she puts a big dollop of strawberry jam onto her second slice of toast, and I get up and go out into the hallway, shrugging on my coat. I think about checking on Adam, but I don't want to risk waking him and disrupting Mom's breakfast. She gets little enough time to herself during the day, so I go back to the kitchen and say goodbye to her before heading out the front door.

The drive to work is really quick this morning, but I guess that's because people have got better things to do with their Christmas Eve than drive around town. My nerves are mounting as I park my car next to Oliver's Jeep, and while there's a part of me that wishes I could've called in sick, I know that would have been impossible. Not only do I have to clear up, but I left all of Mom's plates here last night… and I owe Oliver an explanation.

I get out, hugging my coat around me against the chill breeze. Considering how cold it is today, I'm grateful Oliver took the trouble to return it to me last night. Even so, the wind is still freezing, and I hurry to the front door, pulling it open and stepping inside. I hook my coat up on the rack, taking in the fact that the reception area is clean and cleared of all the debris from yesterday. Oliver must've come in really early, and I feel even more guilty now, as I go over to my desk and switch on my computer. Baxter is already in his basket, but doesn't even raise an eyebrow at my presence and I wander into the surgery to find his master.

The door might be open, but he's not in here, so I go down the hallway to the kitchen, where I discover him, still wearing his jeans, with a white shirt, washing up my mom's platters in the sink.

"Hello," I say and I notice his muscles stiffen at the sound of my voice, which doesn't feel very promising.

"Hi," he says, although his voice is cool, not warm, like it was when we were in here yesterday.

"C—Can we talk?" He sucks in a breath before shaking the water and soapsuds from his hands and turning around. My breath catches in my throat. He's still gorgeous, but there's something in his eyes... something wounded, and I'm surprised by how much that hurts.

"Sure." He waits, like he's expecting me to add something. When I don't, he says, "I had something I needed to talk to you about, anyway."

"You did?" Is he going to fire me?

"Yeah," he says, without elaborating.

"Well, do you think we could go into your office?" I ask. I don't want to be reminded of the conversation we had in here yesterday, or how different everything felt then. That felt hopeful, and this feels desolate.

"Okay." He dries off his hands on the towel, and leads me back to his office, waiting by the door until I've gone through ahead of him. He doesn't make eye contact with me, though. He stares at the floor instead, and I wonder for a moment about just handing in my resignation and making this easier for both of us.

The thing is, I don't want to resign. I don't want to be fired either. Despite everything that happened last night, I still want to be with him. It might be illogical, unwise, and very possibly dangerous, in terms of the damage he could do to my heart, but that doesn't stop me from wanting him.

He follows me into the room and I turn to face him, noticing he's left the door ajar. I wonder why, until I realize that he probably thinks I'll feel safer this way, rather than being confined in a closed room with the man who hit on me last night.

Doesn't he get it?

Doesn't he know that, despite my fear, I already feel safer with him than I've ever felt with anyone else?

Of course he doesn't. Why would he? When he offered me everything I've ever wanted, I ran away from him.

And I need to explain that to him... if I can.

"I—I know you said you wanted to talk, but can I go first?" I gaze up into his face, even though he's now staring out the window and still won't look directly at me.

"Sure. If that's what you want."

"Thank you." He shakes his head but doesn't say anything. "I feel like I owe you an explanation."

"You don't," he says. "You don't owe me anything."

"Yeah, I do."

He moves away, leaning up against the steel countertop that borders two sides of the room, folding his arms across his broad chest and looking straight at me for the first time.

I clasp my hands to hide the fact that they're shaking, and gaze down at them for a moment before looking up at him. I want to explain why I ran, but I'm not sure how… and besides, I think this story has to go further back than that… right to the very beginning.

"I—I met Adam's father when I was at college."

Oliver frowns, like he didn't expect me to say that. "You went to college?"

"Yes."

"You didn't mention it on your resume."

"No. That's because I didn't complete my degree." His frown deepens.

"What were you studying?" he asks.

"History. I'd always wanted to be a teacher." Like my mom. "Obviously, that didn't happen, because I met Adam's father. Well, I didn't exactly *meet* him. I already knew him. We both came from the same town, in Connecticut."

"Eastford?" he says, and I wonder to myself whether he memorized my resume.

"Yes. We'd known each other for years, but it wasn't until we went away to college in Boston that we started dating… and even that didn't happen straight away."

"Why not?"

"Because he dated other people for the first two years… quite a lot of other people." That probably should've told me something, but it didn't, and there's no point in worrying about it now.

"But I'm guessing he stopped fooling around with 'other people' and asked you out?"

"Yes. He said he wanted me and no-one else, and gave me a line about not knowing why he hadn't noticed me before… and then he told me I was beautiful."

"Because you are," he says, and then frowns again, like he didn't mean to say that out loud.

"I don't know if that's true, but I believed him at the time, and let him sweep me off of my feet… and into his bed."

I can hear Oliver's sigh from this side of the room, and he turns, looking out the window again. I follow his line of sight, although I'm not really looking at anything… I'm remembering how it felt to be swept off of my feet. Those blissful, joyous weeks, when I imagined myself to be in love, when everything in life seemed so perfect.

"We'd been together for three months when I found out I was pregnant," I say, not daring to look back at him, but keeping my eyes fixed on the windowpane, rather than anything on the other side of it. "It wasn't planned… not even vaguely. I was twenty years old, two years into my degree course, supposedly with my whole life ahead of me. I had plans, and getting pregnant wasn't one of them."

"What did you do?" he asks and I turn to face him again, discovering that he's no longer looking out the window. He's staring at me, bemused. "I get that you had Adam, but before that… when you found out…"

"I went to Donavan and told him," I say, interrupting Oliver. "He was stupidly incredulous about the whole thing, and kept asking how it could have happened, ignoring the fact that he'd been less than careful on more than one occasion. Like any of that mattered after the event. We spent the next week discussing it – sometimes arguing about it – and then we decided to keep the baby and stay together. We knew it was gonna be hard to study too, but we were young and stupid, and thought we'd be able to cope."

"But you couldn't?" he says, tilting his head.

"Oh, we didn't even get as far as the coping part."

"What does that mean?"

"It means Donavan cheated on me."

"Fucking idiot," he whispers under his breath, and then looks up and says, "Sorry."

I know he's apologizing for swearing, but I couldn't care less. "I was five months pregnant, when I discovered he'd been sleeping around."

"Sleeping around? So he was an idiot more than once?" Oliver sounds surprised, but I can't help smiling, simply because of the way he's phrased his question.

"Yeah, he was. I found out from one of his friends that there had been at least two other girls. I thought the guy was trying to make trouble, but when I confronted Donavan, he admitted it, and said he couldn't help himself. The first girl had thrown herself at him after football practice, evidently. It had happened quite near the beginning of the pregnancy and he claimed it was my fault, because I was tired all the time. I was being sick a lot too, and I wasn't always…" I leave my sentence hanging, unable to complete it.

"You were pregnant, for Christ's sake," Oliver says, angrily. "You were carrying his child and suffering from morning sickness. If that meant you were tired and didn't feel like having sex, your boyfriend should have been there for you, helping you. The very last thing he should've been doing was sleeping around, and then blaming you for his stupidity."

I smile. I can't help it, and I let out a half laugh. "Well, Donavan didn't see it that way, which I guess is why he did it again… and probably again, and again. Like I say, I only knew for sure about two of them, but I don't doubt there were more. He reasoned that if I didn't know, it didn't count."

"Seriously?"

"That's what he said. Except, of course, I found out… and it did count. We had a huge fight about it, at the end of which, I asked him what he wanted to do. I know it was naïve of me, but I honestly thought he was gonna say sorry and beg my forgiveness. I thought he wanted me more than anything."

"Based on his track record of being an idiot, I'm gonna guess he didn't?"

"No. He said he was too young to be tied down. He was too young to be a father."

"He should have thought about that before he got you pregnant." Oliver sounds angry still and I think about going over to him and telling him it's okay. It's not, but I feel the need to soothe him. I don't need to worry though, because he takes a couple of deep breaths, calming himself, and says, "What did you say to him?"

"I told him I was too young as well. I said that we'd agreed. We'd decided together that we were gonna have the baby. That was when he told me he'd changed his mind. Just like that. So, I did the only thing I could. I dropped out and went home to my mom."

"You couldn't stay on at college?" he asks.

"No. I guess, in the same circumstances, some people might, but I had no means of supporting myself. I was five months pregnant and Donavan was the one who was working to pay our bills."

"You were living together then?"

"Yeah. I'd been sharing a house with a couple of other girls, but Donavan and I agreed I should move into his place when we found out I was pregnant. It was a tiny studio apartment and God knows how we ever thought we were gonna fit a baby in there, but we were young and in—"

"In love?" he says, interrupting me, his eyes fixed on mine.

"No. I was gonna say 'insane'."

His lips twitch upwards at the corners and then he says, "So, you moved back home with your mom?"

"Yeah."

"I take it she knew you were pregnant?"

I nod my head. "I'd told her right from the beginning. She wasn't exactly pleased about it, but she was very supportive."

"And when you went home?" he asks.

"She was still supportive. I think she was kinda disappointed too, though."

"In you?" He frowns.

"No. In Donavan. Eastford is a really small town. Everyone there knows everyone else, which meant we knew Donavan's mom. There was some kind of history between her and my mom, although I don't know what that was. Either way, she said some really hurtful things and accused me of putting myself ahead of my child. Mom argued with her that it was Donavan's fault, not mine. It was kinda ugly, but Mom stood by me, and she was there for me when Adam was born. She even persuaded me to call Donavan to let him know he was a father."

"What happened?" Oliver asks, taking a deep breath.

"A woman answered his phone and told me he was in the bathroom. So I left a message, telling her he had a son."

"How did she react to that?"

I smile. "She went kinda quiet, but she said she'd let him know. He didn't contact me for two weeks, but then he sent a text message which just said he was with someone else, and he needed to concentrate on studying. He didn't have time for anything else."

"Asshole," Oliver whispers, and it's hard not to agree.

"I talked it through with Mom and decided that I wouldn't bother contacting him again. We also reached the decision that we were gonna move; to start again. It saved there being any more awkwardness between us and Donavan's mom."

"So you came here?"

"Yes. Not a million miles away, I know, but we needed some distance between us and them. I'd never deny my child the right to see his father, or Donavan the right to see his son, but we couldn't live there anymore. Mom sold her house and bought a much smaller place, so she had some money to spare. Neither of us was very sure what we were gonna do about work, you see. I had Adam to think about, and I'd never had a full-time job. Mom had been working as a teacher in the local elementary school for years, but she was fed up with doing that, so she resigned, hoping to find something else when we got here. Then the job with you came up, and although she thought about applying herself, Mom said I should go for it, and that she'd look after Adam for me. She felt like a break from working – or that's what she said, anyway – and she thought it would do me good to get out of the house and get some experience. So I applied…" I let my voice fade and stare across the room at him, hoping he still wants my lips, and the rest of me, and that I haven't just ruined everything.

Oliver

I'm so angry I can hardly control myself. How could Adam's father have been so irresponsible? Didn't he care about Jemima at all? Clearly not. Any more than he cared about his son. None of that is her fault, though, and I need to calm down and focus on what's happening right in front of me; not what happened before she even moved here.

I can't believe what I've just heard, considering I spent all of last night thinking it was all over between us. Not that there was an 'us' to be over, but I convinced myself I'd have to swallow my pride – what little I had left of it – and explain to her partner that I'd been hitting on her… and then probably find myself a new receptionist.

As it is, there's no partner for me to explain anything to, and while I don't want to second-guess Jemima's motives, I need to understand why she's told me all of this… because it matters now, more than ever.

"I'm glad you did," I say, smiling across the room at her, as I push myself off of the countertop and walk around the examining table, until I'm standing right in front of her.

She smiles up at me and then whispers, "So am I," and my heart skips a beat.

"Thank you for telling me your story, Jemima. You didn't have to."

"Yes, I did." She tilts her head, like she's confused. "You looked really shocked when you came to my house last night."

"That's because I was. You've worked for me for nearly a year now, and I had no idea you've got a baby."

"I know."

"Is there a reason for that?"

"Only that I've gotten used to keeping myself to myself. I don't know why. I just have."

"Probably because of the way your ex treated you." I can't say the guy's name. Hell, even thinking about him makes my blood boil.

"Maybe. Or maybe I'm just wary of getting hurt again."

I'm not sure how to take that. Is she talking about guys in general, or me in particular? If it's me, does that mean she's interested? Does it mean she cares about me? I've got no idea, and I have a feeling that if I think about it too much I'll go crazy.

"You wanted to say something to me, didn't you?" The change of subject catches me by surprise.

"I did?"

"Yeah, when I asked if I could talk to you, you said you had something you needed to say to me, too."

Oh, God. I'd forgotten all about that. "It doesn't matter."

"Yes, it does." She sighs and then says, "If you're gonna fire me, can you just do it, Oliver. I need to know where I stand."

"Fire you?" What the hell is she talking about? "Why would wanna I fire you?"

"Because…" She falls silent and looks down at the space between us. "I don't know. I just assumed you would."

"Why? Because you've got a baby I didn't know about?" She looks up again and shrugs her shoulders. "I wasn't gonna fire you, Jemima. Okay?"

"Then what were you gonna say?"

I'm going to have to tell her, even though I'm not sure what the consequences will be, so I put my hands behind my back and cross my fingers, hoping for the best. "I noticed you'd been crying last night, when I came to your house."

"Yes," she says simply, like it's the most natural thing in the world.

"Well, I wasn't sure why. But when I thought it through, I jumped to several conclusions."

"Such as?"

"Such as… the fact that you've got a baby probably meant you lived with his father, and that, if you'd told him I'd hit on you last night, he wouldn't have been thrilled. I imagined my actions might have caused a problem between the two of you, and I was gonna offer to put things right – or try to – if that was what you wanted."

There… I've said it. For a moment, she just looks at me, before a smile twitches at her lips.

"I see," she says. "Well... I guess you were right."

"What about?"

"When you said it doesn't matter. I don't live with anyone, other than my mom and Adam, so there's no-one to be upset about what happened."

"Apart from you... evidently." I take a half step closer to her, uncrossing my fingers now and letting my arms fall to my sides. "Why did you run away, Jemima? Why were you crying? Was it what I said... about you biting your lip?"

She shakes her head slowly. "No."

"Then why?"

"I honestly don't know. I spent a lot of time last night trying to work it out... and getting nowhere. But I—I really liked what you said." My cock hardens, while butterflies flit around my stomach. Can I have heard that right? She liked me saying I wanted to own her lips?

"You did?"

"Yes. I think it just came as a bit of a shock."

"Why? Why would you be shocked that I want you?" She stares at me and blinks and I wonder whether my request to own her lips was enough of a hint that I want so much more. Judging from the look on her face, I'm not sure it was, because she appears to be in shock again. "It's not just your lips I want, Jem. You do understand that, don't you?"

I've shortened her name and made it intimate in doing so. I've told her what I want. She can't be confused now. Except it seems she can, because she's still looking at me, bewildered and doubtful.

"But why?" she says. "Men like you don't look twice at women like me."

"Excuse me? Men like me?"

"Yes." She studies my face, and then lets her eyes roam downwards, over my chest and arms, before she gazes back into my eyes again. "Men who look as good as you don't normally go for women like me."

"Have you used a mirror lately?" I ask her, noticing the blush on her cheeks.

"No. I try to avoid them."

"Why? You're beautiful."

She shakes her head. "I've had a baby, Oliver. I know I'm not the shape I used to be."

I reach out and take her hand, holding it between my own. "I don't know what you used to look like, and frankly, I don't care. But I can tell you, I've spent a lot longer on this earth than you have, and I've never seen anyone who looks as good as you do."

"D—Do you really mean that?" she says.

"Yes. Every damn word."

I step closer, so our bodies are almost touching, and I let go of her hand, cupping her face instead. I can hear her breath stuttering, and although I'd like to think it's anticipation, or even excitement, I think there's more to it than that.

"What's wrong?" I ask, brushing the side of my thumb against her soft cheek.

"I—I'm scared," she whispers, gazing into my eyes.

"Of me?"

"No. Of being left again. I'm scared of being abandoned. My dad walked out on my mom before I was born. He didn't want me enough to even stick around and meet me, let alone be a part of my life. Then Donavan did exactly the same thing. He abandoned me and our son. I—"

"I'm not gonna leave you," I say, interrupting her.

"Everyone says that at the start. I think some people even believe it. My dad probably promised my mom he'd always be there. Donavan definitely said he'd take care of me, and that we'd make a life together. Neither of them saw it through though, did they? I—I guess I've just gotten used to men putting themselves first, and leaving when the going gets tough. And I'm not sure I could bear it if…" She snaps her mouth shut, like she didn't mean to say that.

"If what?" I ask, moving even closer to her, so my feet are either side of hers, our bodies touching now. I don't care if she can feel how turned on I am. She knows I want her, so what difference does it make?

"If you did the same thing," she says, blurting out the words and then trying to look away, even though I'm still holding her face in my hands.

I pull her back, turning her head and raising it, so she's forced to look at me.

"Why?" I ask. "Why couldn't you bear it?"

She sighs, looking utterly desolate. "Because this time, it would really matter."

My heart soars, my body alight and burning with need for her, as I rest my forehead against hers and whisper, "I. Will. Never. Leave. You." She leans back and looks up at me. "I mean it, Jem. You're not talking to a kid now, making silly, idle promises. I'm a man of my word and I won't leave you, no matter what happens." She bites her lip, and unable to help myself, I growl, "You need to stop doing that."

"Doing what?" she replies.

"Biting your lip."

"Why? Do you still want it to be yours?"

There's a twinkle in her eyes, and her voice sounds kinda husky, and I wonder whether maybe I read her wrong; whether maybe she won't be too shocked by the way I go about things. I guess there's only one way to find out…

"Yes, I do. But, like I said, it's not just your lips I want." I need to warn her… so she knows what she's letting herself in for. "It's kinda hard to explain…"

"Try."

"Okay. When you bite your lip like that, I get this urge."

"Urge?" she says, taking a deep breath, so her breasts heave against my chest.

"Yeah. I get this urge to slam you up against the nearest wall and kiss you so damn hard, you'll be begging me to stop."

I hear the hitch of her breath and see her pupils dilate. "I—I don't think I've ever begged anyone… for anything."

I lower one hand, putting it behind her, in the small of her back, and pull her closer to me. "You will," I say, and then I let her go, taking a half step away. "But, if you don't feel like letting any of that happen, my advice would be to refrain from biting your lip in my presence."

She gazes up at me, still breathing hard, and I note the shy, but sexy look in her eyes, as she very deliberately bites on her bottom lip.

I hear myself groan as I move forward and lift her off of her feet, hitching up her skirt as she wraps her legs around my hips and I walk forward, slamming her against the wall beside the door at exactly the same moment that I claim her lips, devouring her, exploring her deeply. She clings to me, her arms around my neck, breathing hard into me, as I change the angle of my head, and she sighs and moans, her fingers twisting into my hair.

I break the kiss eventually, holding on to her, and she looks up into my eyes and whispers, "Why did you stop? I didn't beg."

I use one arm to support her weight, while I raise the other hand, caressing the side of her neck. "I know. But, like I said, you will."

I kiss her again, harder still this time, and while it's difficult to resist the temptation to undo my zipper and move her underwear aside to make her mine completely, I manage it. Just. I don't want our first time to be like this, no matter how much my body craves her.

I turn around, walking us over to the examining table, where I sit her on the edge, because I need to slow things down and she's not showing any signs of begging me to stop. Then I pull back from her and she looks up at me, letting her legs drop from around my hips, although she keeps them parted, her skirt still hitched up, and I stand in the space she's made for me, nestled against her. I let my hands rest right at the tops of her stockings, my fingertips dusting against her bare skin as she stutters in a breath.

"Y—You're not put off by my story, then?"

I smile. "No. I wouldn't have kissed you if I was."

"So you don't go around randomly kissing women who bite their bottom lips?" she says, and I know she's fishing. She wants to know what I'm like with women; how reliable I am... whether she can trust me. I can't blame her for that. She has a child. She's been hurt before, and I guess there's only one way to reassure her I'm serious about this.

"No, just the ones I'm in love with."

She startles, blinking rapidly and tilts her head. "Sorry? Did you just say 'love'?"

"Yes."

"Are you saying you're in love with me?"

"Yes. I am. I'm deeply in love with you. That's why I'll never leave you, Jem. I can't. I'd have to rip my own heart out first."

"Oh, my God," she murmurs, throwing her arms around my neck and hanging on for dear life. I hold her, giving her the reassurance I think she needs, and then she pulls back and gazes up at me. "Is this something you do often? Fall in love, I mean?"

She's fishing again. "No. It's a first for me."

She snuggles into me again. "Good," she whispers into my chest.

"Why is that good?"

She tilts her head, looking upwards. "Because it is."

I place my finger beneath her chin so she can't look away again and shake my head. "No, I want a proper explanation. Why is it good that I haven't been in love before?"

She bites her lip, just for a second or two, and I gaze at it and raise my eyebrows, which makes her smile. "Because I'm in love with you too, and I really don't like sharing."

For a moment, I'm stunned and I just stare at her, my heart beating fast, my breathing labored, until my need overcomes everything else and I lean down and kiss her, biting on her lip just hard enough to make her whimper, before I pull back. "You'll never have to share."

"Are you always like this?" she asks.

"Like what?"

"Like this... passionate, intense... romantic."

"No. I'm not gonna say I've always been a saint. I haven't. I've always had a wild side. But I've never been like this before. Not with anyone. I've never wanted to be."

"Wild side? What does that mean?" I like the fact that she picked up on that. It's promising...

"You'll find out. If you want to."

"I—I want to," she says, on a faltering breath.

"Good."

"Why is that good?" She repeats my question back at me and I smile.

"Because I really wanna be wild with you. More than I've ever wanted to before... with anyone."

"I like the sound of that," she says.

"So do I."

"And I like the fact that you're different with me."

"Of course I am." I lean back just enough to cup her face in my hands and raise it up, so she's looking right at me. "We both have a past, Jem, but to be honest, I don't care."

"Neither do I. What does that past matter, when the present is like this?"

I smile down at her. "It's not just about the present. It's about the future." I bend and brush my lips over hers, nibbling at her bottom lip, more gently this time, although she still moans and sighs, arching her back.

"D—Do you have a thing about bottom lips?" she asks, as I stand again.

"No. Not usually. It's just yours I'm addicted to."

"I'm glad to hear that."

"Why?" I ask, caressing her cheeks with the sides of my thumbs.

"Because I like what you do to my bottom lip."

I rest my forehead against hers again and suck in a breath. "I know you say you're not worried about the past, but I want you to know you've got nothing to fear. There are no skeletons in my closet. Nothing's gonna come back and bite us."

"You don't have to explain," she murmurs.

"Yeah, I do. You've been fishing for the last ten minutes. So, do you want me to just tell you my life story and get it over with?"

She hesitates for a moment and then nods her head, pulling back and looking up at me expectantly.

I quickly check the clock to make sure we've got time, but before I can say anything, she puts her hand on my chest. "Am I gonna regret this?"

"No. Like I said, I've got nothing to hide. I just don't want there to be any secrets between us."

She nods her head again. "When was your first kiss?" It seems she wants to direct the flow of the conversation rather than just letting me talk, and I'm okay with that.

"First kiss?" I say with a smile. "That would have been in eighth grade, just before my fourteenth birthday."

"Clearly memorable," she says, her lips twitching slightly.

"It was okay."

"Only okay?"

"Yeah. I can't honestly say it was better than that."

She looks at me for a moment. "I take it you progressed from kissing?"

"Eventually, yeah. I found most of the girls around here were quite tame…"

"And we've already established you're the opposite," she says, interrupting me.

"I hadn't developed my wilder tendencies back then, but going to college had its benefits."

"You found your wild side?" She's teasing, but I think that's probably a good thing. It's keeping the conversation light, and not too serious.

"Not straight away, but I did lose my virginity in my second week."

"And how was that?"

"Not great."

She frowns. "Why not?"

"Because I didn't really know what I was doing."

Her frown fades and she smiles again. "Oh, dear."

"Fortunately, it was only her second time, and if she noticed my inadequacies, she didn't mention them. We stayed together for about four months, I guess, so it can't have been all bad… but then we both got kinda bored."

"With the sex?"

"With everything."

She nods her head, thinking for a moment. "Have you ever been in a long-term relationship?"

That's a slightly more serious question, so I give it a slightly more serious answer. "Not really. I've never gone into a relationship thinking 'this won't last'; but equally, I've never found anyone I want to spend all my time with… until now."

She smiles, looking kinda shy. "Did you get better?" she asks, in a whisper.

"Better at what?"

"You said your first time wasn't great because you didn't know what you were doing. So… did you get better?"

I can't help grinning. "You'll find out. If you want to." She doesn't reply. In fact, she doesn't move, or even blink, and after a moment or two, I say, "Do you still want to?" my heart in my mouth.

"Yes," she murmurs, and I heave out a sigh of relief.

"Thank God for that. I've waited so long for you."

"You have?" She seems surprised.

"Yes. I've been in love with you since the day you walked into my office for your interview."

"But that was over a year ago." She's more than surprised now. She's shocked.

"I know. I was dating someone else at the time, and then I met you, and I knew I couldn't keep seeing her… not when I'd fallen so hard for you. So I ended it with her that same evening."

"Really?"

"Yeah."

"And you haven't been with anyone since?"

"No. Like I said, I've been waiting for you."

She smiles and leans in to me. "It… It took me a little longer to work out how I feel about you," she says, biting her lip again, which is very distracting, and I have to pull it free with my thumb, just so I can concentrate on what she's saying.

"When did you realize then?" I ask her.

"I'd been here for about six months, I think. It was one day last summer, and I just looked at you… and I knew…" She gazes into my eyes. "Sorry."

"Hey, don't be sorry. I don't care how long it took you. The point is, you got there in the end."

"Hmm… even though I've spent ages fighting my feelings."

"You have?" Why?

"I need someone reliable in my life, Oliver. It's not just me. I have to think about Adam, too."

"I know. I get that. And I promise, I am reliable. Although I'd like to know why you think I'm not."

"I don't."

"Yes, you do, or we wouldn't be having this conversation."

She hesitates, blushing, and then swallows hard. "It's not that I don't think you're reliable... honestly. It's just that every woman who comes in here seems to think you're their property."

"I'm not. I'm yours. And you have nothing to fear. I don't want any of them."

"I know. You don't flirt back."

"No, I don't. Why would I, when I want you so much?"

I lean in to kiss her, but she places her hands on my chest, stopping me. "Don't you need me to bite my bottom lip?" she says, teasing.

"You can if you want, but I'm sure I can improvise." And with that, I grab her hands, pulling them around behind her back and holding them there, while I kiss her, so damn hard.

Chapter Four

Jemima

We eventually come up for air, although I'll admit, I'm struggling to breathe.

Oliver releases my hands, placing his on my cheeks again and looks into my eyes, which doesn't help at all with my breathing, his gaze is so intense.

"I hate to break this up," he murmurs, sighing. "But my first appointment is at nine-fifteen, and I think we ought to straighten ourselves up a little, don't you?"

He has a point. Although it's me who looks a mess, not him. My skirt is rucked up around my hips, my legs exposed right up to my stocking tops, and my blouse has come out at the back, from when he lifted me up into his arms, and slammed me up against the wall... just like he said he would.

God, that was good.

"You look fine," I tell him. He does. He looks gorgeous.

"So do you." He smirks and although I'm fairly sure my blouse is gaping and I know I'm exposed to him, I don't care in the slightest.

He loves me. He said so himself. Several times, I think. And all my fears and doubts and worries feel like hazy clouds in a sunlit sky. I'm in his arms, and I've never felt safer... or more wanted.

"I guess I had better make myself look presentable," I say, and he pouts, which makes me giggle, although I quieten when he rests his forehead against mine again, like he did earlier.

"I like that sound," he whispers.

"The sound of me giggling?"

"Yes. I think I'd like to make you giggle more often."

"I think I'd like that too."

"Do you need any help?" he asks.

"What with?"

"With making yourself look presentable?"

"Why? Do you think your help is gonna make it any quicker?"

"Hell, no," he says, smiling. "But I can guarantee it'll be more fun."

I giggle again. "If you can help me down from here, I think I can manage the rest."

He puts his hands on my waist and lifts me down onto the floor, watching while I tuck my blouse back in and straighten my skirt.

"I'm gonna need to find something to occupy myself for five minutes," he says, looking around the room.

"Why?"

"Because I can't take a cold shower at work… and I need to."

I laugh, leaning into him, which I doubt will help with his problem, and I whisper, "Sorry."

"Don't be," he says, and then tilts his head to one side. "I wasn't sure whether it was a good idea to tell you I'm in love with you. I wasn't sure whether it would reassure you or scare you off. But when it came down to it…" He doesn't finish his sentence, but places his finger beneath my chin, raising my face and holding it there, while he leans down and kisses me, his tongue finding mine in a delicate dance, until he straightens again, and murmurs, "God, I love you."

I'm breathless again, and for a moment I stare at him, until I find my voice and whisper, "I love you," in return, and he rewards me with a perfect smile.

"How did I ever get this lucky?" He still hasn't let go of me, even though time's moving on. "Last night, I thought I'd blown it, and today…"

"Can we forget about last night?" I interrupt him.

"No."

"Why not? Surely you don't want to remember that, do you?"

"Yes. I want to remember how close I came to getting it wrong, so I never make that mistake again."

"But you didn't get anything wrong, Oliver. I did. You didn't make any mistakes. It was me who overreacted. I ran when I should've stayed and talked. I misjudged—"

He shakes his head. "Stop," he says.

"Stop what?"

"Blaming yourself. It was a misunderstanding, that's all."

"Then why are you blaming yourself?"

"I'm not. Not really. I'm just saying I don't wanna forget what it felt like last night, when I got home and sat by myself, contemplating a life without you. I imagined you with the man I believed to be your partner – Adam's father – and I tortured myself all night, thinking about you and him together. It was painful... really painful thinking about never being able to hold you, and kiss you, and tell you how beautiful you are... and how much I love you. And now I've told you all of that, I don't wanna take it for granted. I don't wanna take you for granted, either. It won't hurt me to remember what it felt like to lose you in my worst nightmare... so I never have to do it for real."

I stare up at him, tears pricking my eyes, and I struggle to speak. "I —I..."

"It's okay," he whispers. "You don't have to say anything."

Good. Because I'm not sure I can.

He kisses me, his tongue darting into my mouth, and I'm just getting breathless again when he pulls back. "Shit!"

"What's wrong?"

"I still need to change." He takes a step back, shaking his head.

"Do you need any help?" I ask, teasing him, because it's fun.

"If you help me, I won't be seeing any clients at all this morning."

"You won't?" I tilt my head to one side, playing with him.

"No."

"Why? What will you be doing?"

"You," he says and I gasp. My skin is tingling, I can hardly breathe and I'm tempted to say, 'Yes please,' but before I can utter a sound, he smiles. "I think you'd better go sit at your desk, and let me deal with getting changed by myself, don't you?"

I'm not sure that's the best idea he's had today, but I do as he suggests, because I'm also not sure I want my first time with him to be in his changing room, or his office, for that matter. I desperately want to see his wild side... but I can wait until the moment's right.

The morning has been filled with clients, almost back to back. I've seen Oliver in between each one, though, when he's come out to the reception area, bringing them with him. Instead of coming over to my desk and giving them any necessary instructions, like he used to, he's walked up behind me every time, and put his hands on my shoulders, letting them rest there. The clients have stared, some more wide-eyed than others, and after the fourth time, I wait until Mrs. Webster has gone, closing the door behind her, and I look up at Oliver. "Why are you doing that?"

"Doing what?" He gazes down at me.

"Touching me."

"Why?" he says, pulling his hands away, like I'm scalding him. "Don't you like it?"

"Yes. Of course I do." I swivel my seat and stand up, putting my arms around his waist, to prove the point, and he relaxes and hugs me. "I just don't understand why you're being so... different. You don't normally behave like that when you come out here."

"Until this morning, I didn't have any reason to," he says, tilting his head to one side, a slight smile forming on his lips. "I know you don't like my clients flirting with me, Jem, but I can't exactly ask them to stop, can I? It would embarrass them. What I can do, is to show them I'm taken, and that their efforts are wasted. They always were, but..."

"Thank you." I stand up on tiptoes so I can kiss him.

He kisses me back, lifting me off the ground at the same time, and I giggle. He breaks the kiss then and just looks at me, sighing.

"This is so damn perfect," he murmurs.

"I know."

He slides me down his body, to the ground, holding me close against him so I can feel his erection, hard against my hip. It's not the first time he's let me know how aroused he is. Telling me he needed a cold shower was a fairly big clue, and I could feel him earlier, in his office. I may not be able to show him in quite the same way, but I want him too… just as much.

"Two more clients to go," he says.

"Yes." As I'm speaking, it occurs to me that we'll be going home soon, and it's the holidays, so I won't see him again until Monday.

"What's wrong?" He looks down into my eyes.

"It's Christmas."

"I know. Didn't we have this discussion once before?"

"Yes. But that was different. Now it means…"

His eyes cloud over and he frowns, realizing as I just have, that we both have family commitments. "It means we're not gonna see each other," he says, letting out a long sigh.

"No."

"We can talk, though, can't we? I can call you?" He sounds kinda desperate, and I can understand that. I feel the same.

"Of course."

At that moment, a car pulls up outside the office and we separate, staring at each other, neither of us happy anymore. "I have to go clean up the surgery," he says, backing away.

"Okay."

He turns and goes into his room, leaving the door ajar, and I wish I could run to him and ask him to spend tomorrow with me. I can't. He's got a family of his own, and he'll want to spend his time with them, just like I want to be with Adam. He's not overly aware of it being Christmas, or that tomorrow is going to be any different to every other day of the week, but I want to be with him and watch him opening his presents, and enjoying the day… like every other mom.

The last client of the day is a man... Mr. Donaldson. He comes out of Oliver's surgery on his own and walks up to my desk, his Dalmatian secured to a bright red leash.

"I'm supposed to make an appointment for two weeks' time," Mr. Donaldson says, smiling down at me.

I check the calendar and find him a suitable appointment, writing it down for him on one of Oliver's calling cards and wishing him a Merry Christmas, before he leaves and I lock the front door. The door to Oliver's surgery is open and I wander over, followed by Baxter, who seems to know when the day's work is over, and as I go into the consulting room, he pads inside, and sits down by the coat stand, where his lead hangs from one of the hooks, looking expectantly at Oliver, who's cleaning down the examining table.

"Is everything okay?" I ask him and he looks up, surprised.

"Yes," he says. "Why wouldn't it be?"

"Because you didn't come out."

"I didn't need to. I don't think I'm Mr. Donaldson's type, so I figured I could let him leave without having to display my affection for you."

"You don't have to display it to anyone, if you don't want to." I get the feeling something's bothering him, even if he says he's okay.

"Yes, I do... and I want to." He comes around the examining table, standing beside me, and takes my arm, turning me around to face him. "Sorry. I'm being grouchy."

"What's wrong?"

"It's just the realization that I'm not gonna see you again until Monday, that's all."

I lean into him, his arms coming around me. "What are your plans for the weekend?" I ask.

"I'm spending tomorrow with Dad, Mason and Isabel, and Isabel's sisters, who are staying with her and Mason for the holidays," he says. "My sister, Destiny, and her husband are going to visit with his sister, Eva and her family in Lexington."

"I've heard you mention your sister before, but I didn't realize she was married."

"She is. As of about six weeks ago."

"And her husband's family come from Lexington?"

"No, they come from England. His sister's married to one of the Crawford brothers."

"Crawford brothers?" I shake my head, unsure who he's talking about.

"You know? Crawford Hotels?"

"Oh." I know exactly who he means now. "Do you mean the one whose wife was kidnapped and killed?"

"No. I mean the other one. Chase. Although Max has remarried recently too."

"So you know these multi-millionaires, do you?" I lean back in his arms, looking up at him.

"Yeah. But I haven't let it change me," he teases and I shake my head at him.

"Apart from seeing your family tomorrow, you're not doing anything else?"

"No, other than missing you." *Oh, that's so sweet.*

"You don't have to." I lower my head slightly.

"I don't have to what?"

"Miss me."

"Yes, I do. I'm not gonna see you again until Monday, so…"

"You could come over tonight, if you want to." The words fall from my lips and I hold my breath, waiting for him to reply.

He cups my face in his hands, raising it to his, his brow furrowing. "Do you mean that?"

"Yes. I want you to meet Adam."

The air stills between us, almost crackling with tension, which Oliver breaks eventually with a cough. "A—Are you sure?" he says, his voice catching.

"Positive. I get that you need to spend time with your family tomorrow, but I really wanna be with you."

"I wanna be with you too," he says, and he leans down, crushing his lips to mine, lowering his hands and pulling my body hard up against his. I love this about him… that he's hungry for me, and isn't afraid to show it. He has me breathless in moments, but pulls back, looking into my eyes. "Are you sure about this? Introducing me to Adam, I mean. It's a really big deal."

"I know."

"And you don't wanna wait?"

"Why? Are you planning on leaving me?"

"No. Never. I told you earlier, I…"

"In that case, I don't see why we need to wait. I want you to meet him, and I want him to meet you."

He sighs and blinks a couple of times, his eyes glistening, and then he says, "I know Adam's father hurt you, and that trusting me is a big step for you, and I realize that introducing me to Adam is huge. I just want you to know I'm not taking any of it lightly. Okay?"

I nod my head, because he's stunned me into silence with his words… again.

He smiles and raises one hand, placing it on my cheek. "As much as I wanna take you to bed and make you whisper my name…"

"Whisper? What do you mean, 'whisper'?" I intend screaming his name, as loudly as possible.

"You have a child, and you live with your mom. There's gonna be a lot of whispering involved."

I giggle, and his smile widens. "Hmm… I see your point. You were saying?"

"Yeah. As much as I wanna take you to bed and make you whisper my name, while you taste yourself on my lips, I think we need to take things slow."

I raise my hands, clinging to his shoulders for support. "A—Are you kidding? You say something like that and expect me to take it slow?"

"Yeah, I do."

"You're actually serious?"

"Yes. I want you. I want you so much, I'm struggling to think straight… but more than anything, I wanna get this right, Jem."

"Given what you're offering, so do I."

"Would that be the offer of tasting yourself on my lips?" he says with a slight smile, his eyes twinkling mischievously.

"No. It would be the offer of your love."

"That's not on offer, babe. That's already yours."

I get home at just after one, having made a quick stop in town. I'm still floating on a cloud of Oliver's words and kisses, struggling to make sense of how different I feel now from when I left here this morning. What started out as desolate and hopeless is now perfect, and so full of hope and love, I have to keep stopping and reminding myself it's real. He loves me just as much as I love him.

Mom pokes her head around the kitchen door, her finger to her lips, and then she points toward Adam's bedroom, bidding me to be quiet.

"Is he asleep?" I whisper, going down the hallway to her.

"Yes, as of about thirty minutes ago. I think he tired himself out yesterday, so I gave him an early lunch and he's having a nap."

I nod my head, smiling as we both go into the kitchen, pushing the door closed. I'm glad Adam's asleep now. It means I'll get to spend some time with him this afternoon.

"Have you eaten?" I ask Mom.

"No. I thought I'd wait for you. But I've made us some sandwiches." She goes over to the refrigerator, pulling out a couple of plates, and putting them down on the kitchen table, before she turns and walks over to the stove, putting the kettle on to boil.

Not being a great fan of tea, I set about making a pot of coffee, putting water into the machine and filling it with grounds, before I turn to her.

"My boss is coming over for dinner tonight, if that's alright?"

She spins around, tilting her head. "Of course it is. I've made a chicken stew in the slow cooker, and there's gonna be far too much for the three of us."

"Are you making dumplings?" I ask, because my mom's dumplings are the best.

"Naturally." She smiles. "They don't take very long. I'll put them in when I get back."

I don't particularly want to talk about Oliver, or why he's coming over, or have my mom question what's going on, so I ask her where she's going this afternoon.

"Nowhere in particular." She's being evasive. "I've just got a few Christmas presents to drop off, and I thought it would be easier without Adam. He'd only get bored."

She has a point. Adam's boredom threshold is fairly low.

"What time is your boss coming over?" she asks, catching me out.

"Six. I thought I could give Adam his bath first, and then we could all eat together."

She frowns slightly, but doesn't comment, because at that moment the kettle boils, distracting her.

We settle at the table and eat our sandwiches, and I keep the conversation about Adam and Christmas, and all the preparations Mom says she's still got to do.

"Can I do any of it this afternoon?" I ask.

"You can make the cranberry sauce, if you like. The cranberries are in the deep freeze, so it's really easy. You just put them in a pan and let them simmer, and then add some sugar, when they're cooked."

"I think I can manage that." I smile over at her.

"I'll only be out for a couple of hours," she says. "So I'll be back in plenty of time to make the dumplings for tonight."

"Okay."

Once she's finished her sandwich, she heads off to her bedroom to get changed, taking her tea with her, and I sit, contemplating the fact that she feels the need to change, just to deliver a couple of Christmas presents. She's being very cagey about where she's going, too, and I wonder whether there might be a man involved. I don't know why she doesn't just say, if that's the case. After all, it wouldn't be surprising. She's very attractive, and she's been on her own all my life, as far as I know…

"I'll be going then," she says, and I glance at the clock, noticing it's not two-thirty yet. She's leaving early, and she's even put her hair up, which she rarely does. She's also put on makeup and a dress – a navy blue one that accentuates her waist, and I smile over at her. *There's definitely a man involved.*

"Have a nice time."

"Thanks." She leaves before I can ask any questions about her appearance, or where specifically she might be going.

She seemed very reluctant to talk, but then I can't complain. I'm not ready to talk about Oliver yet. Still, I'm sure we'll both rectify that… when we're ready.

I clear away and stack the plates into the dishwasher, getting the cranberries from the deep freeze and putting them on to simmer, and then going through to the living room to make sure it's tidy. Mom's very house proud, so I don't need to do much, other than straighten the magazines on the table and turn on the Christmas tree lights, which makes the room feel a lot more festive. I check on the cranberries, lowering the heat, just as I hear a noise from Adam's room, signaling that he's awake. He no longer cries on waking, he just talks to himself, in his own way, or makes some kind of noise to let us know he's with us again.

I wander down to his room and open the door, peeking around, a smile settling on my face as I see him, sitting up in his cot, gazing over at me.

"Mama," he says, which makes my smile widen.

"Hey, baby boy. Did you have a good sleep?"

He raises his arms, and I bend down, lifting him out of his cot, holding him close to me. I love the feeling of him, especially when he's just woken up, and he nestles against me, his head on my shoulder.

"Let's get you something to drink, shall we?"

I take him back to the kitchen, sitting him in his high chair, and pour some water into his beaker, giving it to him. He's very good with drinking and raises the beaker to his lips, taking a sip, before slamming it down on the tray of his highchair again.

"Mommy's just gonna finish the cranberry sauce, and then we'll go play." He bangs his beaker on the tray again, with such a sweet smile on his lips, it makes me giggle. I don't know what it all means, but he's happy, and that's all that counts.

*

I've been playing with Adam all afternoon, which means the living room is a mess again, but I can deal with that later. For now, he's in the bath, because I want to have him ready for bed before Adam arrives. He's due in forty-five minutes, and the only worrying thing is that Mom isn't home yet.

I finish washing Adam's hair, which he hates, and am just rinsing out the last of the suds, when the front door opens.

"It's only me. Sorry I'm late back." Mom's voice rings out through the house.

"We're in the bathroom," I reply.

"Okay. I'm just gonna make the dumplings," she says, and I turn my attention back to Adam, who's splashing water everywhere.

"I don't think so." I lift him out of the bath before we get flooded, wrapping him up in a fluffy towel and pulling him into my arms. "Let's get you dry." I rub my hands over him, which makes him giggle, and I laugh myself, because a baby's giggle has to be the most glorious sound in the world.

The moment I release him, he takes off, toddling straight past me and I get to my feet, going after him.

"What are you doing with no clothes on?" Mom says with a laugh in her voice as he heads straight into the kitchen. He does this every night, but she goes through the same routine with him, and it always makes him chuckle.

"Get back here," I call out and he laughs even louder.

Before long, we're all in fits of giggles, but I have at least caught Adam, and haul him up into my arms, carrying him through to his bedroom, where I get him ready for bed. Once he's in his pajamas, I let him go, and change myself, into jeans and a blouse. I don't need to dress up for tonight, but I would like Oliver to see me in something other than work clothes, for once.

I come out again, going into the kitchen, where Mom's just putting the lid back onto the slow cooker, while Adam sits at her feet, playing with a couple of building bricks which he must've brought in from the living room.

"Did you have a nice time?" I ask her and she turns to look at me.

"Yes, thanks." She folds her arms, leaning back against the countertop, and tilts her head to one side. "I've been thinking…"

"Oh?"

"Yes. About your boss coming to dinner."

I feel myself blush, but I hope Mom doesn't notice, or that she puts it down to the heat in the kitchen.

"What about it?"

"I'm just wondering why he's coming?" she says. "He's been your boss for nearly a year and, to my knowledge, you've never seen him outside of work, have you?"

"No."

"And yet he's coming over for a family dinner… on Christmas Eve?"

"Yes."

"Is there something going on between the two of you?" she asks outright, which makes the question kinda hard to dodge. Even so, I'm not sure I want to tell her how serious things are. It's all been so quick, and I don't want Mom to think I'm being hasty again, like I was with Donavan.

"Yes," I murmur. But I don't give her anything else.

"Are you sure about letting him meet Adam?" She frowns. "Don't you think you should wait a while, before you…"

"No, Mom. It's fine." I hate that she's questioning my judgement. She hasn't even met Oliver yet. Why does she have to assume the worst about him? It's not like I'm suggesting he'll become Adam's father, is it? That's Donavan's job… or it would be, if he wanted it.

She pauses and then lets out a sigh. "Okay… if you're sure."

"I am."

She smiles at last. "I'm glad you've met someone, Jemima. It's about time."

"And what about you, Mom?" I say, turning the tables. "Have you met someone?"

"I might have done." She raises her eyebrows, grinning, and I know I'm right. She's got a man in her life. All I can say to that is, good for her.

We're still clearing up Adam's toys when Oliver arrives, ringing on the doorbell at exactly six o'clock. I answer it, and gaze up at him, noting the intensely passionate look in his eyes, and I wonder to myself how on earth he expects us to take it slow, when he looks at me like that.

"Hi," he says.

"Hello." I step back, letting him into the house and he comes inside, waiting while I close the door. I turn to face him again, only now realizing the difference in our height, when I'm not wearing my heels. "You're very tall."

He smiles and lifts me into his arms, kissing me all too briefly, before he puts me down again.

"I've missed you, beautiful."

"I've missed you, too." I bite on my bottom lip and he narrows his eyes.

"What did I tell you about that?" He reaches out, freeing my lip with his thumb.

"I can't remember now. Would you like to remind me?"

"Later. Maybe," he says, and my body tingles with anticipation.

"Shall I take your jacket?" I ask, out of a desperate need to change the subject, and he nods, shrugging it off. I hang it up on the hook and he takes my hand.

"Nervous?"

"Yes. Does it show?"

"Yes." He gives my hand a squeeze, as I take a deep breath and lead him down the hallway and into the living room, on the right. Mom's kneeling on the floor, collecting up building bricks, and Adam's beside her, still trying to play with them. They both look up at once, and while Adam simply stares at Oliver, Mom gets to her feet and comes over, holding out her hand for Oliver to shake.

"I'm Heather," she says.

"It's a pleasure to meet you," Oliver replies, as I let go of him and go over to Adam, lifting him into my arms and bringing him back.

"This is Adam." I make the introductions, although Adam just stares, while Oliver smiles at my son.

"Hey," he says, reaching out for Adam's hand. Adam lets him, and gives him a smile, which warms my heart, right before he starts wriggling because he wants to get down again.

"I'll go finish the dinner," Mom says, her slight frown betraying the fact that she still doesn't approve of the way I'm handling things, before she disappears into the kitchen, leaving the three of us alone.

I put Adam down and take over Mom's job of clearing away his toys. Oliver joins me, crouching and handing me bricks to put into the bag I'm filling.

"These are his favorites," I say, and Oliver nods, giving me a red square brick.

"Is your mom okay? Does she have a problem with me coming to dinner on Christmas Eve, at such short notice?"

"No, it's nothing like that. I think she's just worried that I shouldn't be introducing you to Adam so early in our relationship, but..."

"Hey, if this is gonna cause a problem." He takes my hand and looks into my eyes as the panic rises inside me.

"Are you backing out already?" My voice cracks, my emotions getting the better of me.

"No, of course not. I'll never back out. Remember? I told you, I'll never leave. I'm just saying, if it's easier for you, we can keep our relationship to ourselves for now... separate from Adam, then involve him later on, when you're more comfortable."

"But that's not easier for me. Don't you see? If we do what you're suggesting, I'll be forced to make too many compromises. I get to spend little enough time with Adam as it is, and now I want to spend as much time as I can with you, too. I want both of you. I don't want to have to choose, and you've promised me you won't leave me, so I don't see what the problem is."

He nods his head and sighs. "As long as you're sure."

"I'm sure."

"Okay." He lets go of my hand and although I miss the contact, I'm so relieved, I can't help letting out a sigh myself, which seems to make him smile as he passes me another couple of bricks. "Does your mom always do the cooking?" he asks, changing the subject.

"Most of the time, yes. When I get home from work, I just wanna be with Adam, so normally Mom cooks while I give him his bath, and get him ready for bed, and then we eat together and I read him a story before bedtime. Then I clear up the kitchen while Mom rests. It's hard work looking after a one-year-old."

"Is that why you rush out of the office every night, so you can get back here to do all that?"

"And to see Adam… yes."

He smiles. "I thought it was to get away from me."

I giggle. "Hardly."

He laughs, shaking his head. "So Adam's one, is he?"

"He's fifteen months, if we're being strictly accurate. His birthday's September nineteenth."

Mom calls us in for dinner, just as we finish clearing away, and I pick up Adam, carrying him through, while smiling up at Oliver.

"I can't believe you're here," I murmur to him and he smiles down at me, placing his hand in the small of my back as we go into the kitchen. His touch is electrifying and I suck in a breath, trying not to respond.

"Do you wanna sit down?" Mom says, taking Adam from me and putting him into his high chair, while I offer Oliver the seat opposite mine. Mom sits at the end of the table, opposite Adam, and starts to dish up. "I hope you like chicken stew," she says to Oliver, as she hands me Adam's smaller dish so I can start feeding him. He has a spoon of his own, but most of the food he takes will end up anywhere other than in his mouth, so we share the task between us.

"I love anything stewed." Oliver takes his own bowl, smiling across at me. "Especially on a cold winter's night like this." He glances down, his eyes lighting up. "And I really like dumplings. My mom used to make the best dumplings ever."

"Maybe I'll get to try them one day," I say, offering Adam a spoonful of stew, which he accepts, while Oliver looks up at me, sadness clouding his eyes now as he shakes his head. "What's wrong?" I'm suddenly scared. Why doesn't he want me to meet his parents, when I've made a point of introducing him to Adam and my mom so early in our relationship?

"My mom died," he says, in a low voice. "When I was ten."

There's an awkward silence, as I remember he's only ever mentioned his dad, and never his mom, and I feel terrible. I should have realized. "I'm so sorry, Oliver."

"Don't be." He makes a valiant attempt at a smile. "It was a long time ago."

"Yes, but you were a child," Mom says. "And your mother died."

I put down Adam's spoon for a moment, and reach across the table, taking Oliver's hand in mine. "How did it happen?" I ask him, just as Adam starts banging his spoon on the tray of his highchair, clearly wanting my attention, and I have to release Oliver's hand to give Adam another spoonful of food.

"She died giving birth to my sister's twin," Oliver says, glancing at Adam and smiling.

"Your sister has a twin?" I struggle to control my shock.

"No, Destiny's twin didn't make it either. She and Mom both died." He takes a deep breath. "Destiny had already been born, and something went wrong, although I was too young to be told exactly what. I asked Dad about it later on, when I was older, and he said Mom had a hemorrhage and the other baby was starved of oxygen. That was enough for me. I didn't need to know any more than that and I stopped him from giving me any other information. I might not be a doctor of human medicine, but I know enough about it to understand that, when it comes to my mom and what happened to her, I'm probably better off not knowing."

I want to hold him, but Mom's sitting here with us, and Adam needs feeding, so I look across the table, trying to convey my sympathy.

"I'm sorry about your mom, and your little sister. It must've been hard."

"It was. But Mason and I got over it."

"Mason is…?" Mom sounds confused, but I can't blame her for that.

"My brother," Oliver explains. "He's two years older than me."

Mom nods her head, frowning. "And you say you both got over it?"

"Okay," Oliver concedes. "Maybe we didn't exactly get over it. We just got used to it. We got used to Mom not being around... eventually, after we'd gone through a period of resenting Destiny, just for being alive."

"Because you blamed her for your mom's death?" Mom asks.

"Yeah. Mason struggled with that more than I did, but Dad helped us get through it."

"And what about your little sister?" I wipe Adam's chin, then give him another spoonful of stew.

"Destiny?" Oliver says, tilting his head.

"No. Your other little sister. Do you ever think about her?"

He sighs and shakes his head. "Oddly enough, no. None of us do. Dad named her Faith, but we've always just referred to her as Destiny's twin sister. We kinda had the faith knocked out of us after what happened, and we don't really talk about her now, or even think about her that much."

"Your father will," Mom says, helping us all to water from the jug on the table, and Oliver gazes at her for a moment, before he nods his head and we all start to eat.

Adam barely makes it through dinner before he's rubbing at his eyes, so once we've finished eating, I take him through to bed, only reading one page of his story before he falls asleep.

When I come back out, Oliver's stacking up the dishes and Mom's nowhere to be seen.

"Where's Mom?" I ask him, bringing a couple of glasses over to the sink.

He doesn't reply and instead grabs my hand, pulling me into a deep, intense kiss, his tongue darting into my open mouth, my body crushed against his. I'm breathless and wanting more, just as he pulls back, looking down into my eyes.

"I told her to go sit down," he says.

"So you could do that?"

"Maybe. I've been desperate to kiss you all evening."

"Well, don't let me stop you." I bite on my bottom lip and he groans as he leans down, kissing me again… so much harder.

∞

Oliver

It's nearly ten-thirty by the time I get home, to be greeted by Baxter, who I take out for a quick walk. I don't normally leave him by himself, but I decided against taking him with me tonight, and he doesn't seem to have minded. He seems grateful for the walk, though, and runs along the lakeside while I walk slowly behind him, both of us familiar with the terrain, after years of doing this in the moonlight.

I have to say, I've had a fabulous evening, right from the moment I arrived at Jemima's house and she looked up at me and made that comment about me being tall. I guess I am, but she's also tiny, especially without her heels on, and I took advantage of the moment and lifted her into my arms for a brief but intimate kiss.

Meeting Adam was better than I'd expected. I'd been kinda nervous, which was weird, considering he's a baby and I imagine he couldn't care less who I am. But I wanted to make a good impression on him. I wanted him to like me. It mattered. It matters even more now, because of Heather's concerns about me meeting her grandson so soon. They mirrored my own, so I didn't blame her for feeling like that. It's Jemima's decision, though, and her mom and I have to respect that. If she's happy, then I'm happy, and I think Heather was too, in the end. She seemed to be, anyway.

There's another reason it matters that Adam liked me… because, having met him, I've kinda fallen for him. I know that's mostly because he's Jemima's son, but he's also incredibly cute, very happy and smiley and clearly adored by his mom. Jemima's pride in him and everything he did was obvious and well-placed and, while I knew I was letting my imagination run away with itself, it was hard not to picture the three of us together, doing all the things that 'normal' families do. Whatever a 'normal' family is.

He went to bed quite early, though, and while I'd have been happy to spend more time with him, I was at least able to enjoy the evening with Jemima.

I wasn't kidding when I told her I'd been desperate to kiss her. I'd missed her more than I'd thought possible, in the few hours since she left the office, and just sitting opposite her at the dinner table was enough to drive me insane. The need to have her in my arms was overwhelming... like the need to draw breath, and judging from the way she deliberately bit her lip, I think she felt the same. We pulled apart eventually, more out of necessity than anything else... at least on my part. I'd promised to take it slow, but kissing her was doing crazy things to my body, and I knew if we kept it going for much longer, I'd have had to break my promise.

As it was, once we'd straightened our clothes, we cleared away and made the coffee, and then we sat in the living room for a while with Heather. She's exactly as I'd expected her to be... basically an older version of Jemima, with slightly shorter hair, which is perhaps a shade darker. She's also very unobtrusive and accommodating. Let's face it, we were out in the kitchen for nearly thirty minutes, so she had to have known we were doing something other than stacking the dishwasher. She didn't come find us, though, or say anything when we finally joined her, and we spent the rest of the evening talking, until Heather pointed out that she and Jemima still had to put out Adam's Christmas presents, which reminded me of something I'd left in the car.

"Can you give me a minute?" I said to both of them and got up, going out into the hallway, before Jemima had the chance to ask what I was doing. I went outside, ignoring the cold, and retrieved the parcels from my car, hiding one in my pocket and carrying the other inside, where I gave it to Jemima, who was standing by the door, looking at me, kinda confused.

"What's this?" she said, glancing down at the brightly wrapped present.

"It's for Adam," I replied and she gazed up at me, tears filling her eyes.

"F—For Adam?"

"Yeah. I didn't bring it in earlier, but I wanted to give him something for Christmas."

"You didn't have to do that," she said, her voice cracking.

"I know. Like I said, I wanted to. He's cute. And he's yours." I wanted to add that he'd already gotten under my skin, but I kept quiet. "Shall I go put it under the tree?" She nodded her head, and gave the present back to me, watching as I took it into the living room. I stepped around the coffee table, between the pale gray couch and two matching chairs, and placed it beneath their Christmas tree, surreptitiously putting the box from my pocket behind it, out of sight, before I stood up again. "I'll leave you to get on," I said, giving Jemima a smile before I turned to Heather. "Thanks for a fantastic meal."

She got up from her seat on one of the chairs, and came over to me. "You're welcome," she said. "Come and see us again soon." That felt like acceptance, and I welcomed it with a smile.

"Oh, I will." She left the room then, going down the hallway to the back of the house, and I turned to Jemima, reaching out for her and pulling her into my arms. "I love you," I murmured, kissing her.

"I love you too," she whispered, when I finally released her. Her eyes were alight, gazing into mine.

"You okay?"

"Apart from wanting you, I'm fine."

"Well... hold the thought," I said, teasing.

"For how long?"

I didn't answer. Instead, I clasped the side of her face with one hand, putting the other behind her back, and kissed her deeply while I flexed my hips, letting her know – as if there could have been any doubt – that the want was entirely mutual...

The cold eventually gets the better of me and I call Baxter, smiling as he bounds back to me and we head for the cabin. He goes straight to his basket, while I take off my jacket and hang it up on the hook behind the door, hearing a thudding sound as something hits the wall. *That's odd.* As far as I'm aware, the pockets are empty, and I pat them down, feeling a square box, which I pull out and examine. It's wrapped in bright red paper, tied with gold ribbon, and there's a gold tag, which I flip over, and read… *'To Oliver, with love, Jemima xxx'.*

I have to smile. She must've snuck this into my pocket during the evening. Maybe even while I was out at my car, fetching hers and Adam's presents.

I grab my phone from my back pocket and look up her details, feeling relieved that I made a note of her cell number last night as I type out a quick message.

— ***Thank you for my present. That was very sneaky. xx***

I wander further into the house, turning on the table lamp by the couch, and sit down, just as my phone beeps. I smile, glancing at the screen, seeing the message is from Jemima.

— ***Thank you for yours too. I found it when I was putting Adam's things under the tree. Shall we open them now? xx***

— ***No. I'll call you in the morning. Early. xx***

— ***Okay. I guess we'd better get some sleep. xx***

I'm not ready for sleep yet. My mind is too full of her kisses, and how sexy she looked tonight, and I'm still smiling as I type…

— ***I can't stop thinking about you, in my arms, in your skin-tight jeans, so that might keep me awake for a while. xx***

— ***Would it help if I told you I'm not wearing my jeans anymore? xx***

I groan out loud, my cock aching.

— ***Not really, no. What are you wearing now?***

— ***Nothing. I've just got into bed. xx***

"Oh, God," I murmur, taking a couple of deep breaths before I reply…

— ***Are you trying to tease me to death? xx***

— ***No. But tell me, if I was there with you, what would you be doing?***

I know I'm repeating myself, but I can't help it. I simply reply with the word…

— *You.*

And I press 'send'.

Jemima responds almost straight away…

— *I wish you would. xx*

— *Is that your idea of begging? xx*

— *No. But is this your idea of taking it slow? Because if it is, it's going to be hard.*

I chuckle and type out…

— *It already is ;) I'll call you in the morning. Now, be a good girl and get some sleep. xx*

She comes back with a message that simply says, 'Love you', and I send one back that says…

— *Love you more. xx*

I set my alarm for six, but I'm already awake when it goes off, having been unable to sleep very well. The thought of Jemima lying naked in her bed kept me awake most of the night, and while I know it was the right thing to do, to suggest we take it slow, I think it's going to prove more difficult than I'd expected. I've never felt a such a deep-seated need for anyone in my life. It might have been less than twenty-four hours since our first kiss, but she's a part of me already.

I grab my phone from the nightstand, unable to wait a moment longer, and look up her details, connecting a call to her. I said 'early' in my message, so I hope she's awake.

"Hello?" She sounds sleepy and I guess I might have miscalculated.

"Did I wake you?"

"Yes. But it doesn't matter. It's nice to hear your voice this early in the morning. I can almost make believe you're here, with me."

"Is that where you want me, then? Lying in bed, beside you?"

"Yes," she replies, without a second's hesitation.

"You know who this is, don't you?" I can't resist teasing her.

"Of course I do, Oliver. Who else do you think I'd want in bed with me?"

"No-one else. Ever again." I'm being completely serious now.

"No. No-one else. Ever again." Her voice is kinda dreamy, like she's imagining the reality of her words. I know I am.

"Shall we open our presents?" I suggest. If we don't, we could end up lying here in silence all day, and I know that's not an option for her. It's not an option for me either. I'm going over to Dad's later on, but I know Adam will probably wake up soon, and I want this time to ourselves.

"Okay," she says. "You go first."

I brought Jemima's present into the bedroom with me last night, leaving it on the nightstand and I reach over and grab it, putting my phone onto speaker while I untie the ribbon and tear into the paper wrapping, to reveal a black box inside. Pulling off the lid, I let out a small gasp.

"Did you know my watch had broken?" I ask, taking the slim, plain-faced watch from its box and wrapping it around my wrist, doing up the buckle on the leather strap.

"No. But you haven't worn one for ages. You keep looking at the clock in the reception when you need to know the time, so I thought…" Her voice fades.

"You are observant, aren't you?"

"When it comes to you, yes."

I smile. "Thank you. It's perfect."

"You like it? I wasn't sure if you'd be one of those guys who prefers a watch that tells you the time on Mars, or whether you'd like something more simple."

"I'm a simple kinda guy, Jem… and yes, I like it."

"Good."

"Your turn," I say, feeling nervous.

I can hear her ripping into the paper I used to wrap her present, and then there's a moment's silence before she says, "Oliver… it's lovely."

"You're sure?"

I know she'll be looking at the white gold necklace I bought her yesterday afternoon, the pendant of which features a dove.

"I'm positive."

"I wasn't sure what to get you, but I was standing outside the jewelry store, feeling kinda desperate, because they were about to close, and I looked up the meaning of your name, hoping to get some inspiration. It turns out Jemima means dove. Did you know that?"

"Yes," she says.

"Ahh, but did you also know that – according to the website I found – in the Bible, Jemima was the eldest of the three daughters of Job, and that they were renowned as the most beautiful women of their time? The necklace already felt right for you, because doves stand for peace, and my name means that too, but when I read about Job's daughters, I knew I'd found the perfect gift for the most beautiful woman of all time."

"Th—Thank you," she says, and I hear the crack in her voice.

"Are you crying?"

"Yes." She sniffles out loud now.

My chest aches at that sound and I wonder if I should've said all that, even though it's true. That's exactly how it happened outside the jewelry store, and that was exactly how I felt. "Do you need me to come over? I hate you crying, Jem. I wanna hold you."

"I want you to hold me, too. And I'd love to say 'yes'… but I've gotta get up soon."

"Are you free tomorrow? Can we do something together?" I know we said we wouldn't see each other until Monday, but I don't think I can wait that long.

"Do you want to?" she asks.

"Desperately." She manages a slight giggle, which sounds a helluva lot better than tears. "Spend the day with me?" There's no point in bothering to hide my desperation, not when I've already put it out there.

"That sounds perfect."

"Good. I'll come over in the morning, shall I?"

"I—If that's okay with you." She sniffles again, and I suck in a breath, struggling to let it out again.

"Please don't cry, Jem. It hurts when I can't hold you."

"Sorry. It's just sometimes, the things you say…"

My heart stops beating. "Am I getting it wrong? Are the things I say upsetting you?"

"No. You say the most perfect things, like just now, and yesterday, when you said you didn't want to forget what happened between us on Thursday, so you'll always remember how it feels to lose me, and you won't do it again." She pauses and I hear a stuttered breath. "No-one's ever spoken to me like that before, Oliver, and sometimes I have to pinch myself to believe this is all real."

"It's real, baby. I mean every single word I say to you. Never doubt that. I love you so much, Jem."

"I love you too." She falls silent for a second and then says, "Damn. Adam's just woken up. I'm gonna have to go."

"Okay. Have a good day."

"You too. Can I call you later?"

I smile, unable to help myself. "Of course."

"What time will you get back from your dad's?"

"I don't know. But call anyway whenever you're free. Even if I'm still there, I'll pick up."

"But we won't be able to talk. Not properly. Not like this."

"Yeah, we will. I don't care who overhears us. I'm so damn proud to have you in my life, I'll shout my love from the rooftops. Having my family around isn't gonna keep me quiet."

She lets out a sob. "Oh, God… you've done it again."

"I'm not gonna change, Jem, so if me saying things like that is gonna make you cry, we'd better get in a supply of Kleenex," I say, and she giggles. "Go get Adam. We'll talk later."

"Okay. I love you," she whispers.

"Hmm… I know. But I still love you more."

Once we've all said 'hello', and wished each other a Merry Christmas, everyone settles in my dad's kitchen, which seems to be the place we always congregate when we're here. That includes Baxter, who has his own basket at the end of the island unit. He's lying there at the moment, watching Dad cook, just in case there are any scraps to be had. Mason is standing over by the sink, leaning against it, with Isabel in front of him, her back to his front, and his arms clasped tightly around her. Isabel's sisters, Ashley and Reagan, are sitting at the island unit. I met them both the other night, at Mason's. They're beautiful, just like their sister, and probably around the same age as Jemima. I got the feeling on Sunday night that Mason and Isabel might have been thinking about pairing me up with one or other of them. That was never gonna happen, of course. Not because they're not very attractive young women, but because there's only one woman for me. I think there always was… even before I met her.

"I missed a call from you the other night," Mason says, looking at me over Isabel's shoulder. "Thursday, I think it was."

"Yeah." I remember making the call now, and wish I hadn't.

"You didn't leave a message," he says. "So I assumed everything was okay."

"It wasn't." I recall my words to Jemima earlier and decide I may as well come clean. "Not at the time."

Dad turns around, facing me, a worried expression on his face, and Isabel's sisters look in my direction too.

"What happened?" Mason asks.

"Thursday was the day of the Christmas party at my surgery."

"Didn't it go very well?" Dad moves a little closer, even though there's still an island unit between us.

"It went perfectly. Right until the end, when I hit on Jemima."

Dad shakes his head and Mason struggles to hide his smirk, failing dismally. "You hit on her? You barely exchange two words with the woman for an entire year, and then you hit on her?"

"I have exchanged words with her. The day had gone really well between us, if you must know… and anyway, it wasn't me who wouldn't talk, it was her."

He nods his head, the smile still etched on his lips. "Okay… so you hit on her. How did she react?"

"She ran."

His smile fades. "Oh." He goes to move away from Isabel, presumably to comfort me, or counsel me, or both, but I hold up my hands, stopping him.

"It's okay. You don't need to worry. I followed her back to her place."

"To apologize?" Dad says, frowning at me.

"I had every intention of apologizing, but it didn't work out quite like that."

"Why not?" Mason asks.

"Because when she opened the door, she was holding a baby, who turned out to be hers."

Everyone stares at me for a moment, until Mason says, "So that was the secret she'd been keeping?"

"Yeah."

"What secret?" Dad says, but before I can say a word, Mason turns to him.

"Oliver's been trying to get Jemima to talk to him for months, but she's been really secretive, holding something back all the time… now he knows why." He looks back at me again.

"How old's the baby?" Isabel asks, and I recall how upset she got on Sunday night when Dad was asking Destiny about the likelihood of her and Ronan making him a grandfather. She and Mason might only be in the early days of trying to start a family, but I guess it has to be hard, hearing about other people's babies, when you want one of your own.

"He's fifteen months old," I say, giving her a slight smile, which she returns.

Mason stares at me, tilting his head. "Right, so let's get this straight… you hit on her, she ran, you went to apologize, and found out she's got a baby son. What happened next?"

"I walked away."

"You what?"

"Are you crazy?"

Mason and Dad both speak at the same time, while Isabel just shakes her head. I don't bother looking to see what Ashley and Reagan make of my response. I doubt it'll be good.

"I was confused. I assumed she was married, or at least living with someone. It wasn't something I was finding easy to contemplate. So I drove home and called you." I look across at Mason, whose face softens.

"You needed to talk?" he says.

"Yeah."

"Sorry I didn't pick up."

"It's okay. I spent a very sleepless night, wondering what the hell I was gonna do, and deciding in the end that it was probably gonna have to involve apologizing, not only to her, but also to her husband, or boyfriend, or whatever he was. She'd been crying when I got to her place, and I assumed he'd given her a hard time about me hitting on her. I was responsible for that, and I knew I had to make it right again. But before I could do anything, she came into work yesterday morning, really early, and asked to talk to me."

"*She* wanted to talk to *you*?" Dad says. "The woman who's barely spoken to you for a year?"

"Yes. She wanted to explain her situation… that she doesn't have a husband, or a boyfriend, and that her ex cheated on her when she was pregnant with Adam."

"Adam's her son?" Isabel asks and I nod my head.

"And she just told you all that?" Mason says.

"Yes, and once I'd heard her out, we talked, and apologized for our misunderstanding. Except… she didn't want my apology."

"What did she want?" Mason asks.

"Me, evidently." I can't stop myself from smiling.

"You mean, you're together?" he says, grinning now.

"Yeah, we are."

"Then why isn't she here?"

"Because she and Adam are spending the day with her mom. And because we're taking it slow… or we're trying to."

"You're not gonna lower the tone again, are you?" Dad says, shaking his head at me.

"No. I'm doing my best to be responsible here. I know it's not my usual style, but Jemima's got a child. A very cute child. She let me meet him properly yesterday evening…"

"She did?" Mason interrupts me. "She let you meet her son already?"

"Yeah. She invited me there for dinner and I met Adam, and Jemima's mom."

"Wow." I can tell he's surprised.

"I know. I fully appreciate how big a deal that is. That's why I'm trying to do the right thing… by both of them."

Dad comes around the island unit and stands beside me, putting his hand on my shoulder. "I'm proud of you, son," he says, which makes me blush more than anything I've said so far. "So, when are we gonna meet this young lady of yours?"

"I don't know." I genuinely don't. We're seeing each other tomorrow, but we've made no further plans, and I don't want to rush Jemima into anything. I don't want her to feel pressured.

"How about at our wedding?" Mason says and we all turn to face him, a stillness falling over us.

"Your wedding?" It's Ashley who breaks the silence.

"Yes. It kinda follows on from getting engaged, you know?" Mason says.

"Obviously," Dad replies, moving away from me. "But you're implying that you're gonna get married soon, if you're suggesting we can all wait until then to meet Oliver's young lady and her son."

"We are gonna get married soon." Mason looks down at Isabel, who turns in his arms and gazes up at him. "I want there to be another Doctor Gould in the family as soon as possible."

"Because there aren't enough of us already?" I say, and he chuckles.

"No, there aren't. So we've decided to hold our wedding on the first Saturday of February. We're avoiding Valentine's day, because that would be too kitsch, but six weeks should give us just about long enough to organize everything." He looks directly at me. "And it should allow enough time for Oliver to persuade Jemima that she's ready to meet us all… and to write his best man's speech."

"Y—You want me to be your best man?"

"Yes. If you think you're up to it."

"Well, I will be the best man there, so…"

"Oh, here we go." Dad rolls his eyes, moving back around the island unit, while Mason and I smile at each other.

I remember sitting at his place, not that long ago, both of us feeling as miserable as sin, pining for the women we thought we'd never have… and now we've both got everything we've ever wanted.

It seems dreams really can come true…

At least they can for us.

Chapter Five

Jemima

We've had a lovely Christmas Day. Adam had a great time playing with all his new toys, especially the wooden bricks Oliver bought for him, which have the letters of the alphabet painted on them. I have no idea how he knew to get bricks, but they've become Adam's new favorite, to the extent that he insisted on bringing a couple of them to the table with him at lunchtime.

Lunch itself was magnificent. Mom had cooked a huge turkey, and I'm fairly sure we're going to be eating it for the next week, as curry, and casseroles, and soups, because there's a lot of it left over. Everything else was really delicious too, except for the cranberry sauce, which I made. Mom dished it up into a bowl, putting it on the table, and as she turned away, she licked the spoon, pulling a face and looking back at me.

"Did you forget the sugar?" she asked, her cheeks puckering.

"Oh, God… I think I might have done."

She chuckled. "You're so distracted," she said, shaking her head. "But I guess that's what love does for you."

I smiled, not bothering to contradict her, and we decided we'd have Christmas lunch without cranberry sauce. It was just as nice.

There wouldn't have been very much point in denying Mom's words. She'd noticed my distraction earlier on, at breakfast, when I'd overfilled my coffee cup, because I was day-dreaming about Oliver, and then she spotted the necklace he'd given me, which I was already wearing, even though I hadn't showered yet, and was still in my pajamas.

"That's pretty," she said.

"Yes. It's from Oliver."

"I guessed that."

"He told me he looked up the meaning of my name, and found out it means dove, which is why he bought the necklace."

I didn't tell her what he'd said about both of our names standing for peace, or that Jemima – Job's daughter – was one of the most beautiful women of her time. I wanted to keep that to myself. Apart from it sounding big-headed, it felt too personal to share.

"That's very romantic," Mom said with a smile, spreading some jam on her toast.

And I couldn't disagree.

Because it was.

Adam's gone to bed an hour earlier than usual, completely exhausted from the day's excitement, and while Mom's watching a movie, I've come into my room to call Oliver, because I need to hear his voice.

He picks up on the second ring, with a very warm, "Hello."

"Hi. Are you home yet?"

"No. I'm still at my dad's."

"Shall I call you back later? Or do you want to call me when you get home?" I can't hide my disappointment. I've been looking forward to a long, private call with him.

"No. We can talk now. I'm sure as hell not waiting until later." It sounds to me like he's smiling and the corners of my lips twitch upwards, too.

"Have you had a good day?" I ask him.

"Yes, thanks… apart from missing you. How about you?"

"I've missed you too, but aside from that, it's been great. Adam loved his bricks, by the way. He can't say thank you himself, but he loves them. He won't put them down."

"That's good. I wasn't sure what to get him, but I figured all kids like bricks… or at least they like knocking them down."

"Yes, they do."

"I love you," he says, unexpectedly.

"I love you, too."

There's a noise in the background, which I can't make out, and then Oliver says, "Oh, yeah... my brother's just reminded me, he and Isabel are getting married on the first Saturday in February, and they'd like you to come."

I'm stunned into silence. I'm invited to his brother's wedding?

"A—Are you sure?" I can't help myself from stuttering.

"Of course."

"But I don't even know your brother."

"You know me. And Mason probably feels like he knows you, too. I've been talking to him about you for the last year... ever since I fell in love with you, but couldn't even work out how we were gonna have a conversation. So you're hardly a stranger."

"You've really been in love with me for that long?" I lower my voice to a whisper, even though there's no-one to overhear me.

"Yes. I told you yesterday, I fell for you the moment you walked into my office."

"I wish I'd worked it out sooner."

He chuckles. "In a way, so do I. But in another way, I wouldn't change a thing. I think I appreciate you so much more, because I had to wait."

"That's such a lovely thing to say," I say, blinking away my threatening tears.

"You're not crying, are you?" he asks.

"Not yet."

"Good. Try not to. I'm not there to hold you."

I wish he was. "I'll do my best."

"And tell me you'll come to the wedding?"

"Is this you begging?" I'm teasing, and maybe trying to distract him.

"No. This is me asking nicely. I don't do begging."

I can hear the smile in his voice, and it feels like my teasing backfired, because no amount of smiling, or begging, is going to alter the facts. "We've only just started seeing each other, Oliver. I'm not sure..." It feels too soon to be meeting his entire family, especially on such a special occasion.

"You have to come," he says. "I don't wanna go without you. I don't wanna do anything without you. Hell, I struggle to function, or even to breathe without you. But when it comes to Mason's wedding, I've gotta be there. Not only is he my brother, but I'm the best man." He pauses and then says, "Please, Jem."

"I thought you didn't do begging."

"I'm making an exception. This is important to me."

"Then I'll come." It matters to him... and that means it matters to me, even if I am nervous about it.

"Thank you," he says. "Mason?" He's clearly talking to his brother now. "Jemima's coming to the wedding."

"Great," I hear in the background.

"Your brother's there with you?" I'd assumed Oliver was alone and that maybe his brother had just poked his head around the door to ask about the wedding. It seems I was wrong.

"Yeah," Oliver says. "We're all sitting in the living room together."

"Y—You mean you've just said all those things about me, in front of your whole family?"

"Not my whole family, no. Destiny and Ronan aren't here. But if you like I can call them up and tell them too." He pauses and then says, "I told you I'll shout my love for you from the rooftops. You're my world, Jem, and I don't care who knows it."

I can't stop the tears from falling this time, and I stutter in a breath. "Oh, Oliver."

"God, you really are crying now, aren't you?"

"Yes," I say, through my tears. "But you don't have to come over. It's okay."

"No, it's not okay."

"It is. Really. I'm happy, not sad."

"I still don't like it," he says.

"Then you can make it up to me tomorrow."

"With pleasure." There's something in his voice that makes my body tingle and I sigh down the phone. "What time shall I come over?" he asks.

"Ten-thirty?" I know how long it takes to get ready in the morning. "I'll be there."

"I can't wait for you to kiss me again," I whisper, that tingle still drifting around my body, making me want him.

He chuckles slightly. "Neither can I."

"Is there anything else you want to do to me?"

"Yes. And we can talk about that tomorrow," he says, sounding a lot more evasive now.

"Is everything okay, Oliver?"

"Of course it is. I'll come over at ten-thirty tomorrow and we'll spend the day together."

"That sounds perfect." It does. Even if I'm still a little confused by the sudden change in him. He was so romantic a few minutes ago, so willing to say anything and everything I could ever want to hear. But he's different now, and I don't know why.

"It will be," he says. "I promise." And the sincerity in his voice makes me feel a lot better, because I can't doubt him... or his love.

"I probably should've told you last night," I say to Mom as we sit at the breakfast table, and Adam chews on a finger of toast, "we're spending the day with Oliver."

"You are?" She's surprised and looks up, across the top of the cup of tea she's holding.

"Yes. We arranged it yesterday morning, but with all the excitement, I forgot to mention it. He's coming over at ten-thirty."

She nods her head, putting her cup down. "And you're spending the day here?"

"I don't know what we're doing. I just know he's coming here at ten-thirty. He might have made plans for after that." I've got no idea, but either way, I'm looking forward to it.

"Does that mean you won't be needing me today?" she says.

"No. Why? Have you got plans of your own?"

"I didn't. But I could have." She gives me a smile as she gets up from the table and goes over to the countertop, where her phone is charging.

She unplugs it and puts it in the back pocket of her jeans before she leaves the room with a spring in her step.

Time's moving on, and Adam seems to have had enough toast, so I lift him from his highchair and carry him out into the hallway, hearing Mom's voice on the phone as we pass her room. I can't help smiling, although I wish she'd tell me about whoever this man is. I'd like to meet him, but I guess she'll get around to that when she's ready.

I'm not dressed yet, and nor is Adam, so I take him through to the bathroom, sitting him on the floor, while I shower, and then we brush our teeth together. He only has five so far, but loves brushing them, although he gets the toothpaste everywhere. Once I've cleaned the sink of all his mess, I take him through to his bedroom and get him dressed in jeans, a t-shirt and a sweater with a truck on the front. It's one of his favorites and he smiles up at me as I put his socks on.

"Do you wanna go find Grandma?" I say and he nods his head, sliding off of the bed and toddling out into the hallway. I follow, noticing that Mom's bedroom door is open and I hear her greet him as he wanders into the living room, so I know he's safe before I go into my room, closing the door behind me.

I dry my hair, leaving it long for a change, because Oliver only ever sees me with my hair in a ponytail, and I put on a white thong and matching bra, stonewashed jeans, high-heeled, black knee-length boots, and a white sleeveless top with a lace trim around the low neckline. Then I add a thick pink and blue check blouse, which I leave open, before I apply a little makeup. I guess I'm as ready as I ever will be, and I go out into the hallway.

"You look pretty," Mom says from her seat on the couch as I enter the living room.

"Thanks."

"I'll be leaving in about ten minutes." She leans down and picks up a building brick which Adam's just knocked flying, then hands it back to him, without making eye contact with me.

"Okay."

"I don't know when I'll be back," she adds, still focusing on Adam.

I'm desperate to ask about the man I know she's going to see, but I restrain myself and just say, "I don't even know what we're doing, but if we go out anywhere, we'll be home in time for Adam's bath, in case you get back here before we do."

She nods her head and gets up. "I'd better go find my shoes," she says, and before I can ask anything else, she's gone.

I sit down, taking her place, and watch Adam trying to build another tower, which keeps toppling over.

"Let me help." I get down on the floor with him, constructing a tall tower of bricks, which he watches avidly, a grin forming on his face as he knocks the whole lot flying. "Well, thanks," I say and we crawl around together, picking up all the blocks and putting them back in a pile in front of the couch again.

"At least he helps," Mom says, and I look up to see her standing in the doorway, her coat already on and her keys in her hand. "When you were little, you'd do the same thing and just sit and watch while I picked up all the pieces."

"Only because you let me," I say and she nods her head, smiling.

"Yeah. Probably." She comes over and bends down, giving Adam a kiss on his forehead. "I'm going now. I'll put the car seat into your car, in case you need it."

"Oh, yes. Thanks." I don't know why I didn't think of that.

"You two have a good day."

"You too." I look up at her, tilting my head, but she doesn't give me any more information, and I guess I'm just gonna have to wait to find out what she's doing... and who she's doing it with.

Once she's gone, we build another tower, which Adam delights in knocking down just as the doorbell rings and I jump to my feet, running to open it. I barely have time to take in Oliver's dark jeans and thick cream sweater before I throw myself into his arms. He catches me, and I wrap my legs around him, clinging on to him as he holds me close.

"God, you feel good," he says into my hair.

"So do you."

He leans back slightly, looking into my eyes, and the air around us stills for a second, before he crushes his lips to mine in a heated kiss, which has me moaning into his mouth within seconds.

"What is it about your kisses?" I ask when he eventually pulls back.

"I don't know. You tell me?"

"They make me want more."

"Good," he says. "Are you ready?"

"Ready for what?" I'm still struggling to make sense of anything after that kiss, including his question.

"I thought I'd take you to my place," he says. "Both of you. We can spend the day there, if that's okay?"

"Oh. That sounds lovely."

"Anywhere you are sounds lovely," he says, and I bite my bottom lip, smiling at the same time. "Leave that lip alone." He lowers me to the floor, pulling it free with his thumb. "It's mine." His eyes drop, and the heat that was already there, bursts into flame. "G—God, Jem," he murmurs.

"What?"

He reaches out, his fingers dusting over the lace trim of my top. He's not even touching my skin, just hinting at it, but my breath catches in my throat.

"You're exquisite."

I'm still trying to get my breath back and having him say something like that isn't helping. I look up at him, his amber eyes boring into mine.

"So, are you ready?" he repeats, letting his hand drop to his side again

"Well, no. I didn't know we were going anywhere, so I guess I need to get a few things together."

"Okay," he says. "Let's do that, and we can get going."

I take his hand and lead him into the house. Adam's still playing in the living room, but when he sees Oliver, he gets up and toddles over to me, putting his arms around my leg. I bend and lift him up and although he nestles into me, he won't take his eyes from Oliver.

"You remember Oliver, don't you?" I say. "He gave you your new bricks." Adam points to the bricks which are spread across the floor. "Yes, that's right. Those bricks. Oliver bought them."

He was fine with Oliver the other night, so I don't understand why he's being shy now.

"What do we need to take?" Oliver asks, and although a part of me is wondering if we should stay here, where Adam's got his toys around him, and everything is more familiar, I want to see where Oliver lives, and I don't want to spoil his plans.

"So much stuff, you wouldn't believe it," I tell him, and he smiles.

"Shall I play with Adam while you get everything together?" he suggests, holding out his hands to take him.

"No." I pull away slightly, my instincts telling me that, with Adam being so shy today, Oliver's plan won't end well. "It's fine. I'm used to holding him and doing all kinds of things. We'll manage."

"You don't have to," Oliver says. "I'm sure he'd be okay with me."

"I know, but it'll be quicker this way."

He nods his head, while shrugging his shoulders, and I move further into the room, gathering up Adam's new bricks and putting them away in their box, so we can take them with us, along with his pretend phone and his set of construction vehicles that Mom gave him for Christmas. That should be enough to keep him entertained.

I put everything on the couch and then turn to Oliver. "Do you wanna put those in your car while I fetch a few things from his bedroom?" He nods his head, gathering Adam's toys and heading for the front door, while I carry Adam toward the back of the house, going into his room, and grabbing the diaper bag from the hook on the back of the door. I put it on the chair in the corner, and check inside, adding some diapers and a change of clothes from his drawers. "We're gonna have a fun day," I say to Adam, who's still clinging to me, as I zip up the bag. At the last minute, I remember to bring Boots – his toy dog, who's brown all over, except for his white paws. He's Adam's favorite, and as I pick him up, Adam takes him from me, holding him tight and putting his thumb into his mouth.

Closing the bedroom door behind us, we go back into the hallway, where Oliver's waiting.

"Shall I take that?" he says, coming forward and reaching out for the diaper bag, which I've slung over my shoulder.

"Thanks." I turn slightly, letting him remove it.

"Is there anything else?"

"Just the car seat, which we can grab on the way out. Fortunately, Mom transferred it from her car before she left, or we'd have been in trouble."

"Your mom's gone out?" Oliver says, holding the door open as I take my keys from the hook.

"Yes. Sorry, do you think you could grab our coats too? And my scarf?"

"Sure."

He turns, reaching for my coat, and Adam's, as well as my long cream scarf, and then we all head out. Oliver puts everything into the trunk of his car while I wander over to mine, opening it as I approach.

"Let me help," he says, coming up behind me.

"Thanks."

He opens the rear passenger door and, with a little difficulty, unfastens the car seat from inside, carrying it to his Jeep, where he takes a little longer, reinstalling it.

"I'll just check the fixings," I say, putting Adam into the seat and making sure Oliver's attached everything properly, before I fasten Adam in place and turn around to face Oliver again.

"Did I do it right?" He shuts Adam's door.

"Yes."

"Can we go now?"

I smile up at him. "Yes. Once I've closed the front door."

He grins. "Good point."

He leans down and kisses me just briefly before I walk back to the house, shutting the front door and making sure it's locked. When I rejoin him, he's standing by the passenger door, holding it open for me and he helps me to get in, making sure I'm comfortable before he closes it again, and walks around the front of the car, climbing in himself.

"Sure we haven't forgotten anything?" he says, smiling over at me.

"Positive."

"Okay. Let's go."

He starts the engine, reversing down the driveway and onto the street, and I turn and check that Adam's okay before we head off.

"Can I ask you a question?" he says, once we're on the main road, heading back into town.

"Sure." I look across at him, although he's concentrating on driving.

"Was there a reason I had to beg you to come to Mason's wedding?"

I turn in my seat, so I'm facing him. "Our relationship is really new, Oliver. We're still getting used to each other."

"I get that," he says, with a slight frown. "But I've met your family."

"Which comprises my mom and Adam. Your family is enormous by comparison. And I've never been great with big gatherings. They scare me."

He reaches over, placing his hand on my leg. "You've got nothing to fear. Aside from the fact that none of my relations is gonna say or do anything to hurt you, I'm gonna be there, and I'll look after you."

"I know. I'm just being silly."

"No, you're not. But I promise, you'll be perfectly safe."

I shift over slightly and lean against him. "I know I will."

"Good," he says, and he bends his head, kissing the top of mine.

"Now, can I ask you a question?" I say, looking up at him.

"Of course you can."

I stare through the windshield as we enter the town, letting the passing buildings distract me. "Why did you change when we were talking on the phone last night?"

"How do you mean?" he says.

"Well, one minute you were saying all those lovely things in front of your family, and the next you clammed up."

"I didn't clam up." He sounds confused, and when I look up at him again, his brow is furrowed.

"It felt like you did. When I asked you if there was anything you wanted to do to me, you didn't give me an answer."

He turns and looks at me, just briefly, smiling now. "Of course I didn't. I'll tell the world I'm in love with you, Jem. I'll tell anyone who'll listen how I feel, and how lucky I am to have you in my life. But I'm not telling a damn soul about how I wanna *show* my love... except you, when we're alone."

"Oh... I see."

I guess this is all part of getting to know each other, but I realize how silly I've been – again – and I lean into him a little closer, resting my head against him as he continues the drive to his place.

Oliver wasn't kidding when he said he lives beside a lake. His cabin is literally right on the banks of a tree-lined stretch of water, at the end of a long, winding lane.

Once he's parked up beside the wood store which runs along one side of the cabin, he gets out and comes around, helping me down, and I stand for a moment, admiring the view across the lake to the woodland on the other side.

"It's beautiful here," I say as he looks down at me.

"It is now." He pulls me into his arms, kissing me.

We keep it short, which is a shame, because I like his kisses. "I'll get Adam," I say and he nods, releasing me.

"Do you want me to unload everything else?"

"Yes, it's probably best."

"Okay."

He goes around to the back of the car, opening it, and before I know it, Baxter is by my feet, nuzzling into me.

"I didn't know he was with us." I look up at Oliver.

"I rarely leave him anywhere," he replies. "I know I did the other night, when I came to see you, but that was only because I didn't want the distraction of thinking about him, when I wanted to concentrate on you. And besides, I knew I wouldn't be out for very long. Normally, he travels in the car with me, but I thought it might be safer for him to be in the trunk today."

"Oh. Sorry, Baxter." I crouch down and stroke the side of his face, and he turns his head, licking my hand.

"He's okay. He's just playing for sympathy."

I smile up at Oliver and then stand, opening the rear door and unfastening Adam from his car seat, before lifting him out and into my arms. Baxter jumps up, wanting to see what I'm holding, and I hug Adam a little closer.

"Down, boy," Oliver says, clearly noticing my reaction, and Baxter calms in an instant, as Oliver turns to me. "Baxter won't hurt him, you know?"

I nod my head, trying to convince myself.

"Baxter… heel," Oliver commands, and Baxter immediately goes to him, sitting right by his leg, making me feel guilty for doubting him. "I can control my dog," he says, tilting his head at me. "And I guarantee nothing will happen to Adam. Baxter's just a big softie, aren't you, boy?" He rubs behind Baxter's ears, even though he's looking at me.

"Sorry," I mumble.

"You don't have to be sorry. Just trust me."

"I do."

"Good." He smiles. "Now, shall we get Adam's things inside?"

I wait, while he picks up everything from the car, noticing that Baxter doesn't move a muscle, which makes me feel even more guilty, and once we're ready, Oliver leads the way into his house. I hear him make a clicking noise with his tongue and Baxter sparks into life, following him up the four steps onto the porch.

"Are you okay?" Oliver says, looking over his shoulder as I bring up the rear.

"Yes."

He pauses by the front door, opening it, and then steps aside to let me enter first. Even Baxter waits his turn, and I smile down at him, hoping he's forgiven me.

I move inside and almost gasp. I'd expected something quite basic, and what greets me is rustic and charming. The roof of the cabin is completely exposed, revealing the wooden framework of the building. The floor is covered with thick rugs, and the furniture is lived-in and soft, and looks really comfortable.

Oliver comes in behind me, closing the door, and leads me into the living area, where I put Adam down on the floor, opening up his box of building bricks for him to play with.

"I didn't realize you lived in the middle of nowhere," I say, turning to Oliver, who's put the rest of Adam's things on the window seat that faces the front of the house, looking out across the lake. "I take it you have hot and cold running water, and heating, and everything?"

He pulls off his sweater, throwing it onto the window seat, too, and then comes over, putting his arms around me. He's wearing a dark gray t-shirt that clings to every muscle, and I want to run my hands over all of them. Slowly…

"I have hot and cold running everything," he says, and waves his arm toward the pale green painted kitchen units that line the back wall of the cabin, separated from the living area by a large oak dining table with benches either side. He turns me around, nodding toward the wood-burning stove. It's set into the wall, between two archways. The left-hand one is filled with shelving, that contains books at the top and wine bottles at the bottom, while the right-hand one leads onto a corridor. "And this place gets more than warm enough."

"For what?" I ask, and he opens his mouth to reply, just as Adam knocks all his bricks over.

"Do you need some help there?" Oliver says, turning his attention to my son in an instant, and although I go to grab his arm, he's too quick for me, and he walks between the two, overstuffed red couches, sitting down on the floor next to Adam, and grabbing hold of a few bricks.

Adam looks up at him as Oliver stacks up the bricks, and I join them. I don't feel like I can leave Oliver by himself. He's not used to babies, and Adam's not used to Oliver either.

Adam looks up at me as I sit down beside him, and then he glances back at Oliver before handing him a brick.

"Thanks," Oliver says, adding it to his tower, just as Baxter appears around the side of the couch, looking kinda sheepish. "Come here, boy," Oliver says. I want to tell him that's not a good idea, that we should probably keep Baxter at arm's length for this visit, but Baxter's already here, sniffing at the bricks, and at Adam's feet. I'm tempted to reach out and pick Adam up again, but Oliver looks at me. "He'll be okay," he says, and with that, he reaches over and picks Adam up off of the floor himself. I come so close to grabbing him back, but before I know it, Adam's perched on Oliver's knee. Oliver turns to Baxter and simply says, "Paw," to which Baxter raises his right leg, holding out his paw to Oliver, who takes it, and then gently touches Adam's hand against it. "See?" he says to Adam. "It's soft."

Adam gazes at Oliver, and then back at Baxter again, his hand resting on Baxter's paw as a smile settles on his lips, which touches my heart. Even so, I'm ready to leap forward, should Baxter make a move, although I don't need to worry, as Oliver turns to me with a smile and lifts Adam up, handing him back to me.

"I'll make some coffee," he says, getting up and wandering over to the kitchen, calling out, "Baxter... here," as he goes.

I watch him walk away and while I know I ought to feel happy, I can't help feeling sad. This is everything I ever dreamed of, not just for Adam, but for myself. If only my father had wanted me enough to stick around. If only Donavan had wanted Adam...

Oliver

I've always loved my cabin, and while there's nothing wrong with Heather's house, or even my Dad's and Mason's Colonial style properties, I prefer open-plan living, and being outside. Having Jemima and Adam here makes it perfect. They make it feel like a proper home... at last.

Jemima doesn't seem as relaxed as I'd hoped she'd be, but I guess that's understandable. She's nervous about Baxter. She might share her work space with him, but letting him near her son is clearly a different matter. There's no reason to be nervous; Baxter's the dopiest dog in the world. He's scared of spiders, and flies, and pretty much everything else that moves... even his own shadow sometimes. There's no way he's going to harm anyone, unless being licked to death counts as harm. But it's easy to see how on edge Jemima is, which is why I wanted to introduce Adam to Baxter properly, so he wouldn't pick up on his mom's fear and share in it. Dogs are great at sensing fear in humans, and it's the very last thing you want to show them. Even a big softie like Baxter. They have to know who's the boss, but I figured letting Adam touch Baxter was enough for now. Give it a little longer and I'll have them rolling around on the floor together, and I know Adam will be tugging on Baxter's tail and trying to ride him like a horse... and Baxter will probably let him, because he's a pushover. But that's the future. For now, we're taking things slow... in more ways than one, because the other thing I've picked up on is how reluctant Jemima is to let me get involved with Adam. She wouldn't leave him with me at her house, while she gathered all his things together, and instead she wandered around with him in her arms, which had to be making hard work of it. And the look on her face when I picked him up just now was a picture. I don't know whether she was more worried by that, or by Baxter being so close to Adam. Either way, it was very clear that, while she may have been happy to introduce me to him within hours of us getting together, that's as far as it goes. I'm going to have to earn her trust with her son... and I guess that's fair enough.

So, at lunchtime, I don't bother suggesting that she comes over to the kitchen with me. I know she'll want to stay with Adam and I make my way over, opening the refrigerator and pulling out a few items.

"I've got chicken and ham and cheese, and some salad. I thought I'd make us sandwiches," I say over my shoulder.

"That sounds lovely, but Adam's not great with anything that organized."

"What should I do then?" I turn to face her and she smiles over at me.

"Just butter him a slice of bread and cut it into fingers, and then give him some sliced ham and cheese and some cucumber."

"No tomatoes?"

"He hates tomatoes," she says with a smile.

"Okay. I'll bear that in mind. And what would Adam's mom like in her sandwich?"

"Ham and tomato, please."

"Coming right up."

I put on a pot of coffee and set about making the lunch, which takes no time at all, and I carry everything through on a tray.

"We didn't bring Adam's high chair." I set the tray down on the coffee table, remembering that he used one on Christmas Eve when I went to Jemima's for dinner. "But I guess we can all sit on the floor, can't we?"

"Won't Baxter want to get involved?" Jemima's clearly recalling how he foraged for scraps in the kitchen at work when she was setting out the platters for the party.

"He might stare at us with doleful eyes, playing on our heartstrings, but he knows better than to try and take food from plates." I give her a reassuring smile and settle on the floor, handing out the food, while Baxter sits over by the end of the couch, looking at us longingly.

Adam tucks into his lunch with gusto, although I notice with a smile that, every time Jemima tries to get him to eat the cucumber, he pushes her hand away, and picks up a piece of cheese or ham.

"You're sure it's just tomatoes he doesn't like?" I say, between mouthfuls.

"Positive. But getting him to eat anything healthy is becoming a battle."

"That's because he's a boy. We're programmed to eat everything that's bad for us."

She giggles and gives up offering him the sliced cucumber, looking over at me. "While still looking incredible, evidently," she murmurs, her eyes raking over me, which feels good.

"If you say so."

"I do."

"In that case, I'll finish my ham and cheese sandwich with extra mayonnaise, shall I?"

"I guess so." She doesn't take her eyes from mine, and while Adam sits next to her, feeding himself from his plate, the heat between us builds to an inferno that I'm not sure I know how to control. I'm not sure I want to either.

Once we've both finished and Jemima is sure Adam's eaten enough, I reward Baxter for his good behavior by giving him a small piece of cheese. He wolfs it down, and then I clear away the dishes, while Jemima fetches the diaper bag, pulling out a trainer cup.

"I'll just give him some water," she says, coming over to the kitchen, where I'm stacking everything into the dishwasher.

"You should've said. I could've got that for him earlier."

"It's okay." She runs the tap for a while and then fills the beaker, taking it back to Adam.

By the time I rejoin them, she's sitting up on the couch, with Adam on her lap.

"He's getting tired," she says.

"Does he wanna go to sleep for a while?"

"Yes. He'll need to, or he'll never survive the afternoon."

"I don't have a crib, but he could sleep on the guest bed, if you think he'll be okay."

She hesitates for a moment, looking down at Adam, whose eyes are fluttering closed, and then she nods her head.

"Let's try it," she says, and although I offer to help her to her feet, she manages by herself, which I've noticed she does a lot, regardless of the situation. I don't comment, even when she struggles to pick up a cuddly brown dog, with white paws, but lead her over to the archway, passing through it and down the hallway that leads to the bedrooms and bathroom.

"In here." I keep my voice quiet, as I open the door to the guest room, waiting for her to pass through.

She carries Adam over to the bed, placing him in the middle and moving the pillows, so they're on either side of him, forming a barrier that she seems to think will keep him enclosed. I don't know how. He can both walk and crawl. He's not going to have any trouble getting out of there if he wants to. Still, it seems to make Jemima happy, and she sits on the edge of the bed, stroking his head while he cuddles the toy dog. I stand and watch for a few minutes, until Adam's breathing changes and it's clear he's asleep, at which point, Jemima stands and looks over at me.

I tilt my head toward the door, raising my eyebrows and she nods, answering my unspoken question about whether it's safe to leave.

We both do, pausing in the hallway.

"I'll leave the door open," she says, in a whisper. "Just so I can hear him."

"No problem."

I take her hand, now we're alone, and while I'm tempted to lead her straight to my bedroom, I don't. We're meant to be taking it slow, so I guide her back into the living room and over to the couch, sitting in the corner and pulling her onto my lap.

"I've just noticed," she says, turning to me. "You don't have a Christmas tree. Did you take it down already?"

"No. I don't usually bother with one."

She frowns. "Really?"

"Yeah. It's just me here, by myself, and I go to my dad's for Christmas Day, so…" I stop talking, noticing the sad expression on her face. "What's wrong?"

"Nothing… it's just that this seems like the perfect place for a family Christmas."

I remember the enormous tree at her mom's house, which they'd stood in the corner of the living room and decorated with white lights and colored baubles, and I smile at her.

"I know, but Dad likes having us over there. He likes doing the whole Christmas 'thing', and we've kinda gotten used to it."

"Even so, I can just picture a huge tree over by the window, and a roaring fire, and…"

"And what? You weren't about to mention eggnog, were you?"

She shakes her head, blushing, and I wonder if she'd been on the verge of saying something about the two of us, or even the three of us, spending Christmas here, together. She seems embarrassed, though, so I change the subject.

"You've done a great job with Adam, you know? He's really well behaved."

"Not all the time, he's not. And I can't take any credit for him behaving himself. He spends far more time with Mom than with me."

"Does that bother you?" I ask, turning her slightly, so she's facing me and I can see her better.

"Sometimes. I miss him when I'm not with him, but I enjoy having a job. I like the freedom it gives me… and I love working with you." She smiles, her eyes sparkling.

"I love working with you too." I lean in and kiss her, just briefly, because if I deepen the kiss, I know I'm going to forget about taking it slow.

As I pull back, Jemima sighs and rests against me, which feels good, and I put my arms tight around her.

"Does your mom not miss working?" I ask, trying to take my mind off of her body, and my hard-on, which is getting kinda uncomfortable.

"I don't think so. After I got the job working for you, and we were talking about how we were gonna manage things, she mentioned she might go back to teaching when Adam starts at school. I think she's enjoying herself at the moment, and of course, not working gives her time to see her new boyfriend."

"Your mom's got a new boyfriend?" I say, although I'm not surprised. Jemima's mom is an attractive woman.

"Yes. But she's being really secretive about him."

"Like mother, like daughter," I say, with a smile and she turns her head, looking up at me.

"I'm not secretive."

I clasp her chin, holding it still. "You kept Adam's existence from me for an entire year. I think that qualifies as secretive."

"That's not being secretive. That's being private. And this is my mother we're talking about. I didn't think she had any secrets from me."

"You'd be amazed at the things parents keep to themselves." I release her chin and let my hand slide down her neck, caressing her jawline with my thumb. "Does it bother you that she's seeing someone?"

"No, of course not. But it would be nice if she told me about him. After all, I've told her about you."

"Oh, yeah? What have you told her?"

"Well," she says, lowering her eyes, like she's shy. "I haven't told her I think you're gorgeous, or how much I want you, or that I'm in love with you… although she kinda worked out that last part for herself. And I haven't told her we're taking it slow, or that I'm finding it really hard to take it slow, especially when you do what you're doing with your thumb."

I can't help smiling, and I keep caressing her, being as it seems she likes it. "You haven't told her anything then, really, have you?"

She shrugs her shoulders. "No. I guess not."

I lean in and kiss her again, a little harder this time. "I'm struggling to take it slow too," I say, pulling back.

She hesitates for a second and then surprises me by sitting up, twisting around and then straddling me. "Then why are we?" she asks, gazing into my eyes. "I want you, Ollie. I think that much is obvious."

I'm distracted by having her sitting astride me, but I still struggle not to laugh, my smile widening, uncontrollably. I've always hated being called 'Ollie', ever since I was a child. Mason used to do it on purpose, just to annoy me, and I'd hit him, to get my own back. Destiny picked up on that and shortened my name sometimes, too. I never used to hit her, obviously. I'd just ignore her until she used my proper name. Eventually, they both got the message, and 'Ollie' was dropped from our vocabulary. For some reason, though, when Jemima says it, it sounds okay. Actually, it sounds fantastic.

"Why are you smiling like that?" she asks.

"No reason." I like her calling me 'Ollie'. I don't want her to feel self-conscious about it.

"Okay… so why are we taking it slow? I know we haven't been together for very long, but we've known each other for a year, and we're in love, and…"

"I told you," I say, interrupting her. "I wanna get this right, and I think you're worth waiting for."

"You can't say that." She lowers her eyes again, her shyness returning. "You can't know…"

"Yeah, I can." I pull her closer and kiss her. Hard. My tongue finds hers in an instant, and before I know it, we're both struggling to breathe. I reach inside her blouse and run my hands up and down her back, feeling her through the thin material of her t-shirt. I touched her earlier, when I first realized how sexy she looked, brushing my fingers over the delicate lace above her breasts, and while that felt incredible, this feels so much more. She lets her hands roam up my arms and onto my shoulders, and although her moans and sighs are soft and low, I can feel the breathless need within them, and I'm grateful to her for breaking the kiss when she does, because I'm about to lose control.

"This waiting thing is all well and good," she says, panting, and gazing up at me. "And I appreciate the sentiment, but I'm not sure you realize quite how much I want you."

She's moved her hands down while she's been talking and they're currently resting on my chest, which is making it hard to concentrate.

"Yeah, I do. I want you too."

"In that case, why are we waiting?"

"You want me to repeat myself?"

She shakes her head. "No. I understand what you're saying about wanting to get it right, and I guess I should be grateful you care…"

"Of course I care." I interrupt her again. "I love you. And you don't have to be grateful."

She tilts her head slightly. "What do I have to do, then? Ask nicely?"

I lower my hands, clasping her ass and pull her closer, flexing my hips so she'll be able to feel my hard-on. She gasps, holding her breath, and then releases it slowly, her mouth open, her eyes glistening.

"You know what you have to do," I tell her, playing with fire.

"Do I?" She grinds her hips into me, in a slow circular movement, playing right back.

"Yeah. I already told you."

She nods her head, looking up at me through her eyelashes. "You want me to beg?" she whispers.

"Yeah, I do," I growl. "I wanna hear about your deepest desires… and I wanna hear you beg for them. On your knees."

Her mouth drops open and I wonder if I've gone too far this time… if I've made an even bigger mistake than when I said I wanted to claim her lips. I think about apologizing, telling her I'm only kidding, but then she sucks in a breath and pulls away from me, sliding off of my lap and onto the floor, kneeling before me, her hands on my thighs as I part my legs and she leans forward and deliberately bites her bottom lip. My cock really hurts, and my body aches for her as I reach forward and free her lip with my thumb.

"Mama! Mama!" Adam's voice rings out and we both startle.

"Damn," Jemima whispers under her breath, letting her head fall onto my leg and leaving it there for a second or two.

"I guess I'll have to wait to hear you beg," I say, and she looks up at me, narrowing her eyes.

"Yeah, I guess you will." She gets up, straightening her clothes and running her fingers through her hair. I didn't even realize I'd mussed her up so much, but before she turns to leave, I grab her hand.

"I love you," I say, and look up into her eyes.

"I love you," she replies, as Adam calls for her again and she pulls her hand away, dashing toward the archway and disappearing from sight.

I take advantage of her brief absence to smarten myself up, and re-arrange the cushions on the sofa, going over to the kitchen and pouring us both a coffee, which I have ready for when Jemima comes back, carrying Adam in her arms. He's still clutching the toy dog and seems kinda sleepy.

"Baxter could do with a walk," I say, once she's sat down with Adam on her lap and given him some water. "So why don't we drink our coffee and go for a stroll by the lake?"

"That sounds like a good idea. It might help me cool off," she says, and I chuckle.

"Do you need to?"

"God, yes."

I can hear the desperation in her voice and I sit down beside her, as close as I can, leaning in and whispering, "Me too."

She smiles and rests her head against my shoulder, and we sit for a while in perfect silence until Adam gets restless. Jemima sits him on the floor then, joining him and taking her coffee with her, drinking it quickly while she plays with him. I take her cue, gulping down my coffee too, and once I'm done, I get up, going over to the window seat and grabbing my sweater, pulling it back on, before I fetch our coats, which I bring back, and drop onto the couch.

"Shall we go?"

Jemima looks up at me. "Yeah. I think Adam could do with getting out too." He seems okay to me, but I guess she knows best, and I hand her his coat, watching while she puts it on him. Then I help her with hers, and wrap her scarf around her neck, using it to pull her closer and plant a kiss on the tip of her nose.

"It's so good, having you here," I whisper.

"It's good being here," she says with a smile. "And I'm sorry Adam interrupted things."

"Hey… it's okay."

"It hasn't put you off?" She sounds kinda wary, and I pull her into my arms.

"Hell, no." I kiss her, letting our tongues collide, but Adam starts grizzling and we break apart, staring over at him.

"He's probably getting hot," Jemima says, going to him, and I shrug on my coat.

"Let's get going then," I reply and she picks him up, following me to the door. "Baxter?" I call and he leaps up from his basket, making it across the threshold before any of us, and as I close the door and we start down the steps, he's already taken off toward the lake.

"Will he be okay?" Jemima says, nodding toward him.

"He'll be fine."

She lowers Adam to the ground, keeping a hold of his hand and he toddles away, wanting to follow Baxter, it seems. While I'd like to hold Jemima's hand, I decide to walk on the other side of Adam, just in case Baxter should get carried away and run into him. He wouldn't do it on purpose, and he wouldn't mean any harm, but I know Jemima would view it as a heinous offense.

"It really is beautiful here," Jemima says, in a kinda dreamy voice, repeating her earlier compliment.

"It's a lovely place to live, but it's better with you in it." She looks at me, smiling and blushing slightly.

I bend, picking up a stick, and throw it for Baxter to chase, which he does, bringing it back to me. Adam clearly thinks this is funny and giggles at Baxter, especially when the stick goes into the lake and Baxter goes straight in after it. Even Jemima seems to relax and laughs at my dog when he loses the stick completely and spends several minutes searching the lakeside, trying to find it. He fails, but brings me another stick instead, seemingly very proud of himself.

Adam soon tires of walking, which doesn't surprise me. Not only is the ground uneven, but he's only little, and Jemima looks at me, a worried expression on her face.

"I didn't bring his stroller," she says.

"Well, that's easily resolved." I pick him up and swing him around, sitting him up on my shoulders. "There. How's that?" I hold him firmly in place and he giggles again, clearly enjoying the view from up there.

"I—I… Oliver, really, I…" I turn to Jemima and see she's paled and is staring at me, her eyes darting up to Adam.

"Is this okay?" I ask her. "I promise I won't drop him."

"I know." She steps closer, making it clear she can barely control the urge to reach up and take him from me. "I—I'm just not used to letting him be with anyone else, other than my mom, obviously."

"Yeah. I noticed you didn't wanna leave him with me earlier, when we were at your place."

"It wasn't that I didn't want to," she says.

"Yeah, it was. And if this is making you uncomfortable, then…"

"It's not," she says quickly, interrupting me.

Her eyes betray her, despite her words, and it's clear to me she's not happy with what I've done. "I can tell how tense you are, Jemima."

"I've never seen Adam with a man before. Not like that," she says, her voice wavering. "It reminds me of all the things I missed out on when I was little."

I know that's not all of it. Her background might be a part of the problem, but there's more to it than that. Even so, I go along with her reasoning… for now. Apart from anything else, I want to get to know her. I want to understand. And that means breaking down her barriers and letting her explain… no matter how long it takes. "Because your dad left?" I say.

"Yeah. When I was little, I used to tell myself that having Mom was enough… that I didn't need a father. But as I grew up and saw what my friends had, I realized I was wrong. I kept hoping he'd change his mind and come back… for me, if not for her. I didn't expect them to get back together, but I hoped he might decide he wanted me enough to at least get in touch."

"Except he never did?"

"No. And now I'm repeating history, aren't I? Donavan left me before Adam was born."

"No, he didn't. You left him… quite rightly, considering what he'd done."

"Who left who isn't what's important here, Oliver. What matters is that Donavan didn't want our child enough to put him first, and Adam will have to grow up just like I did… never knowing what it feels like to have a father."

"Hey. I'm not going anywhere, you know?" She smiles, but it's impossible not to notice the doubt and confusion in her eyes. I don't understand why she's being like this, but I want to make her feel safe, so I keep a firm hold on Adam and lean down, kissing her lips very gently, before I pull back. "I get that this is a big deal for you, but please believe me, you can trust me… with yourself and with Adam. And you can talk to me, and lean on me, whenever you need to… because I will never leave you, Jem. Okay?"

I pull her in close, feeling her body against mine and while I'm not going to deny I still want to have wild, crazy, breathless sex with her, for the rest of my life, I also want to be there for her, and for Adam… just like this. I want to be the one they lean on and hold on to… always.

Chapter Six

Jemima

Working with Oliver and wanting him so much is a lot harder than I ever thought it would be. I keep reliving that moment yesterday afternoon, while Adam was asleep, when Oliver told me to get on my knees and beg for my deepest desires. I'm not even sure what my deepest desires are – other than to be with him – but there was something about the look in his eyes and the way he said those words that made me want to obey. I might have already been on my knees, straddling him, but I knew what he meant, and even though I had no idea what I was going to say, I slid to the floor without giving it a second thought.

God, I wanted him so much then; I was burning up with need for him, and if Adam hadn't interrupted us, I know we wouldn't have bothered taking things slowly anymore. I could see my need reflected right back at me in Oliver's face, and while he may have given me some perfectly sound reasons for taking it slow, his kisses were consuming me. His touch was like fire, and I know we couldn't have stopped ourselves. I don't think we'd have bothered trying.

As it was, we didn't get that far, and now I'm going crazy. Twenty-four hours have passed since I got down on my knees before him, and I swear to God, if he doesn't take me to bed soon, I'm going to crawl into his office and beg him, even if he's got a client with him... like he has now.

I stare at his closed door, my body tingling. This is a first for me. I've never wanted anyone like I want Oliver. I'm breathless just looking at him, and when he kisses me, it feels like I've got no control over anything... not words, movements, or thoughts. He could ask anything of me, and I'd submit.

I'd have done so this morning when I got into work and he pulled me into his office. I hadn't even removed my coat, but he pushed me back against the wall by the door, kissing me so hard I struggled to stand, and clung to him for support.

"God, I've missed you," he murmured into me, biting on my bottom lip

"I've missed you too." He was already wearing his scrubs and I let my hands wander up inside his top, my fingers brushing over his muscular back, just as the phone rang.

"Dammit," he groaned, his eyes alight, and he pulled away, releasing me, so I could run back into the reception and take the call. It was Mr. Donaldson, whose Dalmatian had taken a turn for the worse over the weekend, so Oliver agreed to see him before surgery, if Mr. Donaldson could bring him in right away.

Our moment was lost, and since then we've been constantly busy.

Oliver's door opens and I startle, and then smile as he comes out, his eyes instantly locking on mine, even though he's talking to Mr. and Mrs. Hardy, who've come in with their two kittens.

"Bring them back in two weeks," Oliver says, still gazing at me as they approach my desk. "We'll get them both spayed together."

"Thank you, Doctor Gould." Mrs. Hardy rests her hand on Oliver's arm, fluttering her eyelashes at him, even though her husband is standing right beside her.

"You're welcome," he says, coming around the desk and standing behind me, placing his hands on my shoulders. It's a struggle not to gasp at his touch, but I manage, and look up at Mr. and Mrs. Hardy, doing my best to ignore the way Mrs. Hardy is narrowing her eyes at me.

"Two weeks?" I say.

"Yes, please." Mr. Hardy gives me his best smile now and I feel Oliver tighten his grip.

"That'll be January tenth."

"That's absolutely fine," Mrs. Hardy says.

"We'll look forward to it." Her husband leans forward as I write the appointment for them on a card, handing it over to him, his eyes twinkling at me. "We'll see you then."

"Yes," Oliver says from behind me, and we watch them leave.

The moment the front door closes, Oliver spins my seat around, his hands resting on its arms as he leans over me.

"I'm starting to understand how you feel," he says.

"You are?"

"Yeah. I didn't like the way Mr. Hardy was looking at you."

"Why's that?" I ask, tilting my head, teasing him.

"Because you're mine."

"Wanna prove that?"

He sighs. "I swear, if I didn't have another client in ten minutes, I would."

I moan out my frustration and grab a hold of the front of his top, pulling him closer and leaning up to kiss him. He deepens the kiss, bruising my lips with his, until my body's humming with need and I whimper, clutching his arms.

He breaks the kiss eventually, his chest heaving as he sucks air into his lungs and I sit up, clinging to him.

"Please, Ollie… please."

He crouches in front of me. "Don't beg me now… not when there's nothing I can do about it."

"But I want you so much."

"I want you too, baby."

"Come over tonight?" I urge, still holding him.

"You want me to?"

"Of course. Mom will probably be going to see her new boyfriend, and hopefully we'll have the place to ourselves."

He breathes deeply. "In that case, I'll be there."

"And will you make me beg?" I ask, looking up at him.

He bends, clasping my face in his hands. "Oh, God, yeah."

I shudder in anticipation, and he smiles. "Can you come over straight after work?" I ask and he tilts his head slightly, making me wonder what's wrong.

"I'll have to take Baxter home first," he says. "Unless you want me to bring him with me?"

I'm torn now. Baxter was really well-behaved yesterday, despite my initial fears, which seem so unfounded now. But it's not my house; it's my mom's, and I don't feel like I can invite Oliver's dog there without asking her.

"I should probably check with Mom," I say, and he nods his head.

"Okay. Why don't I take him home, give him a walk and come over afterwards? My last appointment is at five, so I can be back with you by six-thirty?"

"That sounds good. I'll ask Mom, and if she's okay with it, you can always bring Baxter tomorrow."

"You're inviting me tomorrow as well, are you?"

"What do you think?" He pulls me to my feet and into his arms, kissing me, until I'm breathless again.

"Oliver's coming over again," I say to Mom, holding Adam in my arms, before I've even taken my coat off. "Sorry. I know I should've called to tell you." Come to think of it, I could've called to ask about Baxter, too. Why didn't I think of that? Probably because I'm so wrapped up in Oliver…

She smiles across at me from the other side of the kitchen.

"I had a feeling he might be, so I made extra meatballs." I can't help chuckling, and she laughs too. "It's good to see you so happy, Jemima," she says, and although I don't reply, I can't fail to notice how much more contented she's looking, too.

I put Adam down, watching him while he toddles off, and I undo my coat. "I also need to ask you about Oliver's dog."

"What about his dog?" Mom says, going over to the stove and lifting the lid on a large pan, stirring the contents and replacing the lid again.

"Oliver's taken him home for tonight, but he doesn't like to leave him for too long. So, I wondered, would it be okay for him to bring Baxter here when he comes to visit?"

Mom leans back against the countertop, folding her arms. "As long as Baxter understands that he's not allowed to get up on the furniture, then yes, it's fine."

"He's very well behaved." I smile to myself, thinking that it's not just Baxter who bows to every word Oliver says. I'm pretty compliant too.

"Good," she says. "Now, do you wanna give your son a bath, while I clear up a bit?"

"Sure."

I go into the living room and grab Adam, hauling him up into my arms and giving him a big kiss, before I carry him through to the bathroom.

Mom comes in halfway through Adam's bath and leans against the door frame, smiling down at him. "How did your day go yesterday?" she says. "I never got around to asking you this morning." She's quite right. She got back really late last night, and this morning was a terrible rush, because I overslept.

"It was lovely. Oliver's house is beautiful. It's right on the lake shore, and it's a lot more comfortable than I thought it would be when he told me he lives in a cabin."

"What did you expect, then?" she asks, shaking her head.

"Oh, I don't know… wooden furniture and a pot-bellied stove, I guess."

"So, something out of an old cowboy movie?"

"Yeah… but it's nothing like that. It's really nice inside."

"What did you do all day?" she asks.

"Adam played for most of the morning, and then after lunch, we went for a walk by the lake. Baxter chased sticks, and… and when Adam got tired, Oliver carried him on his shoulders."

"I'll bet he liked that." Mom glances back at Adam, who's splashing in the bath.

"Yeah, he did."

I make it sound like I was equally happy with that arrangement, even though I wasn't. That's not something I can say out loud though, because I can't explain it… especially to her. I can't tell her that seeing Oliver carry Adam like that reminded me so much of the father I never had… and I can't tell her how much it upset me. It hit a raw nerve, though, and I think Oliver noticed. He was very understanding about it, even though I struggled to explain why I find it so hard to accept that I've repeated my mom's mistakes. I've wanted my father in my life for so long, and I've denied that to my son. It makes me feel like such a failure. Oliver told me he wasn't going anywhere, which was nice, and even though he's not Adam's father, it was reassuring that he's there for me. He said I could lean on him too. I liked that. It's not something I've ever had before, from anyone… except Mom, and it was comforting to know he cares about me.

"You really love him, don't you?" Mom says in a quiet, considered voice. She hinted at my feelings for Oliver on Christmas Day, and I didn't deny them then, so there's no point in doing so now.

"Yes."

She smiles. "He's a good man."

"I know he is." I look up at her. "And speaking of love, what about you?"

"What about me?" She blushes slightly.

"Are you in love?"

She hesitates for a moment, looking down at her fingernails, and then says, "Yes, I am."

I'm astounded, she's actually admitted it, and I get up off of the floor, going over to her, although I keep an eye on Adam still.

"Tell me more," I say, and she smiles.

"I've been seeing someone for quite a while now," she replies. 'Quite a while'? I hadn't expected that. I thought this was something new. But what does it matter?

"Does this someone have a name?"

"Yes. Dale. We knew each other years ago, but drifted apart…" Her voice fades.

"And you've got back together?"

"Yes."

"But that's fabulous, Mom." She gives me a shy smile. "Are you going over there tonight?"

"No. Dale's gone to visit with relatives until New Year's Eve, so I'm afraid you're gonna have to put up with my company for the next few nights. I'll try not to cramp your style, though."

I rest my hand on her arm. "Oh, don't worry about that. I'm just so happy for you."

"As I am for—" She stops talking suddenly. "Meatballs!" she cries and runs down the hallway, disappearing into the kitchen.

I chuckle and go back to Adam, who gripes about me washing his hair, as usual, but seems quite happy when I get him out of the bath and wrap him up in a towel, which I do right before Oliver arrives.

I let him in, still clutching a dripping Adam. "Sorry, we're running a little late," I tell him, as he leans down and kisses me. "I haven't even changed yet."

"Don't worry. You look lovely as you are."

I want to tell him that Mom's not going out as I'd expected and that our plans for the evening are, therefore, on hold, but before I get the chance to say anything, Mom appears in the kitchen doorway.

"Why don't you get Adam ready for bed, and Oliver can come help me lay the table?" she says. "Dinner's almost ready."

"Sounds good to me," Oliver replies with a smile.

He gives me a slight wink, and I nestle into him for a moment before moving away. I won't deny, I'm disappointed that I'm not going to get the chance to beg him this evening, but I love the fact that he's slotted into our lives so well, that Mom's accepted him, and that even Adam doesn't seem to mind his presence.

All in all, this is about as perfect as it could be.

The last two days have been even more perfect, I think. If that were possible.

Oliver spends every spare minute with me, either at work, in between patients, or in the evenings at home. While he and I cleared away the dishes on Monday evening, I explained to him about Mom's boyfriend, Dale, and that he's gone away for a few days.

"So Mom won't be going out, I'm afraid," I said, keeping my voice down, so Mom wouldn't hear me.

He came over to me, putting down the glasses he was holding and taking me in his arms. "It's okay. We can wait."

"Can we? You speak for yourself." He chuckled and leaned back slightly.

"I told you, it'll be worth it."

"Will it?"

"Yeah. I guarantee it."

I sighed deeply then. "I wish you wouldn't say things like that."

"No, you don't," he said, and kissed me.

And while it wasn't what I'd hoped for from our evening, it was still lovely, and very romantic.

Today, Oliver's had an emergency to deal with, so it's been even more chaotic than usual. It all happened this morning, when a man came in carrying his dog. I couldn't tell what breed it was, but it was small, and the man was distraught, saying the dog had been hit by a car right outside his house. Oliver was with someone, but I called him out immediately, and he took over, bringing the dog straight into his surgery. I dealt with the man and Oliver's other client, Mrs. Jordan, who was only there to get her dog's toenails cut, and I gave them both a cup of coffee while they waited.

Oliver didn't come out until about forty-five minutes later, by which time his next client was also waiting, although he ignored them, and Mrs. Jordan, going over to the man who'd brought in the injured dog.

"I've been able to stabilize her," he said. "If you wanna come through, we can talk about what happens next."

The man got up and followed Oliver back into his room, and I sat there, watching as his door closed, thinking about how much I admire him… not just as a man, but as a veterinary. It's at times like that he comes into his own, showing not just how good he is at doing his job, but how much he cares.

It took a while before the man came out again. He was pale, but shook Oliver's hand before walking out through the front door.

Oliver gave me a very slight smile and then turned to Mrs. Jordan. He apologized for keeping her waiting, although she didn't seem to mind, and then took her back into his surgery.

The result of all that was that Oliver's appointments have run late all day, and by the time the last of his clients leaves, he's exhausted.

"Do you want to skip coming over tonight?" I ask him as he sits on the edge of my desk, looking down at me.

"No. But I'm gonna have to. Brandy – the dog that came in earlier – needs surgery, but unfortunately, it's not the kind of thing I can do here. So I'm gonna take her over to Bob Watkins' place in Southbridge and we'll work on her together. I called him earlier, and he's all set up for it."

"Is she that badly hurt?"

"Yeah. One of her legs is completely shattered, and it's gonna need to be pinned. It's really intricate work."

"And you're gonna do this tonight?"

"Yeah. I'm sorry."

"No." I get up, standing right in front of him, and he parts his legs, pulling me into the space, his arms tight around me. "I only meant, you're tired. I'm worried about you."

He smiles. "I'll be fine," he says. "This happens every so often."

"You're sure you'll be okay?"

"Yes… other than missing you."

"Well, I'll miss you too, if that helps."

"It does," he says, and reaches up, caressing my cheek with his fingertips. "I'd better get ready to go."

"What about Baxter?" I ask.

"Don't worry. I'll take him over to my dad's."

"I could have him, if you want."

He smiles again, even wider. "I'll bear that in mind next time," he says. "But it's already set up for tonight. I wasn't sure you'd want to take him by yourself, and he normally goes to Dad's when something like this happens. They're both kinda used to it."

"Okay. As long as you're sure."

"I'm positive. But thank you for offering. I appreciate it."

"You do?"

"Yes. I know you were uneasy about Baxter, but…"

"I just wanna help," I say.

"I know. And you will be."

"How?"

"By kissing me."

I giggle and he leans in, kissing me hard and fast, making me breathless in a heartbeat, his hands wandering over my body as he pulls me closer, letting me feel his arousal, which makes me moan and sigh, because I want him more than ever.

"I love you so much," I say to him as we break the kiss.

"And I still love you more," he replies with a grin, and I step back, letting him stand, because I know he needs to go.

"Will you be okay with working tomorrow?" I ask him, as he moves away from my desk.

"I'll have to be. I can hardly cancel all my other appointments." He comes back to me and puts his hands on my waist. "Although I might not be up to coming over to your place in the evening."

"Because you'll need to sleep?" I say, despite my disappointment at the thought of not seeing him two nights in a row.

"Yeah. I'm too old to stay up all night."

I chuckle. "Really?"

"Well, I'm too old to stay up all night operating on a dog, anyway."

"Are there other reasons to stay up all night, then?" I ask, leaning in to him.

He raises his eyebrows. "You'll find out. If you want to."

"I think you know I want to."

"In that case, what are you doing on Friday?"

"New Year's Eve?"

"Yeah."

"I'm not doing anything. I've got a baby, remember?"

He chuckles. "Yeah. Point taken. Would you like to find out if I can stay awake all night, and see in the New Year with me?"

"I'd love to."

"Good," he says, letting me go and walking backwards toward his office. "We'll talk about it tomorrow. Okay?"

I nod my head and he blows me a kiss, which I return, as he spins around and goes into his room, and I sit down again, feeling such a maelstrom of emotions I can hardly work them out. I'm disappointed that I won't be spending the next two evenings with him, because even after just a couple of nights, I've gotten used to having him around. But I'm also really proud of him for being able to save this dog's life, and for wanting to. And I'm still reeling from the fact that he said he wanted stay up all night with me, and that we're going to be seeing in the New Year together, because I know what those two things suggest, when they're put together... and I can't wait.

"Oliver won't be coming over tonight," I say to Mom the moment I get in and have taken off my coat.

"Oh?" She pokes her head around the kitchen door, frowning.

"Sorry. I would've told you sooner, but I didn't know myself until just before I left work."

"Has something happened?" She comes into the hallway, holding a cloth in her hand. Adam toddles out from the living room at the same time and I pick him up, giving him a hug. "You two haven't had a fight, have you?" Mom asks, and I turn back to her.

"No, Mom." Why would she think that? "He's got to operate on an injured dog."

"Tonight?"

"Yeah. And that means he probably won't be here tomorrow night either, because he'll need to catch up on his sleep."

She nods her head, turning back into the kitchen again, and I follow her.

"I see." She walks over to the stove. "But I assume you'll be seeing him on Friday, being as it's New Year's Eve?"

"Yes." I'm about to ask whether she'd mind looking after Adam for me, so I can go over to Oliver's place for the night, when she turns, with a shy smile on her face.

"I was hoping you'd say that, because Dale's coming back on Friday morning, and... well, we kinda planned on spending the evening together."

"Oh."

"Is that a problem?" she says.

"No." What can I say? Adam's my son, not hers. If she wants to go out, I can hardly stop her.

"Good." She smiles, clearly not noticing my disappointment. "I—I might stay over, if you're okay with that?"

She's blushing and, despite my feelings of growing frustration, I can't help smiling. "Of course I'm okay with it, Mom. You don't have to ask."

I feel kinda jealous that my mom's going to spend the night with her boyfriend and I'm not, but I can't begrudge her this. She's so happy... and that makes me happy too.

I get in early, desperate to see Oliver, although he looks so tired, my heart aches for him.

"Did you get any sleep at all?" I ask, throwing my arms around him and letting him hold me close.

"No." He looks down into my eyes with a smile that melts my insides. "We didn't finish the surgery until three-thirty, then we had to clear up and make sure Brandy was stable and comfortable, so I didn't get home until nearly five. It didn't seem worth going to bed for an hour, so I sat out on the porch, drinking coffee."

"You must've been freezing."

"No. I was thinking about you."

"Does that keep you warm, then?"

"You bet it does." He leans down and kisses me, all too briefly, before he pulls back again. "I definitely won't be coming over tonight, though. My dad agreed to keep Baxter for the day, because I wasn't sure I'd feel like walking him, but I'll have to go over there and pick him up after work. Then I think I'm just gonna want to sleep for ten hours straight."

"Only ten?"

"That'll probably be enough, yes."

"Enough for what?" I tilt my head slightly, looking up into his sparkling eyes.

"Enough that I'll be able to stay awake all night tomorrow."

I feel my heart sink. "Yeah… about that."

He frowns. "What about it?"

"I'd hoped Mom could babysit Adam for me, so I could come to your place, but she's spending the evening with Dale, and she said she's gonna be staying over."

"Oh?" he says, his lips twitching upward.

"Yeah."

"Are you okay with that?" He frowns again, clearly misunderstanding my disappointment.

"Of course. I'd like to meet the guy, but Mom's happy with him and that's what matters. She's been alone for a long time."

"Hasn't she been with anyone else before, then?"

"No. Not to my knowledge."

"Because she loved your father so much?"

"I don't know. It was me that wanted him to come back to us, not her. She never talked about him. Even when I asked her questions, she'd just change the subject. I've never known whether he was the love of her life, or whether he hurt her so much, she couldn't let him back in. That always felt kinda sad to me. After all, even if they ended up hating each other, they could've tried to be civil, for me."

"Have you ever thought of contacting him yourself?" Oliver asks.

"No. I don't even know his name."

"Really?" I can tell he's surprised by that. "Your mom never told you?"

"No. Like I said, she refuses to talk about him. They never married, and I share my mom's surname, not my dad's."

He pulls me a little closer to him. "Don't take this the wrong way, but how do you know there was a relationship, or any kind of love between them? Hell… for all you know, you could've been the result of a one-night stand."

"I don't think so."

"Why not? Your mom won't talk about him, so…"

"She may not talk about my dad, but she has told me how much she wanted me. I was planned, Oliver… I wasn't an accident." I feel the tears building behind my eyes and blink them back.

"I'm sorry. I didn't mean…"

"It's okay."

It's not, but I can't expect him to understand how it feels to have been abandoned out of choice. Especially as the same thing has happened to Adam. As I stare up at Oliver, I wonder if that's why I reacted so strangely to seeing Adam with him on Sunday… because I'm feeling guilty for not making Donavan want his son more. And because Oliver's taking all of this in his stride… which is easy for him, when he comes from a happy, loving family, and has no idea what abandonment feels like.

"Hey…" he says, interrupting my train of thought. "Didn't you say your mom and Dale dated years ago?"

"Yes. What about it?"

"You… You don't think…?" He leaves his sentence hanging, looking at me and raising his eyebrows, until eventually the penny drops.

"You think Dale might be my father?"

"I don't know, but it's possible, isn't it?"

"I guess." My stomach flips over at the thought of my dream coming true. "Wouldn't she have introduced us, though?"

"Not necessarily. She might want to get to know him again herself first."

That makes sense. "I suppose it would explain why she's being so secretive," I murmur.

"It might," he says. "But don't read too much into it. We could be completely wrong."

We could. But the thought of finally having a father after all these years is almost too much to hope for.

"Do you think I should ask her?"

"No. It's her relationship, and while I get it could be yours too, with your father, you have to let them work things out… in their own way."

He clasps my face in his hands. "Always assuming this guy is even your father."

I nod my head, even while he's holding me, because he's right. As much as I want to get to know my father, I have to wait. I have to let Mom come to me… when she's ready.

"What are we gonna do about tomorrow night?" I ask him, changing the subject. It seems like the best idea for now. I can't spend my life anticipating something that might take months to happen… if it happens at all.

Oliver frowns. "Can't I come to your place?" he says.

"Of course. Only now Mom's going out, we won't be alone. Adam will be there."

"Yeah. Sleeping." He smiles, reaching around behind me and pulling my body hard up against his, so I can feel his arousal pressing into me. "I'm sure you can beg quietly, can't you?"

I struggle not to smile. "You'll find out. If you want to," I say, using his own words right back at him.

He shakes his head, and narrows his eyes, right before he slaps my ass, making me squeal, as a jolt of electricity rocks through me, making me tingle.

"Damn, I really wanna kiss you right now," he murmurs, taking my breath away.

"Why don't you?"

"Because I'm not talking about kissing your lips," he says, although that doesn't stop him.

Oliver

"You have a great New Year, Bob. Thanks for the update. I'll call the owner and let him know."

Bob hangs up and I smile to myself, going out into the reception and over to Jemima's desk, where I sit down and turn on her computer. She left ten minutes ago, and while I'm impatient to follow her, I need to make this call.

I find Mr. Yates's details and dial his number. He answers straight away and I give him the good news.

"Brandy's making a good recovery. I've just spoken to my colleague in Southbridge and it looks like she'll be able to come home after the weekend."

"Oh, that's such a relief," he says, and I hear the emotion in his voice. I don't blame him. I'd be the same if Baxter was involved in an accident.

"I'll call you on Monday morning, but you should be able to go over there and collect her in the afternoon."

"I'll look forward to hearing from you. And Happy New Year."

"The same to you."

I end the call, and shut down the computer again, before returning to the surgery and quickly changing back into my jeans and shirt. It's been a long day. Actually, it's been a long week. But it's over now. It's New Year's Eve and I'm going to spend the evening with Jemima. I've missed her over the last couple of days, but she was really understanding about me having to work, and then needing to catch up with my sleep.

And now, I just want to hold her and kiss her, and see how quietly she can beg, because although I said we'd take it slow, I'm done waiting… and I think she is too.

I smile to myself as I close up the surgery, Baxter following me around. He missed me the other night, when I left him at my dad's and he's been kinda clingy since. But that's okay. I missed him, too. I shrug on my coat and hold the door open while Baxter goes out, waiting while I lock the door, and then he follows me down the steps and over to my car.

Jumping up onto the rear passenger seat, he settles down on his blanket and I get into the driver's seat and set off for Jemima's place.

I'm feeling kinda wired, which I know isn't entirely down to tiredness. I've been waiting for this night for so long, I'm nervous and excited, and impatient, all at the same time. Fortunately, it doesn't take long to get there, and by the time I've parked on the driveway, retrieved Baxter's blanket from the back seat and got him out of the car, Jemima's standing at the door, waiting to greet me. She's wearing a simple black dress, which clings to her figure and ends just above her knees, and she's left her hair hanging loose around her shoulders, which I like, because I want to run my fingers through it while I make love to her.

She throws her arms around my neck as I lean down and kiss her, and judging from the look in her eyes, I'd say she's feeling excited and impatient, too. She doesn't seem nervous, but then I guess there's less pressure on her. I could screw this up in so many ways, especially as it's been over a year. And it matters this time… more than ever.

"Come in," she says, caressing my cheek and gazing into my eyes.

"Thanks. Has your mom already gone?"

"Yeah. She left about twenty minutes ago." We walk into the house, Baxter following, and I shut the door. "I've already given Adam his bath, and dinner's nearly ready," she says as I put the blanket down for a minute to take off my coat and hang it up.

"It is?"

"Yeah." She lowers her head, looking shy. "You said you liked stew, so I left one in the slow cooker before I came to work this morning. I haven't made dumplings, because I can't hope to compete with either of our moms, but I've got some bread to have with it instead."

"You made me stew?" I ignore her comments about our mothers and put my arms around her, resting my hands just above her ass, pulling her close to me.

"Yes."

The words 'Marry me,' are on my lips, but I'm scared she'll think I'm joking when I'm not. Still, I guess it's probably too soon for proposals, so instead I bring my right hand around and place my finger beneath her chin, raising her face to mine, and kissing her.

"Mama…" Adam interrupts us, and we turn and look down at him, Jemima pulling away from me. He's on all fours, having crawled out here from the living room, rather than walked, and she goes over to him, lifting him into her arms.

"Are you hungry?" she says, and he smiles, which she obviously takes to be a 'yes', because she turns to me and says, "Shall we?" nodding toward the kitchen.

I settle Baxter onto his blanket in the living room. It's one I've brought from home after Jemima told me Heather had agreed he could come over here. I thought it best he should have somewhere of his own to sleep, and that it should smell of home. He turns around in circles for a moment or two and then settles down, resting his head on his paws.

"You're so damn lazy," I say to him, with a smile as I scratch behind his ears and he closes his eyes, proving me right.

Out in the kitchen, Jemima's already put Adam into his high chair, and is standing on the other side of the kitchen, with her back to me. I wander over, putting my arms around her waist, pulling her back onto me, and she sighs, twisting around with a serving spoon in her hand, and looking up at me.

"Do you want to sit down?" she says.

"Not particularly."

She smiles. "I'd kinda like to get dinner over and done with."

"Oh? Is there any reason for that?"

"There are lots of reasons, but if we don't have dinner and get Adam to bed, we'll never find out."

She has a point, and I leave her to dish up our stew while I go sit down. Adam looks at me and tilts his head, like he's trying to remember me, and then he smiles, which I take to be a good sign. I want him to remember me. I want him to get used to me. As I smile back, he reaches forward, seeming to want some of the bread that's on the table.

"Shall I cut the bread?" I offer to Jemima.

"Oh. Yes, please."

She doesn't turn around, but I start cutting up the bread. Adam reaches forward again and I hand him a slice, which he holds to his mouth, just as Jemima comes over.

"What are you doing?" she says, taking the bread from him. "That's far too big for you, and you know you're not allowed bread before dinner, only with it." She places his bowl on the table, out of his reach, and puts the bread down beside it.

"That's my fault." I look up at her. "I gave the bread to him, and I forgot I needed to cut it up…"

"It's just better if he has it in smaller pieces."

"Why can't he have bread before dinner?" I ask, wanting to learn, hoping she'll teach me.

"He's a bread addict. If I let him have it before dinner, he'll get full up and won't eat his meal."

I nod my head, and while I appreciate the lesson, I can't help feeling a little chastised as she turns away, going back to the other side of the kitchen and returning with our meals, which she places in front of us, taking her seat opposite me.

"I'm sorry I got it wrong," I whisper, reaching across the table for her hand. She places it in mine and smiles.

"You weren't to know."

"Are there any other rules I should know about?"

"Probably hundreds." She doesn't elaborate, and instead, she picks up Adam's spoon and helps him to a mouthful of stew, before having some of her own.

Over dinner, we talk about Brandy. I update her on the dog's progress, and she asks me about my training, and why I went into this profession.

"My dad's a surgeon. Mom was too."

"She was?" Jemima says.

"Yeah. They met at a surgical conference and fell madly in love… according to Dad, anyway. I toyed with following in their professional footsteps for a while, but in the end I decided I'd rather practice medicine on animals. They don't answer back."

She chuckles. "Yeah, but they can't tell you what's wrong, either."

"Nor can humans most of the time. They just give you a list of symptoms and you have to work out what's wrong with them. It's not so very different, working with animals. It's mostly detective work, with a little knowledge and skill thrown in."

She shakes her head, gazing at me. "You saved Brandy's life the other day, and you call that a 'little knowledge and skill'?"

"That's all it is, Jem… honestly."

"Well, I don't agree," she says. "I think you're…" She stops talking and a blush creeps up her cheeks.

"You think I'm what? Being modest?"

"No. I was gonna say I think you're wonderful."

"I think you're pretty damn amazing too," I say and she looks up at me.

"Yes, but I don't go around saving animals all the time, do I?"

"Just doing my job, babe."

She stares at me for a long moment until Adam grizzles and she remembers to keep feeding him. I smile to myself, because let's face it, a little hero-worship goes a long way… especially given how nervous I am about tonight.

Once we've finished eating, Jemima takes Adam through to bed while I set about clearing up. I'm fairly familiar with the kitchen now, having cleared the table every night I've eaten here, and I load the dishwasher and wipe down the countertop before Jemima comes back, letting me know she's there with a slight cough. I turn and see her standing in the doorway, staring at me, and I put down the cloth I'm holding and walk straight over to her, my nerves forgotten.

"You're beautiful," I say, my voice a little lower than usual.

"Please, Ollie…" she whispers.

"What do you want?"

"You." She blinks, her lips parting, and I smile.

"Is this your idea of begging?"

She shakes her head. "I'm so desperate for you, it's the best I can do."

I pull her into my arms, holding her body tight against mine. "You only had to ask, you know…"

She slaps my arm playfully. "You're such a tease."

"Yeah, I know. But you love it."

"I do," she says. "And I love you too."

Flicking off the lights, I take her hand and lead her toward the back of the house, to the room beyond Adam's, which I know to be hers. I push the door open and she enters ahead of me. I can feel the heat between us already, and I shut the door, turning her and pushing her back up against it as I lean down and kiss her, raising her hands above her head at the same time and holding them there with one of mine, while I let the other roam over her body. She moans quietly into my mouth as my fingers graze over the swell of her breast, down her side and around behind her, settling on her ass and holding her still while I grind my hips into her.

I'm tempted to turn the lights on. The switch is right beside the door. But I recall how self-conscious she was about her body, and I don't want to raise any doubts in her mind… not now. Besides, I don't need artificial light… I can see her perfectly well in the moonlight.

"I wanna taste you," I whisper, biting on her bottom lip as I break the kiss. There's a deep longing in her eyes, and I release her hands, letting her arms fall to her sides, and then reach behind her, undoing the zipper on her dress and pulling it from her shoulders. She wriggles out of it, and it falls to the floor, leaving her in a black lace bra, garter belt, stockings and thong… oh, and the three-inch heels she always wears, and I suck in a breath. "Is this for my benefit?" I stare down at her.

"No," she says and I smile. "I enjoy wearing underwear like this."

"Good. You look incredible, but if you don't mind, I'm still gonna peel you out of it, because I know you're gonna look even better naked."

She swallows hard and bites her bottom lip, which is almost enough to distract me… but not quite, and I kneel, placing my thumbs in the top of her thong and slowly pulling it down to her ankles.

"Step out," I say, holding her hand to make sure she doesn't fall, as I pull her clothes to one side, letting my eyes wander over her perfect hourglass figure before they settle on that neat blonde triangle at the apex of her shapely thighs. "Part your legs a little." She does as I say, moving her feet, and I look up at her to find she's gazing down at me, her eyes wide. I don't break that intimate contact, but spread her lips with my fingers and lean in, finding her exposed, swollen clit with ease, and flicking my tongue across it.

"Yes… yes…" She hisses out the word between clenched teeth and flexes her hips into me as I lick her, tasting her intoxicating honeyed sweetness for the first time, and I shift a little closer, wanting more. As she reaches down, placing her hand on the back of my head, I suck on her clit, and then insert my middle finger into her tight hole, feeling her clamp down on it as I make very gentle 'come hither' movements against the front wall of her vagina. Her knees buckle slightly, but I don't relent. I devour her, alternating between licking and sucking, while still maintaining eye contact. She's breathing hard, circling her hips, and suddenly, she raises her hand, biting down on her forefinger as her legs quiver and she comes, trying not to scream. She's a picture of ecstasy, her body trembling, her pussy dripping hot come down my fingers and onto my hand. I keep going, pleasuring her, until I know she's calming, and then I pull my finger from her and stand. I'm inches from her, no more, and I gaze into her eyes as I move even closer and crush my lips to hers in the deepest of kisses.

"O—Oliver," she whispers into my mouth, bringing her hands up around my neck, clinging to me. I pull her closer, and then lift her up into my arms, wrapping her legs around my hips as I turn and walk over to her bed, which is against the far wall. She's still feasting on my lips as I kick off my shoes and, placing my knee on the bed, I lower us both, her body beneath mine.

"You like the taste of you?" I say, looking down at her.

She nods her head and I smile, kneeling up and bringing her with me, so I can reach behind her and undo her bra, pulling it from her shoulders before I lie her back down again. As I throw the lacy garment over my shoulder, I give myself a moment to take in her generous breasts, before I lean down and capture her right nipple between my teeth, tweaking her left one between my thumb and forefinger.

She's writhing beneath me already, and it's more than I can take. I kneel again, and then shimmy backwards and stand. She leans up on her elbows, watching as I unbutton my shirt, shrugging it off before I pull my wallet from my back pocket and throw it onto the bed and then unfasten my jeans and lower them to the floor, along with my underwear. As I stand, naked, I hear her breath catch and I look up to see her staring at me, wide eyed.

I don't say a word. Instead, I reach over for my wallet, pulling out a condom, and I tear into the foil pack, keeping my eyes fixed on hers as I roll it over my aching cock. She licks her lips, and as I kneel up on the bed again, she lies down, parting her legs as far as they'll go. I settle between them, raising myself above her, balanced on one arm as I rub the tip of my dick along her folds, finding her entrance with ease and sinking into her, feeling her tight walls surrounding me.

She gasps and I still; half in, half out.

"Is that hurting?" I ask, in a whisper, my hands either side of her head now.

"A little. It's been a long time and you're… you're so big."

I smile. Who wouldn't? "Thanks." I keep as still as I can, despite the temptation to move. "We'll take it slow."

She shakes her head. "To hell with taking it slow." And with that she brings her hands up, clamping my ass, and pulls me into her, sighing out a sharp, "Yes," as I hit home, my cock buried deep inside her.

She clearly needs this as much as I do, and I don't wait to be asked, or told, or begged. I ease out of her, almost all the way, and slam back inside again. She has to stifle her cry, biting on her lip and then covering her mouth with her hand as I move, harder and faster with every stroke. Breathing heavily, she pulls her hand away again, slapping it down on the mattress and grabbing at the bedding. She clenches it in her fists as her body succumbs, her walls tightening around me in a deep, shuddering orgasm that wracks through her. I know she's struggling not to cry out and I lean down, kissing her, swallowing her desperate moans as she bucks beneath me.

Eventually, she calms and I lean up again, staring down at her.

"Sorry," she whimpers and I slow my pace, although I keep moving. It's an instinct… like breathing.

"Never say sorry. Not for that. I love watching you come."

"It's just really hard to do it quietly."

"I'm sure with enough practice, you'll get there." She smiles as I move faster again, and she stutters in a breath, her head rocking back. "No. I want you to watch." I place my hand behind her head, tipping it forward, supporting her neck. She raises her eyes, staring into mine, biting on her lip. "That's mine," I growl and she nods her head. "You're all mine."

"Yes. All yours."

We both look downwards, gazing at the place where we're joined, my cock stretching her, pounding into her.

"Watch me fuck you, Jem. Watch my cock sink into you."

"Oh, God... yes."

She shifts slightly, raising herself up on her elbows, so she can get a better view, I think. I move my hand from her neck and put it between us, rubbing her drenched clit with my thumb.

"That looks so good," she says, mesmerized, raising her legs, which makes me realize she's still wearing her stockings and sexy heels. *How could I have forgotten?*

"I hope to God you're close," I whisper and she gives a slight nod of her head. *Thank God for that.* I thrust deep inside her, unable to hold back, and manage not to cry out as I let go, pouring myself deep inside her as I feel her convulse around me, her body clenching and pulsing through another orgasm.

I told her I'd never leave her, and I meant it... but I know now I can't. It would break me.

We're both breathless and I pull out of her, falling to her side, while she collapses down onto the mattress again.

"That was..." she mumbles, gasping for air.

"That was what?" I need to know.

"So good," she says, and I turn onto my side so I can see her properly. "So, so good."

"Worth begging for?" I whisper, and she chuckles.

"I don't remember begging, but if I'd had to, it would've been worth it."

I run my fingertip around her hardened nipple, and she gasps. "Good," I murmur, feeling kinda pleased with myself that at least I didn't screw up.

"Are you thirsty?" She turns onto her side, smiling at me.

"Are you?"

"Yes."

"Do you want me to get some water?"

She shakes her head, shifting away from me toward the edge of the bed. "I'll go. You'd have to get dressed."

"I would?"

"Yeah. In case Adam wakes up."

"He's a baby. I very much doubt he notices what I'm wearing."

She's standing already and looks down at me. "I'm up now," she says, kicking off her shoes and gazing over me, her eyes halting when they reach my still-hard cock. "I won't be long."

"I'm not going anywhere." Evidently.

She crosses to the door and grabs a robe from the hook on the back, pulling it on before she ducks outside.

Once I'm alone, I dispose of the condom and twist around on the bed, lying back on the pillows, one arm behind my head. I can't help smiling. Jemima wasn't wrong. That was good. In fact, it was the best. With that in mind, I sit up, reaching to the bottom of the bed, where I threw my wallet, and I grab the remaining three condoms I brought with me, wondering if four was enough, as I put them on the nightstand… because I'm nowhere near done yet.

Jemima returns within a couple of minutes, carrying two tall glasses of water, and I get up, going to her.

"Here, I'll take those," I say to her and she hands them over, undoing her robe as I turn away and put the glasses down beside the condoms. When I turn back, she's standing before me in her stockings and garter belt. "Do you want to take those off?" She may look as sexy as hell, but I want her to be comfortable, too.

"Do you want me to?" she asks.

I smile, going over and standing in front of her. "Why don't we compromise? I'll take them off for you."

She nods her head and I kneel, just like I did earlier, only this time, I unfasten her stockings, rolling them down her legs, one at a time. She raises her foot, and I peel them from her, kissing the tips of her toes, before I undo the clasp of her garter belt, letting it fall to the floor. I can hear her breathing hard, and I stand, gazing down at her naked body, aching with need for her again.

She's about to step forward, toward the bed, when I stop her.

"We've got a problem."

She frowns, looking up at me. "We have?"

"Yeah. It seems your legs are still working."

She tilts her head, the corners of her mouth twitching upward. "Why is that a problem?"

"Because it means I didn't make you come hard enough yet."

"You didn't?"

"No." I grab her, pulling her close to me. "And that means I'm gonna have to keep fucking you..."

"Until my legs don't work?"

"Precisely."

I pick her up and turn, dropping her down onto the mattress, and as I grab a condom from the nightstand and crawl over her body, she gazes up at me, resting a hand on my chest.

"Ollie?" she whispers and I stop, the foil packet poised in one hand.

"Yeah?"

"I love you."

I drop the condom, lowering myself down and clasping her face in my hands. "I love you, Jem. So much."

She grins, running her tongue over her lower lip. "Now," she whispers, "will you please, please fuck me again? Really hard. I need to feel you inside me."

"Well, when you ask like that..."

"That wasn't asking. That was begging," she says, with a smile.

"No, it wasn't. That was nowhere close to begging... but it'll do for now."

I wake early and check the time on my watch. The one Jemima gave me for Christmas. It's just before six, and still dark outside.

She's lying, her body curled into mine, her hair half covering her beautiful face, and I gently brush it aside, revealing her still slightly swollen lips and flushed cheeks. I'm not that surprised by her appearance. I did as she asked last night, and fucked her really hard for at least another hour, after which we both dozed for a while, and then I woke in the early hours, kissed her awake and wished her a Happy

140

New Year, because I'd forgotten all about what day it was. She gazed up at me and asked, "Did you wake me just to say that?"

"No." I smiled, and then I kissed her some more, because she seemed to like it.

After a while, she broke the kiss and pushed me onto my back, straddling me as she reached over to the nightstand for a condom, which she held out to me, wordlessly.

I didn't take it, but smiled up at her. "If you want me, you're gonna have to put that on me first," I whispered, and she gazed at my cock for a moment or two, before tearing into the foil packet and doing her level best to roll the condom over my dick. She struggled, and I thought about helping her out at least twice, my need to be inside her almost overcoming my enjoyment of the games we seemed to have gotten into. But she got there in the end, with a triumphant smile on her face.

"I think I've earned a reward now," she said in a soft whisper.

"Yeah, so do I." She shimmied forward a little, raising herself up over my dick, but I stopped her just as she went to lower herself down. "Not yet."

"Why not?"

"Because you've earned a reward."

"I know. I was just about to…"

"Not that. Come up here."

She looked down at me, confused, so I grabbed her ass, pulling her a little further up my body. She seemed to get the message then and shifted upwards, until she was straddling my face and I leaned up and licked her intimately, hearing her gasp at the contact.

"Oh… that's so good," she murmured, grinding down into me.

I sucked on her clit, then licked and even bit on her occasionally as she rode my face, and I reached up, cupping her breasts, and tweaking her nipples, making her squeal with pleasure. It didn't take long for her to come, and when she did, her juices flowed straight into my mouth, and I drank them down.

She came really hard that time, and I could hear her struggling to catch her breath. That didn't stop me from wanting more, and after she'd taken a few moments to recover, so did she, and she shifted down the bed, impaling herself on my dick. She took me one slow inch at a time, letting out a deep sigh when she finally settled herself down on me. I wanted her nearer to me though, so I sat up, my hands on her ass, and she grabbed my shoulders.

"Fuck me... please, please, fuck me," she groaned into my ear, as I pulled her down onto me so hard she yelped. I didn't stop though... and neither did she. We took each other, in a haze of deep kisses, whispered entreaties, longing touches and – finally – shattering orgasms, as we came together.

Afterwards, she fell right back to sleep again, clearly exhausted and I guess I must've dozed off too. But I know Adam will be awake soon and that means I can't lie here forever gazing at Jemima, even though I want to.

I lean over and kiss her tender lips. She doesn't react, so I kiss them again, a little harder, and she snuffles slightly and opens her eyes, focusing on me with a smile.

"Good morning," I say in a soft whisper.

"Hello. Did you just kiss me?"

"Yes."

She sighs and snuggles into me. "Thank you for last night," she murmurs and I lean back, looking down at her.

"You don't have to thank me, Jem."

"Yes, I do. You were very considerate. And... and thank you for using a condom."

God, her ex was a loser. "Why are you thanking me? Of course I was gonna use a condom. And that's no reflection on you. Or on me. You've been used before. You ended up pregnant when you didn't want to be, and while I know you love Adam, and you wouldn't change a thing about him, I don't think this is the life you planned, or the one you would have chosen for yourself, or for him."

"No, it's not," she whispers, and she leans up, kissing me.

I roll her onto her back, wanting her again, my need undimmed. I trace a line of kisses along her jawline to her ear. "How long have we got?" I ask her.

"Until what?" she says.

"Until breakfast. I mean until Adam wakes up and demands his breakfast, because I could happily feast on you all day."

I nibble on her earlobe, but feel her stiffen and tense beneath me and I raise myself up, straightening my arms, and gaze down at her beautiful face, her eyes misted with uncertainty.

"I didn't realize you were planning on staying," she murmurs.

"You... you mean you want me to leave?" I'm kinda stunned and struggling to hide it.

"I think it's for the best."

It had never occurred to me she'd have a problem with me being here when Adam wakes, or him seeing me over breakfast, and I'm not sure how to respond.

"Is that okay?" she asks, when the silence has stretched a little too far.

"To be honest, not really," I say and she tilts her head, frowning.

"Why not?"

"Because I want to stay. I want to be a part of your lives. Yours and Adam's."

"You are."

"Really? You're saying you want me to leave before he wakes up in one breath, and then you expect me to believe I'm part of his life the next?"

She lowers her eyes, looking at my chest. "I'm just not sure about him seeing you here in the morning yet, that's all."

"Yeah. I kinda got that. But he's one, Jem. He's not gonna know whether I spent the night, or just turned up to have toast and coffee with you."

She looks up at me again, blinking a few times and then says, "Is this a deal-breaker for you?"

"No." I can't deny her attitude hurts... especially given everything we did and said last night. "I guess it's just too soon for you to let me in, isn't it?"

She takes a breath. "Do you still love me?" Her voice is pitifully quiet, but I notice she hasn't denied what I said. It is too soon... at least for her.

"You know I love you, Jem."

I lean down and kiss her, and then kneel up, moving to the edge of the bed.

"Where are you going?" she asks.

"I'd better get dressed and get out of here."

She sits up, grabbing my arm. "But Adam won't wake up for at least another thirty minutes. Can't we…?" She leaves her sentence hanging and I turn to look at her, taking in the sadness behind her eyes as she bites her bottom lip. That's all it takes and I reach over, picking up the last of the condoms before I push her down onto the mattress again, settling between her parted legs.

"Thirty minutes, you say? I guess we'd better make this quick…"

Chapter Seven

Jemima

The last few weeks have been amazing. They've been better than anything I could have imagined. That's all because of Oliver, of course. As a lover, he's gentle, but he's also masterful and relentless. I love the way he is with me, and the things he says to me. He makes me feel desired and wanted; lusted after and loved... and over the last few weeks, he's shown me pleasure I didn't even know existed. Sex with Oliver is like a whole other country, with no borders or boundaries, and I'm having fun exploring it.

He's stayed with me every night since New Year's Eve, although after that first morning, I wondered whether he'd ever want to sleep with me again. I know we'd talked and joked about staying awake all night, but that was when we thought I'd be going to his place. At mine, I anticipated things would be different... I thought he'd leave after we'd made love. Except we fell asleep, thoroughly exhausted, and although he woke me in the early hours, the thought of him leaving wasn't foremost in my mind at the time. Being rewarded, and feeling him inside me again were all I could think about, because there's nothing in the world that feels as glorious as being joined to him.

In the cold light of day, though, when he kissed me awake, and made it clear he intended staying for breakfast, I had to tell him I didn't think it was a good idea. It was pure maternal instinct; a need to protect my child... nothing more. It wasn't anything personal against Oliver. He seemed hurt, though, and for a moment I wondered about changing my mind and letting him stay. Except my instincts still said 'no', and I couldn't go against them. Oliver made it clear he wasn't happy, but he accepted what I had to say, and then he made love to me. Hard and fast… and I have to say, it was breathtaking.

If the last few weeks are anything to go by, it seems it's always breathtaking with Oliver.

He left after that, but when he came back later that day, he brought the biggest box of condoms I've ever seen, and left them in my nightstand. "So we never run out," he said, with a smile, and I think I knew then we'd be okay. He hasn't mentioned that morning since, and nor has he moved anything else in here, but I guess he doesn't need to. He leaves every morning before Adam gets up, and goes home to grab a quick shower before work. Of course, the moment I get into the office, we're in each other's arms again, like we've been parted for days, rather than a little over an hour. He's like an addiction, and I know I can't give him up. What's more, I don't intend trying.

There have been a couple of nights when I've wished we could've gone to his place, even if only for the evening. Having quiet sex is kinda hard. It's harder than I thought it would be, anyway. Oliver makes me want to scream my way through every orgasm, and having to lose my mind quietly is my only regret about our relationship. Still, it is what it is, and going to Oliver's place isn't an option… especially as Mom seems to be getting even closer to Dale.

I'm trying not to think of him as my father, and although I'm excited at the prospect of finally having someone to call 'Dad', I'm also bewildered about why he's stayed away for so long, and why Mom is taking her time introducing us to each other. She's stayed over at his place almost every night since the New Year too, and I can't help feeling a little left out.

"Try not to take it personally," was Oliver's answer when I raised the subject with him last night in bed.

"How can I take it any other way? I know you said she might need some time to get to know him first, but how long does it take?"

He turned to face me, pulling me into his arms. My hand seemed to find itself right by his erection and I held it, giving it a gentle caress as we talked.

"We don't even know for sure that Dale is your father," Oliver reasoned, sucking in a breath, presumably distracted by my actions, which made me smile.

"Even if he isn't, you'd think she'd introduce us."

"Why? It's her business, isn't it? Do you tell her everything we do?" he said, sounding a little worried, and I giggled.

"Of course not."

"So you didn't tell her you sucked my cock this morning before I left for work?" I love it when he says things like that and my body tingled, remembering…

It was the first time I'd done anything like that, but as he lay there on the bed, looking so glorious and masculine, I couldn't resist. I couldn't take much of him, but it was still a fabulous experience, having him hold my hair behind my head and raise his hips up off the mattress, taking my mouth. He was as gentle as ever, but there was something kinda wild and abandoned about him, too. He didn't come, because he said it was my first time and he didn't know how I'd react, but I want him to come the next time, and I told him that.

"No, I didn't," I replied, smiling back, as he nodded his head and then sat up, forcing me to release him. Before I knew it, he'd pulled me down the bed a little and flipped around, lying back down again, but facing the other way, with his erection right by my mouth. He edged closer, and I circled my tongue around the enlarged tip of his arousal, which made him groan, just as he raised my leg, exposing me. I gasped, feeling his tongue connect with me intimately, and I instinctively moved nearer to him, taking more of him into my mouth. We licked and sucked at each other, becoming more and more frenzied as we both drew nearer to our climaxes. I wanted to warn him I was going to come, but I had my mouth full, and as I clamped my thighs together around his head, he stiffened and I knew he was going to come too. I braced myself, unsure what to expect, and then I felt a surge of hot liquid hitting the back of my throat. It was tempting to pull back, but I swallowed, as another stream of come filled my mouth. I was struggling for control myself and it was difficult to know what to concentrate on, as Oliver's tongue flicked over me, and I swallowed him down.

Eventually, we both finished, and I released him from my mouth, leaning back slightly to catch my breath. He turned around, so he was facing me again and, with a smile on his lips, he kissed me, letting me taste myself. Neither of us said a word, but we didn't need to, and within moments, we were fast asleep.

This morning, I'm awake before Oliver for once and I gaze at his beautiful face, his lips slightly parted as he sleeps beside me. He's on his back and I'm snuggled up beside him, enjoying the warmth of his body, even though my mind is otherwise occupied.

I'm feeling kinda nervous. Tomorrow is his brother's wedding, and I'm anxious about meeting his family. Oliver and I may have been together for six weeks, but I haven't met any of them yet… not even his dad. That's partly because work has been quite busy, and obviously Adam takes up a lot of my time. On top of which, there's also the minor point that, whatever time Oliver and I get, we want to spend alone… and preferably in bed.

I've bought myself a new dress, which Oliver hasn't seen yet. It's pale pink and quite figure-hugging, because while I don't think I have a body to write home about, Oliver does, and I want to look nice for him.

He stirs beside me, his legs stretching to the very end of the bed, and then he turns, facing me, and I smile. I can't help it. I don't think I'll ever get tired of this.

"Hello," he murmurs and leans over, kissing me.

"Hello."

He frowns. "Are you okay?"

"Yes. I was just thinking about tomorrow."

"The wedding?" he says.

"Yeah. I'm kinda nervous about meeting your family."

He pulls me closer to him, being protective, as usual. "Like I said to you before, you've got nothing to fear. My family are gonna love you."

I frown at him. "You can't say that, Oliver."

"Yeah, I can. They won't be able to help themselves." He nuzzles into me. "You're irresistible."

I shake my head at him, even though I'm smiling. "I wish you didn't have to be the best man."

"How can you doubt I'd be anything but the best man?" he says, wiggling his eyebrows, which makes me giggle.

"I'm being serious, Ollie. You'll have duties to perform... I won't get to see very much of you."

"Yeah, you will. My most important duty will be looking after you." He cups my face with his hand. "You don't have to worry. I'm not gonna abandon you. Okay?"

"Okay. But I guess I will have to do without your company for tonight." I can't keep the sadness out of my voice, and he hugs me tighter.

"Would you miss me if I wasn't here?" he says.

"You know I would."

"In that case, you'll be relieved to know that you won't have to do without me at all."

"But I assumed you be staying with Mason."

"So did I," he admits, with a slight shrug. "But I talked to him about it earlier in the week, and he said that, while he knows it's traditional for the bride and groom to be apart for the night before their wedding, he needs to be with Isabel." Oliver smiles. "I told him I was fine with that, because I need to be with you too."

"You told him that?" I don't know why I'm questioning him. Oliver's about the most open-hearted person I know.

"Yeah, I did. He didn't seem remotely surprised."

"Is that because he feels the same about Isabel?"

"Partly. But mainly it's because he knows how I feel about you. I haven't kept it a secret."

I wrap my arms around him and pull myself up, kissing him. He deepens the kiss in seconds and I push him onto his back, straddling him, right before he rolls me the other way, settling between my legs, his erection pressing into me.

"I'll have to leave a little earlier than usual tomorrow morning," he says, breathing hard as he raises himself up, gazing down at me.

"You will?"

"Yeah. I've gotta go home and shower and then get over to Dad's place. Mason's going there for about eight-thirty, to give Isabel time to get ready. You are gonna be okay getting to Mason's by yourself, aren't you? It's kinda out of the way."

"I know. But you've explained the route I need to take."

The wedding's being held at Mason's house, and Oliver's already given me directions and shown me on a map, too. I'm fairly confident I can find it.

"It'll be good that you'll have your car there. If Adam gets tired before I can officially leave, you can always bring him home, and I can follow on later."

I pull away, forcing myself into the pillows behind me as I look up into his eyes. "I'm not bringing Adam to the wedding. Mom's having him for the day. I arranged it with her at the end of last week."

He frowns and kneels right back on his ankles. "I—I assumed you'd be bringing him," he says, shaking his head.

I reach out, touching his arm and letting my fingers trail down it. "I thought it would be easier without him."

He takes a breath and studies me for a moment before he leans over again, his hands resting either side of my head.

"Okay." I can tell it's not 'okay' at all.

"Don't you see?" I say. "I'll be able to relax more if I'm not worrying about Adam all the time, and like you said, if he got tired, or bored, I'd have had to bring him home again."

He nods his head. "I know. I said okay."

"Then why doesn't it feel like it's okay?"

"Because you're still not letting me in."

"I am, Oliver. This has nothing to do with that. I'm just being practical." I pause for a second, sensing the tension between us. "Are you mad at me?"

"No." He shakes his head. "No, I'm not mad."

"In that case, how would you feel about me spending the night with you?" I don't know why this didn't occur to me before, but hopefully it'll make him realize how committed I am to us.

"Spending the night?" he says, tilting his head. "We already spend every night together."

"I meant at your place," I whisper, suddenly feeling a little uncertain. "If you'll have me."

He smiles. "Of course. Sorry. I didn't understand what you meant. I'd love for you to stay at my place."

"I'll have to check with Mom first that she's happy to look after Adam overnight," I say, thinking through the practicalities.

"But if she says yes, can you stay all night? Including for breakfast?"

"Yes. As long as we can have it in bed."

He leans down, his lips almost touching mine. "We can have it anywhere you damn well please."

∞

Oliver

I've been awake for about an hour already, holding Jemima in my arms.

Today is Mason's wedding day and I have to go soon, although I'm hanging on for as long as possible, savoring every second with her, even though she's not awake.

She'll be at the wedding later on, obviously, but I can't help feeling disappointed still that she won't be bringing Adam with her. I'd assumed she would and hadn't thought to raise the subject until she actually told me yesterday morning that she's coming alone.

To me, this is just another example of how she's keeping Adam away from me... and believe me, there have been plenty.

Sure, I spend every night here at her place and I have done for the last six weeks, but she never lets me get involved with Adam when he's around. Since New Year's Eve, when I gave him that slice of bread, she's watched me like a hawk at the dinner table, which makes me think she's worried I'm going to poison him or something. Whenever I offer to play with him, or help at bath time, she refuses, usually with an, "It's fine," which doesn't help, because it's not fine at all… not for me. I want to be involved, and no matter what she says, I'm not.

They've been over to my place on a couple of Sunday afternoons, but Jemima's made a point of bringing Adam's stroller. It's really hard to push it on the lakeside, but that hasn't stopped her, and I've assumed she doesn't want me to carry him again… because it seems she doesn't. Wherever we go, she always takes him, and keeps a firm hold of him, saying, "It's easier," or "He prefers it."

It hurts when she does that and I'll admit there's a part of me that wishes she hadn't introduced me to Adam so early in our relationship. I knew it was a big step, but she said she wanted me to meet him 'properly'… and I believed her. What I hadn't expected was that she'd dangle him like a carrot, only to take him away again. I get that, as his mother, she has every right to do that, but what I don't understand is why she can't see how much her actions are getting to me. I can't switch off my feelings for Adam, any more than I could for Jemima, and I wish now that she hadn't let me get attached to him. It would have been easier. We could have got to know each other, gotten used to being together as a couple, and then she could've introduced me to her son, once she was sure about me. Doing it this way around just makes me feel inadequate.

Still… it's too late now.

In the meantime, at least I've got tonight to look forward to, because Jemima's going to be staying at my place. Her mom's agreed to look after Adam, which means we've got all night together. We can be ourselves, we can make some noise… and for once, we can even have breakfast.

She stretches, slowly waking, and I turn to face her, pulling her closer, her naked body warm and soft against mine.

"Good morning," I say the moment she opens her eyes.

"Hello." She smiles and I lean in and kiss her, just briefly.

"I've gotta go."

She pouts playfully and flexes her hips into mine. "Sure you can't spare a few minutes?"

"Sorry. I have to go home and shower, and then get over to Dad's place."

She nods her head, and while I'm tempted to say that things could be very different – that I could stay longer today and every other morning, if she was willing to let me keep a few of my things here, and risk Adam seeing me at the breakfast table, or coming out of the bathroom – I don't. It's not a subject I've raised with her since New Year's Day, and I don't intend doing so now. I'm feeling a little fragile, and I'm scared she'll say, "No," again… and that this time it'll hurt so much more.

I kiss her again and get out of bed, pulling on my underwear and jeans. "Don't forget to pack a bag and bring it with you," I remind her as she lies back, letting her eyes graze over my body.

"Oh, I won't," she whispers and I chuckle, pulling on my shirt and leaning over her, my lips brushing against hers.

"I'm gonna miss you," I say, and she brings her arms up around my neck, holding me in place as we both deepen the kiss.

"I don't wanna let you go," she replies, pulling back eventually.

"I know, but duty calls."

It really does. I'm going to be late if I'm not careful. I give her one last kiss, telling her I'll see her later, and head out the door, creeping past Adam's bedroom, and clicking my fingers as I get to the living room, which is enough to rouse Baxter from his sleep. He raises his head and then jumps up, coming over to me.

"Hey, boy." I crouch and scratch behind his ears, my voice a low whisper. "C'mon, let's go."

I let us out, pulling the door closed behind us, and open my Jeep, letting Baxter onto the rear seat, before climbing up in front. I know Baxter would probably like to go for a run, but he's going to have to wait until we get back to my place. He should know that by now. It's his new routine. As of New Year... as of when our lives changed to include Jemima and Adam.

Well... Jemima.

Baxter and I arrive at Dad's place to find Mason already there, and while Baxter settles in his basket in the kitchen, tired out from his run along the lakeside, Dad pours me a coffee and I sit down beside Mason, who's still wearing jeans and a shirt, looking really relaxed, considering it's his wedding day.

"How's everything going at your place?" I ask him, taking a sip of my coffee.

"Fairly awful," he says, with a smile. "I hated leaving Isabel behind, but Destiny's already there helping, and Ronan's gone over to the florist's to pick up the flowers."

"I thought they were being delivered," Dad says from the other side of the island unit.

"They were. But they haven't been. Ronan said he'd deal with it."

"Sounds like you're in the best place," I tell him with a pat on his shoulder.

He nods his head. "I'm starting to think that having the wedding at our house was about the dumbest idea we ever had," he says. "When I left to come over here, the living room had been transformed so it could accommodate the seats for the ceremony, and the kitchen was a hive of activity, with the caterers milling around. I couldn't even get a damn coffee."

Dad smiles, topping up his cup.

"Be grateful you kept it small," I say, and Mason nods his head. They have kept it small, too. There are only a handful of guests coming, and he didn't even have a bachelor party... not that I minded. It was one less thing for me to worry about.

"We couldn't have organized it so quickly if we'd gone for anything bigger, what with work being so busy, and..." He falls silent, turning to look at me. "What's wrong?" he asks.

"Nothing. Why?"

"It's just you look kinda thoughtful."

"Do I?"

Dad steps nearer, studying me. "Are you sure you're okay?" he says.

"Yeah. I'm fine."

"You're *fine*?" Mason says, and I turn back to him. He's frowning now. "You've finally got the woman of your dreams, who you've been pining for since heaven knows when, and the best you can muster is 'fine'? What happened to the love struck, dewy eyed guy who was here at Christmas, whispering sweet nothings down the phone?"

"I wasn't whispering."

"No, you weren't. That's the whole point. What's happened, man?"

"Nothing's 'happened'."

"But something's wrong?" Dad says.

"No. Well… yes, I suppose."

"Do you wanna start that again?" Mason says. "Only this time try making some sense. You're clearly unhappy about something."

"I'm not unhappy. It's just that I want us to be a family and Jemima doesn't."

"What does that mean?" Dad says.

"Are you saying she doesn't wanna have kids with you?" Mason asks, and I shake my head.

"No. We haven't even talked about having kids yet. She's got a little boy of her own, remember?"

He nods his head. "And he's the problem?"

"In a way…" I let my voice fade and take a sip of coffee while they both stare at me, making it very clear they're not going to let this go. "I think I told you, Jemima introduced me to her son right at the very beginning… and she made a big deal out of it."

"It is a big deal," Dad says.

"I know, and I get that. When she first suggested it, I told her she didn't have to do it. I wanted her to know she had a way out if she needed it. But she said she wanted me to meet him. I guess I thought that meant she was serious… that she wanted me to be involved, or at least to participate in some way. That was a mistake, though, because she won't let me near him. I'm not allowed to help, or play with him…

155

and, even though I sleep there every night, she won't let me stay for breakfast in case Adam sees me."

"You sleep there every night?" Dad seems surprised.

"Yes, Dad."

"I see," he murmurs, and I glance at Mason, noting the slight smile on his lips.

"The problem is, I'm getting kinda fed up with having to sneak out of the house every morning."

"You never minded when we were younger," Mason says.

"I don't wanna hear this." Dad raises his voice, clearly detecting that, between us, Mason and I might be about to lower the tone.

"I was a lot younger then. When you're eighteen or nineteen, there's something kinda exciting about sneaking around, trying not to get caught out, but I'm too old for that shit now."

"Has Jemima given you a reason why she doesn't want you to stay for breakfast?" Mason asks.

"Not really. She just said she thought it was for the best. And whenever I offer to help with Adam, she says it's easier if she does things."

Dad nods his head. "You need to give her time, son," he says. "She needs to know you're not gonna leave her, like the baby's father did. It's one thing to get involved herself. She's only risking her own heart, but to let her child get attached is something else."

"I get that, Dad. But if she's worried I'm gonna leave and end up hurting Adam, why did she introduce us in the first place? If she was that worried, she should have kept us apart until she was sure."

Neither of them says anything for a moment or two, and I know, without them having to say a word, that they agree with me.

"It's early days," Mason says eventually, echoing Dad's words. "You've only been seeing her for six weeks."

"Yeah, and that's roughly two weeks longer than it took for you to propose to Isabel, so I don't think time has much to do with it, do you?"

"No," he says.

"And besides, I've been in love with her for over a year. It's not like I'm ever gonna change my mind about her. We work together, too, just like you and Isabel… which makes a difference, doesn't it?"

"Yeah," he says. "Spending so much time with the person you love seems to make things happen more quickly."

I nudge into him and he smiles. "Like this wedding, you mean?" I say, trying to forget my problems for a while, and focus on him. It is his day, after all.

With forty-five minutes to go, we all get changed into our tuxes, after which we drive over to Mason's house, taking Dad's car as well as mine, because I'll be going back to my place with Jemima later on.

I've got Mason in the car with me, but there's something I need to do, and I hand him my phone as we start the journey, following behind Dad's BMW.

"Can you call Destiny for me?" I ask him, and he finds her number, connecting the call and putting the phone onto speaker.

She answers quickly, sounding a little breathless.

"What is it?" she says.

"Hi to you too," I reply.

"Things are a little crazy here, Oliver. Was it something important?"

"I'm just calling to let you know we're on our way, so you can keep Isabel out of sight, and also to ask a favor."

"Because I don't have anything else to do," she mumbles, and then takes a deep breath and says, "What do you need?"

I smile to myself. "Can you keep an eye on Jemima for me? She was feeling kinda nervous about meeting everyone, and I've obviously gotta hold Mason's hand – at least until he's married. So do you think you could make sure she's okay?"

"Of course." I can hear the smile in her voice now. "What does she look like?"

"She'll be the most beautiful woman in the room…"

"No, that would be Isabel," Mason interrupts, and I chuckle.

"I guess we have to let you have that one, just for today," Destiny replies, and then says, "What's Jemima wearing?"

"I've got no idea. I know she bought a new dress, but I haven't been allowed to see it."

"Great." I can imagine Destiny rolling her eyes.

"She's got blonde hair, and she's about five foot four, but she usually wears heels, and her face just takes your breath away."

Destiny chuckles. "That's not very helpful, Oliver, but I'm sure I'll find her. And I'll look after her, don't worry."

"Thanks, Sis. I owe you."

We end our call, and Mason flips my phone over a couple of times. "You don't have to hold my hand, you know," he says, staring out through the windshield as I take the turning into town.

"I know. But I want to."

He smiles across at me, and I smile back.

Mason was right; his living room has been transformed. There are a few rows of chairs, each with a pale blue ribbon tied at the back, and down the center of the room is a make-shift aisle. All the furniture has been put into the garage for now, and the room is surprisingly large, most of the surfaces filled with either candles or flowers. It looks pretty and romantic, and just right for Mason and Isabel.

We're standing at the front, most of the chairs now filled with guests. Although I've kept my eye on the door, I haven't seen Jemima yet, and I'm getting nervous that she's found a reason not to come. I've contemplated calling her a couple of times to see if there's something wrong with Adam, or if she's lost, despite her telling me the directions I gave her were fine. I reach into my pocket for a third time, feeling for my phone, just as she appears in the doorway to the hall, and looks around the room, taking a second or two until her eyes lock on mine. She smiles, but almost immediately, Destiny makes her way over, followed by Ronan, and they introduce themselves, shaking hands. Jemima looks a little surprised to start with, but Destiny says something, which makes Jemima laugh. She glances in my direction, and I imagine that whatever my sister just said, it was some kind of insult, aimed at me. I don't care though. Jemima's here, and that's all that matters.

"What's wrong?" Mason whispers.

"Nothing. I've just seen Jemima, that's all."

Mason turns as well, taking a moment before he sees her at the back of the room with Destiny and Ronan.

"I can see why you're so enamored," he says, nudging into me, and I sigh. Because, despite the problems with Adam, I'm so in love with Jemima, it sometimes surprises me.

"It's an amazing feeling, isn't it?" I reply, watching Jemima, as Destiny guides her toward the front of the room, leaving Ronan behind to make sure that people get to their seats. As Jemima approaches, I get to see her dress for the first time, my breath catching in my throat as I take in the way the pale pink material clings to her figure, hugging every curve and contour.

When they get to the front, Jemima seems to waver. Destiny's talking to Dad though and doesn't seem to notice. Jemima's just a few feet from me, and seeing the doubt in her eyes, I can't stand here and do nothing. "Give me a minute," I murmur to Mason and he nods his head, stepping back slightly so I can get around him and go to Jemima, who's almost backing down the aisle now.

"Hey," I say, putting my hand on her waist and looking down into her eyes. "What's wrong?"

"Your sister's brought me up here, but I can't sit at the front," she whispers.

"Yeah, you can." I guide her forward again, but she pulls away from me and I turn back to her.

"No. The front is where members of the family are supposed to sit," she says.

"I know. That's why you belong there. You're my family."

She looks up at me, tears filling her eyes. "Family?" she whispers.

"Yeah. That's how I think of you. That's how I've always thought of you." She blinks, her tears threatening to fall. "Don't cry, Jem."

"It's hard not to, when you say such lovely things."

"I say them because they're true, and because I love you." She smiles. "Come and meet my dad. You'll make his day."

"I will?"

"Yeah. He's dying to meet you."

I lead her forward, right to the very front, a few feet behind where Mason's standing. Dad's sitting, looking up and talking to Destiny, with Baxter at his feet.

"I'm sorry," my sister says, as we approach. "I didn't mean to leave you behind." She's talking to Jemima, although she glances at me with a smile, which I take as her approval.

"Don't worry," Jemima says.

"No, don't worry," I add. "It gave me the chance to come to the rescue."

Destiny slaps me on the arm. "You're such an idiot," she murmurs as my dad gets to his feet, turning to face us.

"Dad, this is my girlfriend, Jemima," I say, making the introductions.

He smiles and as Jemima holds out her hand, he takes it and raises it, touching his lips to her fingers in a very old-fashioned gesture, which makes her blush.

"It's a pleasure to meet you," he says. "You must call me John. If you called me Doctor Gould, half the family would answer, including your boyfriend here." We all laugh, including Jemima, which is a relief. She's so tense, I can feel it. "Would you like to come sit with me?" Dad asks. "You can keep Baxter company too."

I left Baxter with Dad, knowing he'd behave himself while I've got other things to do, and Jemima glances up at me and then smiles, turning to my dad.

"I'd love to," she says and goes to sit beside him, just as Ronan appears at my shoulder.

"D?" he says, clearly addressing my sister, which makes me smile. "I think everyone's here now. Do you wanna let Isabel know?"

Destiny nods her head and makes her way to the back of the room and out through the door, heading up the stairs, I guess, while Ronan takes his seat behind Jemima, leaving space for his wife.

I take that as my cue to get back to my best man duties and, with a wink to Jemima, who's listening to my dad, I return to Mason, who smiles at me.

"You're so in love, it's pitiful," he murmurs.

"You can talk," I reply and he chuckles, just as the room falls silent and we turn to see his bride enter.

Chapter Eight

Jemima

Isabel looks stunning, walking down the aisle in an off-the-shoulder column dress, although it's hard not to notice that she's by herself; no father holding her arm, and no bridesmaids, either. Oliver's told me next to nothing about her, so I'm left wondering whether she has any family, or whether she's alone in the world.

As she reaches the front and turns to face Mason, her face lights up, and I see the love in her eyes, and realize she's not alone, and she never will be... not when she's got a love like that.

I'm sitting beside Oliver's dad, in the front row of the seats, trying to control my nerves and wondering what I'm doing here. I was surprised to be invited to the wedding in the first place, but to be asked to sit with Oliver's family has been very unexpected. Almost as unexpected as that moment just now, when Oliver told me he looks upon me as his family too. I nearly cried when he said that, and I wanted more than anything for him to hold me. All my life, it's just been me and my mom, and Adam, too, since his birth. Like me, my mom is an only child and her parents died before I was born, so I've never understood the idea of belonging to a bigger family, with brothers and sisters, uncles and aunts... and goodness knows what else. It's a little overwhelming. Good, I guess... but overwhelming.

Everyone is studying the bride and groom, who are just in front of us. Oliver is standing right behind Mason, and that gives me the chance to stare at him, to admire the way he looks in a tux, and I smile, thinking about how much I want to see him take it off later, at his place. He turns and looks straight at me, as though he can feel me watching him, and he gives me a smile that melts my heart, just as the celebrant begins the service.

Mason and Isabel don't take their eyes from each other, and when the time comes for them to say their vows, Isabel goes first, sucking in a sharp breath and gazing up into his eyes.

"I feel like I've had a life of two unequal halves. The time before I met you, and the time after. Before, my life was dark and lonely. I was looking for a part of me I always felt was missing. Then I met you, and you made me complete. You fill my life with so much love and happiness that when I look back, I don't even recognize my old self. And now, when I look forward, I see a life beyond my wildest dreams, full of light and wonder. All because of you." She reaches out and takes Mason's hand. "I will love you, honor you, and cherish you, until the light fades from my life, and dims from this most perfect world you've made for us."

Mason smiles down at his bride before he squares his shoulders and says, "The thought of you being lonely hurts me, and I guarantee it will never happen again. I will always be there for you, no matter what. I promise to keep our lives alight, to keep our love burning just as strong as it is now, to protect you, to keep you, to worship you. You've given me everything I ever wanted, and more than I dreamed possible, and as our family grows, I will support you, care for you, and – if it were possible – I will love you more and more… every single day. There isn't a moment in my life when I'm not thinking about you… and until the second after the last breath leaves my body, there never will be."

Everyone seems to let out a collective sigh, and I struggle with the tears that are brimming in my eyes at such beautiful words, trying to concentrate on the celebrant as she completes the ceremony and Mason kisses Isabel for the first time as husband and wife.

The guests all stand and applaud, which makes Baxter bark, and Oliver comes over, crouching down and calming him, before he stands again and looks down into my eyes.

"Okay?" he says and I nod my head as he puts his arm around me and gets Mason's attention. "Let me introduce my brother," Oliver says, and I smile up at Mason. "This is Jemima." Mason nods his head, holding out his free hand.

We shake and then I turn to Isabel as Mason says, "This is my wife," a broad grin on his face.

"I guess that makes you another Doctor Gould," Oliver says as we're joined by Destiny and her husband, Ronan. I met them earlier when Destiny came up and introduced herself to me, almost the moment I walked through the door. I'd forgotten that Ronan's British and for a moment, his accent took me by surprise, but Destiny soon put me at my ease. She told me she had no idea what I saw in her brother, but she could see why he'd fallen for me, which made me laugh. I liked her straight away, and now she comes and stands beside me, nudging into me with her elbow.

"Just what this family needs," she says, rolling her eyes. "Another doctor."

She's smiling at Isabel as she speaks, and although I know they're both older than me, there's a part of me wondering if we might all become friends... maybe.

"Yes, but I'm the only Doc in your life," Ronan says, standing behind Destiny and pulling her close to him, his arms around her. She turns and smiles up at him, nodding her head, just as two young women approach, accompanied by two very handsome men, who I guess are in their early thirties, and Isabel stands to one side, making room for them in our group.

The two women are probably around my age, and while one is a brunette, the other has slightly lighter hair. It's easy to see a resemblance to Isabel though, and I revise my opinion about her having no family, especially when Oliver says, "These are Isabel's sisters, Reagan and Ashley."

They both nod their greetings, and I wonder if the two men might be their boyfriends, before the one called Reagan says, "This is Isabel's oldest friend, Noah." She smiles up at the man right beside her and he narrows his eyes at her, shaking his dark head.

"Less of the old," he says and Reagan chuckles, turning to the last man of the group, who's around the same height, but is blond.

"Aaron is Noah's… friend." She hesitates over her words, and Noah rolls his eyes.

"We're among family," he says. "I think we can be honest." He turns to me. "Aaron's my boyfriend, but we're still getting used to being open about it."

I nod my head, feeling a little overwhelmed again, and I look around the assembled group. "Ollie's told me so much about you all." That's not even remotely true. I didn't even know half of these people existed until today. Still, I had to say something, although I wonder if I should've kept quiet, as I feel Oliver tense slightly, and notice the look of surprise on his dad's face, right before Destiny bursts out laughing.

"He lets you call him 'Ollie'?" Mason speaks up before his sister can.

"Yes. Doesn't everyone?"

"No."

"Not if we want him to answer," Destiny says, joining in.

"Or we don't wanna get hit." Mason and I both look at Oliver, although I'm the only one who's blushing.

"You don't like being called 'Ollie'?"

He turns me, so I'm facing him and then takes me in his arms, holding me against him, regardless of the people gathered around us. "Not by anyone else, no. I never have. But I like it when you call me 'Ollie'. So don't even think about stopping."

Did he really say that in front of everyone? I turn and notice them all staring, and looking a little surprised as well.

"Ignore them." Oliver grins at me. "They're just not used to romance."

"Not from you, we're not," Mason says. "But after that phone call we all sat through on Christmas Day, I don't know why we're surprised anymore."

Oliver holds me a little tighter, chuckling. "Neither do I."

Destiny reaches out, touching my arm. "I meant to ask you earlier, why didn't you bring your little boy? Adam, isn't it? We were hoping to meet him."

I smile at her, realizing Oliver hasn't limited his conversation to me, but has clearly been talking about my son, too. "I left him at home with my mom today."

I turn back and can't fail to notice a strange exchange of glances between Oliver, his dad, and Mason, which has me a little bewildered. It feels like there's something going on I don't know about. It clearly concerns me, and maybe Adam as well, and I wish I could be alone with Oliver to ask him whether I imagined that. I don't want to make a scene and am just wondering what to do when Mason whispers something to Isabel. She nods her head and he turns to face us all again. "As all the family's together for once, we may as well take the chance to tell you… Isabel's pregnant."

Oliver's dad gets in first with his congratulations, before Oliver says, "I knew it wouldn't take long," and Mason shakes his head, grinning. I feel a little in the dark – again – but I offer my congratulations anyway. This seems to be such wanted news, and I try to bury the memory of that 'end of the world' feeling I went through when I discovered I was pregnant. That was so different to this happy scene.

"Is that why you wanted to be here last night?" Oliver asks his brother, while everyone else is still congratulating Isabel.

"Yeah," Mason says. "Isabel's suffering with morning sickness, and I wanted to be around when she woke up today to bring her some orange juice and make sure she was okay."

I can't help thinking how loving and supportive that sounds, recalling that Donavan had seemed quite caring at the beginning…

I look up at Oliver and smile, and he smiles back. It's evening now and we're still at the wedding, sitting on the stairs cuddled up together. Baxter is on the next step down, his head resting between our feet, exhausted from running around in the woodlands for the last half hour. I'd rather be at Oliver's place, curled up in front of his fire, or – better still – on his bed, but we're quite secluded here, and it's the next best thing.

"Can I ask you something?" I say, keeping my voice down, even though there's no-one near us.

"Sure."

"When your sister asked me about Adam, I noticed you and your brother exchanging a look with your dad. What was that about?"

"Nothing," he says. "It was just that I'd been talking to them earlier today, and they'd said they wanted to meet him. That's all."

That's not all. I can tell. But I don't really feel like I can argue with him. Not here. Not now. So instead I nod my head and say, "I didn't realize Isabel had sisters."

"Yeah. They're a lot younger than her."

I smile up at him. "I'm glad you didn't say that in front of her. You've just made her sound ancient."

He chuckles. "Yeah. That probably came out wrong. But it's an easy mistake to make, considering she practically raised them."

"She did?" He nods his head. "Are her parents dead, then?" I ask, lowering my voice still further.

"No. They just don't bother with the parenting part of their lives too much."

"What does that mean?"

He shrugs his shoulders. "It means they walked out when Isabel was sixteen, and they've been absent for most of the time ever since."

"Including on their daughter's wedding day?"

"Yeah." He frowns. "That wasn't their choice, though. Isabel decided against inviting them in the end. To be honest, I'm not sure they even know she's getting married." I can't contain my surprise, and I guess it shows. "You have to understand how much they hurt her," he says. "We both have loving parents, even if we only have two between us. Hers abandoned her and left her to care for her sisters."

"And yet she didn't want them as bridesmaids?" I say, feeling bemused again by other people's families.

"No. But that wasn't a reflection on them. It was just because she wanted to keep the wedding very small and low-key."

"Oh, I see." I guess I can understand that. "And the pregnancy? Was that planned?"

"Yes. Very. They may not have been together for very long, but they worked out right from the beginning that they wanted to have kids, and they didn't want to wait." I sigh, wondering how it must feel to plan something like that, as opposed to having it thrust upon you. "Hey... are you okay?" he says, clearly noting my sadness... somehow.

"I—I was just thinking about the contrast between their happiness, and how I felt when I found out I was pregnant with Adam."

"You weren't happy?" he says. "Not even a little?"

"I was scared. That's the only thing I remember feeling. It was like my world had ended, which I guess it had. At least my world, as I knew it, because it was never gonna be the same again, was it?"

"I guess not."

"Obviously, I didn't know Donavan was gonna cheat, and at the beginning – once I'd got over the shock – I kidded myself that, even if our lives were never gonna be the same, it was just the start of a new chapter, not the ending of everything." I pause for a second. "Mason saying he wanted to be there for Isabel during her morning sickness reminded me a little of Donavan."

"Was he there for you?" Oliver asks.

"Yes. Most of the time. He didn't like being in the bathroom with me while I threw up, but he'd make me cups of tea and let me sleep on him, and for a while I let myself believe it would all be okay."

"I'm sorry," he says.

"What for?" I twist slightly, looking up into his eyes.

"I'm sorry I wasn't there for you. If you'd wanted me to, I'd have come into the bathroom with you. I'd have done anything... anything at all. I wish... I wish..."

I put my fingers over his lips. "Don't," I whisper. "There's no point in wishing for things that can't be."

Oliver

I pull Jemima's hand away, kissing her palm and although I don't say a word, I still wish to myself that things could have been different, that I could have made her life easier and happier... that I could have been Adam's father.

But I know she's right. I can't change the past.

So maybe there is no point in wishing... for anything. Maybe I'm better off just letting things happen...

"Do you want to go?" I say and her eyes light up, which makes me smile.

"Can we?" She's so eager, my smile becomes a grin.

"Of course we can. Come on, let's go find my brother and let him know."

I stand, pulling her to her feet, and help her down the stairs, telling Baxter to stay at the bottom, which he does. Then, keeping my arm around Jemima, we go into the living room, and beyond into the kitchen, where Mason's sitting on one of the stools at the island unit, with Isabel nestled between his legs. They're talking to Ash and Reagan, and we walk over, Mason turning as we approach.

"We're gonna head off," I say, and he gives me a smile, which speaks volumes to me, but hopefully means nothing to Jemima, because I think she'd be embarrassed if she knew my brother has almost certainly worked out why we want to get back to my place.

He stands, Isabel moving aside as he does, and pulls me over to my right. "Thanks for everything," he says, not that I feel as though I've done very much.

"Anytime."

"There won't be another time for me, but I'll return the favor, if you want me to."

I nod my head. "I'll bear that in mind."

"She's lovely." He nods toward Jemima, who's deep in conversation with Isabel and her sisters.

"I know."

"If you're really worried about the situation with Adam, you can talk to me… but my advice would be that you discuss it with Jemima first. Tell her how you really feel."

"I will. But maybe not tonight." Tonight I'm in the mood for letting things happen. We move back toward Jemima and Isabel, who both smile up at us. "Tell Dad and Destiny and Ronan we've gone, will you?" I say to Mason. "We'll be here for another hour at least if we have to say goodbye to everyone."

"And you've got better things to do with your time?" he says, raising his eyebrows.

"Yeah, we have."

I don't wait for his answer, but I grab Jemima around the waist and steer her from the room.

"I apologize for my brother," I say, as I guide her to the front of the house.

She looks back at me, and although her cheeks are flushed, I'm not sure it's with embarrassment. It looks more like anticipation, like the sparkle in her eyes. "Don't worry," she murmurs, and I let us both out through the front door, Baxter following behind as I close it softly.

Jemima's followed me back to my place in her car, and she parks up beside my Jeep, as I let Baxter out and he runs around in the dark for a few minutes, while I help Jemima from her Honda, and grab her bag from the rear seat.

"You've undone your tie," she says, looking up at me.

"Yes." She doesn't say a word, but just stares appreciatively, and I pull her closer with my free arm. "I'm so glad you're here."

"So am I." She looks up at me, and while I'd like to stand here forever and just stare into her eyes, it's freezing, and I can think of far better places to be… and far better things to do.

I take her hand in mine and lead her up the steps and into the cabin, flicking on the lights. Baxter dallies for a few moments, sniffing at something by the bottom step, but then bounds inside, lapping up some water from his bowl.

"I just have to feed him," I say to Jemima, as I put her bag down by the couch. "It won't take a minute."

She nods her head and I go over to the kitchen, preparing Baxter's food, while he sits right by my leg, staring up at me.

Jemima comes over, leaning against the countertop beside me and after a moment or two, she breaks the silence. "That look, between you, your dad and Mason, was it really just about them wanting to meet Adam?"

I carry on with what I'm doing, playing for time, and wondering whether I should lie again. I didn't like lying to her earlier, so doing it again feels wrong... especially when I love her so much.

"No, not really."

"I didn't think so." I can hear the disappointment in her voice and I put Baxter's bowl down on the floor, before turning to her and facing the sadness in her eyes. "What was it really about?"

So much for letting things happen.

"I'd told Mason and Dad how I feel about not being able to stay at your place for breakfast every day, and why you won't let me." That's not all I told them, but I'm not sure now is the right time to confess my true feelings for Adam, not after she closed me down earlier, when I was trying to tell her I wished I could have been his father.

"So they know you're sleeping at my place, then?"

"Yes. Is that a problem?" I hadn't foreseen that. "Your mom knows about me sleeping with you," I reason and she nods her head, clearly seeing the logic in my argument, now I've made it.

"And how do you feel?" she asks. "About not staying for breakfast, I mean."

"You know how I feel, Jem. I hate it. I hate sneaking around. It's the kind of thing I did when I was younger, and fooling around with girls, trying not to get caught out by their parents. Except I'm not fooling around with you, and I hate pretending we're not serious about each other, when we are… or at least, I am."

She grabs my arm, a look of alarm in her eyes. "I am too," she says.

"In that case, why can't I stay with you for breakfast? We've been together for six weeks now, and I know that's not long by some people's standards, but it's long enough for me to know I wanna be with you all the time."

"You are… practically. We're barely apart for more than an hour each day."

I gaze down at her. "Don't you like it that way?"

"Yes."

"Then why can't you take that last step? Why do I have to keep sneaking out of your house every morning? You know I love you, Jem, so why can't you trust me?"

"I do," she says. "You know I do."

"I'm sensing a 'but'." It's filling my heart with fear.

"There isn't one. Honestly. And I understand how you feel." She sighs. "I'd have to run it by Mom first, being as it's her house, but why don't we try it next weekend?"

"Excuse me?" Did I hear that right?

"I said, why don't we try it next weekend? Weekdays can be kinda tricky, with having to get ready for work, and Mom staying over at Dale's so much. But we can try on Saturday morning, if you like?"

I pick her up off the floor, twirling her around. "Thank you," I whisper, between frantic kisses, holding her body close to mine, my cock responding, as I imagine all the things I want to do with her… all the things I've planned to do with her. As we stop spinning, she leans back in my arms and tilts her head, staring at me, her brow furrowing at the same time.

"What's wrong?" she asks.

"Nothing. Why?"

"You've got a strange expression on your face."

"Sorry. It's just that you're so naked in my head right now, I'm finding it confusing."

She giggles and I lower her to the floor, and take her hand, leading her to the front of the house, where I flick off the lights again, before I start down the hallway to my bedroom.

Once we're inside, I close the door, switching on the dim bedside lamps, and then I turn back to her. She's looking up at me, her eyes on fire, and I go over, kissing her hard as I reach behind her, unzipping her dress and pulling it from her shoulders. She's breathless and desperate in an instant, and I like that.

"I—I can't wait," she murmurs, as I shrug off my jacket and let it fall to the floor. She undoes my shirt buttons, fumbling and looking up into my eyes. "I need this so much."

"I know, baby."

I push her dress down over her hips and it falls around her ankles, revealing her black lace underwear, and although she's only halfway through my buttons, I lean down and lift her into my arms, carrying her over to the bed and dropping her onto the mattress. She squeals and I chuckle, shaking my head.

"There's nothing for it. I'm gonna have to buy a new bed," I mutter, undoing the last of my buttons and taking off my shirt, kicking off my shoes at the same time.

She gazes hungrily at my chest, and then says, "Why? What's wrong with this one?"

"Nothing." I kneel up, pulling off her panties, which I throw over my shoulder. "Except I think we might break it tonight."

She giggles again, but I keep a straight face, and she gazes up at me as I bend over her, taking both of her hands and holding them above her head with one of mine. Then I pull down the cups of her bra, revealing her full breasts, and I dip my head, biting at her nipples. She squirms beneath me, but I don't stop. Instead, I let my hand wander south, to her exposed pussy, and she gasps as I touch her swollen clit, stroking it.

"Y—You're not kidding, are you?" she stutters and I lean up, looking down at her.

"Hell, no." I insert a finger into her soaking entrance, while my thumb works its magic around her clit, making her writhe and buck and moan.

"P—Please," she whimpers.

"Please what? Tell me your deepest desires… beg me for them."

"I wanna feel you inside me. I want you to make me come… hard. Please, Ollie. Please. I need this so much…"

I curl my finger inside her, rubbing her g-spot, and she throws her head back, letting out a low moan, which builds and builds, as I circle my thumb around her clit. She's close, so I insert a second finger, scissoring them, stretching her.

"Oh, God… Oh, God." She grinds out the words, raising her legs and planting her feet on the mattress as she lifts her hips high off the bed, desperate for more. I rub a little harder against her clit and she screams, a plaintive cry, followed by my name, as her thighs shudder, her body trembling through her orgasm. I watch her, seeing the ecstasy on her face, the blush on her skin, and feel her juices drip down over my hand. That's too much for me, and although she hasn't calmed yet, I pull my fingers from her, releasing her hands as I move down the bed, lying between her legs. "W—Where are you going?" she asks, leaning up and looking at me.

"I wanna taste you," I say, and bury my head between her legs. She's divinely sweet, and she places her hand on the back of my head, holding me there, while she bucks her hips up into me.

"More…. give me more, Ollie. I'm begging you."

I put my fingers back inside her, pumping them in and out this time, while I bite and lick her clit, and within moments, she's gone again, squealing something incoherent as her thighs lock against the sides of my head and she comes hard. I lap her up, swallowing down as much of her as I can, and once she's spent, and I can hear her breathing even out, I kneel up and move backwards off of the bed, unfastening my pants, and pulling them off, along with my trunks and socks. Jemima watches as I grab a condom from the nightstand and roll it over my cock, biting on her bottom lip, her eyes feasting on me. Then I pull off her shoes, and undo her garter belt, removing it and her stockings as she reaches behind her back, unfastening her bra and discarding it, so she's lying naked before me, her legs parted, her pussy glistening.

"I'm gonna make you come so fucking hard," I murmur as I kneel up over her body.

"You just did," she says, smiling. "Twice."

"That wasn't coming hard." I put an arm around each of her thighs, parting her legs and pulling her up off the mattress toward me. "*This* will be coming hard." I impale her suspended body and she lets out a long guttural groan, her pussy gripping me as I take her.

She closes her eyes, her lips moving, although I can't make out what she's saying.

"There's no-one to hear you, Jem. Whatever you're saying, you can say it out loud. You can scream it, if you want."

She opens her eyes again, staring into mine. "Fuck me," she says and I smile. "Fuck my pussy, Ollie. Please."

I lower her body to the bed, pushing her legs upwards toward her chest, and holding them in place, my hands in the crooks of her knees as I lean over her.

"You want fucking?" I say, my cock half in and half out of her, in a wicked tease.

"Yes. Hard."

"You've got it." I pull all the way out and she opens her mouth, presumably to object, just as I sink all the way back into her again, stretching her, filling her.

"That's... that's so good."

"You want more?"

"Yes. I want it all. Give me everything you've got."

I don't say a word. I just lean over a little more, so I can take her deeper, and then I up the tempo, pounding into her, so hard and so fast, she's struggling to catch her breath and beads of sweat form on my back.

"You like it this hard? This deep?"

"Yes," she yells.

"You like my cock inside you?"

"Yes!"

I hope to God she's close, because I'm not sure how much longer I can keep going, and I'm just about to ask, when she suddenly comes apart, without warning, her body twitching and quivering against mine as she screams out her pleasure. I take another couple of strokes, burying myself as deep as I can go, and I howl her name, over and over as I come, harder than ever.

I take a moment or two to recover and pull out of her, falling onto the mattress at her side, and she looks across at me, biting her bottom lip.

"Was that kinda slutty of me?" she says, sounding doubtful, and I lean up on one elbow, turning her onto her side and pulling her close to me.

"No. Why ever would you think that?"

"I was begging you to… to… I mean, I know I've said things like that to you in the past…"

"Pretty much every time we've made love," I say, with a smile and she nods her head.

"I know. But that was… so much more."

I lean in and kiss her. "This is the first time we've been alone, baby. It was always gonna be different. You just need to remember that what we do… everything we do, is beautiful, Jem. There's nothing slutty about it, and there's certainly nothing wrong with you voicing your desires. I don't have a problem with you asking to be fucked… or begging to be fucked. It's all part of what we are. I like that. I like being able to say anything to you, and that you can say anything to me. So, whatever you want, or need, just tell me, and it's yours."

"I—I've never been like this before," she says, still harboring doubts, it seems.

"And?"

"And I don't understand why I'm so different with you."

"Maybe because this is how you're meant to be," I say. "I've never been like this before either, you know?"

"Haven't you?"

"No. I don't routinely ask women to beg me."

"So, it's just me, then?"

"Yes."

She smiles. "That's good to know."

"It is?"

"Yes."

"Why?"

"Because I know you have your wild side, and you're more experienced than I am, but I like the idea that what we have is different."

I hug her closer, her breasts pressed against my chest. "Oh, baby… this is so different, sometimes it blows my mind." She bites her bottom lip and I lean in, freeing it with my teeth, which makes her moan and flex her hips into mine.

"C—Can we do all that again?" she asks, gazing up at me.

"Of course. Just give me two minutes to go to the bathroom, and then I'll give you anything you want."

"Anything?" she says, her eyes sparkling.

"Yeah. Absolutely anything."

I wake slowly, like I'm coming out a dream, but as I focus on Jemima's beautiful face beside my own, I realize that's not the case at all. I'm waking into a dream… a perfect dream, and even though she can't see me, I have to smile, because I'm so in love with her.

Last night was amazing, and my smile widens as I remember her idea of 'anything', which became apparent when I walked back into the bedroom and found her kneeling up on the mattress, her ass in the air. Her intentions were obvious, and I gazed at her perfectly rounded hips and ass while I rolled another condom over my cock, contemplating keeping it simple and just kneeling up behind her. Except 'simple' isn't really my style, and I hate being predictable. So I grabbed her and pulled her across to the edge of the bed, slapping her ass with one hand while I palmed my cock with the other and rubbed the tip against her entrance until she was grinding back into me, squealing and moaning.

"You want this?" I said.

"Yes," she murmured, her face buried in the covers, which we'd scattered over the bed. I hesitated, waiting… hoping she'd tell me what she wanted, because despite her earlier doubts, I wanted to hear it. I needed to hear it. "Please," she whimpered, turning her head. "Give me your cock."

I pushed inside her, just by an inch or two, and then pulled out again. She edged backwards, clearly wanting more.

"Tell me what you want."

"I want you to fill me. I want your enormous cock deep in my pussy."

I gave her exactly what she'd asked for, ramming home, spanking her ass again, and making her scream out her pleasure as she rocked back and forth, taking my dick.

"More," she cried, looking back at me over her shoulder. "Give me more…"

She seemed to want everything, and so did I. I wanted all of her. I slowed my pace slightly, leaning over her, and teased my thumb between her lips.

"Suck," I said, and she did, her tongue working over me and her eyes on fire, until I pulled my thumb back out again. "Still want more?"

"Yes!"

Maintaining that steady pace inside her, I stroked my moistened thumb against her tight anus, and she stilled for a moment, making me wonder if she was going to object. She didn't, though. She groaned, a deep guttural noise coming from somewhere deep inside her.

"More?" I said.

"Please, Ollie… please."

She smiled at me as I pushed inside that tightest hole, and then she gasped, and after just a second's hesitation, she nudged back against me, wriggling her ass.

"You like that?"

"Yes… I like that."

Slowly, taking care not to hurt her, I increased the pace, until my cock was hammering into her, my thumb delving deeper with every stroke. I felt like my heart was going to burst, but I kept going until she let out a plaintive cry, her body stiffening and her pussy clenching around me as she came, really hard.

"Now," she cried. "Come now, Ollie. Please."

That was more than I could take, and I exploded deep inside her, giving her what she wanted, and what I needed... more than anything.

Looking back now, regardless of her doubts last night, I don't think we know any other way of being together. She brings out the wildest side of my nature, and it seems I do the same for her. And I love that part of us. To me, it means we're perfect for each other.

"Hello." Her voice awakens me from my daydream, and I smile down at her.

"Hi." I lean over and kiss her gently. "Did you sleep okay?"

She nods her head. "Your bed is very comfortable." She stretches her arms and legs. "So, please don't buy a new one."

I chuckle, remembering my comment last night.

"If you say so."

"I do." She smiles and sighs at the same time, which feels kinda gratifying.

"Are you okay?" I ask her.

"Yes, I'm fine."

She seems confused by my question, so I clarify. "I didn't hurt you last night... your ass, I mean?"

"No... although I have a question."

"Okay."

She looks up at me. "Have you ever done that before?"

"No... what about you?" I ask, intrigued.

"No," she says, and then frowns. "Can I ask... what made you wanna do it with me?"

I lean down and kiss her. "Because I want all of you."

Her lips twitch up into a perfect smile. "I'm yours," she whispers.

"I'm glad to hear it... now, would you like some breakfast?" I ask her, and her smile fades slightly.

"Have we got time? I promised Mom we'd be back by nine."

"We've got plenty of time. I'll get us some toast and coffee, and then we can shower together."

Her eyes sparkle into life again, and she bites her bottom lip.

"Really?" she says, on a breath.

"Yeah." I lean over and free her lip with my thumb.

"Do you mean shower? Or do you mean something else?"

"You'll find out. If you want to," I tease, and she smiles.

"Oh, I want to," she says, and I kiss her, wondering – not for the first time – how the hell I got this lucky.

Chapter Nine

Jemima

"It's been such a lovely weekend." I turn and smile at Oliver as he holds me in his arms. He's going to have to get up soon, but we can enjoy this moment… for now.

"What was the best part?" he says, shifting onto his side and pulling me closer to him, his ever-present erection prodding into my hip.

I pause, pretending to give some serious thought to his question. "Well… yesterday was nice, just hanging out here with Adam. And, of course, there was meeting your family at the wedding…"

He pushes me onto my back, holding my hands either side of my head and pinning me to the bed with his body.

"*What* was the best part?" he repeats, his lips barely an inch from mine.

"Staying with you, at your place, and all the new things we did together." We both know what I'm talking about, even if I haven't put it into words.

"Any new things in particular?" He's not going to let this go.

"Yes… taking a shower." He looks down at me and smiles, and although that's not what either of us is thinking about, our shower yesterday morning was spectacular. The moment we got in there, and he'd turned on the water, he spun me around, facing away from him and pulled me onto his erection, lifting my right leg off of the floor and hooking it over his arm. In that position, I could lean back into him for support and twist my head around so we could kiss really tenderly. It was romantic, but it felt so promiscuous… and I liked it, screaming for him to take me harder. Except I think I told him to fuck me harder, because it seems that's the kind of thing I say when I'm with him. That's the kind of person I am.

"Anything else?" he says, tilting his head.

"Yes. Finally realizing I don't have to feel embarrassed about voicing my needs and desires."

"No, you don't." He lowers himself still further, his body crushing mine in the nicest possible way. "If you can't tell me what you want, who can you tell?"

"No-one."

"Good," he says, smiling. "In which case, will you tell me whether you liked me playing with your ass as much as you seemed to?"

"I did," I murmur, blushing.

"And would you like me to do that again?"

"Yes, please."

"It'll be my pleasure… but I think we might have to save it for when we're at my place. I'm not sure you can come quietly when we're doing that."

I laugh, which makes us both shake, being as he's lying right on top of me. "Neither am I." I lean up and kiss him. "Thank you for letting me be me, Ollie. I didn't realize who I was until now."

"You didn't?"

"No. Like I said to you, I was never like this before. I think you've brought me out of myself, and I'm grateful for that."

He brushes his lips across mine. "You don't have to be grateful," he says. "Believe me, I wouldn't want you any other way. You're sexy, you're fun, you're everything I could ever want. You're my idea of what love should be."

His words bring tears to my eyes… again. "Th—That's such a lovely thing to say."

"It's the truth."

He kisses me, crushing his lips to mine, pushing my legs apart with his own and nestling into me, our bodies grinding and pulsing together, until the alarm goes off, signaling it's time for him to leave, and we both still.

"I—I guess I'd better go," he says, releasing my hands with obvious reluctance.

Reaching up, I caress his cheek with my fingertips. "I'll talk to Mom this morning about you staying for breakfast on Saturday. I promise."

He smiles. "Thank you."

"Don't thank me. I should have done it sooner."

I should. Looking back, I know why I refused to let him stay. I know it was a maternal instinct to protect Adam. But what did I think I was protecting him from? What did I think Oliver was going to do to him? It was silly, and selfish, and I know it hurt Oliver. I shouldn't have done it, and now I just want to make amends.

I help Adam to a finger of toast, as Mom pours her tea, a slight smile on her face.

"I feel like I've hardly seen you over the last few weeks," I say to her. We don't always have breakfast together anymore. Sometimes she only gets back from Dale's just before I leave for work.

"I know," she replies, her smile widening.

"So, things are going okay with Dale?"

"Yes." Her voice is kinda dreamy, and while I desperately want to ask for more information, I don't feel like I can. I know she'll tell me when she's ready, which I guess means she isn't yet. So, even though I really want to know if this guy is my father, I can't ask her.

"I wanted to ask a favor," I say instead.

"Oh?" She raises her eyebrows.

"I was wondering if it would be okay for Oliver to stay for breakfast?"

She tilts her head and sighs. "Of course it would. You don't need to ask."

"Yeah, I do. It's your house, Mom."

"I know and I appreciate you respecting that. But he's been sleeping here for weeks now, and to be honest, I'm surprised not to have seen him at the breakfast table before now."

I can feel myself blushing. "I—I thought it was better for Adam not to see him in the mornings," I say and she frowns.

"Why?"

"Well… because Oliver's not his father, and…"

"And what?" Her frown deepens. "Honestly, Jemima." She sounds disappointed, or frustrated. I'm not sure which. "Dale stayed here on Saturday night, when you were over at Oliver's place, and Adam didn't have any trouble over breakfast. We all just got on with it."

That must mean Dale left not long before we got back here yesterday morning. I missed meeting him by minutes… but more importantly, if Dale is my father, does Mom really think it's fair to introduce him to Adam before me? Surely not. So does that mean Dale isn't my father? Or that Mom doesn't think it matters? I have to know now…

"Can I ask…" My phone rings, interrupting me, and while I consider ignoring it, I realize it might be Oliver. It's too early in the morning to be anyone else. And I guess if he's calling, it must be important. There might be an emergency at the surgery… "I'd better get that." I get up and go over to the countertop, where my phone is charging. Checking the screen, I let out a gasp as I see the word 'Donavan' lit up before me.

"What's wrong?" Mom says from her seat at the table.

"I—It's Donavan," I whisper, still in shock.

"You'd better answer it." She nods to the phone, still resting in my shaking hand, and I unplug it, pressing the green button and holding it to my ear.

"Hello?" I whisper.

"Hi," says the familiar voice at the other end of the line. "It's me. Donavan."

"I know. Your name came up."

There's a moment's pause and then he says, "So you kept my number then?"

"Yes."

"And I'll bet you're wondering why I called you."

"Of course I am. We broke up, and the last time we spoke, you told me you wanted nothing to do with our son, so what's changed?"

"Everything," he says. "I got it wrong, Jemima."

I feel like the air's been sucked from my lungs and I turn, clutching the countertop for support.

"Which part?"

"Like I said… everything."

Suddenly I see red. "Are you kidding me? You slept around while I was pregnant, you abandoned me—"

"No, I didn't," he says, interrupting me, mid-flow. "You're the one who left."

I remember Oliver saying the same thing, but it makes no difference. "Yeah. Because you cheated. What did you expect me to do? Stay and watch you sleep with every girl you came across, while I struggled to make ends meet and had our baby by myself?"

"It wouldn't have been like that," he says, sounding regretful. "I'd have come to my senses, eventually."

"Really?"

"Yeah. I made a mistake."

"You made more than one," I remind him.

"Okay. But that was then, Jemima."

"And?"

"And I've changed. Like I said, I got it wrong. I wanna try and make it right."

"It's a bit late for that. I'm with someone else now, so I don't know what you expect me to do about it."

There's a pause. Quite a long one. And then he says, "You can let me see my son."

"Is this some kind of joke? You can't just call me up and say that. Not after such a long time."

"Yes, I can. He's my son."

"I know. I knew that all along. You're the one who conveniently forgot that when you cheated on me, and then ignored Adam from the moment he was born."

"Well, I wanna make up for lost time," Donavan says. "Is that such a sin?"

I can't think what to say to that, and although I'm still angry, I can see the logic behind his words. People do change, after all, and rather than continuing our pointless argument, I just say, "No. I guess not."

"So, can we meet up? Can I see him?"

"I don't know. You'll have to let me think about it." I can't just say 'yes', no matter how much I want Adam to have his father in his life. It's all too much to contemplate on the spur of the moment.

"Okay," Donavan replies. "You've got my number. Call me back when you've decided."

I hang up, tears welling in my eyes, which I don't want him to hear, and as I let the phone fall from my hand, my legs start to give way.

"Jemima?" Mom comes over, putting her arm round my shoulders. "What did he want?"

"To see Adam?"

"Is he serious? After all this time?" She's as confused as I am.

"Yeah."

"You told him you'd think about it?"

I nod my head. "I didn't feel like I could just say 'no', anymore than I could say 'yes'."

"I know." She takes a breath. "This isn't something you can rush into."

"No."

"You should probably discuss it with Oliver, too."

I tilt my head, frowning, unsure why she thinks that's necessary. This concerns Adam, and that makes it my decision, not Oliver's. But at the mention of his name, I realize I'm going to be late for work.

"I've gotta go," I whisper, picking up my phone again and swallowing down my tears.

"Okay," she says. "Call me if you wanna talk."

I nod, going over to Adam and lifting him from his high chair, even though he's still finishing his toast. He seems confused, but that's not surprising. I don't normally do this. I normally just give him a quick hug and a kiss, but today, I feel the need to hold him… and I do, his little body tight against mine.

"You be good," I murmur, as I kiss his cheek. "Mommy will see you later."

He stares at me and blinks, before putting the soggy toast into his mouth again, as Mom comes and takes him from me.

"He'll be fine," she says, and I console myself with the thought that Donavan doesn't know where we live, so he can't do anything drastic. Adam will be safe…

My drive to work is filled with confused thoughts. I honestly never thought I'd hear from Donavan again, but hearing his voice, hearing his request, has left me anxious and panicky. What should I do? I feel like if I say 'no', there's a real danger that Donavan could fight me for access to his son, but if I say 'yes', I'm opening a whole other can of worms. I'm only just getting my head around letting Oliver into Adam's life, and now his father wants to be let in as well? It's too much for me, and as I park my car beside Oliver's, I start sobbing…

Oliver

I get out of the shower, feeling disgruntled.

Okay, so maybe disgruntled is too strong a word… after all, we've had a fantastic weekend. It's just that I'm kinda fed up with coming back here every morning to shower and give Baxter a run along the lakeside, before I leave again, pick up breakfast at the diner and head into work. I don't bother having breakfast here, because it's not worth stocking up my refrigerator. I don't spend any time here anymore. In fact, my home is kinda redundant these days. Every evening, I go to Jemima's place straight after work, by which time Heather's usually left to spend her evening with Dale, and while Jemima gives Adam his bath,

I clear up his toys and cook our dinner, which we all eat together. I'm not allowed to feed Adam... heaven forbid. In fact, I'm not allowed to do anything with him. I'm a bystander in his life; observing, rather than participating.

With a towel wrapped around my hips, I pad back into my bedroom, looking at the pile of laundry in the corner. I'm getting by, putting washing into the machine one morning, and then into the dryer the next. But some days I run out of time, and in any case, it's a long process and very far from ideal, which is why I'm so far behind. It's another reminder that, while I love spending every night at Jemima's place, in Jemima's bed, I wish we could work things out; that we had a place of our own, where we lived like a 'normal' family, instead of this half-and-half life.

I find some clean jeans – which is a miracle in itself – and grab a t-shirt from the closet, throwing them onto the bed and sitting down, reminding myself that Mason and Dad were right. I can't rush this. Jemima and I have only been together for a few weeks, and it's a huge transition for her. I need to be patient and give her time. She'll get there. And besides, she's going to talk to her mom today about me staying for breakfast on Saturday morning. She promised she would before I got out of bed, and again when I kissed her on the doorstep. So, who knows? Maybe that might be the start of something new.

I've already changed into my scrubs and am finishing the last of the coffee I picked up at the diner, sitting at the countertop in my surgery, while I go over Brandy's file. She's making a good recovery and Mr. Yates is bringing her in first thing this morning for a check-up.

I look up at the sound of a car pulling up outside, the smile automatically forming on my lips when I see Jemima's Honda, which she parks beside my Jeep.

I've missed her, even though we've only been apart for a little over an hour, and while I know that's kinda sappy, I don't care. I love spending time with her. It's just that I just want to do it more often.

I lean forward slightly, waiting for her to get out of her car, but she doesn't and I stand, going out into the reception area, where I can get a better view, noticing straight away that Jemima's head is bent over the steering wheel, and that her shoulders are shaking.

She's crying?

What the hell?

I run out, pulling open her door, and she startles, looking up.

"What's wrong?" I crouch down, brushing a loose hair from her cheek, as I rest my arm across her lap, wishing I could hold her properly. Surely this can't be about me staying over, can it? Heather can't have said 'no'. She's not that kind of person. And even if she did refuse, that wouldn't be enough to make Jemima cry like this, would it? "You're scaring me, Jem. Please, tell me what's wrong."

She sucks in a stuttering breath, trying to calm herself, and looks at me, her eyes filled with tears still. "M—My phone rang while we were having breakfast this morning," she says, her bottom lip trembling.

"Okay."

"I thought it was probably you, being as it was so early. I guessed there might be an emergency or something. But... But it was Donavan's name on the screen, not yours."

"D—Donavan?" I'm struggling to breathe, let alone speak.

"Yeah. Adam's father."

I want to tell her I know who the guy is. I remember her story, and I'm not likely to forget her ex's name, even if I find it hard to say out loud. But I can't say any of that, any more than I can ask her why she's still got his details on her phone. She's breaking apart in front of me, and I need to keep my emotions in check. I need to bury my fear and insecurity, and my jealousy, and focus on her instead.

"What did he want?" I ask.

"T—To see Adam," she says, barely able to control herself.

"Now? After all this time?"

"Yes."

"What are you gonna do?" It's her decision, not mine.

"I don't know." She shakes her head. "I'm not sure I even have a choice in the matter."

"Why not?"

"Because if I don't let him see Adam, Donavan might go to court and get legal access, which wouldn't be on my terms, would it? It would be on his."

I reach up and caress her cheek. "It doesn't work like that, baby. He doesn't get to call the shots just because he's finally decided to step up and do the right thing. But you… you have to go with your gut." Which I hope is telling her to run a mile from this guy. She doesn't say anything for a moment, so I add, "If you don't think he should see Adam, then…"

"I don't know what I think," she interrupts, letting out a sigh. "There's a part of me that says he's left it too late." *Good. That's just what she should be thinking.* "But then another part of me keeps remembering how it felt to grow up without a father, and I have to question my right to take that away from Adam. Either way, I'm not sure I have any choice. Donovan's entitled to see his son." 'Entitled'? Really? That's not how I see it, but I sense I'm fighting a losing battle here. I get the feeling her history is going to defeat her common sense.

"Okay, but if you're gonna go ahead with this, you have to be there with them," I say and she turns, glaring at me.

"I know that!" she barks. "I'm not a complete idiot."

I pull back, releasing her, and holding up my hands at the same time. "Okay. Sorry I spoke."

"Stop sulking, Oliver," she says, bitterness lacing her voice. "This isn't about you."

That hurts, and I stand, putting a necessary distance between us as she stares out the windshield, rather than at me. "I know. I get that this is about Adam, and you… and his father, I guess." She still doesn't look at me, and I can't see the point of standing here anymore. She's not interested in anything I've got to say. That much is obvious. "I'll be inside. Take your time and come in whenever you're ready." I step away from her car and close the door, walking slowly back into the office.

I lean against the wall beside the door in my surgery, feeling a little guilty for leaving Jemima outside in her car by herself when she's still so upset. At the same time, though, I can't help feeling hurt by her attitude. Yeah, it's about Adam and her, and her ex, like I just said. They're the family unit in this. But can't she see? I want to be part of that family, too.

Chapter Ten

Jemima

I stare out the window, feeling guilty for snapping at Oliver like that, for accusing him of sulking. He wasn't. But I didn't ask for his opinion, did I? And whether he likes it or not, Adam is my son. He's not Oliver's. He's mine and Donavan's. There's no getting away from that, and in reality, I don't think I want to. Isn't this what I've always wanted for Adam? To have his father in his life?

Even if I didn't want it, I'm not sure I have a choice. Like I said to Oliver, Donavan has rights. He could take me to court if he wanted, and that's the last thing I need.

No… if we're going to do this, I'd rather keep it informal and on my terms. I'd rather not involve the courts and have it all be made official and inflexible.

With a shaking hand, I delve into my purse and pull out my phone, connecting a call to Donavan, before I can change my mind.

He answers on the fourth ring, sounding surprised to hear from me.

"I've decided," I say, not bothering with a 'hello'.

"And?" He sounds impatient.

"You can see him."

I hear him sigh. "Thank you," he says, and my heart swells in my chest as I realize how much he wanted this. It's a shame it's taken him so long, but I feel kinda relieved that Adam will have something I never had. He'll have a father. And because he's so young, he won't remember the time when his father didn't want him. He'll never have to know how it feels to be abandoned.

"I—I don't know how you wanna work this," I say.

"Saturdays are gonna be best for me. I've got a job in the city."

I don't know why that surprises me, but it does.

"Okay. But I can't do this Saturday."

"Oh?" He sounds disappointed and inquisitive at the same time, but I'm not about to explain that Oliver is due to have breakfast with us this Saturday, for the first time. There's no way I want Donavan knowing that much about my life with Oliver. It's none of his business. "Can you make Friday afternoon?" he says, once it's become clear I'm not going to give him an explanation.

"I guess. If I can get some time off… but I thought you said you were working."

"If I make up the hours, they won't mind me taking the afternoon off." His employers sound very flexible. "So, what do you say?"

"I'll speak to my boss."

"Good." He pauses for a moment and then says, "Do you wanna come to my place? I'm not in Eastford anymore. I've got a little house just outside of Boston, but you're very welcome to come… both of you, obviously."

"I—I think it's gonna be better if we meet up somewhere neutral to start off with." I can't help stuttering, just at the thought of how wrong this could all go.

"Okay. If that's what you want." He's being very accommodating, but then I guess he has to be. "How about Whitehall State Park? We could go for a walk."

"Okay."

"I can get there for around two-thirty, if that works for you."

"That should be fine. I'll call if it's gonna be a problem."

"Okay. Otherwise, I'll see you on Friday."

"You will."

I'm about to hang up when I hear him say, "Thanks, Jemima. It'll work out, I promise," and my breath catches in my throat. I can't speak, so I don't, and I end the call, hoping I've done the right thing.

Taking a deep breath, I gather my thoughts as I put my phone away and rummage through my purse for a Kleenex to wipe my nose and eyes. I wanted this so much when Adam was born, and I guess those feelings have never gone away. I've always wanted him to have his father in his life, because I know what it feels like to grow up without one. Now it's really happening, though, it doesn't feel real. Maybe that's because I'm scared Donavan will let me down again. It wouldn't surprise me if he did. He's got a track record, after all.

"Stop being so negative." I mustn't think like that.

I have to give him the benefit of the doubt.

At least until he proves me wrong.

I open the car door, climbing out and locking it behind me as I walk over to the office, the Kleenex still clutched in my hand, my stomach churning and my mind in turmoil.

Pushing the door open, I go inside, just as Oliver comes out from his surgery and leans against the doorframe. It's obvious he's been waiting for me to come in, and he stares right at me, not saying a word.

"I—I've spoken to Donavan," I mutter.

"Already?" He's shocked and folds his arms across his chest defensively.

"Yes."

"And?"

"I've arranged to take Adam to see him at Whitehall State Park on Friday at two-thirty. It seemed sensible to meet somewhere neutral, but it means I'll need the afternoon off. I—I hope that's okay."

"It's fine," he says, his voice really monotone, like he couldn't care less. "Take the whole damn day."

He steps back into his office, but I rush over, grabbing his arm.

"Are you mad at me?" I tug on him, although he won't be moved and just stands, stock still.

"I don't know." His words are like a hammer-blow, right at my heart, and I stagger slightly. He reaches out, holding onto me until I'm steady, and then he releases me again. "I—I don't know how I feel right now, Jem... other than disappointed. But, hell... it's not about me, is it?"

He turns to go again, but I put my hand on his arm, and he stops. "Please, Oliver. Don't be like that. This doesn't affect us."

"Yeah, right." I can hear the hurt and confusion in his voice, but I don't know what to do... how to make it better.

"It doesn't. Can't you see?"

"See what?"

"What happens with Adam and Donavan is nothing to do with us... with our relationship."

His eyes cloud, and he purses his lips. "You really believe that?"

"Yes. Donavan is Adam's father and I can't deny them the right to see each other, but that doesn't mean I love you any less."

"I know that," he says, raising his voice slightly and I take a half step back, a little startled.

"Then why are you so cross?" I say, seeing the man before me, but not knowing him at all. "Why can't you understand... I don't have any choice in this."

He stares at me for a moment, like he doesn't believe me... or he doesn't want to. I'm not sure which. Then he pulls his arm away and turns, going into his office, and although he doesn't close the door, I don't follow him. I don't know what I'd say. He's the man I can say anything to, and I've got no words. None at all.

Oliver

I can't focus, even though Brandy's standing perfectly still on the examination table, and I'm doing my best to look like the professional I'm pretending to be. I can't get my brain to work, because all I can think about is the look on Jemima's face when she said that what happens between Adam and Donavan has nothing to do with us... or with me, to be more precise. That's what she was saying. That's what she was meaning. Because it relates to her, doesn't it? She's Adam's mother, so it has to relate to her. It's just me who's out in the cold... evidently.

"She's doing well, don't you think?" Mr. Yates says, bringing me back to reality.

"Yes, she is." I concentrate a little harder on what I'm doing, completing my examination of Brandy's rear leg. The wounds have all healed and although the pins are a permanent fixture now, she should lead a perfectly normal life. "You're not letting her jump up and down yet, are you?" I ask.

"No, not yet." He gives me a smile. "She's gotten kinda used to being lifted on and off of the couch and carried out to the car. I get the feeling she might not want to go back to using her own legs, even when she's allowed."

"Oh, I don't know. Border Terriers are very agile, and she's still quite young. I imagine she'll be keen to get her freedom back." Brandy's youth was the reason I was so keen to do the surgery. It works best on young animals. They have a greater chance of recovery. "I think you should be okay for another month now, but bring her back if you've got any doubts."

Mr. Yates nods his head and picks up the dog, lowering her to the floor and putting her leash back onto her collar. I take a moment to watch how she walks, seeing that there's no sign of a limp now, and I give him a nod of my head.

"She's doing very well," I say, and he smiles.

"Thanks to you."

"Not entirely. I had a lot of help."

I open the door to the reception and wait for him to exit ahead of me, following him outside and showing him to the front door.

Jemima's at her desk, typing something on her computer, but I don't go to her. I can't. I don't even know how I feel right now. Instead, I go back into my room and close the door behind me, trying to occupy myself by cleaning down the examination table, even though I don't have another appointment for thirty minutes. It doesn't work though, and after a moment or two, I stop and sit up on it.

Why can't Jemima understand? Donavan isn't a father, other than biologically. He's ignored his son so far, leaving her to pick up the pieces of a life she never asked for. Yet, he clicks his fingers, and she's willing to forget his lies and give him a second chance... just like that. There's more to this than meets the eye. I'm sure there is. I've got no idea what his game is, but I'm fairly sure it's got nothing to do with being a good father. He's had more than enough chances to do that, if it was what he really wanted.

I know I do. I'd welcome the chance to be Adam's father, if only she'd let me. Except now Donavan's back, I might as well be invisible as far as a relationship with Adam is concerned. She made that very clear when she told me it's not about me. I'm not even entitled to an opinion, it seems. This is about the three of them, and while I might be in a relationship with Jemima, that's as far as it goes...

"C—Can I come in?" Jemima pushes open my door and looks over at me, stepping inside my office, doubt written all over her face.

"Sure."

I gaze across at her, the sadness in her eyes breaking my heart, and while I want to go to her and take her in my arms, I can't. I'm still too full of hurt and anger, jealousy and disappointment.

"I—I forgot to tell you earlier," she says, stuttering. "I spoke to Mom about you staying for breakfast on Saturday."

"Oh?" I'd forgotten all about breakfast on Saturday, although that's not surprising. "What did she say?"

"She said she's fine with it. She told me Dale stayed over on the night of Mason's wedding and had breakfast with her and Adam, and he didn't have a problem with it."

The night of Mason's wedding... I can't help thinking about everything we did on the night of Mason's wedding and how perfect it all felt. The contrast between then and now is almost too great to contemplate, but I know Dale's role in her mom's life is important to Jemima, and no matter how hurt I am, I can hear the uncertainty in her voice, and I can't ignore it.

"So Adam's met Dale?" I say.

"Yes. I—I'm not sure how I feel about that."

"Because Dale might be your father?"

"Yes."

"Did you say anything about it to your mom?" I ask.

"No. I was going to, but I didn't get the chance. That was when Donavan phoned."

"I see." Great. We're back to Adam's father again.

She bites on her bottom lip for a moment and then, with tears in her eyes, she says, "D—Do you still wanna stay for breakfast on Saturday? Or are you too disappointed in me?"

Oh, shit…

I jump down from the examination table and walk across to her, placing one hand on her waist and the other on her cheek. Then I walk her backwards to the wall beside the door until she hits it, and I press my body hard against hers.

"I'm sorry," I murmur and she blinks, gazing up at me.

"You're sorry? What for?"

"I don't know. But I hate seeing you like this."

"I hate being like this. I've spent the last half hour trying to work out how to make things better between us, and I don't know what to do, Ollie. What do I say to make it right?" She's clearly desperate; it shows in her eyes and I move my feet either side of hers, so I'm closer still, brushing my thumb against her soft cheek.

"It's okay," I say, even though the situation is the polar opposite of okay. "I understand you want Adam to have his father in his life. I even understand why."

"And do you understand how much I love you? How frightened I am of losing you?"

I pull back just slightly and move my other hand up, clasping her face, holding her steady. "You're not gonna lose me. I told you I'll never leave you, and I won't."

She puts her arms around my waist, clinging to me. "I need you so much, Ollie. I—I'm thrilled that Adam's gonna have his father in his life at last, but I'm so scared."

"Of?"

"Aside from losing you, I'm scared of it all going wrong with Donavan, and Adam getting hurt. Believe me, it's bad enough knowing your father never wanted you. I can only imagine how awful it would be if Donavan got close to him and then walked away."

I don't say a word, but I stroke her hair as she rests her head against my chest and I resist the temptation to tell her she might not be feeling like that it she hadn't been so quick to agree to her ex's request. If she'd talked it through with me first, we might have been able to come up with a better solution, like maybe setting up a meeting between Jemima, her mom, and her ex, so they could gage the guy's intentions before involving her son. But what do I know? I'm not a father.

She leans back in my arms. "Y—You didn't answer my question."

"Which one?"

"About Saturday morning. Do you want to stay for breakfast? Or am I still a disappointment?"

"Yes, I want to stay." I don't say anything else, because I can't lie. I'm still disappointed... and hurt.

"And do you still love me?"

"I never stopped." That's not a lie either. I can't stop loving her... not while I'm still breathing.

She smiles, despite the tears in her eyes, and I lean down and crush my lips to hers, kissing her harder than ever. I pull her body closer to mine, wishing I could turn the clock back and that Donavan had never called; that he'd stayed out of our lives. For all her talk of love and fear of losing me, I feel like I'm the one who's lost... like I'm the one who's in danger here.

I'm nowhere with Adam, and there's a very real danger I could lose Jemima too, if she found the chance to give her son the one thing she never had...

A family.

I feel like this week has been spent walking on eggshells, trying hard not to say what I really think, and struggling with my own emotions. I want the meeting between Adam and his father to go well, for Adam's sake – and Jemima's too, I guess – but I can't escape my own fears that, if it does, I'll lose them both.

Now the day is here, I'm finding it harder than ever, and I wish I could stay for breakfast and spend a little more time with Jemima, just for my own reassurance, if nothing else.

She's not meeting her ex until this afternoon, but she's decided to take the whole day off. I can't complain about that. I offered, after all. But that's something I'm regretting now. It feels like she's turning this into a special occasion and part of me – the jealous and strangely insecure part – can't help wondering why.

Her decision means I won't see her until this evening, and I'm not looking forward to a day by myself, wondering what's going on.

"Will you call me?" I ask her as I get dressed. "When you get home, I mean?"

"Sure. If you want me to."

Why does she even need to ask me that? This is the longest amount of time we've spent apart since the New Year. Why wouldn't I want her to call me?

I fasten my jeans and lean over her, kneeling on the bed and kissing her. "Of course I want you to," I murmur into her mouth. She brings her arms up around my neck, which feels good, and I pull her body up, crushing it to mine, until she's breathless.

"Do you really have to leave?" she asks, her eyes sparkling.

"Yeah. My receptionist's not coming in today, so I've gotta get to work a little earlier than usual." I try to make light of the situation, for my benefit more than hers.

She smiles, struggling to look contrite, and I have to smile back, because she's so damn cute. And because I love her... so damn much.

"I'll let you know when I'm home," she says. "And I'll cook us something nice for dinner."

"I'll look forward to it."

She reaches up, caressing my bare chest with her fingertips and biting on her bottom lip, which makes my cock ache. "Is that all you're gonna be looking forward to?" she says in a low whisper.

"No. I'm also looking forward to coming back here later on and making love to you."

"Making love?" she queries, almost sounding disappointed. "Not fucking?"

"They're the same thing, where you're concerned."

"Good. You had me worried then."

"Why? Do you want me to fuck you?"

"Always," she murmurs, sighing deeply.

It takes all my willpower to stand and finish getting dressed, especially as she's watching me so closely, her eyes raking over my body. But it has to be done, and when I'm fully clothed, I lean over her again.

"Have a good day," I say, putting as much enthusiasm into my words as I can muster.

"You too."

"Without you? I doubt it."

She smiles. "It's only one day, and I'm sure we'll make up for it later."

"You can count on it."

So far, my day has been okay, I guess. It's been nowhere near as good as my days usually are, when they're spent with Jemima. But that's because she's not here, and I'm reminded of that fact every time I go outside of my surgery and see her empty seat in the reception.

Of course, that makes me think about where she is, and what she's doing, and I'll admit, I've been finding that a struggle. My imagination has drifted from the whole thing being a disaster, resulting in Jemima and Adam going home in tears, to it being an enormous success, and her walking around the park, hand-in-hand with her ex, reminiscing about old times. I'm not sure which scenario is worse. The former would be terrible for her and Adam, but the latter would probably be the end of our relationship. After all, how can I compete with someone she's already got on a pedestal, just because he showed her so little respect that he got her pregnant?

The problem now is that it's nearly six o'clock, and I still haven't heard from her. And that means my imagination is going into overdrive, and rather than imagining them walking around the park, hand-in-hand, I keep wondering whether he's persuaded her to go somewhere else… like maybe back to his place.

I'm cleaning down my examination table for the last time, wondering if I should head over to Jemima's or go home, and wait to hear from her, when my phone beeps, telling me I've got a text. I grab it from my desk and heave out a sigh of relief when I see the message is from her, although I can't help wondering why she didn't call as we arranged.

Even so, I click on the message app, and read…

— Hi. Sorry to text, but Adam's being a nightmare. He's exhausted and grizzly. Wanted to let you know I'm home. When do you think you'll be coming over? Love you, Jem xx

I smile, because at least she still loves me, and type out a reply.

— Don't worry, it's just good to hear from you. I'll be over in twenty minutes. How did it go? Love you more. Ollie xx

I've never signed my name like that before and it feels strange, but somehow right with her, and I press 'send', taking my phone with me as I go into the changing room at the back of my surgery and strip out of my scrubs. I'm just fastening my shirt when Jemima's reply comes in.

— It went well. I'll tell you about it when you get here. Jem xx

I'm not sure what to make of that, so I just send her a couple of kisses, and quickly finish dressing, closing up the surgery and calling Baxter to follow me. He looks a little miserable, his head drooping and his eyes kinda doleful, and I can't say I blame him. He misses the long walks I used to take him on when we got home, and no matter how complicated our lives have become, I need to talk this through with Jemima. We need to work out a better routine than this, because at the moment, I've got a house I don't live in and a dog who's not getting enough exercise. And as I get behind the wheel of my Jeep, I wonder about suggesting to Jemima that, once we've gotten this whole 'staying for breakfast' thing out of the way, and she feels a bit more comfortable having me around all the time, she and Adam could come stay with me for a few nights a week. Maybe over the weekends, or something. It feels like a reasonable compromise to me… somewhere between moving in together, and not quite moving in together, and it would mean Heather could have her house back, for at least a part of the week.

I pull up outside Jemima's place, noticing that Heather's car isn't here, my nerves competing with my desperation to find out what happened, and as I know there's only one way to resolve the issue, I don't hang around. I get out, opening the rear door, and letting Baxter out too. He runs around the front garden, and I let him, while I grab the bag I brought with me from home, being as I'm going to be staying here overnight, *and* into tomorrow, for once.

"C'mon, boy," I call and Baxter obeys, as usual, following me to the front door, and waiting, while I ring the doorbell.

Jemima answers quickly, giving me a smile, and I step across the threshold, dropping my bag, pulling her into my arms and kissing her. She responds, her tongue clashing with mine, her breasts heaving into my chest, and I feel reassured. We're here… we're where we belong.

It's going to be okay.

Baxter's still sitting by my heel, knowing not to go anywhere yet, but as we break the kiss and walk further into the house, he pads through to the living room and goes over to his blanket. Adam's on the floor, rubbing his eyes.

"Is he tired?" I ask, my arm around Jemima.

"Only so as you'd notice," she says, sounding kinda tired herself.

"It went okay though, didn't it? You said…"

"It went fine," she says, smiling, her eyes sparkling as she looks up at me. "But we got back a lot later than I expected. Adam didn't sleep at all on the way there, and I think he got overtired, because he only slept for about ten minutes on the way back, and woke up screaming… and now I need to give him his bath."

"Then go ahead."

"But I wanted to cook us something nice," she says, sounding undecided.

I'd offer to bathe Adam myself, but I know she won't let me. "Shall I cook?" I say instead.

"It was supposed to be my treat."

"Well, it can be mine. I'm not promising anything spectacular…"

"At the moment, I don't think I care."

"Okay. I'll just make spaghetti, shall I?"

"Sounds wonderful." She rests her head against me for a moment and then releases herself from my grasp and wanders over to Adam, picking him up from the floor and holding him on her hip. As she does, I notice for the first time that, rather than wearing her usual casual skin-tight jeans and sweater or blouse, she's got on a short dress that finishes in the middle of her thighs, and thick black pantyhose, or leggings maybe. I can't tell. Not from here, because she's also wearing high-heeled knee-length boots, and she looks really sexy. I wonder for a moment, if she did this for her ex's benefit, a tidal wave of jealousy threatening to overwhelm me. It heightens still further when she walks past me, going back toward the bathroom, and I notice her face is made up like it is when she comes to work, with heavier lipstick and mascara, which she doesn't normally wear when we're by ourselves.

What the fuck is going on here?

I cook the spaghetti with a quick tomato sauce, because Adam's tired, and I can't concentrate on anything too difficult, and by the time it's ready, Jemima's just getting Adam into his pajamas.

"We'll be there in a second," she says, when I tell her everything's on the table, and while I want to offer to help, I don't, and I make my way back into the kitchen and pour us both a glass of wine.

They both join me within minutes and she sits Adam in his high chair, taking her own seat beside him, and although I've already cut up his spaghetti, she makes a point of cutting it up some more, making me feel inadequate… again.

I gaze at her, waiting until she's started feeding Adam, and then I take a sip of wine and say, "So, how did it go?" unable to hold back any longer.

She looks up, her eyes twinkling with happiness to match the smile that's forming on her lips. "I don't think it could've gone any better."

"That's good." I twirl some spaghetti around my fork, although I don't feel like eating it. My stomach feels like lead.

"I couldn't believe how much Donavan had changed," she says, taking a forkful of spaghetti for herself. "I mean, he still looks the same, but he's got a steady job, which pays really well, and he's so much more reliable."

I wonder how she can possibly know that, based on just one meeting, but I don't say a word.

"What does he do?" I ask her.

"He works in the sales department for a technology company. To be honest, I didn't really understand most of it. But he was always into that kind of thing, even when we were kids."

I remember now that, not only did she date him, but she's known him for years, having grown up with him, in the same small town, and my heart sinks a little further.

"He's just bought himself a house in Boston. It's not very big, evidently, but Donavan says it's got a small backyard that Adam can play in when we go to visit."

"E—Excuse me?" I can't have heard that right. "Did you say when you go to visit?"

She helps Adam to some more pasta and then puts down his spoon, staring at me. "Yes. It's gonna be so much easier. Adam really enjoyed playing with Donavan, but it was kinda awkward being outside for such a long time, especially when it's so cold. So we decided I'd take Adam to Boston next time around."

"And when will that be?" I ask, still reeling from the fact that Donavan obviously got to be a lot more hands-on with Adam than I'm ever allowed to be.

She purses her lips and then nibbles at the bottom one, looking unsure of herself. "I—I didn't think you'd want me to keep taking time off, so I've arranged to go next Saturday."

"Next Saturday?"

"Yes." She reaches across the table, but I can't take her hand. I can't move. "We're gonna go there in the morning, probably around nine, and stay until two, or thereabouts. That way, Adam can sleep at something closer to his usual time on the way home and it won't mess up his routine, like we did today."

She's clearly worked this out already, without even discussing it with me, even though it means my plans for the two of them spending weekends at my place are now blown out of the water. I guess she didn't know I had any plans, so I can't blame her for that. But it would have been nice to be asked.

She pulls her hand away, twirling some more pasta around her fork, and I watch, mesmerized, unable to swallow, or breathe, or see straight. I don't get it. She's giving this guy so much time with Adam – and with her – after just one meeting, but it's taken her weeks to let me have breakfast in her son's presence. As for anything else, like playing with him, or helping at bath time, or bedtime, I don't have a chance.

This guy let her down in the worst possible way, and she's gushing about how wonderful he is.

I didn't do anything except fall in love with her, and I feel like yesterday's news.

I stand in the darkness, in Jemima's bedroom, holding her naked body against my own, and while I know I should kiss her and touch her, make her whisper her needs and desires – because she can't scream them out when we're here with Adam – this is all I can do.

I want to make love to her. Being inside her feels as natural to me as breathing, but I feel so uncertain... so insecure, and those are both alien concepts to me. I'm in unknown territory here... lost and floundering, unsure where to find the answers.

She pulls back in my arms and looks up at me, her eyes sparkling in the moonlight.

"Take me to bed," she murmurs. "Please?"

I'm tempted to say 'no', because I'm still trying to work out the questions, let alone find the answers. But I can't resist her, not when she looks at me like this, all beautiful and pleading... and submissive.

So, I lift her, wrapping her legs around my hips and I carry her over to the bed, lowering her to the mattress. For a moment, I think about foregoing the condom and claiming her as my own, but the knowledge of what her ex did to her is still there in my mind. I'm not that man. I can't do that to her. So I reach over to the nightstand and grab a condom, rolling it onto my cock, before I crawl up over her body, entering her gently as I lean down and kiss her, wrapping her up in my arms and holding her as I love her, slowly and tenderly. There's nothing wild about this, and although I half expect her to beg me for more, she doesn't. She sighs and moans as I thrust into her, and when she comes, her body curls into mine, and she clings to me, sending me over the edge into a silent climax that almost breaks me.

I made a huge mistake. I created a fantasy in my head that our first morning together at Jemima's place would be romantic. In my fantasy, I imagined we'd prepare breakfast together, and then eat around the table, stealing furtive kisses and gentle caresses, whispering remembrances of a night, and a morning spent in the deepest ecstasy. I thought we'd gaze longingly at each other, and spend the morning – or the better part of it – in a haze of loving intimacy.

The reality has been so different.

When it came down to it, I had to get up early to take Baxter for a walk. Jemima was still asleep, and I didn't have the heart to wake her, so I took a quick shower and got dressed in the bathroom – into clean clothes for once – and then, making as little noise as possible, I crept out of the house, taking Jemima's keys from the hook, so I could let myself back in again. Baxter seemed excited and went straight to the car, presumably thinking I was taking him home, like I normally do, and that he'd be able to have a run by the lakeside. He seemed most disheartened when I attached his leash to his collar and led him toward the street. He kept looking up at me, as though to ask what was going on, and why we were still here, but I didn't say anything. I didn't have any answers for him, because I don't know them myself.

I've got no idea what's happening, or how I feel about it.

All I know is nothing's the same, and if I'm being honest, I'm not sure he and I belong in this picture anymore.

"I guessed you'd taken Baxter for a walk," Jemima says as I let myself into the house.

I look down the hall, to where she's standing, by Adam's bedroom door, holding him in her arms. She's wearing a robe and her hair looks messed up, like she just got out of bed.

"Sorry. I should've left a note, or something."

"Oh, don't worry. Adam only woke me five minutes ago, and I noticed Baxter and his leash were gone, and put two and two together." She looks up at me. "It would have been nice if Adam could have stayed asleep a little longer, so you could have come back to bed for a while… but it seems the fates are against us." She rolls her eyes, stepping forward, but going into the kitchen, rather than coming up to me, and I take off Baxter's leash, putting it down on the hall table and following her.

"What do you want for breakfast?" she asks as she puts Adam into his high chair.

"A kiss?" I say and she smiles again, coming over and standing on her tiptoes, giving me a quick kiss on the lips. I'm about to reach out, to hold her, when she pulls away.

"Toast and coffee?" she suggests, getting back to practicalities, and I nod my head.

"What can I do to help?"

"You can make the coffee, if you want?"

"Sure."

I pour some water into the jug, adding it to the machine and am just spooning in the coffee grounds, when Jemima's phone rings. She glances at the screen and then looks up at me.

"Can you excuse me for a second?" she says and, grabbing Adam, she runs from the room.

I stare after her, struggling to process what just happened, and why she couldn't leave Adam with me while she went to take her call. Come to that, why did she even have to take the call without me being present? I'm not sure I want to think about what that means, but until I know who was phoning her, I guess I could be over-reacting… or at least over-thinking.

She's back within five minutes, a smile on her face, and she puts Adam back in his high chair before turning to me.

"Is there a problem with the coffee?" she says, looking at the machine, which I still haven't turned on yet.

"No. Who was on the phone?" I hate how suspicious I sound, but I can't help myself.

"Donavan," she replies, a slight blush appearing on her cheeks.

I try not to over-react... or over-think.

"And? What did he want?"

"He just called to check we made it home okay."

Seriously? I'm meant to buy that? If the guy cared that much, he'd have called last night. He wouldn't have waited until this morning.

I nod my head and walk over to her, my pace slow and measured. She looks up into my face, her own clouded with uncertainty. "Can I ask you something?" I say, standing in front of her, but keeping my distance.

"Sure."

"Why did you leave the room to talk to him?"

She tilts her head to one side. "Because I figured you wouldn't want to listen to us." She reaches out and touches my arm, her hand burning my icy skin. "I thought it might be awkward for you."

"Why?"

"Because he's my ex. I wouldn't wanna listen to you talking to one of your exes."

"Well, that's never gonna happen, so..."

"I know. But the fact is, I have to talk to Donavan, and I just assumed you'd find it easier if I went into the bedroom, so you didn't have to hear us."

It sounds kinda reasonable when she puts it like that. It even sounds considerate, except for one small thing... it also makes me feel like she's keeping me on the outside of their family unit.

She steps closer, her body almost touching mine. "You know I love you, right?" she whispers.

"Yes." It's true. I do know that. I'm just not sure if love is enough anymore.

She leans in to me, snaking her arms around my waist. I hold her, feeling her naked body through the thin material of her robe, and I wonder how much longer I can keep pretending I'm okay with this, when I'm not. The thing is, if I tell her the truth; if I tell her I'm really not okay with this, if I ask her to choose, will that mean the end for us?

I hold her tighter as I realize, of course it will be.

She'll put Adam first, just like she always does… just like she should, as his mom. And that means, if I ask her to choose between me and Donavan, she'll choose Donavan, because he's Adam's father, and I'm not.

Chapter Eleven

Jemima

It's been ages since I've driven into Boston, so I'm having to concentrate on the unfamiliar roads, especially as Donavan's house isn't anywhere near the campus where we studied together. Even so, as I take Adam to visit his father, I can't help thinking about last week, and how well things went between them. Like I said to Oliver, it was kinda difficult being outside all the time, which is why we've decided to meet up at Donavan's place this time around. Adam got tired and grizzly, and it transpired that meeting in the afternoon wasn't such a good idea, because it messed with his routine. Donavan was really patient with him, though, which surprised me. In fact, a lot of things surprised me about Donavan. He still looked as handsome as ever, but he'd matured, and as I explained to Oliver, when we spoke over dinner, he was much more reliable. He'd grown up. That much was obvious, just from his attitude and from the way he spoke to me. He was attentive and kind, and considerate, and he was fantastic with Adam too. I'll be honest, there was a part of me that wished he could've been like that before, rather than being so selfish and always putting himself first. That way, Adam could have had his father in his life all along. I'm not saying it would have made a difference to my relationship with Donavan. It wouldn't. I couldn't have forgiven his cheating, and I didn't love him. So, I wouldn't want to turn the clock back in that way. I wouldn't want to give up what I have with Oliver, either. But I can't help thinking about all the things Donavan's missed out on. Which is why I'm determined to let him see his son now, when he so clearly wants to.

He's making the effort, that's for sure. He's called a couple of times since our last meeting. The first time was on Saturday morning while Oliver and I were preparing breakfast, which was just to make sure Adam and I had got home okay. I thought that was really sweet of him, and it showed how much more considerate he is now. The second time he called was on Thursday evening, just after I'd put Adam to bed, to double-check the arrangements for today. He wanted to confirm the time of our arrival, and I told him I'd bring Adam's lunch with me.

"You don't need to," he said, surprising me.

"Why not?"

"Because I thought I'd take you both out somewhere. Nothing fancy… just pizza. Will Adam be able to handle that?"

I've never taken Adam out anywhere, and the idea of the three of us having lunch somewhere was kinda exciting. I was also impressed that he'd thought through the venue and come up with the sensible option of pizza.

"He'll be fine with pizza. It's one of his favorites."

"Okay." I could hear him smiling.

"As long as we can still leave by about two," I said, reminding him of the schedule in case he'd forgotten.

"Why? Have you and your boyfriend got plans?" he asked.

"Not that I'm aware of, but if you remember, Adam's routine got kinda screwed up last time. I want to be on our way back by two so he can sleep in the car. It just makes the evening a lot less stressful."

"Sure," he said. "We'll have an early lunch and take it from there."

"Thanks, Donavan."

"That's okay. I'll see you Saturday."

We hung up, and I went out of the bedroom and back into the living room, where Oliver was sitting on the couch, staring into space. I went over and sat beside him, but he didn't move or put his arm around me and I turned and looked up into his face.

"Is everything okay?" I asked.

He nodded. "I take it that was Adam's father?"

"Yes."

"What did he want?"

"Just to confirm the details for Saturday." He didn't respond, and just continued to stare straight ahead. "Ollie? Will you look at me?" He turned his head, his eyes giving away his sadness, and I shifted in my seat, kneeling up and straddling him. He rested his hands on my ass, but it was more of an instinct than anything else, and I clasped his face between my hands, gazing into his eyes. "I love you," I said slowly. "You. No-one else. Okay?"

"I know," he said.

"Then why do you look so sad?"

He took a deep breath and let his hands fall to his sides again. "Because I feel sad."

"Because of Donavan?"

"Yes."

I shifted back slightly. "He's Adam's father, Ollie. There's nothing I can do about that."

He opened his mouth to speak, but then closed it again and after a second's hesitation, he whispered, "I know," and then leaned in to me and kissed me, before he stood up, lifting me with ease, and carried me through to the bedroom.

My Sat/Nav tells me to take the next left, so I do, turning into a tree-lined road, with single-story houses on either side. They've all got small front yards, and I drive slowly, looking for number 340, which is on the right-hand side.

Before I've even climbed out of my car, Donavan is at the door, a smile on his face as he comes out, walking down the narrow path toward us, his jeans hanging from his hips, seemingly oblivious to the cold, in just a t-shirt. He still looks great, still gorgeous, and he strides up to me, all confidence and swagger... just like Donavan.

"Hi," he says.

"Hello."

"You found me okay, then?"

"Yes. It was quite straightforward in the end."

He nods his head and then, unexpectedly, leans in and kisses my cheek. "It's good to see you," he says, and before I can answer or comment on the kiss, he opens the back door of the car. "Shall I get him out?" he says, nodding to Adam, who's in his car seat.

"Sure," I say, still reeling, and he leans in, unbuckling the straps and pulling Adam out and into his arms.

"I like his dungarees," he says with a grin, studying the bright green dinosaur on the front of Adam's denim dungarees.

"Mom bought them," I tell him, going around to the trunk and getting out the diaper bag, and the toys I brought with me.

"Do you need any help?" Donavan offers.

"No. I'm fine." I sling the diaper bag over my shoulder, closing the trunk, and he walks ahead of me up the garden path. I can't help smiling as I watch the two of them together, recalling how Donavan held onto Adam last week, and how it touched my heart to see them like that for the first time. Will it always feel like this, I wonder. Will it always feel so special to see them together, or will it one day become normal to watch my son and his father interact with each other? I'm not sure, but then I also wonder whether I'd like it to be 'normal', or whether I'd prefer it to always be 'special'.

Donavan crosses the threshold before I've had time to think that through, and then waits for me as I close the door behind us. He wasn't kidding… his home is small, but the living room that we walk straight into is very neat and tidy. It has a couch, which faces the fireplace, and a TV in the corner, while an archway leads to the kitchen, that has a dining table with four chairs.

"This is nice," I say, putting Adam's toys on the floor in front of the couch.

Donavan sits Adam down beside them and turns to me. "I liked the neighborhood as much as the house," he says. "It's fairly quiet, but close enough to the city if I want to go out."

"How long have you lived here?"

"About four months," he replies, and then moves toward the kitchen. "Would you like a coffee?"

"Hmm… yes please."

I help Adam with his toys, getting out his bricks and his wooden trains, joining them together so he can push them along.

Donavan returns within a couple of minutes, carrying two cups of coffee, and I stand, taking one from him. It feels kinda awkward for a moment, and I focus on Adam, who seems happy, playing on the floor.

"How does your boyfriend feel about you coming to see me?" Donavan asks out of the blue and I turn, studying his handsome face, his dark hair still as messy as ever. "Or are you guys not that serious?"

"He's fine about it," I reply, not giving him an answer about the seriousness of my relationship with Oliver. That's none of Donavan's business, although I'm also well aware that I'm lying, and that Oliver's not entirely happy with the setup. He was certainly very quiet this morning over breakfast. He held me, and kissed me before he left, though, and when I asked, he told me he was going to spend the day at his place, catching up with his laundry. We've arranged that I'm going to call him when I get home, and he'll come back over so we can spend the evening together, and he'll stay the night with me, like he always does. He'll stay for breakfast too. He's been doing that every morning this week, since last Saturday, when he did it for the first time, and I have to say, we're getting better at it. That first morning was kinda weird, not helped by the fact that I woke up to Adam crying, and an empty bed, and went into a panic. I didn't know where Oliver had gone, and I shot out of bed and threw on a robe, going to fetch Adam and then wandering around the house, trying to work out whether Oliver had forgotten our arrangement, or whether he'd decided he didn't want to stay, after all. I was about to call him when I noticed Baxter and his leash were missing, but that my keys were gone too, and I realized he must've taken the dog for a walk. My relief was overwhelming, although when Oliver came through the door a couple of minutes later, I tried not to let it show and we started making breakfast together. I honestly think everything would've been perfect… well, okay, not perfect, because perfect would have been Oliver waking me and making love to me before our day got started. But I think things would have been a lot better if Donavan hadn't phoned. While it was sweet of him to want to make sure we'd got home safely, Oliver clearly didn't like him calling. He didn't like the fact that I'd taken the call in my bedroom, either. Once I explained the situation to him, that I was only trying to be considerate of his feelings, and how I'd hate it if I had to listen to him talking to an ex of his, I think he understood.

Our mornings have definitely been a lot better since then. We've fallen into a routine which is nowhere near as boring as it sounds, and although it means waking up really early, it does at least mean we get to make love before Oliver takes Baxter for his walk, and Adam wakes up. Once he does, I start the breakfast and usually have it ready by the time Oliver gets back. It's a good compromise, which seems to work for everyone, and while it's not perhaps as romantic and playful as we'd hoped, I like the contrast between the sex we have in the mornings, which is kinda slow and sleepy, and the sex we have at night, which is just as intense and passionate as it was the first time.

Best of all, though, is the fact that Adam has accepted Oliver's presence and taken the change in our routine in his stride. And because of that, I can't help thinking that, if things carry on like this, once Oliver accepts the setup with Donavan, I'll be able to juggle everything, and fit everyone in perfectly. Donavan will slot seamlessly into our lives, he'll develop his relationship with Adam, and we'll all get along just fine.

"He must be a very understanding guy," Donavan says, staring at me. "I don't think I'd be so willing to share you, if you were still mine."

How am I supposed to reply to that? I don't regard myself as being shared. I'm Oliver's. Period. I'm not sure I was ever Donavan's... not in the way he means. He was far too willing to share himself around for me to have considered myself that. Fortunately, I'm saved the effort of saying anything by Adam, who's pulled his trains apart and holds them up for me to put them back together again. I kneel on the floor and Donavan comes over, sitting on the couch, watching us.

"What does your boyfriend do?" he asks.

"He a veterinary. I work for him."

I look up as Donavan smiles at me, those familiar dimples forming in his cheeks, reminding me why I fell for him... or at least why I fell into bed with him. "So it's just an office romance, then? Nothing serious…" His voice fades into the background and I wonder what to do or say. I don't particularly want to share the details of my personal life with him, but he's making such an effort with Adam, I feel as though I should at least be honest…

Just at that moment, Adam's trains fall apart again and he bashes them together, impatience getting the better of him.

"I think we need a man to work this out," Donavan says, sliding off of the couch and joining us.

"Chauvinist," I mutter under my breath and he chuckles, while putting Adam's trains back together yet again. I'm not complaining – not really. I love watching him with Adam, and at least I've been saved the trouble of having to answer his questions.

"Lunch was great, wasn't it?" Donavan says as we leave the restaurant.

"Yes, it was." It's true. We had a great time. Adam was fascinated by the whole thing and behaved really well, probably helped by the waitress making a tremendous fuss of him.

"Shall we go for a walk?" he suggests. He's carrying Adam in his arms, but puts him down on the ground between us.

"Where?" I glance around at the parking lot, our two cars parked beside each other, over on the far side. We drove here together so I could head off home once we'd eaten.

"There's a playing field," he says, pointing to the patch of green on the other side of the road. "We could go over there. It's only one-thirty, so you don't need to go yet, do you?"

"No. I guess not."

I lift Adam into my arms, feeling Donavan's hand in the small of my back as he guides us across the narrow road to the other side, where I put Adam down again and let him walk for a while.

"Thank you for lunch," I say, looking up at Donavan as he falls into step beside me. He insisted on paying, even though I offered.

"It's my pleasure," he says. "Maybe we'll come back again next weekend."

"If you want to."

He smiles down at me. "I want to. I like taking you out."

I'm about to check that he means Adam and not me, when Adam topples over and although he's not hurt, his bottom lip starts to tremble.

"You're okay," I say, going straight to him and lifting him up.

"He's fine," Donavan says, following me.

I tweak Adam's nose to distract him and then hold him out to Donavan. "Why don't you go to Daddy?" I say, and while Donavan takes him willingly, he frowns.

"That sounds weird," he says.

"What does?"

"Being called 'Daddy'."

"Well, you are his father, so…"

"I know," he says, his frown deepening. "Does… does he ever call your boyfriend 'Daddy'?" He sounds uncertain, maybe even insecure, which is a first for Donavan in my experience.

"No. 'Mama' and 'dink', which means 'drink', are about the limits of his vocabulary at the moment. He's never needed to use the word 'Daddy' before, but I'm sure he'll get there, eventually."

"And when he does, will you let him call the veterinary, 'Daddy'?"

"I don't know. It's not something we've talked about."

"I don't want him to," he says firmly, surprising me.

"Oh… okay. Well, when the time comes, we'll work something out."

I'm not sure what, but I guess there's no reason Adam can't call Oliver by his christian name, or a version of it, if it makes Donavan more comfortable. I'm sure Oliver won't mind…

"Good," he says, with a smile and we carry on walking.

"Why don't you put him on your shoulders?" I suggest, after a few minutes, looking up at Donavan, who turns Adam around and then tries lifting him up. Adam's legs get caught between Donavan's arm and his head, and because Donavan's not holding onto him properly, he almost falls, forcing me to reach out and grab him, and I chuckle as I help set him straight.

"Thanks," Donavan says, looking down at me.

"That's okay. You're just not used to him."

"No," he says. "But with practice, and your help, I soon will be."

We smile at each other and my heart sings at the thought of Adam having his father in his life… permanently.

Oliver

I'm getting sick of hearing about how great Jemima's ex is. She's been taking Adam into Boston on Saturday mornings for four weeks now. I guess I can't object to that. What I'm really fed up with, though, is that she comes home in the afternoons, and I go over to her place and have to listen to her telling me what a 'great father' the man is.

If I'm being honest, I'm not sure how much more I can take.

I didn't realize until last weekend that every time she goes there, her ex takes them both out for lunch. I'm not sure why she hadn't told me this before – other than that she never stops talking about how good he is at playing with Adam, and looking after him – but last Saturday, she revealed that he's been taking them to a pizza place just around the corner from where he lives, and that Adam really enjoys it.

I'd like the chance for us to do things like that too, but whenever I've suggested it, she always says we don't have time. She's not wrong, either. On weekdays, Adam's too tired by the time we get home from work. They spend their Saturdays with Jemima's ex, and our Sundays over the last few weeks have been about relaxing, because Jemima's been exhausted too, which I put down to her having to rush around so much on Saturdays. I don't think it would hurt her ex to come here once in a while, but he seems to like things the way they are. Who can blame him? He's got Jemima running around after him… and I think he likes it that way.

What can I do, though?

It's not like I have any say in things, so I don't even bother commenting.

I just focus on Jemima and our relationship, and trying to keep it together.

Our mornings are definitely better than they were, I'll say that much, and right now, it's the only thing that gives me any hope. We've found a way to make things work, which means we can make love before Adam wakes up. I always keep it slow and gentle, and very much about our love, showing her how I feel, or at least how much I love her. If I were truly showing her how I feel, we'd probably be arguing about her ex, and my insecurity. So I stick to love, more than feelings. Our nights together are just as fiery and urgent as they ever were, and I need them. I need to know she wants me enough to plead and to beg for whatever she desires. I need to hear that passion in her voice, even if it is whispered… and I need to know she's mine.

I watch her sleep for hours sometimes, wondering what's going on in her head. I torture myself with unasked questions; the ones I'm too scared to put into words, for fear her answers might break me. I picture them together, the family that they are – that she doesn't want me to be a part of – and I wonder sometimes if great sex is enough. Can that alone keep us together, and can it make up for being deprived of involvement in every other aspect of Jemima's life? I don't know anymore, but I wonder how much longer I can take having to hear about the father of the year, every time she goes to see him and I know, if I don't talk to someone soon, I'm going to go crazy.

I've caught up with all my laundry over the last few weekends, and my house has never looked so tidy, so today I'm going over to see Mason, because I can't afford to go crazy. I called first to make sure it was okay for me to visit, and I think he guessed something was wrong, because I rarely do that. That's one advantage of having a brother who's a psychologist. You don't have to explain to him when you're feeling low. He just kinda gets it. And you can get advice for free… and outside of office hours.

I park up beside his Mercedes, noticing that Isabel's Lexus isn't here, and I get out and walk up to the front door, ringing on the bell. Mason answers within moments and looks at me, tilting his head to one side.

"The coffee's already on," he says. "Come in and tell me about it."

"Where's your wife?" I ask, following him into the house and he turns, smiling.

"Do you think I'll ever get used to that?" he says, leading me into the kitchen.

"What? Hearing Isabel referred to as your wife?"

"Yeah."

"Who knows?" I shrug my shoulders and he sighs.

"She's gone to check out some furniture for the nursery," he says, reaching into the cabinet for some mugs.

"Isn't that something you'd normally do together?"

"Yes, and we were going to, until my brother called, sounding like he needed to talk."

He stares over at me. "You didn't have to cancel your plans for me."

"Yeah, I did… and now I think you'd better tell me what's wrong."

"Is it that obvious?"

He nods his head and pours our coffee and then we sit at the island unit, side by side. "Is this about Jemima?" he asks, when I don't say anything.

"Yeah."

"Has something happened?"

"You could say that."

He turns slightly. "You're gonna have to help me out here," he says. "I mean, I can guess at what's wrong, but it's gonna be a lot quicker if you just tell me."

I turn too, so we're almost facing, although I can't bring myself to look at him, and keep my eyes fixed on the mug in my hand. "I—I haven't mentioned anything until now, but Adam's father got in touch."

"He did?" I can hear the surprise in Mason's voice.

"Yeah. He called Jemima and asked to see Adam."

"How did she react?"

I suck in a breath and let it out, remembering her reaction in the parking lot at work. "She got it into her head that, if she didn't do what he wanted, he'd take her to court to get access."

"So she agreed?" he says.

"Yeah. And when I told her she needed to be there with them, she flew into a rage at me. I mean, I know I was kinda stating the obvious, but even when she'd calmed down, she told me that what happens between Adam and his father is nothing to do with us... with her and me, and our relationship."

"It isn't?"

I heave out a sigh of relief. "Do you know... I'm so glad you said that. I've been wondering if maybe it was me, if maybe I was expecting too much."

"Well, that rather depends on what you were expecting," he says, sounding like the shrink he is. "But I'd say that what happens between her son and his father is bound to affect your relationship."

"It is. It does."

"In what ways?" he asks, taking a sip of coffee.

"More ways than I can think about."

"Okay. But if you want me to advise you – which I'm kinda assuming you do – then you're gonna have to give me a little more than that."

I sip my own coffee and sit back in my seat. "The first time she met up with him was at Whitehall State Park. They kept it neutral, and they took Adam for a walk together."

"And?"

"And it went really well. She came back singing the guy's praises, telling me how he'd bought himself a house and had settled down."

"He's with someone?"

"No, but he's a lot more responsible than he used to be... according to Jemima, anyway."

"I see... and they've met up since?" he says.

"Yes. At his place, near Boston. Jemima's been driving up there every Saturday."

"Oh."

The way he says that makes me glance up at him for the first time and I see a look in his eyes which kinda mirrors how I'm feeling. It speaks of confusion and doubt.

"Yeah... oh." I say, letting out a sigh. "She and Adam have been going there for a month now, and every week, her ex takes them for lunch, and they have a great time... evidently."

"She comes back and tells you all about this?"

"Yes."

"In detail?"

"Yes."

He nods his head. "Well, at least she's not hiding things from you."

"No." I'm not sure that feels like much of a consolation. "Although whenever he calls, which he seems to do at least two or three times a week, she always goes into the bedroom to speak to him."

"Away from you?"

"Yeah. She says it's because, if the roles were reversed, she wouldn't want to listen to me talking with an ex. And I can see that. I'm not sure I wanna actually hear their conversations."

"But you feel like she's sneaking around?" he says.

"I—I don't know. Sneaking around sounds like cheating, and I don't think she'd cheat." *Do I?*

"Don't you?" he says, like he can see right through me. "You sound jealous."

"I am jealous."

"What of, though? Her relationship with her ex, or her son's relationship with his father?"

"Both?" I say, shaking my head and then letting it drop into my hands. "I don't trust the guy's motives, I know that much."

"Have you talked to Jemima about this?" he asks, and I raise my head again, looking at him.

"Not really. Not properly."

"You need to. You're bubbling over, Oliver, because you're not able to express yourself. But you can't keep doing that without reaching a boiling point. And if Jemima doesn't know how you feel, and how hard you're finding the situation, she can't do anything about it."

"What if she doesn't want to do anything about it, though? She seems to like things the way they are."

"How do you know that?"

"The big clue is that, whenever she gets back from seeing him, she spends at least a couple of hours telling me how damn perfect this guy is, and how wonderfully well everything's working out, how relieved she is that we're all fitting in just fine with each other... like I'm even a part of this. I'm not. I've got nothing to do with it. Her ex is fitting in with her and Adam just nicely, and I'm still on the outside... the whole fucking time."

"Are you on the outside with Jemima?" Mason asks.

"How do you mean?"

"Other than telling you about her visits to Adam's father, has she treated you any differently since they've started seeing each other? Has this affected your relationship?"

"I'm still her boyfriend. I'm still her lover, if that's what you mean. But that's it. That's all I am."

"Is she still keeping you at arm's length with Adam?" he asks.

"Yes. I'm not allowed to play with him, or help out with him, but his father can do whatever he likes. He's the one she wants in Adam's life... not me."

"That doesn't mean she wants him in her life," he says, reasonably.

"I know. But I don't see why I have to be excluded. Why can't we both be involved with Adam... her ex, *and* me? Why does it have to one or the other? I don't know... maybe it would be easier if Adam's father had been involved all the way through, and it was me who'd come onto the scene, rather than him."

"Do you think you'd feel like less of an outsider then?" he asks.

"I don't know. I guess they'd already have a setup going, and at least I wouldn't be left wondering if this is really about him and Adam, or if it's really about him and Jemima."

"Do you honestly think that?"

I sigh, deeply, shrugging my shoulders, "She tells me she loves me and I believe her. I know she does. It's just that she gets so damn excited whenever they're going to see him."

"You're asking her to trust you with her son," he says, sighing himself and tipping his head to one side, like he's thinking things through. "You need to trust her, too. I've never seen you this insecure before."

"I've never felt this insecure before. But then I've never been in love, have I?"

"Well, love and trust go together, so… talk to her," he says firmly. "Tell her what you've told me, about how jealous and insecure you're feeling. She loves you, Oliver. She's gonna want to help put your mind at rest."

"You're sure about that?"

"Yeah. I may have been kinda wrapped up in my wife at our wedding, but I still had time to observe the two of you together, and she's just as in love with you as you are with her. She's not a mind-reader, Oliver. You need to tell her you're unhappy."

"I'm not unhappy."

"Yeah, you are."

Mason's words ring in my ears all the way home and although I'm still scared, I know he's right. I need to tell Jemima how I'm feeling.

When she calls at just after three to let me know she's home, I decide to sow the seeds…

"C—Can we talk, later on, when Adam's gone to bed?" I say, trying to ignore the nervous tension in my stomach.

"Sure. Is everything okay?" She sounds concerned.

"Of course. Everything's fine," I lie. "There are just a couple of things I need to talk to you about."

"Okay. Well, my period started earlier, and I'm not feeling great, so…"

"It can wait," I say, interrupting her. I want to hold her and try to make her feel better, not bother her with my problems.

"No, it's fine. I was just gonna say that I'll probably wanna go to bed early, but as long as you're okay with having our conversation while I lie in your arms, then that's perfect."

"When am I not okay with holding you in my arms?"

"Never," she says and I can hear her smiling. And while I don't like the idea of her being in pain, I'm almost relieved that her period's started. It means we can keep sex off the agenda, and focus on what needs to be said, and hopefully find a solution that works for both of us.

"I'll just take Baxter for a walk, and then I'll come over," I tell her.

"Okay. Love you."

"Love you more."

I hang up, hoping for once that my words aren't true, and then I call Baxter and open the front door, letting him run out to the lakeside, barking like mad and wagging his tail, and I wish life could be so simple for all of us.

"Hmm… I needed that," Jemima says, as I pull back from our kiss.

"Me too." I did. I needed her kiss. Not just for the kiss, but for the reassurance of what lies behind it. Mason was right. I am feeling insecure and jealous. And I need to work things out before I boil over and either say or do something I know I'll regret. "How was today?" I ask.

"It was fantastic, even if my period started two days early, about twenty minutes after we arrived at Donovan's."

"I guess that's better than it being late," I say with a smile.

"Yeah, you're not kidding." She rolls her eyes, shuddering, and I can't help feeling disappointed. I know the thought of being unexpectedly pregnant wouldn't fill her with joy, but I hadn't anticipated such negativity… not when the child concerned would be mine. I open my mouth to say something, but she gets there first. "But it did cause a problem."

"What did?"

"My period starting."

"Oh?"

She nods her head. "I didn't have any sanitary pads with me."

"What did you do?"

"The only thing I could... I left Adam with Donovan while I went out to buy some."

My skin tingles. Was that really the 'only' thing she could do? Couldn't she have taken Adam with her? She'd have done that if she'd been here, rather than leaving him with me, I know that. Or couldn't her ex have gone to buy what she needed for her? That's what I'd have done...

I don't reply. I can't, because I know this is one of those times where my response is likely to be something I'll later regret. Instead, I let her lead me into the living room, where Adam's sitting on the floor, pushing a toy truck around. "Is that new?" I ask.

"Yes. Donavan bought it for him."

"It's a bit complicated for him, isn't it?" It looks like one of those toys where parts of it can be removed... way too easily.

"I don't know. Donavan had already taken it out of the packaging by the time we got there. But Adam seems to like it."

She looks down at her son, her eyes filled with love, and I shake my head, wondering why she can't see what's wrong with this situation, and I decide to check the toy out for myself a little later on, maybe while Adam's in the bath, to make sure it's safe.

"So, apart from having to rush out to the drugstore, how was it today?" I ask, as we both sit down, side by side, on the couch. I might feel nervous about asking, but I still need to know.

"It was great," she says, smiling at me, her eyes sparkling.

"I take it you went out for lunch?"

"Yeah. Adam's gotten used to it now. To be honest, I think he'd object if we did anything else." She chuckles and looks up at me, although I can't even smile. "He really enjoys being with his father, you know? And it's so good to see them together."

I'm tempted to say something to her now about how this is making me feel, rather than waiting until we're in bed, but right at that moment, Adam turns and looks over at us, giving me a smile, and then he says, "Dada," and gets to his feet, toddling toward us.

"Did… Did he just say what I think he just said?" I ask, my heart swelling in my chest.

"No," Jemima says, sounding unsure of herself. "No, he can't have done."

Adam gets to us, and Jemima lifts him up onto her lap, even though Adam's gazing at me. "Dada," he repeats, pointing right at me, and then he holds out his arms to me, so there can be no doubt about it.

"That's not 'Dada'," Jemima says, before I can utter a sound, giving him a hug and pulling him away from me. "That's Oliver."

Talk about rain on my parade. "Do you wanna tell him I'm just a friend as well?" I say, unable to hide my disappointment.

She turns to me, blinking quickly and bites her bottom lip, although this time – for the first time – I'm completely unaffected. "I'm sorry," she whispers. "But this is really difficult for me."

"It's difficult for *you*?" I get up and step away, pushing my fingers back through my hair.

"Yes. That's the first time Adam's ever said that."

"I know."

"And he said it to you."

"I know. I heard him."

"But you're not his father."

I sigh and shake my head. "I'm aware of that, Jemima." She reminds me often enough. How can she think I could've forgotten?

"But that's the problem. You see, Donavan told me a few weeks ago that he doesn't want Adam to call you 'Daddy'. He…"

"Excuse me?" I interrupt her.

"Donavan said he——"

"I heard what you said. I'm just a little surprised I'm only hearing about it now. And I'm wondering how you feel about this demand of his. I'm guessing you agree with it, being as you've just told Adam that I'm Oliver and not 'Daddy'."

"It's not a demand," she says, defending her ex, which hurts more than I'll ever be able to tell her. "And I don't feel it's that unreasonable, to be honest. If Donavan doesn't want his son to call you 'Daddy', then I think we have to respect that. Don't you?"

"I don't know why you're bothering to ask. It's not like I get any say in it, do I, Jem?"

"Does it make you unhappy?" she asks.

"Does it matter?"

She sighs. "Please don't be like this, Oliver." I don't know what to say to her, so I turn away, stepping toward the door. "Where are you going?" she asks, panicking and getting to her feet, resting Adam on her hip.

"I'm gonna make a start on dinner. We're having chicken, aren't we?"

She nods her head, relaxing. "It will get better," she whispers.

"Will it?"

"Yes. Just give it time. I know this is hard for you too."

"Do you, Jem?"

"Yes. But you'll get used to it."

Will I? Will I get used to how this feels? I doubt it. And I'm not sure I want to. I'm not even sure I can understand why I should have to.

I'm browning the chicken breasts and cutting up some onions while trying really hard not to think, when I hear Jemima cough and I turn toward the door. She's standing, leaning against the frame, with Adam still perched on her hip.

"I'm just gonna give Adam his bath," she murmurs, and the sadness in her voice tears at my heart. I put down the knife I'm holding, and walk over to her, placing my hand on her waist. We sigh in unison, and it feels like an admission that we're both unhappy with the situation, and both kinda powerless. It doesn't make it any easier, but it helps to know I'm not alone.

"Okay," I murmur. "How are the cramps?"

"Bearable," she says, and then pulls back slightly, looking up at me. "How was your day? I meant to ask."

"It was okay. I went over to Mason's."

I don't explain why, because I know I can't tell her how I feel now. It's only going to make things worse... for both of us.

"I know we said we'd talk later, in bed, but I think I'm likely to fall asleep, so what was it you wanted to say?"

She gazes up at me and I shake my head. "Nothing. It doesn't matter."

"Was it about Donavan?" she asks, frowning.

"Yeah, it was. But, I'm not sure I wanna talk about him anymore… not today."

She moves closer. "You know you've got nothing to fear from him, don't you?" she says.

I can't answer her, because as far as I'm concerned, I have everything to fear, so I lean in and kiss her, which makes Adam chuckle and as I pull back, smiling myself, he says, "Dada," again.

"Oh, God…" Jemima whispers, making it very clear this is a problem for her.

"Your ex might not be happy with Adam calling me that, but I don't see what either of us can do about it… unless this is something he's gonna start saying to every man he sees."

"Let's hope so," she says, turning and walking toward the bathroom.

I stand and watch her, wondering if this is what it's like for every step-parent; whether it's normal to feel like an outsider, but as I turn back in to the kitchen, I stop in my tracks, realizing that I'm not even a step-parent. I'm Jemima's boyfriend… that's all. When it comes to Adam, I'm nothing. I'm certainly not his 'Dada'. Evidently, I never will be. And that's kinda depressing.

It's been a tough week. Making it to Friday feels like an achievement in itself. Although, to be fair, today has been a lot better than the rest of the week. I guess that's because Jemima has spent most of it flirting with me… and I've been flirting back. She told me after she'd showered this morning that her period had finished, and she's been dropping not very subtle hints all day that she can't wait for tonight. I'll be honest, I can't wait either. This isn't the first period she's had since we've been together, but I've missed her more than ever this time around. We may have kissed and hugged our way through the last few days, but I've missed being intimate. I've missed being inside her, and the feeling that she's mine and I'm hers, and that we belong together. And if that makes me insecure, then so be it. I am insecure. What I'm going to do about that is still a mystery to me, but at least if Jemima and I can get back to normal, I'll hopefully feel better. We can work on everything else.

I park up outside her house, letting Baxter out and noting that her mom's car isn't here. It's been a few weeks since I've seen Heather. She still looks after Adam during the day, but because I have my surgery to clear up, and usually take Baxter for a quick walk, she's often left for Dale's by the time I get here. She hasn't mentioned anything about him to Jemima yet, and to be honest, we've got enough problems of our own, so it's not something we've had time to talk about.

I knock on the door, thinking that this weekend might be a good time to ask if Jemima would consider letting me have a key to this place, because having to knock, or remember to take her keys whenever Baxter and I go for a walk is getting to be tiresome. She answers quickly though, and while I'd hoped for a deep kiss, as a prelude to our longed-for intimacy, I'm halted by the fact that she's got her phone to her ear.

"Can you hang on?" she says into the mouthpiece as she lets me in, and I close the door behind me.

There's an awkward silence and then she looks up and smiles a little half-heartedly before she nods over her shoulder toward the bedroom and I realize who she's talking to. It's him.

I shrug my shoulders because I'm not happy that he's called her, or that she's obviously going to disappear to her room to speak to him, but what can I say? She nods her head and hurries to the back of the house, letting herself into her room and closing the door behind her. I understand why she does that. She did it on Tuesday night when he rang for no apparent reason. I can even appreciate it sometimes, because she's right; I don't want to hear their conversations. But that doesn't mean I'm happy. I wish he'd never called her in the first place. I wish he'd crawl back under whatever rock he came out from and leave us alone. Jemima might not have been willing to let me get close to Adam, but we were doing okay before he came on the scene. Now, I'm not sure anything will ever be okay again.

Left to myself, I wander into the living room, where Adam's sitting on the floor, and while I'm surprised to be alone with him for once, I take advantage of the situation and sit too, joining a couple of his trains together for him, and watching while he pushes them around. Baxter comes over and sits beside me, and although Adam is initially keen on playing, he eventually looks up, notices Baxter, and shifts closer, patting him on the back.

"Good boy," I say, to both of them really. Baxter's being very patient and Adam's being very gentle, so they both deserve praise.

"Dada," he says, still patting the dog, and I laugh. It seems even Baxter is 'Dada' at the moment, so for all Jemima's worrying about how her ex is going to react to Adam calling me by that name, it looks like he's just gonna have to accept it. At least until Adam can differentiate who his real 'Dada' is.

I hear the bedroom door open and get to my feet, not wanting to antagonize Jemima by playing with Adam, and I turn as she comes into the room. I'm about to tell her Adam just called Baxter 'Dada', when I notice the look on her face.

"What's wrong?" I say, stepping closer to her, taking in her slightly widened eyes and pale complexion.

"That was Donavan," she whispers, looking up at me.

"I guessed that."

She nods. "He... He asked if he can have Adam by himself tomorrow, without me being there."

I feel confused and conflicted. I've assumed from the beginning that her ex's motive in all of this was something to do with Jemima. Can I have been wrong? It looks like it, if he wants to see his son without her. And from my perspective, that has to be a good thing. Except it doesn't feel good. There's a nagging doubt in the pit of my stomach and, even though I've never met him, I'm not sure I like the idea of him having Adam by himself. I don't trust him, even if Jemima does.

"Why?" I ask, remembering to speak at last.

"He wants Adam to meet his mom," she says.

"And you can't be there for that?"

"No. Things ended kinda badly between her and me, and my mom. Donavan thinks it could be difficult."

At least he's being considerate, I guess. But I'm not happy about it.

"I hope you said 'no'." I think this needs a lot more planning, and I don't understand why he's left it until tonight to bring it up as part of tomorrow's visit. Why can't his mom wait until next Saturday?

"Actually, I said 'yes'."

"You did what?" I can't believe I'm hearing this, but as I see the anger building behind Jemima's eyes, I realize I've spoken out of turn… again.

"I told you ages ago about the hurtful things Donavan's mom said when he and I broke up. I think he's right. It would be best if I'm not there when Adam meets her."

It strikes me it would be better still if Adam didn't meet her at all, but that's not for me to say. Instead, I look for an excuse – any excuse – for her to rethink her decision.

"It doesn't seem odd that he called you on Tuesday and didn't mention this?"

"No. Why should it?"

"Because he's not giving you any time to think it through."

"I don't need to think it through." She tilts her head to one side. "I thought you'd be happy. I know you don't like me going to see him, and this way, we'll get some time to ourselves. We haven't been alone for ages, Ollie. This is the perfect opportunity. Unless you don't want to…" Her voice fades to silence as she looks up at me, doubt clouding her eyes.

"You know I want to be alone with you. And you're right; I don't like you going to see him, but that's not the point here."

"Then what is?" she asks.

"You don't know this guy."

"I do," she counters, frowning at me. "I've known him as a friend since I was a child, and when we dated, we were together for eight months, which is five months longer than I've been with you."

Wow… that didn't hurt. Much. "Thanks for that," I say, stepping back from her. "Thanks for reminding me how much more Donavan means to you than I do. Not that I need reminding."

"W—What does that mean?" she says, blinking.

"It means, it's nice to know why you got dressed up to meet him that first time, and why you wear so much makeup every single time you get together. It also makes sense of why you still had his number on your phone. Because I have to tell you, I don't have any of my ex girlfriends' numbers. None at all." I sound like a jealous idiot, but I'm not sure I care. I am jealous, and she may as well know it.

"Yes, but you don't have children with your exes, do you?" she snaps. "I only kept Donavan's number because he's Adam's father. And for your information, I wore that dress on the day he and I first met up because I was behind with my laundry and didn't have a top to wear with my jeans."

I can't deny her answers make sense, considering how far behind I was at the time. But anger has blinded me and I'm still not satisfied. "And the makeup?" I say.

"What about it?"

"Why do you wear so much?"

"I don't," she says, raising her voice. "I don't wear any more than I do when I go to work."

I know that's true. "But you still wear more than you do when you're with me."

"And? Do you need me to wear makeup? I certainly don't feel like I have to wear it with you, because with you, I can be myself. I don't need a mask."

That's exactly how I want her to feel around me, and I'm tempted to take her in my arms and tell her to forget the whole thing... except that won't resolve the problem.

"Okay," I say, lowering my voice, calming down, and resolving to talk reasonably, rather than argue. "I understand that. But I still think you're missing the point."

"What point? That you're jealous?"

"No. Well, yes. I am jealous. And I'm feeling really insecure... about us." She tilts her head, like she doesn't understand. "I hate the way you are around him, Jemima. I hate that he's even a part of our lives."

"He's part of Adam's life," she says, shaking her head.

"No. He's part of our lives, but the point is, no matter how much you think you know him, no matter what you remember from when you were together, people change."

"I know that." She raises her voice again. *So much for not arguing.* "That's the point *you're* refusing to see in all this. Donavan has changed. He's not the same man he was before."

"He was a boy before," I tell her, but she waves aside my comment.

"Whatever. He's more considerate now. More reliable. You don't know him, Oliver. You don't have the right to judge him."

"I know you're constantly singing his praises," I say, hurt getting the better of my good intentions. "I know you're very willing to defend him… very willing to agree to his demands."

She steps closer, her body only an inch or two from mine now as she glares up at me. "He's not the one making demands," she says in a low whisper. "He's not the one telling me to get on my knees and beg."

I grab her arms, just above the elbow, but she pulls free of me, and I let her. "You never had to beg, or get on your knees. That was just…"

"Just what?"

"It wasn't me making demands, that's for sure. Not in the proper sense of the word. And if you thought it was, then you don't know me… not as well as you seem to know your ex." We stare at each other for a moment, both breathing hard, until I say, "Why don't you trust me?"

"I do," she says.

"No, you don't. You say you do, but you don't. Not with Adam. I always knew I'd have to earn your trust with him, but how can I? You never let me play with him, I'm not allowed to feed him or do anything at all to help out. And if I do, and I get just the slightest thing wrong, you pick me up on it, like I'm the child in this relationship. But from what you tell me when you come back from your visits, it seems your ex is allowed to do whatever he wants, and any mistakes he might make are turned into funny anecdotes."

"He's got no experience with babies. I can't expect him to know what he's doing."

"I've got no experience with babies either, but you don't cut me any slack. You just don't let me do anything. And that doesn't alter the fact that you let him do whatever he wants."

"Of course I do. How can I stop him? He's Adam's father." She rolls her eyes at me and I step further away.

"And that means you trust him, does it? Just like that? Regardless of what he did to you? Christ... do you think so little of yourself?" I suck in a breath. "Do you think I haven't wanted to make love to you without a condom? Do you think I don't ache to know what it would be like to feel you, with no barriers?" I push my fingers back through my hair. "I haven't done it, Jem, because I love you, and that means I care about what happens to you. But you show more trust in the guy who didn't care enough about you not to get you pregnant. You trust him, even though he put his own needs first at every turn... even though he cheated on you when you were carrying his child. And you give him that trust, simply because he's Adam's father?"

"It's not about trust," she says, blinking hard.

"What is it about then?"

"It's about Adam having the chances I never had as a child... to be with his father. You don't understand..." Her voice fades.

"What don't I understand?"

"What it feels like to be abandoned."

I shake my head at her, stepping closer again. "My mom *died*, Jemima. Believe me, you don't get to feel any more abandoned than that. There's no way back from death. There's no hope, no future... no nothing. And when you're ten years old, and you lose someone like that... trust me, it really fucking hurts."

She swallows hard and blinks a few times. "S—Sorry. I didn't mean it like that. I just don't understand why you're so down on Donavan all the time."

"I'm down on him because I don't like him. I don't like what he's doing to us... what you're letting him do to us."

"I'm not letting him do anything, Oliver. How many times do I have to say this? He's Adam's father..."

"Really?" I say, interrupting her.

She glares at me. "What the hell does that mean? Are you accusing me of sleeping around?"

"No, of course I'm not."

"Then what are you saying?"

"That being a father isn't something you get to play at, like your ex is doing. It's not a badge you can put on and take off when it suits you. It's a responsibility for life, from the moment you get a woman pregnant, and if your ex was any kind of man, he'd know that."

She blinks up at me, her bottom lip trembling.

"He's trying, Ollie. If you'd only…"

I hold up my hand to stop her, knowing she's never going to relent on this… and neither am I. We've reached a point of no return.

I promised I'd never leave her, but I'm about to break that promise, and I walk around her, calling out to Baxter as I get to the door.

"Where are you going?" she whimpers from behind me.

"Home. I can't do this anymore."

"O—Ollie?" I hear her sob as I step outside, but I don't look back. I'm done here.

Chapter Twelve

Jemima

I make it to the couch, dropping my phone as my legs give way and I flop on to the seat, tears flowing down my cheeks, and then onto my blouse as I catch gulps of breath.

Oliver's gone. He's really gone.

I'm torn between fear that he won't come back, guilt for doubting he'd understand abandonment, and anger that he can't see what I've been trying to tell him.

Why did he think he needed to define fatherhood to me? I know it's not a game, or a badge. I understand that better than anyone. That's the whole damn point. I didn't have a father, and now Donavan's back, I want to grab this opportunity with both hands... for Adam's sake, not mine.

I thought Oliver understood that. I thought he was on my side in this... but evidently not.

Adam crashes two trains together, making a lot of noise about it and bringing me to my senses. I need to think about giving him his bath, but as I'm here by myself, I also need to make us something to eat. I'm quite capable of managing alone, but the thought of it makes me sob, and I cover my mouth with my hand, and reach out for my phone, turning it over and staring at the screen for a moment.

I could call Oliver and ask him to come back. Except I'm not sure he would. He said he couldn't do this anymore, which I guess means he's done with me. I never thought he'd say something like that, but I never thought he'd leave either. He told me he wouldn't… and yet he has. So why would he come back?

Because I love him?

No. That's not enough. I know it isn't. I told him often enough, and he still left me, so why would saying it all again make any difference?

My stomach feels heavy, and there's a pain in the middle of my chest that's like a cold, dark ache… like there's no hope left in the world.

Adam rubs his eyes, and grizzles, saying, "Dada," in between incoherent noises and I cry even harder, wishing Oliver could be here, and wondering if Adam misses him too. I don't care if Donavan doesn't like it, not when his absence hurts this much.

I found a lasagne in the deep freeze and heated it up while I gave Adam his bath. Not that I ate very much, but I fed him, and then put him to bed.

Clearing up the kitchen, I miss Oliver more than ever. I've gotten used to him being here, and the house feels so empty without him. I feel empty without him, and I can't see the point in staying up, so I come into the bedroom, not bothering to switch on the light, but undressing and climbing into bed.

This is the loneliest I've ever been. It's even worse than when I discovered Donavan was cheating, and I faced the prospect of life as a single parent. It's worse than when I left him and went home to my mom, not knowing what the future held. I feel so alone, and although it's a struggle not to remember the fun interludes we've shared today, when I've teased and flirted with Oliver about how much I wanted him, it's just his presence that I want now, more than anything.

I turn over, the wide, empty bed stretching out before me and I wish he could be here, so we could talk. We need to talk. That much is obvious. I think we've needed to talk for quite a while. Probably since Donavan first got in touch, because it's clear to me that Oliver's not happy with the situation, and hasn't been since the beginning.

I've been fooling myself that everything was okay. It's not. Not for Oliver, and hearing him say how insecure he feels was hard. He's got no reason to feel like that. Like I told him earlier, I love him. I don't love Donavan. I never did. But I guess, lying here alone and thinking through his accusations, I can see how he could have misinterpreted at least some of my actions. I don't think there was anything wrong with still having Donavan's number on my phone, or with wearing that dress when I first went to meet him. And as for his thing about my makeup, that was kinda silly. I will admit, I have been singing Donavan's praises, and if I put myself in Oliver's shoes and try to imagine how I'd feel if our roles were reversed, I can see how difficult it must've been for him. If he was visiting an ex girlfriend of his, with his child, and came back, telling me how wonderful she was, I don't think I'd like it either. He's borne it in silence, though… until now.

That was probably a mistake, and it might have been better if he'd told me sooner how he felt. I could've reassured him that the only reason I've been so fulsome in my praise of Donavan is because he's changed so much. He's not the irresponsible guy I used to know, and that I feared he might still be. But that change in him doesn't mean I want him back. Surely Oliver can see that? Surely he can understand that his resentment of Donavan is completely unfounded. My only interest in him is as Adam's father. Nothing more. Nothing less.

I just wish Oliver was here, lying beside me now, so I could tell him that… and maybe find a way to show him I mean it.

I wake with a start, hearing Adam cry out from his room next door, and glance at the clock as I get up. It's nearly seven. I ought to feel great… I've been in bed for almost eleven hours. The problem is, I've only been asleep for the last two, so I feel dreadful, and I stagger to the door, pulling on my robe and making my way to Adam's room.

He's standing in his crib, holding the rails and grinning at me. I smile back, although it's an effort.

"Morning, baby boy," I say, opening the drapes before I reach over and pull him up into my arms. He feels warm and snuggly against me and I hold him close for a moment or two, savoring the feeling of his body against mine, before he starts to wriggle, desperate to be let down onto the floor. He's at that age where cuddles have become less important than independence, and I've given up fighting him over it. Besides, I don't have the energy this morning. "Mommy's gonna make breakfast," I say, offering my hand. He looks up at me, studies my hand and then toddles off toward the kitchen by himself, and although I know it's unreasonable of me, I can't help but feel rejected… again.

I make Adam a slice of toast and pour him some milk into a beaker, while my coffee brews. I'm not hungry, even though I didn't eat last night, and I sit and watch him chew on his toast, wishing Oliver could be opposite me, his eyes fixed on mine, like they usually are, and the afterglow of our slow, lazy, early morning love-making could still be fresh in my mind, instead of a distant memory.

Tears fill my eyes again, but I get up and pour myself a coffee, bringing it back to the table and keeping half an eye on the clock. I've still got to shower and get Adam's things ready before Donavan arrives at nine, so once Adam's finished, I lift him from his high chair and carry him through to the bathroom, sitting him on the floor while I take a quick shower.

I'm working on auto-pilot at the moment, going through the motions of drying my hair and pulling on a pair of jeans and a blouse, while trying not to think about how my life is going to be without Oliver in it. Because I can't. I can't bear that thought.

So, I occupy myself with putting Adam's toys into a bag, making sure his diaper bag is filled with everything Donavan could possibly need, and going out to the car to remove Adam's seat, so it's ready for Donavan, who arrives exactly on time.

He rings on the doorbell and I pick up Adam and answer it as quickly as I can.

"Hi," he says, his smile fading as he looks down at me. "Are you okay?"

"Yes, I'm fine."

"You don't look it." He comes into the house, even though I haven't invited him, and closes the door, frowning. "You look like you've been crying."

"That's because I have." There's no point in denying it. I glimpsed myself in the mirror when I was brushing my teeth. My eyes are red-rimmed and I've got dark bags underneath them... not to mention a puffy nose.

"Has this got anything to do with your boyfriend?"

"Yes."

He moves closer. Close enough to make me uncomfortable, and I step back, bumping into the wall behind me. "He hasn't hit you, has he?" Donavan asks.

"No, of course not. Oliver's not like that. We just had an argument, that's all." *About you.*

He nods his head. "Well, why don't I stay here for the day? I can keep you company."

"What about your mom? We've set this whole thing up so she could meet Adam..." I let my voice fade and he tilts his head, smiling.

"Oh, don't worry about Mom. You're more important. Why don't we do something together... just the three of us? We are a family, after all."

I feel uneasy and move along the wall slightly. "No, we're not. You're Adam's father."

"Yeah. And you're his mom, so we're a family."

I know he thinks he's being funny and logical, and I'm too tired to argue with him. Besides, I can't speak right now. I've just remembered that Oliver once said I was his family. It was at his brother's wedding, and it made me feel like I truly belonged, for the first time in my life.

I loved that feeling, nearly as much as I love Oliver, but look where it got me.

He still left me... because he hated this setup, and for that reason alone, no matter how much I don't want to spend the day by myself, I can't say 'yes' to Donovan's suggestion.

"I don't wanna cause a problem with your mom." That sounds like a reasonable excuse, that won't offend him. "You know how badly things ended between us. I don't wanna give her an excuse to accuse me of trying to cause problems."

"You're not," he says.

"Even so, I think it's best if we stick to the plan. It'll give me a chance to catch up on my sleep." It won't, but he doesn't need to know that.

He hesitates for a second, his mouth opening, and then closing again, before he nods his head in acceptance, and I struggle not to sigh out my relief. After all, if Oliver comes back, I can't think of anything worse than for him to find Donavan here.

"Do you wanna grab the car seat and the bag of toys?" I suggest and Donavan bends over to pick them up, while I go back into the kitchen to retrieve the diaper bag, which I left on the table.

I rejoin him and we go out together, putting the bags into the trunk of his car, before he takes Adam from me and I fix the car seat, making sure it's secured properly, and then put Adam in. As I'm doing so, I wonder about telling Donavan that Adam's started saying 'Dada'. I know he won't be happy that he said it to Oliver, though, and there's no point in rocking the boat, so I keep quiet. Donavan will find out soon enough, when Adam says it to him.

"Don't forget," I say as I stand and turn to face Donavan. "You need to leave your place by two, and no later."

"I won't forget," he says. "You've told me about a hundred times already."

"There's no harm in saying it again. You've never looked after him by yourself." I glance down at Adam. "Is there anything you're not sure about?" I ask his father. "Anything you need me to tell you?"

"No." He shakes his head. "But you need to chill. You always were a worrier."

I'm not sure that's true, but I smile anyway, leaning into the car and giving Adam a kiss.

"Two o'clock," Donavan says, giving me a mock salute. "I'll even text you when we're leaving, if it sets your mind at rest."

I smile my thanks. "See you later, and call if you need anything."

He doesn't reply, but gets into the car, reversing off of the driveway. I wave, and he waves back, driving away, and I stand for a moment, wondering what to do with the rest of my day.

I'd expected to be spending it with Oliver, preferably naked, and begging him to do all kinds of things to me, and as I sigh and tears well in my eyes again, I make my way back into the house, closing the door and drowning in the deafening silence.

"Oh, Ollie," I whimper, sinking to the floor.

Why did I accuse him of making demands of me? Why did I make it sound like I don't like them, when I do? Especially as I know they're not really demands at all. They're fun. They're part of who we are, and they've helped me to understand myself so much better than I did before.

I lean back against the door, tears falling fast. I miss him so much, I ache, and I'd happily crawl to him on my hands and knees and do anything he asked of me... anything at all, if he'd just tell me he loves me. And that I'm forgiven.

∞

Oliver

I stayed at my place last night for the first time since Mason's wedding, when I spent the night here with Jemima.

On neither occasion did I sleep very much. When Jemima was here, that was because we spent most of the night making love. Last night, it was because I sat out on the deck, looking at the stars and gazing at the lake, and missing her. So. Damn. Much.

I thought about going back over there roughly once a minute. Or maybe more often than that. I can't be sure. I didn't go, though. What would have been the point? No matter how much this hurts, it hurts so much more to witness the way she fawns over Donavan. That's not my jealousy or insecurity talking. That's how it is.

And I can't take it anymore.

Baxter's sat with me, all night, loyal as ever, and we watch the sun come up together, while I close my eyes and wish Jemima could be here too, to see the pink and purple hues streaking across the dawn sky, their reflections shimmering on the lake's surface, and that we could have shared this moment. When I open them, I'm still alone, and I don't mind admitting, the sky and the lake and the trees become a blur.

I sigh, whispering her name under my breath, as I wipe my eyes with the back of my hand, and then get to my feet, going inside and giving Baxter his breakfast.

I didn't eat last night, and I still can't face food, so I make my way through to the bathroom, stripping out of my clothes and stepping into the shower. I've been in here many times since Jemima stayed with me, but now all I can picture is the two of us, naked beneath the cascading water, and the yelp of surprise that left her lips when I turned her around and entered her from behind. Bending her over was the most obvious option, but I wanted to feel her close to me, so I lifted her leg, exposing her, and held her body against mine. She ground back into me and then turned her head, so I could kiss her. There was something free and yet intimate about that. And when she yelled at me to fuck her harder, I realized I couldn't lose her.

And yet I have.

"Fuck it, J—Jem…" I slam my hand against the tiled wall, tripping over her name, unable to control the sob that leaves my mouth.

I make quick work of washing and get out, wrapping a towel around my hips and going out into my bedroom, where I grab my phone and dial Mason's number.

He answers promptly on the second ring.

"C—Can I come over?" I say, still struggling.

"Sure. Are you okay?"

"No. I need to talk."

"Okay." There's a pause before he says, "Isabel's gonna be here. She was really sick this morning, and she's not up to going out."

"You don't have to send Isabel out, just because I'm coming over."

"I know. But if you wanna talk…"

"I can talk in front of her. Can't I?"

"Of course. I just wasn't sure you'd want to."

I shake my head, even though he can't see me. "Who knows? A female perspective might be useful," I murmur. "It might help me make sense of all this. Nothing else is working."

"Has something happened?" he asks.

"Yeah… but I'll tell you about it when I get there."

"Okay. I'll put the coffee on."

I knock on Mason's door a little under an hour later, with Baxter sitting by my feet, having had a run down by the lake. He'll sleep happily for the next hour or so, and while I could do with some sleep myself, I know that won't be happening for a while yet.

Mason opens the door and steps aside for me to enter, frowning as he looks at me. "What happened to you?"

"I got hit by a truck. Metaphorically."

"It looks like it was literally." He closes the door and leads the way into the living room, where Isabel's sitting on their L-shaped couch, with her feet up. She's kinda pale and is clutching a glass of orange juice.

"Are you okay?" I ask her.

"I've been worse," she says with a smile. "And I think I'm doing better than you are."

I wander in and take a seat at the opposite end of the couch, leaving space for Mason in the corner between us.

"I know I promised you coffee," he says from the doorway and I turn to look at him. "But would tea be okay? It's just that the smell of coffee is enough to make Isabel feel sick at the moment."

"Tea's fine." I don't honestly care, but I think he can sense that, and he gives me a smile before he disappears toward the kitchen.

"Mason told me about your conversation the other day," Isabel says once we're alone. "I hope you don't mind."

"No, of course not."

She smiles. "Can I assume things have gotten worse?"

"That would be the understatement of the century."

Her smile fades and she shifts slightly, getting more comfortable, just as Mason comes in carrying a tray, laden with cups and a teapot, some milk and a plate of lemon slices, which I have to assume are for Isabel. He sets everything down on the table in front of us and then kneels on the floor, leaning forward so he can pour.

"What's happened?" he says, without turning to me.

"We've… We've split up."

He stops what he's doing and faces me. "Permanently?"

"I don't know." Isabel sits up now, putting her orange juice on the table and her feet on the floor, moving closer to Mason, and they both stare at me, making me feel like a prize exhibit.

"How can you not know?" Mason asks.

"Because I'm the one who left her, and I don't know if I wanna go back."

He raises his eyebrows, but before he can say anything, Isabel asks, "Why?"

"Because there are only so many times a guy can take being told he's not good enough."

"Did she tell you that?"

"Not in so many words. She didn't need to. It was in everything she did, and everything she said. Implied, if not explicit."

"What actually happened?" Mason asks, getting back to pouring the tea.

"Sh—She had another call from her ex," I say, taking the cup he offers me. "He phoned last night, wanting to take Adam by himself today, without Jemima being there, and while I know that ought to have made me delirious, I felt uneasy about the whole thing. I wasn't comfortable with the idea of Adam going to this guy's place without someone being there to supervise, and I didn't like the way he'd sprung it on her at the last minute."

"Did you tell her that?" Isabel asks.

"Yeah, but only after she'd said 'yes' to him."

Mason turns to me, putting down the teapot. "She said yes?"

"Yeah."

"You… you mean she's allowed this man to take her son, even though he's had almost no contact with Adam since he was born?" Isabel says, looking slightly fearful.

"Thank you," I say, leaning back. "It's good to know I'm not the only one who thinks it's a really dumb idea."

"Well, I didn't say it was dumb, but I'm not sure I'd trust a man like that to look after my child."

"That was my point exactly. He let her down, he cheated and lied, and yet she's trusting him... with Adam. She can't see it that way, of course. In her eyes, her ex is the perfect father, so she agreed with what he wanted."

"She didn't talk it through with you first?" Mason asks

"No. She never talks to me about anything to do with Adam. She just went straight ahead and did what he asked."

"So Adam's there now?" Isabel says.

"Yeah. As far as I know."

"What do you mean? Don't you know where he is?"

"No. We argued... badly. I told her I didn't like the way she just bows to this guy, or the way she comes home and sings his praises. She denied doing any of that, even though she's literally done everything he's ever asked of her, and she never stops talking about him." I shake my head, sitting back. "I told her I didn't like the guy being involved in our lives. She told me it wasn't optional."

"And you left?" Isabel says.

"Yeah. I'm not proud of walking out on her. I promised her I'd never leave her, and I have. But..." I struggle to finish my sentence and stare out the window for a moment or two, trying to get it together.

"If she was here now, what would you say to her?" Isabel asks, trying to make it easier.

"I don't think I'd say anything," I reply, turning back to face her. "I don't think I'd wanna talk to her."

"Not at all?" Mason says.

"No."

"Because you're angry, or because you're hurt?" Isabel asks.

"Both. Being without her is so painful, I can't even begin to describe it. I always knew leaving her would break me, but what else can I do? I'm so mad at her. She won't let me do anything with Adam. Not one thing. And yet this guy can do whatever he likes… simply because he was inconsiderate enough to get her pregnant."

"Are you jealous?" Isabel says.

"Yes. I've had this conversation with Mason already, and with Jemima. I know I'm jealous… and insecure."

Her lips twitch up into a half smile. "At least that was honest."

"I can't see the point in denying it. It's eating away at me… and before you ask, I don't think Jemima's cheating. I'll admit, I wasn't sure about that when I first talked it through with Mason, but having had more time, I think it's her ex's role in Adam's life that I'm jealous of, and Jemima's blind support of that. I also think the guy has an ulterior motive, which might revolve around Jemima, rather than his son, but I've got no evidence of that."

They both stare at me and then look at each other for a moment, before Mason says, "Most jealous people are a lot less rational than that."

"Well, I've had all night to think about it."

"You haven't slept?" he says.

"No. I've been sitting out on the deck at home, going over everything in my mind, right from his first phone call, when I realized she still had his number stored on her phone, to…"

"She still had his number?" Isabel interrupts.

"Yeah. Do you think that's odd too?"

"I don't know." She turns to Mason. "Would you keep an ex-girlfriend's number on your phone?"

"Other than the ex I told you about… the one who needed counseling, no."

"Your ex needed counseling?" I say, picking up on that.

"Not because she'd been dating me, no." He shakes his head, knowing that's where I'm going. "She had a lot of problems to do with her past, and I got her some help, and then stayed in touch with her until I knew she was okay."

Isabel leans in to him and they both turn to look at me again. "What about you?" Isabel asks. "I'm guessing you don't keep your exes' numbers either?"

"No."

I focus on Isabel, half expecting her to confirm that she's the same, but she doesn't say a word, and instead, she blushes, which feels kinda odd, considering she started this.

"Neither do you, do you?" Mason says, putting a lot of emphasis into his words as he turns to her, and I feel like something's a bit off between them.

Isabel lowers her head and then shakes it before she looks up, turning to Mason. "You're a useless liar," she says and then glances over at me. "I should probably explain that your brother was my first boyfriend, so I can't really comment on this, except to say I think I'd feel uncomfortable if Mason had his former girlfriends' numbers still."

I'm a little taken aback, and in normal circumstances, I'd probably say something about that revelation. But these aren't normal circumstances.

"Did Jemima give you a reason for having her ex's number on her phone?" Mason asks. "Or haven't you talked about it?"

"No. We talked about it – or, to be more precise, we argued about it – and she said it was because of Donavan being Adam's father."

"Well, I guess that makes sense," Isabel says.

"I thought so too… except I remembered she'd already told me that, after Donavan rejected Adam when he was born, she decided she wasn't gonna contact him again."

"Stop it," Mason says.

"Stop what?" I stare at him.

"Overthinking this. She probably didn't wanna speak to him, or hear from him ever again, after what he did. But it's possible she realized she might need to contact him, if Adam got really sick, or something… or maybe she just forgot to delete his details."

"I know all that, and I'm not overthinking it… I'm jealous, and I'm not handling it very well. I think we've already established that."

"What do you want to do?" Isabel asks.

"I don't know." I sit back, letting out a long sigh. "Like I said, I'm not sure I wanna speak to her right now."

"That's only because you're angry," Mason says.

"Even so, I can't see much of a future for us, if it's gonna be like this. I can't live a life where I'm on the periphery of her family, fitting in with the rules laid down by her child's father."

"What does that mean?" Mason sits back too, pulling Isabel with him and puts his arm around her.

"It means that Adam called me 'Dada' the other day."

"He did?" Mason smiles at me.

"Yeah. Don't read anything into it. I did at the time, but yesterday he called Baxter 'Dada' too, so it doesn't mean anything."

"So? What's the significance?" he asks.

"That when it happened, Jemima went into a mild panic. At first she tried to pretend he hadn't even said it, but then, when he did it again, she told me her ex wouldn't like it, because he'd evidently told her that under no circumstances is Adam to be allowed to call me 'Dada', or 'Daddy', or any other 'father' substitute."

"It sounds to me like you're not the only one who's jealous," Mason says.

"You think her ex is jealous of me?"

"Yeah, I do."

That hadn't occurred to me before. But even if it's true, I doubt it makes any difference.

"It's unfortunate," Isabel says, like she's thinking out loud. "You've both got what the other one wants. You've got Jemima, and he's got her son."

"I don't just want Jemima. I want both of them. And in any case, I'm not sure I have got her," I whisper. "But even if I do, when it comes down to it, he'll win, won't he? She'll do whatever's best for Adam… every time. And that's how it should be. He's her son, and she has to put him first. I get that. It's just that, in her head, what's best for Adam doesn't include me, because I'm not his biological father."

We sit in silence for a moment or two, but when Mason opens his mouth again, I hold up my hand.

"Sorry. Can we change the subject? I—I'm kinda done."

He stares at me, tilting his head and narrowing his eyes just slightly. "Done talking, or done with Jemima?"

I take a breath, struggling for control. "Both... I think. I've given her everything I have to give... and it's still not enough."

He sighs, but before he can say anything, Isabel puts her hand on his arm. "Don't give up yet," she says. "We can pick this up later, if you change your mind. And don't feel you need to leave. You can stay as long as you like."

"Thanks. I appreciate that." I'm not sure I want to go home and face the memories that seem to seep out of every pore of my house, reminding me of what I've lost.

I've made myself useful, and spent the day helping Mason paint the nursery. They've ordered the furniture, and although it won't be here for a few weeks, he thought he ought to make a start on decorating. By noon, Isabel was feeling a lot better, and she offered to take Baxter for a walk in the woods, after which she made us all some sandwiches, which we ate in the kitchen, before getting back to work.

"I know it's nearly four, but if you can stay for another couple of hours, I think we can get most of this done today," Mason says, surveying the pale yellow walls. They've gone for a neutral color, being as they don't know the baby's sex yet.

"I can stay for as long as you want." It's tempting to add that I don't have anything else to do, but I refrain. I'm fed up with feeling sorry for myself.

"We'll feed you," he adds with a smile.

"I already said yes," I tell him, shaking my head while I concentrate on painting around the window, just as my phone rings and I put down my brush, pulling my cell from my back pocket and letting out a groan as I see the word 'Jem' on the screen.

"What's wrong?" he asks, coming over.

"It's Jemima."

"Answer it, for Christ's sake," he says. "You love her, don't you?"

"Yes, but..."

"Then talk to her."

I press the green button, holding the phone to my ear, my hand shaking and my heart pounding in my chest.

"He didn't come, Ollie." She starts talking before I can even open my mouth, and I can hear the panic in her voice.

"Who?"

"Donavan."

I feel my anger rising. How could he do this? How could he let his son down? "And you're surprised?"

"No, you don't understand." Her words are pouring out, almost too fast for her mouth to keep up with them. "He came at nine this morning, just as we planned, and he took Adam. Then he sent me a text just after ten-fifteen to say they'd got back to his place, which I hadn't expected him to do. And I haven't seen or heard from him since."

"When was he supposed to bring Adam back?" I ask, aware of Mason coming closer, standing right beside me.

"An hour ago, at least," Jemima says. "I told Donavan to leave his place by two. He was supposed to text me when they were leaving, but he didn't. Even if he forgot, they should have been here no later than three. And it's gone four, Ollie. I know it's only an hour, but I've tried calling and he's not answering his phone."

"Do you mean he's not answering, or his phone is dead?"

"He's not answering. It rings five times and goes to voicemail."

"Have you left a message?"

"I've left four, and I've sent three text messages as well, but he hasn't come back to me." He's choosing to ignore her. "Do you think something's happened to them?"

"If it had, I think you'd have heard…"

"How? No-one would know to call me." She's really panicking now.

"I know, but if there was an accident, they'd call Donavan's mom as his next of kin, and while I know you don't get along with her, I'm sure she's not so heartless that she wouldn't contact you."

She sighs, seeming to calm, just a little. "Do you think I should drive down there? Or am I overreacting?"

"You're asking my opinion? Now?"

"Don't be like that, please, Oliver. I'm scared. I don't know what to do."

Her voice cracks, and I wish I was there with her. I need to hold her, even if I am still mad at her. "Sorry. I shouldn't have said that. And for the record, I don't think you're overreacting. But I also don't think you should drive. You're too upset."

"Then what am I…?"

"Give me your ex's address and I'll go get Adam."

She starts to reel it off, but then says, "It'll be easier if I text it to you, won't it?"

"Yeah."

"A—Are you sure about this?" she asks.

"Yes." I check the time again, thinking about how long it's going to take to drive into Boston. "I'll do my best to have Adam back with you by seven, but if I'm gonna be any later than that, I'll call you. Okay?"

"Yes," she whispers.

"Obviously, if your ex should bring Adam back in the next hour, call me and let me know."

"Do you think he will?" She sounds so hopeful, it breaks my heart.

"No." I can't lie to her. "If he was gonna do that, he'd have done it… and besides, why isn't he taking your calls, or returning them?" She falls silent, although I can hear her sniffling. "Try not to cry," I say. "And call your mom. Get her to come over. I don't like the idea of you sitting there all by yourself, worrying."

I hear her whisper, "O—Okay," but before she can say anything else, I hang up.

"What's happened?" Mason asks as I put my phone back in my pocket.

"Jemima's ex hasn't brought Adam back at the time she designated and he's not taking or returning her calls."

He pales. "Has she called the cops?"

"Not yet. I'm gonna go to this guy's address and find out what's going on… and get Adam back."

He puts down his paintbrush, that he's been holding all this time.

"Are you hoping to get Jemima back too?" he says, as we start down the stairs.

"No. I left her, remember? I still don't know how I feel about her."

"Yeah, you do. How did it feel to hear her voice?" he asks.

"Painful."

"Hmm… that's because you're in love with her."

"I know." It's pointless trying to deny it. "But right now, I don't know if that's enough."

"Do you want me to come with you?"

"No. You should be here with Isabel. And anyway, I need to do this by myself."

"You're sure?" he asks.

"Absolutely positive."

Chapter Thirteen

⁓

Jemima

"Jemima? Where are you?" My mom's voice echoes through the house and I sit up.

"In the living room," I call and she appears in the doorway, her face lined with worry.

I did as Oliver suggested and, the moment he'd hung up, after I'd texted Donovan's address to him, I called her. I'm not sure how much sense I was making, but it was enough for her to say she'd be home in ten minutes, although I don't think it's even taken her that long. As I get up and run to her, I notice a woman standing directly behind her. I don't know who she is, and for the moment, I don't care. I just need a hug.

"Mom," I say, throwing my arms around her.

She hugs me back, rocking me slightly at the same time.

"It'll be okay," she says in a soft whisper.

I pull back and look over her shoulder at the woman, who's still standing there. She's about the same age as Mom, maybe a couple of inches taller, and is wearing jeans and a pale yellow blouse. Her dark hair is tied back in a ponytail, and she's undeniably attractive, with piercing blue eyes.

I look back at mom again, hoping for an introduction to this stranger, and notice a flush on Mom's cheeks as she turns and takes the woman's hand in hers.

"Th—This is Dale," she says.

I stare, first at Mom, and then at the other woman.

"You're Dale?" I whisper.

She nods her head and I turn to Mom, who's gazing at me, biting her bottom lip and looking uncertain. "I know this is a shock for you," she says. "But can we deal with one thing at a time? Can you tell me what's going on with Adam?"

I'm reeling, my stomach churning more than ever, but I step back, letting them into the room, and we all sit down; Mom and Dale beside each other on the couch, while I resume my seat on the chair, where I've been holding onto Boots. We've never taken him to Donavan's, just in case he gets left behind, and I clasp him to my chest again, for comfort.

"Donavan didn't bring him home," I say, tears forming in my eyes.

"You said that on the phone, but what do you mean?" Mom asks.

"He came and collected Adam at nine this morning, but he didn't bring him home, like we planned."

She sits forward, releasing Dale's hand. "Are you telling me you let Donavan have Adam by himself?"

"Yes. We arranged it last night... right before Oliver walked out on me."

"He what?" Mom frowns.

"He walked out on me. He flew off the handle about Donavan having Adam, and about how I never let him do anything to help, and we both said a whole heap of things..." I let my voice fade, choking back my tears.

"And he walked out?" Mom says.

"Yeah."

"And you're surprised?"

I look up at her, stunned by her reaction. "He was being jealous," I say. "He didn't like the fact that I still had Donavan's number on my phone, or that I spend time with him, or even that he's a part of our lives."

"I don't blame him," she says. "Donovan's turned your lives upside down, and you've let him... not that any of that matters right now.

What matters is why on earth you agreed to let him have Adam, by himself."

"Because he asked."

She shakes her head. "And that means you have to agree, does it?"

Dale reaches out, touching Mom's arm. "Calm down, Heather," she says in the softest of voices. "Jemima's upset."

She's not wrong. I thought my mom was here to support me, not argue with me.

"I know she's upset," Mom says, lowering her voice just a little. "What I don't get is why she'd trust Donavan over Oliver." She turns to me. "Why would you do that? Donavan has done nothing but let you down, and Oliver's been there for you since the day you first set eyes on him."

"Yes, but Donavan is Adam's father," I explain. Why can't anyone else see this? Why is it only me who understands how this feels?

"And?" Mom glares at me, and I sit forward.

"Do you know what it felt like, wishing my dad would come back to me?" I say, raising my voice now, because I'm done with being judged. "Do you know how it felt, wishing he'd want me enough to come and find me? I never got to experience that. So, when Donavan got in touch and wanted to see Adam, it was like my dream coming true. Not for me, but for my son... and I didn't wanna do anything to ruin it for him."

"But... but that's ludicrous," Mom says, dismissing my argument with a wave of her hand. "I don't know what Donavan's motives were for contacting you, but if he wanted to be a father to that baby boy, he should've been here with you from the beginning. He should've put you first... all day, every day. He should never have left it to me to help you raise your son, and whatever he's playing at right now, that proves he's not fatherhood material... unlike the man you're doing your best to push away."

I sit back again, her words piercing my heart. "No, I'm not. I'm not pushing Oliver away."

"Really? You introduced him to Adam the very first time he came here. You knew I thought that was crazy, and I think Oliver might have done too, but you did it anyway. Then, when Oliver started sleeping here, wouldn't let him stay for breakfast. You made him get up and leave every morning. How do you think that made him feel?"

I know perfectly well how it made him feel. He told me... it hurt. "I just needed time before I let Adam see him here in the mornings... you know that."

"In which case, why did you introduce them to each other in the first place? If you weren't sure about Oliver, you should've kept them apart until you were. Except you didn't, did you? You made the introduction, and then you didn't let him get involved at all. You've never let him do a thing, even though he so clearly wanted to. It was written all over that man's face how much he wanted to be involved with Adam, but you've made him feel second-rate, every step of the way. He didn't deserve that, Jemima. Especially when – despite your best efforts – he's been more of a father to Adam than Donavan could ever be. So, no matter what you say, you've pushed him away."

Tears fill my eyes, hearing her repeat Oliver's accusations, almost word-for-word. "I—I didn't push him away. He left."

"Yeah. Because there's only so much rejection a man can take."

"I didn't reject him. I love him... I told him that, over and over."

"I'm sure you did, and I know you love him. Oliver probably knows it, too. The thing is, I'm not talking about whether you rejected him as a man, but as a parent."

"He's not a parent, though, is he?" How many times do I have to explain this? "He's not Adam's father. Donovan is."

"Biologically, maybe, but being a parent is about a lot more than that. Do you honestly think Oliver only wanted you in this deal, and not Adam? He knew nothing about you having a child until that night when he came around here. A lot of men would've run a mile at that point, but he didn't. He stuck around, knowing that if he wanted to be with you, he had to accept Adam, too. That takes guts and commitment, but he did it. He accepted Adam, and he stayed. Except you only gave him part of the deal."

"Heather," Dale says, grabbing Mom's arm again, and she sits back, shaking her head.

"I'm sorry, Jemima," she whispers. "I don't mean to get angry with you. Especially not when it's... it's my fault."

"What is?"

"This." She waves her hand around. "None of this would have happened if I'd told you the truth about your father from the beginning. You'd have known where you stood and probably had a more realistic outlook on life... and fatherhood. It would have helped if I'd been more honest about myself, too."

"I—I don't understand," I murmur. My brain feels like it's in danger of spontaneous combustion right now, and I gaze at her across the room as she turns slightly in her seat and takes Dale's hand in hers again.

"I've let you believe Dale was a man," she says, blushing, as Dale smiles.

"I actually thought Dale might be my father," I admit and they both turn, frowning at me.

"Why?" Mom asks.

"Because you said Dale was someone you'd known before, a long time ago. I put two and two together..."

"And made five." Mom shakes her head.

"So you haven't known each other very long?" I ask.

"Yeah, we have," Dale replies.

"I didn't lie to you. Dale was my first love," Mom says. "We met when we were in high school, just outside Boston, and we just fell for each other. We spent as much time together as we could, and it was everything I'd ever dreamed it could be."

"Y—You mean you've always been a lesbian? It's not a recent thing?" I clutch Adam's toy dog a little tighter, hoping to gain some comfort, or at least a little understanding, because nothing's making sense to me right now.

"No. It's not recent," Mom says. "I've never liked men... not sexually. I like them as people. At least some of them. But sexually, they do nothing for me. They never have. I realized that when I was growing up, but it wasn't until I got together with Dale that I understood why."

"If that's the case, and you were so happy, why didn't you stay together?"

"Because Dale's family moved here, to Sturbridge. We couldn't keep seeing each other after that."

"Why not? Boston isn't that far away."

"No… but we were young. It wasn't easy back then. People weren't as tolerant as they are now, and our families would've been outraged."

"At least that's what we told ourselves," Dale says in a quiet voice. "We probably could've stayed together, but we were scared of how people would react. We didn't realize how precious love is."

She gazes at my Mom, who gives her a soft smile before she turns back to me again.

"It was hard enough being together when we lived in the same town, but being apart made it impossible. So, we both moved on. Dale found someone else, and so did I, for a while. But that broke up after a couple of years, and it was then, when I was in my early twenties, that I decided I wanted to have a baby." She takes a breath and then says, "There are a few ways of going about that… some more mechanical than others."

"Did you use a mechanical method?" I ask, feeling fascinated and bemused in equal measure.

"Yes. I couldn't bring myself to have sex with a man, but I knew a couple – a gay couple – and I'd talked it through with them on several occasions, trying to decide how to go about it. Then one night, when I was at their place having dinner, one of them suggested becoming my sperm donor, if that was what I really wanted. I'd never thought about it before, not in terms of the donor being someone I actually knew. To be fair, we were kinda drunk that night, but the next morning, they evidently talked it through and then came to see me, and the guy reiterated his offer. We were all completely sober then, and we discussed the consequences while they sat on my couch, holding hands. He told me he was just doing it to help me out. He didn't want to be a father, and he wanted nothing to do with the baby we were gonna make. Once we'd established that, and I'd agreed to his terms, all we had to decide was how to go about it. He didn't wanna have sex with me any more than I wanted to have sex with him. So, it was all done artificially. He helped a friend, and I got what I wanted… namely you."

She gazes at me with a loving smile. "Because I wanted you, Jemima. More than anything."

"W—What was his name?" I ask.

"I'm not allowed to tell you his full name," she says. "That was one of his conditions. But his first name was Matthew. He said I could tell you that much, if you ever asked."

"Matthew." I repeat the word, even though it means nothing, and then I look up at her. "Why did you tell me my dad left?"

"I didn't." She sits forward again. "I never told you anything about your father. I was tied by my agreement with Matthew."

"But, I remember…"

She shakes her head. "Think back over what we said, Jemima. What did I actually tell you?"

I take a deep breath and replay a few of our conversations in my head, realizing how one-sided they were; how I'd ask questions, and she'd skirt around the answers.

"I never told you anything, did I?" she says, after a moment or two. "I avoided your questions, and you made up the answers by yourself." She lowers her head. "I shouldn't have let you do that. I should have told you the truth as soon as you started coming up with your own version of it. But you were very young then, and I wasn't sure you'd understand. I didn't think the fairytale version of reality you'd created would do you any harm, so I let it slide. I—I regret that now," she says, stuttering over her words. "More than ever."

So do I, but I can't say that… not to her face. She clearly feels guilty enough as it is.

"Why is it I've never noticed you having a relationship with a woman before now?" I ask instead, and she looks up at me again.

"Because I was on my own for a very long time. Not long after you were born, I moved us to Eastford, knowing it wasn't too far from Sturbridge. I'd realized by then that Dale was the only woman for me and I didn't want to be with anyone else. I couldn't contact her, though, because she was in a relationship. I just liked being close to her."

Dale puts her arm around my mom and smiles at her, and it's easy to see how in love they are.

"Unfortunately, my partner died of cancer about seven years ago," Dale says. "She was quite a few years older than me, but I loved her… not in the same way as I loved your mom, but we'd been together for a long time, and I'm not gonna say it wasn't hard losing her."

"I heard about Dale's loss from a mutual friend." Mom takes over the story. "And I reached out to Dale to see if I could help her. We met up, and that was when I discovered Dale's capacity for making jam."

They both sigh in unison, and I tilt my head. "So, you're the one who makes the jam?"

"Yes. I took it up when Bethany died, just for something to do, but it's kinda taken over my life and it's turned into a full-scale business. I've outgrown my apartment now, so I'm gonna have to sell it and I'll use the proceeds to buy some commercial premises, while I find somewhere else to live…" She stops talking and glances at my mom.

"We can talk about that later," Mom says, looking back at me. "The point right now is that Dale and I became friends again, and we stayed that way for quite a long time, while she mourned Bethany."

"And you helped me," Dale says, leaning into my mom.

"And then, when the time was right, and Dale was ready, we became lovers again. We couldn't live together, obviously, but I'd drive here to Sturbridge, or she'd come to Eastford to see me. It wasn't ideal, and we'd have liked to see more of each other, but we both had commitments and we were so happy, just being together…" Her voice fades and she looks at Dale, smiling.

"So it wasn't a coincidence that we moved to Sturbridge then?" I say, and Mom turns to me.

"No. We needed to get away from Donavan's mom after Adam was born, but we could've gone anywhere to do that. I chose Sturbridge so I could be closer to Dale."

"And now you wanna live together?" I guess, and Mom nods her head.

"Yeah, we do. If you're okay with that."

"O—Of course I'm okay with it." I say, and then without any warning, I burst into tears and Mom gets up, coming over to me. She crouches down and looks into my eyes right before she pulls me into a hug.

"I'm sorry, Jemima," she whispers, holding onto me.

"You don't need to say sorry," I mutter between sobs. "You've got nothing to be sorry for."

Dale joins us, kneeling next to Mom and we all hug each other, Boots crushed between us.

"It'll be okay," Mom says. "Adam will be okay."

I lean back, stuttering in a breath. "D—Do you think Oliver will get him back?"

She smiles and reaches out, caressing my cheek with her hand. "Of course he will. He'd do anything for you."

I let her hold me again, hoping she's right. I hope Oliver can bring Adam home, and that he loves me enough to forgive me for all the stupid things I've said and done.

Oliver

I find the house and, as I park up outside, I have to admit, it's nicer than I'd expected. I've spent the entire journey here wondering what to expect, and picturing Mason and Isabel's worried faces, as I waved them goodbye. With hindsight, I'm not sure I made the right decision in turning down Mason's offer of help. I think his calm, reasoned abilities might be useful, but as I climb out of the car, telling Baxter I won't be long, I realize it's too late now. I'm here, and I've just got to face whatever comes next, no matter how hostile Jemima's ex is. Because there's no way I'm leaving here without Adam.

I knock on the door, feeling apprehensive, although I don't have long to wait. It's opened within moments by a tall, dark-haired young guy, who's undeniably handsome. Annoyingly so, in fact. He stares at me, frowning.

"Yeah?" he says.

"Are you Donavan?" I ask.

"Yeah. Who are you?"

I can hear Adam crying somewhere in the background, although the man standing in front of me doesn't seem fazed and just continues to stare at me, waiting.

"You don't know me, but Jemima asked me to come and collect Adam, and take him home." I give him what sounds like a reasonable explanation for my appearance at his door, even if Jemima didn't actually ask for my help. She never does where Adam's concerned.

He looks over my shoulder. "Jemima didn't come with you?" I'm surprised that he looks more fearful than I'd expected.

"She's too upset to drive. You took her son."

He stands up straight, puffing out his chest. "He's my son too."

I'm riled now, probably because Adam's still crying and this guy doesn't seem to care. "Then act like his goddamn father," I say, raising my voice. "And in case you don't know what that means – and you don't seem to – it means you don't take him from his mother, you take her calls, and you do what she says, when she says it." Adam really screams, even more loudly and I wonder if he's heard my voice. "What's wrong with him?"

"How should I know?" He shrugs his shoulders. "He's been screaming like that for the last couple of hours. It's driving me crazy, but he just won't quieten down."

"Okay. Let me in." I barge past him, although he doesn't object, and closes the door.

I find myself in a small living room, with a couch in front of a fireplace, and an archway that leads through to what seems to be a kitchen. Adam's on the floor, surrounded by toys, in front of the couch, his face red and blotchy, his eyes streaming with tears.

"Hey," I say softly, going over and picking him up. "What's wrong? Why all the tears?"

He looks at me, sniffling, and then starts crying again, and as I hold him closer, I realize what the problem is.

"He needs his diaper changing," I say, turning to Jemima's ex, who's still standing over by the door. "Do you have diapers?" I'm sure Jemima will have given him some, but I can hardly search his house for them.

"Yeah," he says, looking around vacantly. "They were in a bag."

He frowns and then, as though he's remembered something, wanders into the kitchen, returning with the diaper bag, which he hands over to me.

"Thanks," I murmur, and kneel on the floor, being as it's the flattest surface available.

I've seen Adam roll around and try desperately to get away from Jemima when she's changing him, but he just lies there, staring at me, gulping great lungfuls of air, as though he senses the diaper change is necessary... and welcome. I've never done this before, but it's not rocket science, and doesn't take more than a few minutes to clean him up and put on a fresh diaper.

I pull up his pants and straighten his clothes, lifting him into my arms again, hoping that will have done the trick, although he soon starts to whimper again.

"See?" Donovan says, a smug expression on his face. "He's still crying."

"When did you last feed him?"

"I took him to the pizza place for lunch, just like we normally do..." His voice fades.

"And?"

He stares at me for a moment. "He seemed kinda nervous without Jemima, and started screaming the place down, so we left."

"Before or after you'd eaten?"

He lowers his eyes. "Before."

"So, you came back here and fed him? When was that?"

"I don't know, but I didn't know what to give him... and he wouldn't stop screaming," he whines, like a pathetic child.

"Y—You mean, you haven't fed him at all? You've had him since nine this morning, and he's had nothing to eat?" I keep my voice as quiet as I can, even though I'm livid. There are more important things to think about. "Do you have some bread?" I ask. "And some cheese or ham?"

"Yes. What should I do? Make him a sandwich?"

"No. Just butter the bread and cut up the ham."

He nods his head and walks over to the archway, disappearing through it into the kitchen. I hang onto Adam, still sitting on the floor with him, and although I try to distract him with his trains, he won't have it and just keeps crying… not that I blame him.

"It's okay," I say, holding him close. "We'll give you something to eat and then I'll take you home to Mommy." That doesn't seem to quieten him down at all, but I hug him, hoping to give him some reassurance.

It takes an inordinate amount of time for Jemima's ex to come back with the food, and I'm about to get up and go find him, when he reappears in the archway, carrying a small plate, which he brings over, handing it to me.

He hasn't cut up the bread, although the ham is in squares, but rather than arguing over it, I just break the bread into pieces, handing one to Adam, who raises it to his mouth straight away, chewing avidly.

"He'll need some water," I say, looking up again. "Did Jemima give you Adam's beaker?"

"I don't know."

"Well, go through his things and find out," I whisper through gritted teeth, desperate not to show my anger to Adam, although he's so engrossed with his food, I'm not sure he'd notice anything at the moment.

Donavan strides away, having first given me a dark look, and returns a minute or two later, carrying Adam's trainer cup, which he's filled with water. At least he got that right. I take it from him and wait for Adam to finish his mouthful before I offer him the water. He looks at it and then at the bread and ham, hesitating before he takes the beaker from me, holding it briefly to his lips.

"Haven't you given him a drink all day either?" I say to Donavan, taking the beaker back and handing Adam a piece of ham, watching him to make sure he doesn't choke.

"I didn't know he'd need one," Donavan replies, looking as pathetic as he sounds, with his hands in his pockets and his head bent.

"Hasn't your mom been here?" I ask, wondering how a mother could've let a situation like this arise.

"No," he says.

"But I thought you told Jemima…"

"I only said that so she'd let me have Adam," he interrupts.

"You mean, you lied to her?" He shrugs his shoulders again. "Even without your mom being here, surely you realized Adam needed to have something to eat and drink, and that he'd need to have his diaper changed. You must've noticed what Jemima does with him when she's here… or are you a total idiot?"

"Don't talk to me like that," he says, narrowing his eyes. "I'm guessing you're her boyfriend, although what she sees in someone as old as you, God knows. But you're the idiot, not me. You're the one who had a fight with her. You're the one who made her cry."

I ignore his comment about my age as a sharp pain strikes at my chest. "H—How do you know that?" I ask.

"Because I saw her this morning when I went to collect Adam. She looked like she'd been crying all night." He shakes his head at me, like I'm the world's biggest loser. "Even I never hurt her that much."

The pain intensifies, knowing I did that to her.

"I offered to stay with her, but she wouldn't let me," he continues, when I don't reply. "So I went back to my plan…"

"What plan?" I say, turning slightly so I can see him better.

"I—I thought, if I told Jemima my mom would be here, she'd let me have Adam for a few hours by myself, which she did. Then I thought that, if I waited a while, I could call her and tell her my car wouldn't start, and she'd have to come here to collect him." He stares at me, a slight smile on his lips. "I know she's not serious about you. She told me herself it's just an office romance, so I figured if I got her here, a bit later in the day, I could persuade her to stay for dinner… and then…" His voice fades and I take on board what he's saying. Is he playing with me, or would she really have called our relationship an 'office romance'? And would she have agreed to his plan? Would she have stayed with him? Do I even need to ask that question? She's agreed to everything else he's asked of her. So why not this?

"Why didn't you?" I ask eventually. "Why didn't you call her and pretend your car wouldn't start?"

He waves his hand at Adam, who's still sitting on my lap, chewing his bread.

"It didn't work out, did it? Adam wouldn't eat at the restaurant, and... and I couldn't figure out what to do with him when we got back here. I didn't want her to see what a mess I'd made of things."

"So you thought you'd keep hold of Adam, rather than taking him home and admitting you couldn't cope by yourself? You thought you'd ignore Jemima's calls and put the fear of God into her instead, did you? Jesus... didn't it occur to you that, when you didn't bring Adam home, she was gonna assume you'd kidnapped him?"

He smiles, looking smug and stupid at the same time. "Don't be so dumb. How can I kidnap someone who's mine?"

I put Adam down on the floor, with the plate of bread and ham beside him, and although I'm still watching him, I turn on Donavan.

"Adam is not a possession. He's a person in his own right, and the fact that you don't understand that shows you don't understand basic human decency. He may be your biological son, but he's not yours to do with as you please."

He doesn't answer me, but he averts his glare now, staring at the fireplace beyond Adam.

"How could you possibly think a plan like that would work?" I say. "Aside from the way you've neglected Adam today – which Jemima would never forgive you for – she was never gonna want to be with a man who would lie to her, and try to use her own son to blackmail her into getting back with him. If you wanted her, you should've treated her right in the first place. You should've stuck by her when she needed you."

"You think I don't know that?" he snarls, taking a step toward me, his anger showing. "You think I don't regret what I did? I've never been with anyone like her since the day she walked away from me. I've tried. God knows, I've tried. But there's no-one who can fuck like Jemima.

That's why I got in touch with her again. That's why I've been doing all this… to get back with her."

He tries to step around me, leaning down as though to pick up Adam, but I get in his way and lift his son into my arms. I glance down, seeing that Adam's eaten more than half the bread and nearly all the ham, and I know that'll be enough to keep him going until we get back to Jemima's place. So I crouch down, with Adam perched on my knee, unwilling to let him go, while I gather up his toys and put them into their bag. Then I hand him his trainer cup to hold and I sling the diaper bag over my shoulder, pick up his toys and stand, turning to face Donovan again.

"We're leaving," I say, which seems to make him jump and spark to life.

"No." He shocks me by getting in the way, putting himself between us and the door. "I might not be the most responsible guy in the world, but I've got no idea who you really are. You could be anybody."

"Hardly," I say, shaking my head. "We've already established I'm Jemima's office romance."

"So? That doesn't mean she asked you to come here."

"Maybe not. But if you don't believe me, why don't you call Jemima and ask her?"

He hesitates for a moment and then pulls his phone from his pocket and flips it over, tapping on the screen a couple of times before he holds it to his ear. He doesn't get the chance to say a word before Jemima yells. I can hear her from here, and although I can't make out what she's saying, she doesn't relent. A couple of minutes pass before he's able to get a word in.

"Can I speak?" he says at last. Jemima says something, although I don't know what, and he replies. "Whatever," like he couldn't care less, and then adds, "There's a guy here. He says you sent him to take Adam back. Is that right?"

Jemima clearly says, "Yes," judging by the expression on her ex's face.

Then I guess she must ask why he kept Adam, because Donavan goes quiet and says, "I'll let your boyfriend explain." He hangs up then, glaring at me, but neither of us says a word.

I move toward the door, and this time, he doesn't try to stop me. As I put my hand on the door handle, though, I turn back to him.

"I'm gonna need Adam's car seat. Can you get it for me?"

He nods and goes to the kitchen, coming back with a set of keys in his hand, and he follows me outside. I go straight to my Jeep, putting Adam's bags in the trunk and then, opening the rear door, I take the seat from Donavan and place it next to Baxter, who raises his head, looking surprised. Normally, I'd move him into the trunk if Adam was in the car, but I don't. I'm fairly sure Adam's going to sleep for most of the journey home, and I trust Baxter to behave himself. I sit Adam in the seat, and I fix it in place and strap him in, double-checking that it's secure, and that he is too. Then I close the back door, turning to find Donavan standing a couple of feet away.

"I'm not gonna tell you what I think of you, because I can't find the words," I say, opening the driver's door and resting my hand on top of it. "But if you ever wanna see your son again, you're gonna need to apologize to Jemima and explain yourself properly to her... and you're gonna need to grow up."

He sneers, shaking his head. "Yeah, like you're ever gonna let me near your girlfriend again, knowing I want her back."

I take a step closer to him, and he moves backwards, fear showing in his eyes. "This isn't about me," I growl. "It's about your son. Or at least, it was meant to be. Except I'm not sure you give a damn, do you?"

He doesn't answer and I can't be bothered to wait for him to work it out, so I turn and climb into my car, shutting the door and starting the engine.

"We'll be home soon," I say to Adam, trying to sound reassuring.

I know I told Jemima I would only call her if we were going to be late, but I decide she could probably do with some reassurance herself, so I send her a quick text message.

— *On our way. Should be back in an hour.*

I'm not sure whether to add a kiss, but decide against it. I don't know where I stand with her, and a text message doesn't seem like the best place to work that out.

I'm about to pull away when my phone beeps and I pick it up and read...

— *Thank you. x*

She's put a kiss on her message and while I want to read something into that, I can't. I don't even know how I feel about her at the moment, especially after Donovan's comments, so overthinking a kiss seems like a dumb move.

Adam grizzles in the back seat and I remember that sound meaning he's tired, so I set off, knowing he'll sleep on the journey, which he does. Baxter does too, and both of them are silent companions for the hour we take to get back to Jemima's place.

That gives me time to think. I'm blown away by how dumb her ex is, although I guess that isn't a tremendous surprise; he cheated on her, after all. I also give some thought to what's been going on between Jemima and me since he came back into her life. I knew from the beginning that he had an ulterior motive, but being proved right doesn't make me feel any better. It just makes me regret everything even more, because Jemima couldn't see him for what he is, even though she claims to have known him so well. Was she so blinded by him that she didn't want to see? Did she want to re-kindle their romance, too? Is that why she told him ours is just an 'office romance'? Was she lying when she said she loved me? Can I have got that so wrong? Or was that Donovan playing with me and was it just Jemima's need for Adam to have his real father in his life that blinkered her to Donavan's games, and to the damage she was doing to us?

It's getting dark by the time I park up on the driveway outside Jemima's house, but she must've been looking out for me, because before I've even switched off the engine, she's opened the door and is running toward the car. She yanks open the back door behind me, and unstraps a sleepy Adam, pulling him up and into her arms, his body hugged close to her chest. I get out, shutting my door and look down at her, noticing the tears welling in her eyes as she looks up at me and mouths, "Thank you," in the softest of whispers.

She looks a little disheveled, like she's been running her fingers through her hair, which she probably has. Her eyes are red and puffy and there's an obvious tiredness in her face, and I feel guilty for causing at least some of that, although her ex has a lot to answer for too.

"That's okay," I murmur, stepping around her and unfastening the car seat, before fetching the rest of Adam's things from the trunk and carrying it all over to the house, leaving everything by the front door. There's no sign of Heather, although her car's here, so I know she must be around somewhere, and I guess she's giving us some privacy.

As I turn back to the car, Jemima's already walking toward me, Adam still clutched in her arms. He's rubbing his eyes, clearly still tired, although he looks up at me and smiles when they get close enough.

"Your ex hadn't fed, or changed him, or given him anything to drink," I say.

"Since when?"

"Since this morning. He'd tried taking him the pizza place you usually go to, but Adam didn't like being there without you, and started screaming, so your ex brought him back home and, from what I could see, he just left Adam playing on the floor. Needless to say, he was crying his eyes out when I got there."

Jemima's mouth drops open, her eyes widening in anger. "How could Donavan do that? What's wrong with him?"

"I don't know." I genuinely don't.

She swallows hard. "What did you do?" she says.

"I resisted the urge to punch your ex in front of your son, and got him to give me some bread and ham, which I fed to Adam. He's had a little water, too, but you'll probably want to give him some more. Oh... and I changed his diaper."

She shifts Adam, moving him to her hip and then reaches out, touching my arm. I struggle to breathe, staring at her pale hand against my darker skin.

"Thank you," she says again, a little louder this time. "D—Donavan said you'd explain. Why he did this, I mean."

"It was simple." I let out a breath as she pulls her hand away, rubbing it across Adam's head and smiling at him. "He wanted you back."

Her eyes dart to mine and she blushes. "Me?" she whispers. "He wanted me?"

"Yes. This was all about you. I'm sorry, Jem, but right from the start, it was always about you, not about Adam."

"But… but why?"

"He said he'd never been with anyone like you." I don't use her ex's exact words. I can't bring myself to say them.

"So? If he wanted me that much, he shouldn't have cheated on me, should he?"

"I did kinda tell him that, but he seemed to think that if he played at being a father, you'd see him differently. Not as a cheat, or a liar, but as Adam's dad."

She rolls her eyes, making a kind of 'humph' sound.

"Why are you scoffing? It worked like a dream, didn't it? Until today, that's exactly how you've seen him. You've been the first one to say how much he's changed." I can't hide the bitterness in my voice, and Jemima looks down at the space between us, blushing and sighing deeply.

"I—I still don't understand… about today, I mean. His mom…"

"Was never gonna be there," I say, interrupting her. "He only told you that so you'd agree to let him have Adam. He came up with a plan that he'd take Adam for pizza and then call you afterwards to say his car wouldn't start, so you'd have to drive there."

"So why didn't he? Call me, I mean?"

"Because he'd screwed up. He hadn't expected Adam not to eat at the restaurant and he knew you'd be mad at him when you saw Adam in the state he was in, and he was too scared to see it through." Those may not have been Donovan's words, but that was his meaning.

"He's not wrong," she says, shaking her head. "What did he think we were gonna do when I got there, assuming everything had gone smoothly? Surely he must have realized I was just gonna collect Adam and come home again."

"No. He had other ideas. He thought he'd be able to persuade you to have dinner with him… and then maybe to stay for a while longer…" I let my voice fade, not wanting to think too hard about that.

She frowns, clearly incredulous. "Did he seriously think I was gonna stay with him? He knows I'm with you…"

"Yeah, but he didn't seem to think you were serious about me, so…"

"Why would he think that?"

"He said you'd told him yourself." I gaze into her eyes, hoping to see the truth in them. "He said you'd explained that ours was just an office romance."

She closes her eyes, so I can't see anything. I can feel the pain in my chest, though, and it cuts right through me.

"He was telling the truth, wasn't he?" I say.

"No." She opens her eyes and reaches out for me, but I step back, fearful of her touch now. "I never said that to him. He asked about us. I said I worked for you... and he assumed it was an office romance. I didn't correct him, because it was none of his business. That's all. You have to believe me..."

"I do." It's impossible not to. The truth is written all over her face.

"I promise, on Adam's life, it's you I love... and I guarantee I've never said or done anything to encourage Donovan to think otherwise."

"Except give in to every request he's ever made." I'm careful not to use the word 'demand', knowing how she feels about that. "I guess he interpreted that as a willingness on your part to do anything to keep him in Adam's life. He told me he nearly changed his plan at the last minute, when he came over here this morning and saw that you'd been crying. He said he offered to stay..."

"Yes, he did, but I said 'no'."

"Which meant he had to go back to his original plan, to persuade you that you belong with him... both of you."

Chapter Fourteen

Jemima

I stare up into his face, my heart aching. He looks so tired and so hurt, and I just want to hold him... or have him hold me... or both.

Except I'm so angry. Not with Oliver, but with Donavan... and with myself. I let this happen. I let myself be blinded and fooled into believing this was all so perfect when it was nothing of the sort.

"But we don't belong with him. Even if I could ignore his cheating and the way he behaved in the past, there's no way I'd even consider being with someone who'd use my son to achieve his aims."

Oliver shakes his head. "I kinda told him that."

"And you told him I'm with you now, surely? You told him I'd never go back to him anyway, no matter what he did?"

"No. No, I didn't say any of that." He sounds so defeated, and I reach out again, putting my hand on his arm. He lets me this time, sucking in a breath as he looks at me, and even in the dim evening light, I can see a glistening in his eyes, which breaks my heart.

"Why not, Oliver?"

"To be honest, I wasn't sure you were with me anymore."

My hand drops to my side and I stagger, clutching Adam, as Oliver reaches out and holds me, his hands on my arms, steadying me. "But... you just said you believe me. I never belittled our relationship to Donavan. I just never talked about it. Please, Ollie... I love you. I've told you I love you, over and over."

"I know… and I believe you," he says, letting me go. "It's just that, ever since your ex came into our lives, you've been like a different person." He pauses and then says, "I even thought about asking you to choose between us."

"You did?"

"Yeah. I was getting so fed up with hearing about how great he was, I was gonna give you an ultimatum. Me, or him."

"But you changed your mind?"

"I decided against it." He looks down for a moment, and when he raises his head again, I can see the hurt in his eyes. "I knew you'd choose him."

I reach out and touch his chest, resting my hand against it. "No, I wouldn't—"

"Yeah, you would. You'd have put Adam's needs first, before your own, and that means you'd have chosen his father over me. You might well have broken your heart in doing it, but that's what you'd have done. That's why I didn't ask. I was too scared of losing you."

A tear hits my cheek and I swallow down the lump in my throat. "I —I'm sorry," I say, realizing the truth of his words. "You're right. If you'd forced me to choose, I would have chosen for Adam to keep his father in his life. It would have broken me, and I'd have hated my life without you, but I'd have done it… and I'd have been so, so wrong."

I let out a sob, unable to hold it in anymore and he steps closer, so he's almost touching me, but not quite. "It's okay," he says softly. "I understand. You got swept away on the idea of Adam having a father, and you kinda lost sight of everything else, including me… and us. I know you wanted it for Adam because you didn't have it for yourself, and I know you honestly thought you could make it work… regardless of your ex's real motives and what it was doing to me."

"I—I didn't…" I stop talking, realizing my denials are stupid now. Hell, he's only saying what I've been thinking myself. "What was it doing to you?" I ask instead.

Rather than answering, he glances around, his eyes settling on Mom's car.

"Is your mom here?" he asks.

"Um… yeah." I'm not sure what his point is.

He nods his head. "I know this is a big ask in the circumstances, but could you take Adam inside and leave him with her for a few minutes? There are things I need to say to you…"

"Without him being here?" My legs feel weak and my skin freezes. This is it. He's going to break up with me… I know it.

"Yeah, if that's okay."

For a moment, I wonder about refusing, but that would make me no better than Donavan, using my son to achieve a goal… in this case, to stop Oliver from breaking my heart.

"Sure," I say, trying to sound like I'm not falling apart, and I turn away, walking slowly into the house, where I find Mom waiting for me in the hallway.

"Is everything okay?" she asks, looking at Adam with a smile.

"No. Oliver wants to talk to me by myself," I say, just about holding back my tears.

"I'll look after Adam, shall I?"

"If that's okay." She reaches out and takes him from me, her face kinda grim. She doesn't say anything more, and I know she's thinking the same thing as me… that I've blown it. "He's probably hungry and thirsty," I say, and she nods her head as I kiss Adam's cheek and take a deep breath before heading back outside.

Oliver's leaning against his Jeep, gazing at the ground, but he must hear me coming because he stands upright and turns to face me.

"Is he okay?" he asks.

"Yes. Mom will take care of him."

He nods.

"You didn't answer my question," I say, desperate to put off the inevitable.

"What question?"

"What was all this doing to you?"

"You know it was hurting me, Jem. I'm not sure you realize how much, but I don't think you can claim to be ignorant of it."

"N—No."

He sighs and moves a little closer. "I don't blame you. I don't think you did it deliberately."

"I didn't." I look up at him through my falling tears.

"But that doesn't make the pain any easier," he says.

"I'm sorry," I whisper. "I'm sorry for all the things I got wrong, and I'm sorry I compared my losses to yours." He shakes his head.

"I'm sorry too."

"What for?"

"I made you cry... and I said some hurtful things to you last night. I shouldn't have don't that."

"I deserved it," I whisper, wondering if I misread things... whether he's not going to break up with me, after all. "Do you wanna come inside?" I ask, biting my bottom lip in a very deliberate move.

"I don't think that's a good idea," he says and my hopes are dashed. I feel the air being sucked from my lungs.

"Don't you love me anymore?"

"Of course I do, but sometimes, love isn't enough."

Oh... God. "Please, Ollie... please. I—"

"I don't wanna hear you beg... not now." He stops talking and lets out a deep breath. "Sometimes it feels like you just want me for sex, Jem... like I don't have any other role in your life. And I'm sorry, but – no matter how great the sex is – I want more. I love you so much." He pauses for a moment, but I heard the emotion in his voice just then, and it makes me cry even harder. "You own my heart, and the only way I'll ever stop loving you is when it stops beating. But sometimes it feels like you don't need me as much as I need you. I get that you've got Adam, and that he's your priority... I understand that, and I'm not asking you to change. I—I just need to be more than someone you sleep with, and if that's not what you want from our relationship, then... then I don't think we have a future."

"A—Are you breaking up with me?" I sob.

"No. I'm asking you to work out what it is you want from me... and from us."

"What is it *you* want?" I ask, stuttering in a breath.

"I want us to be the family you were trying so hard to create with your ex," he says, his voice a low whisper. "I'd like for you to share your life with me, not just your body. And while you're deciding if you can do that, I don't think we should see each other."

"But I work for you."

"Then take some time out. Be with Adam. I'll manage at the surgery by myself."

"You don't wanna see me?"

"I didn't say that." He tips his head backward, looking up at the sky for a moment, before he gazes back at me, his eyes filled with tears. "I said I didn't think we *should* see each other, not that I don't want to. Seeing you is so damn hard, Jem." He raises his voice a little. "We've been apart for one night, and my body aches so much... just standing here, like this, I'm burning for you. But no matter how much I want you, or how much I love you, we need to look at the bigger picture, and there's no use pretending; things weren't right between us even before your ex came onto the scene."

"I—I never meant..." He holds up his hand and I stop talking.

"It doesn't matter what you meant; it's what you did. You introduced me to Adam, but then snatched him away again. It took weeks before you'd agree to let me stay for breakfast, and even now, you'd rather struggle to do everything yourself than let me help. You won't let me do anything... and yet, you let that fucking idiot take your son and starve him." He takes a breath, his bottom lip trembling. "I— I don't wanna be on the outside anymore, Jem. But I need you to work out whether you can let me in. All the way in. I need you to decide if you can let me be a part of your life. Yours and Adam's. And when you've decided, call me."

He doesn't give me a chance to reply, but steps around me and gets into his car, driving away, the tires kicking up dirt as he goes.

I stand, staring, unsure what to do, my heart hurting, tears rolling down my cheeks. I want to go after him, to beg his forgiveness, but his anger and my shame have me rooted to the spot.

I jump as I feel an arm come around me and I turn to see my mom looking down at me.

"Come inside," she says, her eyes filled with sadness.

She turns me around, and I notice Dale standing by the front door, holding Adam in her arms. Someone has moved Adam's bags and his car seat into the house, and we step around them as we pass through and Dale closes the door behind us.

"He's had an oatmeal muffin and a banana," she says. "Do you want me to get him ready for bed now?" I'd like to take him and hold on to him forever, but I realize we need to be practical, and I'm grateful. He needs changing, and I'm not sure I'm the best person to do it.

Adam goes with her willingly, and she hums a tune to him as she takes him down the hallway toward his bedroom, reminding me that she's not only familiar with the house, but with my son. God... how foolish I've been.

"Oh, Mom." I turn and throw my arms around her neck, letting her hold me. "I've been so stupid."

She doesn't reply, because we both know I'm right, but she leads me into the living room and sits me down on the couch, taking a seat beside me and holding my hand in hers.

"What did Oliver say?" she asks.

"About Donavan, or us?"

"Both. I mean, why did your stupid ex decide to keep Adam?" I can tell she's angry, but I am too.

"He had some twisted idea in his head that I'd get back together with him."

"If he kidnapped your child?" she says, raising her voice.

"He didn't see it as kidnapping, but yeah." I'm not in the mood for explaining Donovan's plan and how he believed it might work out. I feel I bear too much responsibility for that myself. I should have put him right and told him how much Oliver means to me.

She pulls back slightly and takes a deep breath. "I hope you've learned your lesson."

"About Donavan?"

"Yeah. He was never any good. When you first told me you were pregnant, I was so disappointed... not because you were pregnant, but because Donavan was the father. I could've told you he'd be a cheat before you told me. It's in his blood."

"How do you work that out?" I ask.

"Because his father cheated on his mother, with just about every woman in town." She smiles. "He even tried it with me once."

"How did that go?"

"It caused the original problem between Donavan's mom and me," she says, rolling her eyes. "Someone in the town told her about her husband flirting with me, and she came and saw me after work one day. She blamed me for the whole thing; accused me of leading him astray, and called me a slut."

"Oh, Mom…"

She shrugs her shoulders. "It's okay. I knew it wasn't true. So did everyone else in town. The man had a reputation that followed him around like a bad smell. His son's no different."

"I know."

"You're not gonna let him see Adam again, are you?"

"From what Oliver said, I don't think he's gonna ask, but if he does, the answer will be 'no'."

"What if he takes you to court?"

"Then I'll fight him. I'll tell the court what he did, and we'll see what a judge has to say about it."

She smiles. "Good. It's taken you long enough to work it out, but you got there in the end."

"Yeah. At a tremendous risk to my son. What kind of mother am I?"

"A human one." She gives my hand a squeeze. "You just wanted what was best for Adam."

"Hmm… but how wrong was I?"

She doesn't contradict me. We both know I couldn't have gotten things more wrong if I'd tried. "H—How was Oliver?" she asks, sounding slightly fearful.

"Angry."

"With Donavan?"

"And with me. I can't blame him for that. I treated him so badly."

Dale comes back in, carrying Adam in her arms. He's wearing his dinosaur pajamas, and he's rubbing his eyes.

"He's tired," I say, pulling my hand from Mom's and reaching out to take him. He settles on my lap and I sit back, holding him close, relishing the feeling of his tiny body against mine as tears fill my eyes.

"I'll get him a beaker of milk," Mom says, getting up and going into the kitchen, while Dale sits down.

"Thanks for changing him," I say, and she smiles.

"He seems none the worse for his adventure," she replies.

"No thanks to me."

She shakes her head. "Don't be so hard on yourself. You were only doing what you thought was right."

"Yeah, and ruining everything into the bargain."

"You didn't ruin anything," Mom says, coming back into the room and picking up on our conversation. She's carrying Adam's blue beaker, and she hands it to me to give to him. He clutches it, and settles back in my arms, drinking down the milk in great gulps.

"You didn't hear Oliver," I murmur, looking down at my son. "You didn't see how hurt he was."

"Did he say he doesn't love you anymore?" she asks, sitting down beside me again.

"No. He said the only way he could stop loving me would be for his heart to stop beating."

Mom smiles, tears forming in her eyes. "I'm no expert on men," she murmurs, "but I don't think they say things like that very often. I know I'm repeating myself, but he's a good man, Jemima, and as long as he still loves you…"

"I know he's a good man, Mom. I've never doubted that. But I'm not sure love is gonna be enough." I quote Oliver's words at her, getting back to reality. "Like I said before, he's angry."

"So angry he couldn't forgive you?"

"I—I don't know. He said he wanted me to take some time to think about what I want from him… from our relationship."

"And?" Mom says. "What do you want?"

"Him."

"I think he already knows that." She shakes her head. "But he wants more, doesn't he?"

"Yeah. He does."

"He always did. So, I guess you need to ask yourself whether you're willing to commit yourself to this man with no holds barred. Whether you're willing to welcome him into your family, and accept his love, not just for yourself, but for your son."

"Of course I am."

She smiles. "Then you need to go tell him that."

"I—I can't."

"Why not? You don't wanna listen to any nonsense about taking time to think things through. If you're sure about how you feel, then get over there and tell him."

"It's not that," I whisper. "It's just that I don't wanna leave Adam... not tonight. I wanna stay until he's asleep."

Mom looks over, craning her neck so she can see him. "I don't think you'll have long to wait," she murmurs. "He's nearly there already."

I glance down to see Adam's eyes fluttering closed and I smile, bending to kiss his forehead as I pull the beaker from his hands and he snuggles in to me.

"I'll put him to bed," I say softly, getting to my feet, cradling him in my arms.

"And then you'll go see Oliver?" Mom says, handing Boots to me.

"I might just sit with Adam for a little while, but yes... then I'll go see Oliver."

I carry Adam down to his bedroom and lay him in his crib with Boots alongside him. He wriggles and whimpers a little, but soon settles, his eyes closing, his lips pouting, and I reach over and stroke his head.

"I'm sorry," I murmur. "Mommy got it wrong – really wrong – but she's not gonna make that mistake again." He snuffles and turns his head toward me. "I'm gonna go see Oliver in a minute," I say, still in a quiet whisper. "And hopefully he can forgive me and I can make things right between us, so we can be a family... like we always should have been."

Oliver

Baxter runs along by the side of the lake, stopping every so often to sniff at something before he sets off once more. He's happiest here, and I feel kinda guilty about keeping him away for so long. Still, I guess we might be spending a lot more time here from now on, if Jemima decides she can't let me into her life in the way I need her to. And while that thought makes it kinda hard to breathe, I allow my mind to drift to a nightmare world without her in it, and I wonder if I should've given her that ultimatum… if it was an ultimatum. I'm not sure now. Either way, I gave her a choice, to be with me fully, completely, in a loving and whole relationship that includes me having a role in Adam's life… or not.

Now I'm back here by myself, I'm wishing I'd just kissed her and held her and told her everything would be okay. I wish I'd said I'd fit in with whatever she wanted, even though I know I'd have been lying, because without that complete relationship, I know I'll never be okay. I can't live a half-life anymore.

Something's nagging at the back of my mind, which I know I need to think through, even though I'm so tired, I can't remember what it is. But it's almost dark now, and there's no moon tonight, so before I lose my dog forever, I call him back. He comes galloping out of the twilight and I smile. Just. It's a struggle, but I manage it, and I crouch down and scratch behind his ears.

"Let's get you something to eat," I say, and his ears prick up, like he can understand me, as he trots beside me on the way back to the cabin.

Inside, I flick on the lights and go over to the kitchen, preparing Baxter's bowl of food, which I put down on the floor, watching while he eats, and then I go back into the living room. I don't feel like eating myself, but as I sit, I remember Mason and my plans to stay there for dinner, and that he and Isabel are probably wondering what happened this afternoon. So, I pull out my phone and connect a call to my brother, who answers on the second ring.

"How did it go?" he says, by way of greeting.

"Okay, I guess. I got Adam home safely. So that's the main thing."

There's a brief pause before he says. "You're on speaker."

"Okay." I guess Isabel wants to know the outcome, too. She was as worried as anyone about what happened.

"So, was it a misunderstanding?" she says.

"No. The guy had come up with a stupid plan to win Jemima back, but it backfired, and now all he's done is alienate her."

"Which benefits you, doesn't it?" Mason says.

"It should," I reply. "But I've asked her to take some time to think about what she really wants." Although I'm not sure 'asked' is the best way of phrasing that. I didn't really give her much choice, and the more I think about it, the more I'm regretting that.

"From you?" Isabel says.

"From our relationship, and from me. I—I think I might have made a mistake there, though."

"How?"

"I put it to her like an ultimatum. You know? Like it was an all-or-nothing thing, and I didn't mean that."

"So, despite everything you said earlier… despite telling us you didn't even want to talk to her, you want her back?" Mason says.

"Yes, I want her back, but…" Suddenly that nagging thought comes to the front of my mind, and I remember what it was I needed to think through.

"But what?" Mason says.

"Oh, it's just something her ex said."

"What was that?"

"He queried why she'd be with someone as old as me. I'm just wondering if maybe we've got different expectations. I—I kind of accused her of just being in this for the sex. But, thinking about it, maybe that's all this is to her. Maybe she doesn't want to settle down."

"Can I remind you that she's the one with the child?" Mason says.

"I know, but that wasn't her choice. She wasn't ready to be a mom, and maybe she's not ready to be a family yet."

"How old is she?" Isabel asks.

"Twenty-two."

"And how old are you?"

"He's thirty-four," Mason replies on my behalf.

"Which is one hell of an age gap," I say, shaking my head even though they can't see me.

"It's not the biggest one we know of, though, is it?" Mason says. "Look at Max Crawford and his wife. Dad said they've got a seventeen year age gap between them. They've got a baby girl and his daughter from his first marriage, and they're deliriously happy. So stop looking for problems where there aren't any... and stop feeling sorry for yourself."

"Who says I'm feeling sorry for myself?"

"I do," he says. "Correct me if I'm wrong, but are you at your place?"

"Yeah."

"You're not at Jemima's?"

"No."

"In which case, you're definitely feeling sorry for yourself... *and* you're doing this wrong. Do you remember at Destiny and Ronan's wedding, when I was so damn miserable because Isabel had left me?"

"Yeah."

"You recall the conversation I had with you and Colt Nelson, and how Colt said I needed to get off my ass and get up to Vermont to talk things through with Isabel?"

"Yeah."

"Well, I'm giving you that talk now. You may not have screwed up like I did. In fact, I don't think you've screwed up at all, but you love Jemima and she loves you, and that means you need to be wherever she is. If she needs thinking time – which I'm not sure she does – then give it to her. If you feel you've given her everything you've got to give, and it's not enough... find something more. But don't leave her while you're working on it. You love her, and we never leave the women we love... do we?"

He's right...

"I've gotta go," I murmur.

"Okay. Call me."

"I will… and thanks."

I hang up and get to my feet, rushing to the kitchen, where I pick up my keys from the countertop. Baxter's asleep in his basket and I wonder for a moment about waking him, or leaving him here. The problem is, if I get this right, I'll be staying with Jemima, so I have to take him with me.

I'm about to lean down to wake him, when a thought crosses my mind. Am I acting too soon?

Yeah, I know I should be with her, but there's no denying I'm also still mad at her. That was why I left in the first place, and that means it might not be wise to go back there… not right now. It might be wiser to wait until the morning.

I stand again, pushing my fingers back through my hair, undecided, as the memory of Jemima's face comes into my mind, and I picture her, hugging Adam to her chest and mouthing her thanks at me. The look she gave me then wasn't just one of gratitude, it was filled with love, too. A kind of unbreakable, everlasting love, and I know no matter how unwise it might be, I have to go to her.

I have to tell her that, even if I'm still mad at her, we'll work it out.

I'm about to bend down to Baxter again, when someone knocks on my front door and I curse quietly under my breath, turning and striding over, thinking to myself that whoever this is, I'm going to have to get rid of them, because I don't have time for callers, or visitors, not now.

I yank open the door, my breath catching in my throat as I look down to see Jemima kneeling on the porch, her head bowed.

"What the hell are you doing down there?" I say, reaching down and taking her hand, pulling her to her feet.

She looks up at me, tears filling her eyes. "I'm begging," she whispers.

"You never have to beg. You never did. I told you that. It was just… just a game, I guess. I never wanted you to take it that seriously. I thought you understood."

"I did," she replies. "I do. And I like your games. They turn me on, and they're part of who we are. But this isn't about that. It's got nothing to do with sex. And I'm sorry if you think that's all I want you for. It's not." She stops talking and swallows hard, blinking back her tears. "Th—that's not what I came to say."

"Okay. What did you come to say?"

"That I've decided what I want, and it's you. I—I can't lose you, Ollie. You're a part of me, and if I lose you, I won't have a life worth living. So I'm begging you to stay."

I step closer. She still looks kinda disheveled, and I brush a stray hair away from her face, tucking it behind her ear. "You think you have to beg for that?" I murmur.

"Yes. I need you to forgive me. I—I need you to come back to me." She pauses and then says, "No, that's wrong. I need you to come back to us. To Adam, and me."

I hold up my hand, revealing my keys. "I was just about to."

She smiles, and bites her bottom lip, and I reach out and free it with my thumb. It's too soon to use my lips or my teeth, but she still gasps at the contact and I gaze into her eyes.

"Y—You were gonna come back?" she says.

"Yeah. I was gonna ask you to forgive me."

Her smile fades as her brow furrows, and she tilts her head slightly. "Forgive you?"

"Yes. I told you I'd never leave you; I said it so many times, and yet that's exactly what I did. And I shouldn't have. Not last night, and certainly not this evening. I should've stayed with you and Adam. I should've made sure you were both okay… and I should never have given you that dumb ultimatum."

She looks confused. "You didn't. You changed your mind about that, remember?"

"Not that ultimatum. I'm talking about tonight, when I told you to decide about us and our relationship. I told you we didn't have a future. That made it sound like, if you didn't give me everything I wanted, I was gonna walk away forever… and I can't do that, Jem. I was just so… so jealous."

"Was that why you walked out last night?"

"I walked out because I was angry."

"At me?"

"Yes. I was angry that you'd given your ex so many chances with Adam, and you'd given me none."

"That was so stupid of me. I don't even know why I did it."

" Yes, you do. It was because you wanted it to be perfect for Adam, in ways that it wasn't for you. You wanted his father to want him, because your father didn't want you."

"I know. I get all of that. What I don't understand is why I kept you at arm's length the whole time."

"To be honest, I'm not sure I understand that myself. Maybe it was because you've never had a father-figure yourself, so for you it's the real thing, or nothing." I'm guessing now, but that kinda makes sense to me, and judging from the look on Jemima's face, I think it makes sense to her, too.

"Well, if that was the case, I was wrong," she says. "In so many ways. Not only have you been a better father to Adam than Donavan could ever be, but it seems I don't actually have a father, so all my silly ideals are just fantasies, anyway."

I stare down at her. "What do you mean, you don't have a father? Your dad might have left before you were born, but he's still your dad, biologically speaking."

"Yes, except that's not how it happened."

"It's not?"

"No."

She glances around and I realize we're still standing on the doorstep, half in and half out of my house.

"Do you wanna come in?" I ask.

"I—If that's okay with you."

God, this is way too formal for us, but I still feel like there are things to be said; like we're on a precipice, and that means I can't just haul her across the threshold and into my arms. All I can do is step aside and let her enter. She does, pausing while I close the door.

"Shall we sit?" I suggest, and she nods, walking over to the couch and sitting down at one end. I put my keys on the table and take a seat beside her; not too close, but not so far away that it looks as though I'm trying to put a distance between us. "You were saying about not having a father?" I prompt her, as she stares at her clasped hands.

"Yes. I was." She twists slightly, so she's facing me and says, "After you'd said you'd go into Boston to find Adam, I called Mom, like you suggested, and she came over, bringing Dale with her."

"So you've met him?"

"Not exactly. Dale's not a man; she's a woman."

"Oh." I wasn't expecting that. "So your mom's…"

"A lesbian," she says, finishing my sentence. "It seems she always has been."

I can feel myself frowning. "In which case, how were you conceived? If that's not a stupid question."

"A friend of hers volunteered to donate his sperm," she says, taking a deep breath. "He was gay, and in a relationship…"

"And he slept with your mom?"

"No. It was all done artificially. Mom told me his name's Matthew, but that's all she's allowed to say. That was their deal. He didn't want a child, or any involvement with me. He just wanted to help her out."

"I see." I don't, really. There's no way I'd get a woman pregnant and walk away, showing no love or responsibility for a child I'd helped create. But I guess if he hadn't done it, there wouldn't be a Jemima in the world, and it would be a sorrier place for that. "Why did she tell you he left then?" I ask.

"She didn't."

"But I thought…"

"I made it all up," she says, biting on her bottom lip again. It takes all my willpower not to lean in and kiss her, to free it and bite it myself, but I hold back, waiting for her explanation. "Mom never told me the truth… not until today. But she never actually lied, either. She just avoided answering my questions. She'd change the subject, or distract me, and I guess I just invented a father for myself… and she let me."

"Which makes you angry?" I guess, and she tilts her head to the right and then the left, like she's thinking about my question.

"Disappointed," she says. "I get Mom had an agreement with Matthew, but that didn't mean she couldn't have explained the situation. She didn't have to go into detail, or name names, she just had to put me straight, rather than let me build up a fantasy father in my head." She stops talking and I sense that there's anger bubbling beneath the surface, as well as the disappointment she's admitted to.

"Maybe you should cut your mom some slack?" I say, moving a little closer to her. She looks up at me, her eyes filled with confusion.

"Why couldn't she have been honest from the start?"

"I don't know. I'm sure she had her reasons, and I'm not saying it's ideal, but you need to remember, you've kept yourself to yourself for a long time, too. You kept Adam's existence from me for ages…"

"Are you telling me off?" she says, looking like she might cry.

"No, of course I'm not. I'm just saying you're two of a kind in some ways. Relationships aren't easy, Jem, so give your mom a break."

"I will. I am."

I smile at her and she smiles back, just briefly. "Tell me about Dale," I say, changing the subject, and her smile widens, which seems promising.

"She's nice. I like her."

"Were she and your mom really together when they were younger?" I ask. "Or was that something your mom made up to throw you off the scent?"

"No. That was completely true. They fell in love at high school, but Dale's family moved here to Sturbridge, and they split up."

"And then found each other again when you moved here?"

"No. Mom always knew Dale was here. So she moved us to Eastford when I was a baby."

"Hoping to get back in touch?"

"No. She knew Dale was in a relationship, but I think Dale has always been my mom's one true love, and from what she said, and the way she said it, I think she just wanted to be close to her… without crowding her."

"So what happened?"

"Dale's partner died of cancer when I was about fifteen, and Mom contacted her then to see if she could help. They became friends… and then lovers."

"And they're happy?"

"Very. Dale is obviously the reason we moved to Sturbridge, and Mom says she wants to live with her now. They were talking about Dale selling her apartment because her business is expanding and she needs to find new premises, or something."

"What does Dale do?" I ask.

"She makes jam. It's her strawberry jam you've been spreading on your toast since you've been staying for breakfast."

"In that case, she can stay," I joke, and Jemima giggles, although it's short-lived as she stops suddenly and frowns.

"D—Do you think they'll wanna live at the house?" she says. "It's Mom's, after all, not mine."

"Did they say they wanted to live there?"

"No. But we didn't go into details. I was kinda upset at the time."

"About Adam?" I guess.

"Yeah. I was scared Donavan would find a way to stop you from bringing Adam home."

I move closer, so we're almost touching, and I reach out and caress her cheek with my fingertips.

"Nothing your ex could've said or done would've stopped me from bringing Adam back to you."

"It wasn't just Adam I was scared about," she murmurs. "I was also scared I'd lost you. You might have agreed to go find Adam, but you were so cold about it."

"I'm sorry. That was unfair of me. I was hurt and angry, but it wasn't about me, it was about Adam. I should've realized that... I—I let you down."

She shakes her head and then blinks a few times, her eyes glistening. "Are you still angry with me?" she murmurs.

"Yes... but I'll get over it. I love you too much to stay mad at you for long, and I've realized since I walked away from you earlier on that I also love you far too much to live without you. I don't know why I thought it was a good idea for us to not see each other, but I was wrong. Whatever's going on between us, we need to work it out together."

She opens her mouth, but before she can say anything, I lean in and kiss her, capturing her lips and biting on the bottom one, making sure she knows it's still mine. I pull her body closer, but it's not enough, so I lift her onto my lap and she nestles against me, her breasts hard against my chest as she rocks against my cock, driving me insane.

"P—Please," she stutters into my mouth, and I pull back, breaking the kiss.

"No. No more begging. We're not gonna do that anymore. I don't want you to feel…"

She leans back herself, staring at me. "But I like begging," she whispers. There are tears in her eyes, and for the first time, I realize how much this means to her. "I'm sorry for what I said about your demands. They're not demands… I know that, and I'm sorry for comparing you to Donavan. You showed me who I am… and I really don't wanna change."

"I don't want you to change either. I love you just as you are, but I need you to understand, I'm not making demands of you."

"I know you're not. You're letting me be myself… for the first time in my life."

"And I wouldn't want you any other way."

She smiles, even though the tears are still glistening in her eyes. "I know. You told me that before… and you made it really clear earlier."

"I did?"

"Yeah. All those things you said…"

"What things?" She blushes. "We've said a lot to each other today, Jem. I need to know what you're talking about."

"When you said you burned for me," she whispers. "I've never felt so needed, or wanted, or loved before… even though you were angry with me."

There's no point in denying it. I was angry with her. "I can't switch off my feelings for you, no matter how mad I am. I long to be inside you… but that doesn't alter the fact that I need more. It's not just about sex for me."

"I know. And it's not just about sex for me either."

"I love you," I say and she opens her mouth to reply, but I put my fingers against her lips, stopping her. "I'm not finished." She stares at me. "I love you, and I love Adam too." Her eyes widen and I put my free hand on her ass and pull her closer, my hard-on pressing against her core. "I know you're not keen on the idea, but if you should change your mind, I want us to have children of our own one day, and…"

She grabs my wrist, pulling my hand away. "What makes you think I don't want to have children with you?"

"You do."

She frowns at me, confusion etched on her face. "How? We've never even talked about having kids."

I gaze down at her. "I know, but don't you remember, when your period started at your ex's place?"

"Yes."

"It was early."

"I know it was."

"And I made that comment about early being better than late… and… let's just say, your reaction made it clear that being pregnant was the last thing you wanted."

"Oh, God…" She shakes her head. "All I meant by that was, I'd rather plan it than have it sprung on me. I didn't mean for you to think I don't want to have children with you. I love you, Ollie. Of course I want to have your children. I just think I'd rather do it properly this time around."

Relief washes over me and I pull her closer again. "So would I… but in that case, if it should happen, I never want Adam to feel like I'm treating him differently, just because he's not my biological son. And that means you've gotta let me in."

"I—I know," she murmurs. "And I want to let you in, more than anything. I should never have trusted Donavan or given him so many chances. You were right. I should've seen through him."

"It's okay." I place my hand behind her head, holding her steady. "You were blinded…"

"Not by him," she says quickly.

"No, by him being Adam's father and what that means to you."

"Except he isn't a father, is he? Not in the proper sense of the word." She gazes at me for a moment as I caress her neck. "The... the next time Adam calls you 'Dada', I'm not going to correct him."

A lump forms in my throat but I manage to talk past it... just. "I—I never told you, because I didn't get the chance, but Adam called Baxter 'Dada' yesterday, so I don't think we can read too much into it. He's making sounds, that's all. He doesn't know how much they mean to the rest of us."

"Well, I know how much they mean to me, and when the time comes, I'll be proud to tell him you're his daddy."

I lose the battle against that lump, and my eyes sting as she blurs before me. "Are you sure you mean that? Don't say it if you don't, just because you know it's what I wanna hear."

She moves her hands up, cupping my face. "I mean it, Ollie."

"What about your ex?"

"What about him?"

"Won't he have something to say about all that?"

"I don't care. And he won't know. I've already thought this through, and talked it over with Mom, and Donavan's gonna have to fight me in court, if he wants to see his son again."

I take her hands in mine, turning them over and kissing her palms, one at a time, before I look into her eyes. "I don't think he will want to see him though, do you? Not when you consider this was all about you."

She blushes and lowers her head, although I'm quick to put my finger beneath her chin and raise it again. "I'm sorry," she whispers. "I should've worked that out for myself."

"How?"

"Because there were things he said that made it obvious. Looking back, I should've noticed them."

"Why? What did he say?"

"Oh, it was just little things. Even right at the beginning, when he first called, he said he wanted to make things right... and it was kinda obvious he was talking about things between him and me, not Adam. He only mentioned seeing Adam *after* I'd said I wasn't interested."

"Well, it was probably easy to miss the signs. You weren't expecting to hear from him, were you?"

"No. But that wasn't all he did. He kept paying me compliments and asking about our relationship. And he kissed me…"

"He what?" I pull away from her.

"It was just on the cheek… nothing untoward, I promise. No more than a 'hello' kiss. But it made me feel uncomfortable. Just being near him made me uncomfortable, and that should have been a red flag for me. If I'd been paying attention. And then yesterday he said we were a family… him, Adam, and me."

"How did you reply?" I ask, trying to relax.

"I didn't agree. He argued we were, because I'm Adam's mom and he's his father. Except that's not what makes a family, is it?"

I smile at last. "No, baby. Family isn't just about the fact that you made a child together. It's so much more than that. It goes so much deeper."

"Is that why you said I'm your family?" she asks.

"Yes. But I didn't just mean you when I said that. Adam's always been part of the deal as far as I'm concerned. The moment I knew you had a child, I worked out that, if we were gonna be together, it was always gonna be about all three of us."

She pulls back slightly, looking down at my chest. "Do you have any idea how much I love you?" She looks up when I don't answer. "Do you? O—Or have you had doubts about me?"

"Sometimes. I doubted your commitment to us. Even before your ex got involved, it felt like I wanted more from this than you were willing to give."

"Why didn't you say something?" she asks.

"I did. Don't you remember? I brought the subject up several times, but you always shut me down. I couldn't force you to let me in, Jem. It had to come from you."

She shakes her head, and a lone tear falls onto her cheek. I brush it away with my thumb as she sucks in a quick breath and says, "How have you put up with me?"

"Easily. I love you."

"I don't know why you haven't left me," she mutters, like she hasn't heard me.

"I did leave you. It was the biggest mistake of my life... and it's not one I'm gonna be repeating."

"But you've offered me everything I've ever wanted for myself, and everything I should've been wanting for Adam... everything any sane mother would want for her child, and I've pushed you away."

"I know. The question is, are you gonna keep pushing?" She shakes her head, sniffling, and I smile. "That's good to know, because I'm never gonna leave you again either."

"Ever?" she looks up at me.

"For as long as I live."

That sounds like a vow. It feels like one too.

"Am I forgiven?"

"Of course. I don't expect things will change overnight, but we'll work it out."

She leans in and kisses me, and I tilt my head, deepening the kiss as she breathes harder, my hands roaming over her back and down to her glorious ass, as I pull her onto my cock. She groans and pulls back.

"You're wearing way too many clothes," I whisper.

"Then take them off," she says.

"You want me to?"

"Yes... please." She bites her bottom lip with a very sexy smile and I shift forward on the couch, getting to my feet and bringing her with me, held in my arms. She wraps her legs around my hips and I kiss her again, even harder this time.

"I'm gonna make you come so hard, you won't be able to remember your own name," I growl as I pull back again, and she shudders.

"Oh, God. Yes... please. Please, Ollie."

I let out a slight whistle, which I know will be enough to wake Baxter, and I bend down a little awkwardly to grab my keys from the table before I head for the door.

"W—Where are we going?" Jemima asks.

"I'm gonna make you come."

"But, I thought..." She glances toward my bedroom and I stop, Baxter at my feet.

"I wanna make love to you, and I wanna wake up beside you tomorrow morning, and that means we need to be at your place... where Adam is."

"You're sure?"

"I'm positive. You can forget your name quietly, can't you?"

She giggles and I kiss her, hard and fast, before I open the door.

Baxter stays right by my side, glancing up at me every few paces, as we go down the steps toward my car. He's clearly confused, having assumed, I guess, that we'd be spending the night here.

"We'll have to come back here tomorrow to collect your car," I say and Jemima nods her head.

"We can come for the day, if that's okay. It'll give us some time together."

"We're gonna have lots of time together, baby. But I don't have a problem with you coming here for the day."

"I'll let Mom know what we're doing, in case she's got plans," she says as I lower her down my body to the ground, so I can open the car door and put Baxter in the back. "She's still at the house, with Dale, by the way."

"Hmm... I kinda worked that out." I turn back to her, closing the door again, once Baxter's settled. "I didn't think you'd have left Adam by himself."

"No." She sounds doubtful.

"Are you okay with me meeting your mom's girlfriend?" I ask, wondering if that's the reason for her sudden change of mood.

"Of course. I was just thinking..."

"Is now the best time for that?"

"No. But, do you remember I said that Dale was talking about selling her apartment, and that I thought she might wanna move in with Mom?"

"Yes."

"Well, don't you think it might get a bit crowded with all four of us there, and Adam, too?"

"It might. But who says we have to live there, anyway? I've got a perfectly good house of my own, in case you haven't noticed." I wave my hand at the cabin.

"Y—You mean we could live here?" she says, gazing up at me.

"Yes. It was something I was gonna talk to you about, before you started going to see your ex at weekends."

"You wanted us to move in with you?"

"Eventually, yes. But at the time, I was just gonna suggest we could spend our weekends here... the three of us, by ourselves. Like I said, I wanted to be more involved... I wanted you to let me in. I thought if we spent some time here, where we could relax and be ourselves, it might work itself out."

"And then I went and ruined it by making all my arrangements with Donavan, and not even asking you... not even thinking you might have plans of your own." Her voice cracks.

"Stop," I say. "It's in the past now, and we're not gonna dwell on it anymore. But if you're okay with it, I'd really like for you and Adam to come live with me. The house is more than big enough, and I know a certain chocolate labrador, who'd be thrilled."

She leans in to me, her arms coming around my waist and, rests her head against my chest.

"Do you know... you're perfect. I really don't think I could ask for anything more."

I pull back just slightly and look down at her upturned face. "Yeah, you could. You can ask for anything you want."

"Can I?" she says, with a tease to her voice.

"Yeah. Anything at all. As long as you're on your knees."

Epilogue

Jemima

"I can't believe you know a multi-millionaire," I say as Oliver parks his Jeep at the front of Max Crawford's enormous house in Lexington, alongside Mason's Mercedes.

"He doesn't act like a millionaire," he replies, giving me a smile. "And besides, it's not just Max. His brother and sister are multi-millionaires too."

"I know you've explained it before, but how exactly are you connected to them?"

"Ronan's sister Eva is married to Chase Crawford."

I nod my head. "It's so much easier when you put names to people."

"Yeah, it is. You'll find it easier still when you can put faces to the names."

He opens the door and climbs out of the car, coming around to my side to help me out, before he opens the one behind and reaches in to get Adam from his seat. Rather than handing him to me, he perches my son on his hip and grabs the diaper bag, slinging it over his shoulder. We've started toilet training at home now, with varying degrees of success, but when we come out, it's simpler to revert to diapers. Adam gets easily confused in strange surroundings and I don't want any accidents today. Not just because we're at the home of a multi-millionaire, but because it's a special occasion.

Today is not only Max Crawford's thirty-ninth birthday, it's also his daughter's first, and as luck would have it, it's Isabel's thirtieth, too. I don't think anyone was aware of the fact that they all share the same birthday until Max's wife sent out invitations to Max's party. Mason then raised the issue that it coincided with Isabel's birthday too, at which point Max declared she had to be part of the celebrations. So, they're having a party here today, for all three of them.

"Come on, Baxter," Oliver says, opening the trunk, and the dog jumps out, sniffing at the ground, before he looks up at Oliver. He waits until we're ready, then he follows, sticking close to Oliver's side, even though the grounds here are extensive and I'm sure he must be desperate to run off and play. I can't believe I ever harbored any doubts about Baxter; he's so well behaved, and he's become Adam's best friend since we moved into the cabin. They're inseparable, and mischievous... and very cute when they fall asleep together, usually with Adam's head resting on Baxter, who often puts a paw around my son, like he's protecting him. Which I know he is, and he would... against anyone.

As for Oliver, he's proved to be the perfect father. He's attentive and kind, and always there when Adam needs him, or when I do. I was absolutely right when I said I couldn't ask for anything more, because I couldn't.

He was wrong about one thing, though. Things did change overnight...

After he'd taken me home and I'd introduced him to Dale, and we'd all eaten the takeout pizza that Oliver ordered, he took me to bed and made me come so hard I struggled not to scream, and I forgot everything, including my name. I forgot all the heartache and pain, all the trouble I'd caused, and I let him pleasure me for hours... and he did. In the end, though, sleep claimed us. Neither of us had slept the night before, so as much as he might have wanted to make love all night, we both needed to rest.

The following morning, we overslept, and got up in a bit of a panic to find that Mom and Dale were already having breakfast, with Adam sitting happily in his high chair at the end of the table.

That was when we sat down, me beside my mom and Oliver next to Dale, and the four of us talked through our plans.

It was obvious Mom was nervous about something, and after a few minutes, it became clear what that 'something' was.

"Do you remember Dale mentioning that she's gonna have to sell her apartment?" Mom said.

"Yeah."

"Well, after she's invested the proceeds in her new business premises, there won't be very much left over for her to find somewhere new, and we want to live together now, so…"

"You want her to move in here?" I said, helping her out.

"Yes. But you and Adam live here too, and so does Oliver most of the time. We can't just…"

"Yeah, you can," Oliver said. "This is your home, Heather, and I've already asked Jemima to come live with me… at the cabin."

Mom's face cleared at that moment, and she turned to me. "Is this true?"

"Yes."

"And is it what you want?"

I reached across the table for Oliver's hand, and he took mine in his, looking into my eyes as I said, "More than anything."

Mom got up then and walked around the table, standing behind Dale. She leaned over, and they hugged, Mom kissing Dale's neck. "This is the perfect solution," she murmured. "You can sell your place and move in here. We can be together."

"I know. And I can take a second look at that warehouse," Dale said, looking up at Mom, who smiled, before returning her gaze to me, across the table.

"I'll still look after Adam for you during the day," she said.

"I'm glad about that, because I don't wanna give up work." I smiled at Oliver, who gave me a slight wink.

"I'd miss him, if he wasn't here," Mom said, glancing down the table toward Adam, who was playing with his toast, rather than eating it.

"He'd miss you too, Mom."

"And he can sleep over here a couple of nights a week, if you like, to give you guys some peace."

"I think we'd appreciate that," Oliver said, raising his eyebrows at me, which made me giggle.

It was then that Adam threw a finger of toast onto the floor, making it clear he'd had enough, and while Mom went to move toward him, I got up myself, noting the look of disappointment in Oliver's eyes.

"I think we'd better get you dressed," I said, lifting Adam from his high chair, and then I waited a moment, until Oliver looked up. "Do you wanna take him?"

"Me?" His surprise was obvious.

"Yes. I haven't finished my toast yet, and you have."

He stood up. "Can I just get this straight? You're asking me to get Adam dressed?"

"Yeah… there are clean jeans and a sweater in the third drawer down."

I tried to make it sound like it meant nothing, but I could tell from the look on Oliver's face that it meant everything, and he came around the table and took Oliver from me, looking down into my eyes. "Thank you," he whispered.

"Don't… I should've done this a long time ago."

He smiled, because we both knew I was right, and then he focused on Adam. "C'mon then, buddy… let's see if we can do this quicker than Mommy, shall we?"

"Trust a man to turn everything into a competition," Mom murmured, and I giggled, watching as Oliver carried Adam from the room.

I feel like I've been giggling ever since.

We didn't wait for Dale's apartment to sell, but she moved in with Mom the next weekend, and Adam and I moved out into Oliver's place… our place, as it is now.

We bought some new nursery furniture and a new high chair, because it made sense to leave Adam's old things at Mom's. He'll be spending a lot of time there still, and once we'd moved things around and got organized, the cabin felt like home straight away. I guess that's because we're a family... so, wherever we are is always gonna be home.

It took a while for Dale to sell her apartment, but it's gone through now and although the original warehouse she was looking to buy had gone, she's now found somewhere even better. It's nearer to Mom's and has a commercial kitchen already installed, which is going to save her a lot of money. She's hoping to get set up there by the end of the month, which will be great, because I know she and Mom have been looking forward to their lives being more settled.

None of that upheaval has affected Adam's routine, though. Oliver and I drive him over to Mom's before we go to work, and then pick him up when we're finished, and bring him home. We take it in turns to cook, or get Adam ready for bed, and then we eat together, and once Adam's asleep, Oliver takes Baxter for a long walk, while I sit out on the porch and watch them. I can't go with them, because we can't both be that far away from the cabin when Adam's sleeping. But I sit, watching one and listening for the other; half way between the two men I love most in this world...

We walk around the side of the huge colonial-style house to find a group of people already gathered, and I'm grateful that at least I know some of them, because otherwise, I think I'd feel a little intimidated.

Mason is the first to notice us, and as we approach, he remarks on us being the last to arrive.

"We had to go over to Heather's to collect Adam," Oliver explains, as everyone gathers around. "He stayed over there last night."

Mason steps forward, giving me a hug, and Isabel follows suit, her bump showing more now.

Oliver's dad is just behind, and he hugs me too, before taking Adam from Oliver. We've spent more time with Oliver's family over the last couple of months, making up for lost time and introducing Adam to everyone. Adam seems to enjoy having a grandfather, and the two of them get along so well, it always brings a smile to my face.

"You come with Grandpa," John says, hugging Adam, although Baxter's keen not to be left out and jumps up wanting attention too, and the three of them wander off toward a couch, which is set against the rear wall of the house, on the huge terrace.

Destiny and Ronan come over next, with hugs and kisses, full of excitement about a dig they're about to embark on, in Wales, of all places.

"I was promised exotic destinations," Destiny says, rolling her eyes with a smile. "And I'm getting Wales."

"Which is very beautiful." Ronan puts his arms around her from behind, holding her close, and she turns to look up into his face. "My old boss has organized this dig, and asked me to go along," he says, before he bends his head and kisses her. She nestles against him for a moment and then he pulls back, looking around. "I guess I should make the introductions…"

He turns slightly, keeping one arm around Destiny, as a striking couple step closer. The woman is blonde with a slim figure, and the man has dark hair and is exceptionally good looking. "This is my sister, Eva," Ronan says. "And her husband Chase."

"Our daughter is behaving herself for once, and is actually asleep," Eva says, with a smile, her British accent taking me by surprise, although I don't know why; she's Ronan's sister, after all. "You'll get to meet her later."

"You'll certainly get to hear her," Chase adds, and we all laugh. "Freya might mean 'noble lady', but she's got a mighty pair of lungs."

"How old is she?" I ask.

"She's coming up for four months," Eva says, looking around. "We've got a son as well. Thomas. He's nearly two. I think he's inside with Tia at the moment. That's Max's daughter from his first marriage." She glances over at Adam, who's still sitting with John. "I imagine your son must be around the same age?"

"He's twenty months. So, close enough."

"We'll have to introduce them later on," she says.

"Knowing Thomas, he'll introduce himself," Chase says, shaking his head with a smile.

They move away slightly, but not completely, and I notice a second couple. This time the woman has a mane of dark hair, which falls in ringlets over her shoulders. She's stunning, and also quite pregnant. Beside her is a giant of a man. He's at least six foot six tall, has close cropped hair and a handsome, chiseled face. He's carrying a little girl, who's got her mother's dark curls, and is wearing a pale blue dress, with a matching ribbon in her hair, and is currently wriggling in her father's arms.

"Willow has just discovered that crawling is the best thing in the world," the man says, explaining his daughter's fidgeting. "And she doesn't like to be held anymore."

"I remember those days," I say, as the woman steps forward and offers her hand.

"I'm Bree," she says, with a smile. "And this is my husband, Colt."

He goes to offer his hand too, but his daughter makes a bid for freedom and he flips her around and holds her above his head. "Oh, no you don't."

"I think we'd better take her out onto the grass and let her crawl around for a while, before she rebels completely."

"Yeah, she's her mother's daughter," Colt says, trying to settle his little girl in his arms, even though she's clearly desperate to get down. "She's a rebel at heart."

Chase laughs as Bree scowls at her husband. "Let's hope her little sister is calmer," she says, placing her hand on her bump. Colt bends down and kisses her gently, and as they move away, she leans in to me. "We'll catch up later," she says, and I nod my head, overwhelmed by how friendly everyone is.

"Ahh… here's the birthday boy," Chase says, as another tall man steps forward. "My brother, Max."

"Thanks for the reminder that I'm a year older," he says.

"Yeah, only one more until you hit forty," Chase jibes and Max narrows his eyes at him, and then turns his attentions to me with a smile. "Don't remind me."

"Happy birthday," I say and then turn back to Isabel, who's still standing to my left. "I'm sorry. I forgot to say that to you too."

"Don't worry. I'm trying my best to forget that I'm thirty."

"Thirty…" Max says wistfully. "That's a distant memory."

"Yeah," Chase replies. "But that's because you're so old."

Max ignores his brother this time and smiles down at me. "I'd introduce you to my wife, Cara, but she's inside at the moment, changing our daughter into her second outfit of the day."

"Is that the prerogative of being the birthday girl?" Oliver asks.

"No. It's because she threw an entire glass of orange juice over herself a few minutes before you arrived. It was Bree's and because we're not used to Sapphire crawling yet, she got hold of it when we weren't looking. I think she was trying to drink it, and failed miserably."

We all laugh and walk further onto the terrace, where I notice there are yet more people – two further couples – who are talking among themselves.

"I'll finish the introductions later," Ronan says in my ear, and I nod my head, feeling a little overwhelmed.

We've been here for nearly an hour now, and I'm halfway through a glass of very nice, chilled white wine. I'm sitting at a table with all the other women, while the men are gathered around the barbecue, beer bottles in their hands. Oliver glances over at me occasionally, and we're both keeping half an eye on Adam, who's playing happily with Thomas and Tia. She's probably about four years old, and seems very well behaved and happy, mothering her two charges. Willow and Sapphire have relented with crawling around and are sitting together on a play mat a few feet away, several toys spread out between them, which they seem to be sharing nicely... for now, at least.

I got to meet Cara, who is very beautiful, with long brown hair that has blonde streaks running through it. I guess she's around the same age as me, as is Eva, and that's quite a relief. When it became clear that today is Max's thirty-ninth birthday, I half expected everyone here to be a lot older than I am. It seems I was wrong, though, and I don't feel out of place at all. In fact, everyone is really friendly.

I've met the other two couples as well. Eli is evidently Chase's bodyguard, and although I hadn't realized it, Colt performs the same role for Max. I'm not sure why they need bodyguards, but I guess when you're worth as much money as these people are, it becomes a necessary part of life. Eli's wife is called Sienna, and after she'd been to the bathroom several times within the first forty-five minutes, she came back and revealed that she's just found out she's pregnant. Eva was particularly thrilled by that piece of news and I gathered they're quite close. The other woman who's here is called Piper. It seems she works for Colt as Tia's bodyguard, and she became a little subdued after Sienna broke her news, and after a while, Cara leans over and asks if she's okay.

"I'm fine," Piper says, glancing over toward her husband; a man called Richard, who Bree informed me earlier on, is a city cop.

"Wanna run that by us again?" Bree says, tilting her head and sipping her orange juice.

"I—It's just that Richard and I have been trying to get pregnant for a while…"

"And it's not happening?" Cara guesses and Piper nods her head.

"I'm so sorry," Sienna says. "If I'd known…"

"It's not your fault. And I'm thrilled for you. Really, I am."

Everyone immediately sits forward, taking an interest.

"Are you seeing anyone?" Bree asks. "Because my gynecologist is fabulous, if you want her number."

"We've been to see a specialist," Piper says. "Colt insisted on paying, because our insurance company refused to cover it."

"He did?" Bree is clearly surprised. "You mean he knew about this?"

"Yeah, but I asked him to keep it to himself, until we knew the test results."

"Which I'm guessing you do?" Eva says, settling her baby girl in her arms.

"Yeah. It's not good." Piper looks down at her hands, which she's got clasped in her lap. "I don't really wanna go into the details, but the problem is with me, not Richard, and it doesn't look like there's much they can do about it." A hush falls over all of us and we wait until she raises her head again. "We're looking into adopting," she says, with a smile that doesn't feel quite genuine.

"It'll happen." Cara leans over, taking one of Piper's hands in hers. "And if you need anything, you just have to ask. You know that, right?"

Piper nods her head, tears forming in her eyes.

At that moment, the men wander over and, as they approach, Bree gets to her feet, struggling slightly. She pushes her chair back and steps closer to Colt, putting her arms around his neck and kissing him deeply, regardless of our presence.

They break the kiss after a while and Colt looks down at her. "What was that for?" he asks with a slight smile.

"It was for being you."

"Okay." He nods. "I'll keep on being me, shall I?"

"Yes."

"I think it was because I've just told everyone about how you paid for Richard and me to visit the specialist," Piper says, and Colt looks over at her, tilting his head. He smiles, just slightly, showing his understanding, as Richard goes to his wife and stands behind her, his hands on her shoulders.

"Which specialist was this?" John asks.

"A guy in the city," Richard explains. "We've been trying to conceive for a year or more, but it seems Piper has a pre-existing condition that makes it almost impossible. That's why our insurance wouldn't cover it."

Piper looks down again, struggling with her emotions, as John walks around the table.

"I wish you'd come to me first," he says, speaking gently.

"You're a surgeon, Dad," Mason says. "Not a gynecologist."

"I know." John looks over at Mason, and then back at Richard and Piper. "But my oldest friend from med school is now one of the foremost gynecologists in the country. He practices out of New York, but if you're willing to travel there, I'm sure he'd see you."

"We… we couldn't afford…"

"If it's a question of money," Max says, stepping forward.

"Don't worry about it." John holds up his hands, looking from Max to Piper. "I'll speak to Charles. He owes me a few favors."

Piper looks up at Richard, taking his hand in hers, before she turns her attention to John. "Could you?" she says. "I—I mean, do you think he'd see us?"

"I know he would. I'll call him on Monday and I'll get back to you. Okay? I'm not guaranteeing he can do anything, you understand. But if anyone can, it'll be Charles."

Richard leans over Piper. "Don't get your hopes up, honey," he whispers.

"I won't," she says. "I just wanna know we tried everything, before we give up."

He nods his head and gently kisses her cheek.

At that moment, I feel Oliver come up behind me, his hand on my shoulder and I tilt my head back, looking up at him.

"You okay?" he says, like there's no-one else here.

"Hmm... just feeling very lucky."

"Me too." He smiles, and I wonder if he's thinking about the same thing as me. I wonder if he's remembering last night. I am. It's not something I'm likely to forget... any more than I'm going to forget how close I came to losing the man I love, and how happy I am that he never gave up on me... or on us.

Oliver

I stare down at Jemima, and although we're surrounded by family and friends, I can't see anyone but her. Sure, I'm aware of Adam, playing a few feet away, with Chase and Eva's son Thomas, but my heart is so full of love for Jemima, it's like nothing else exists.

It's been that way since the moment I met her, but ever since that day back in March, when my brother reminded me how close I'd come to losing her, and that I should never have left her, I've made a point of keeping her close. Not in an insecure or jealous way, because I've got nothing to be insecure or jealous about. I know that now. I just keep her close in a way that lets her know I'm here if she needs me, and in a way that lets her know I need her… all the time.

Her eyes are sparkling and she's got a sexy smile on her lips, and I wonder if she's thinking about last night. I know I am. Because last night was very special. It marked a turning point for us, and I know I'll never forget it.

We had the cabin to ourselves, which is normal for a Friday, since Adam stays with Heather and Dale overnight into Saturday. It gives us an evening to ourselves, and we get the chance to sleep in before we have to pick him up. And because Dale works during the week, she gets to spend some time with Adam too. She really loves him; that much is easy to see, and they have a great time together.

Yesterday evening, we got home at around six-thirty, and I took Baxter for a walk, while Jemima changed into shorts and a t-shirt and made us a chicken salad. It's been really hot over the last few days; much hotter than usual for May, and we sat out on the porch and ate, rather than confining ourselves to being indoors.

Afterwards, once we'd cleared away, we finished the bottle of wine we'd started with dinner, sitting and watching the sunset over the lake.

It was still humid and airless, and I felt the need to cool down, so I stood and turned to Jemima, holding out my hand.

"Wanna come swimming with me?" I said and her eyes lit up, a smile settling on her lips.

"In the lake?" Her voice was hushed, but there was something urgent behind it, and I grinned.

"Yeah. In the lake."

"Should I get a bathing suit?"

"Hell, no."

I hauled her to her feet, which turned her giggle into a yelp, and she followed me down the steps and out to the lakeside, where I pulled off her t-shirt and shorts, her underwear following quickly behind, to make a small pile on the shore. Finally, I stripped off myself, as she stood, gazing at me, her eyes alight, and then I took her hand.

"Kick off your shoes," I said, and she did, before I led her into the chilled water.

"I—It's freezing," she stuttered, hesitating.

"No, it's just cold. And you'll get used to it."

She stared at me and I gave her hand a tug, and after a moment's hesitation, she took another step before stopping again.

"Are you seriously telling me you go swimming in this?" she said.

"Yeah." I let go of her hand and bent down, lifting her into my arms. She squealed, kicking her legs, as I walked us both out into the water, until I was submerged up to my waist.

"Don't you dare," she warned, glaring up at me, just as I dropped her, and she fell with a splash and a scream.

She ducked right under, but righted herself straight away, coming up and lunging at me.

"I hate you, Oliver Gould," she yelled.

"No, you don't." I grabbed her and pulled her close to me, and she calmed in an instant, her hands resting against my bare chest as I leaned in and kissed her.

Within seconds, the atmosphere changed between us and I placed my hands on her ass, pulling her onto me.

"Oh... God," she murmured, breaking the kiss for a moment. "You're so hard."

"I know. I wanna fuck you."

"Here?" she said.

"Yeah. Right here."

She breathed in, her lips trembling, although I'm not sure whether that was from the cold, or from excitement, as she jumped up into my arms and wrapped her legs around me.

"Then fuck me," she whispered, and I raised her up slightly, before settling her down on my cock, that moment of direct contact sparking off every nerve in my body, as realization hit me and I raised her up again, separating us. "What are you doing?" she said, frowning.

"I don't have a condom."

"I don't care. I need you inside me."

313

I leaned back, gazing into her face. "I know, and I need you too, baby. But…"

"I said, I don't care. You told me you wanted us to have kids one day, so why can't that day be now?"

I unwrapped her legs and set her down on the ground, because I needed to concentrate; to be sure.

"Are you saying you want us to have a baby?"

"Yes."

"Now?"

"Well, not this minute," she said. "If memory serves, it takes around nine months."

I cupped her face in my hands. "You know what I mean. And I'm serious, Jem. I need to know. Do you want this?"

"Yes," she said, nodding her head, as though to reassure me. "I want this. I want to have your baby, and I want Adam to have a little brother or sister. Is that clear enough?"

When she put it like that, it was more than clear enough, and I lifted her again, only this time I bent her legs over my arms, reaching beneath her to palm my cock and impale her in one swift movement.

She threw her head back, clinging to my shoulders for support, and let out a loud moan, and as I started to move and take her harder and harder, she begged me for more, pleading with me to go deeper. She felt warm and tight, and as I stood, holding her in the cool water, our bodies highlighted in the silvery twilight, I was overwhelmed with a need for something more. I ground into her, keeping her steady with one hand, while I held onto her head with the other.

"I need you to come. Now," I said, through gritted teeth.

"Then fuck me," she repeated, but this time, she said it like a command.

"You want fucking?"

"Yes," she yelled.

I put both hands on her ass and walked us out of the lake, leaving our clothes and shoes on the shore, and going straight into the house. I ignored the droplets of water we were leaving on the floor, and took her through to the bedroom, lowering us both onto the mattress and shifting her legs up onto my shoulders as I raised myself over her.

"You want this?" I asked. "You want me to come inside you?" I had to be sure, after what her ex had done to her.

"Yes. I want you. I want all of you," she said. "Please, Ollie."

I pushed her hands above her head, holding them there, and pounded into her, taking her harder than ever. She held my gaze, her body surrendering to mine, until I felt her tighten around me, her body tensing, as she let out a wild cry and came apart, thrashing and writhing against me. That was more than I could take, and I buried myself deep inside her and let go, howling out her name as I filled her with everything I had.

It took me a while to recover, but when I did, I released her hands and lowered her legs, and although we were still both wet, I turned us onto our sides.

"I love you," I whispered. "I love you so damn much."

"I love you too."

"And you're really sure?"

She smiled. "I'm really, really sure."

With no condom to dispose of, I stayed inside her, holding her in my arms, and we made love again, more slowly, more tenderly, gazing deep into each other's eyes, our bodies joined. She came twice more before I did, and then we had to change the bedding, because we'd soaked it, and I rescued our clothes from the lake shore, before we fell into bed, sometime around midnight.

We woke this morning, and I think we both knew, without either of us saying a word, that something had changed between us.

We've been in love forever – or at least it feels that way – but knowing that we want to make a new life together makes everything feel different. And after we'd made love again, we dozed in each other's arms, and then woke with a start, remembering we had to get to Heather's to collect Adam, before coming over here for the party.

That didn't stop us from showering together, or from gazing at each other while we dressed, or holding hands all the way to Heather's place.

And, even just now, while I was standing with the guys by the barbecue, and Max was recounting the story of his proposal to Cara, which took place on this very day, one year ago, my eyes kept drifting over to Jemima. When he told us about how Cara had gone into labor almost the moment she'd said 'yes' to him, I knew what I was going to do.

I bought the ring ages ago, not long after Jemima and Adam moved into the cabin with me. I've just been waiting for the perfect moment. Only, as Max told his story, I realized there's no such thing as a 'perfect' moment, and waiting for it was just a waste of time. So, I decided to just seize the opportunity whenever one next came along…

We're sitting around the table, having enjoyed steaks and chicken, and we're surrounded by children playing and happy, smiling faces, and I have to say, I hope it doesn't take too long for Jemima to get pregnant. Because, as much as I'm enjoying getting there, I want a big, happy family, all of our own. I want more of this.

"Can I get down, Mommy?" Tia says to Cara, and for a moment, everyone around the table falls silent.

"Of course," Cara says, smiling, and Tia hops down from her chair, running into the house.

It's impossible not to notice the altered atmosphere, and although I'm not about to say anything, Chase doesn't feel so restrained.

"Tia calls you Mommy now?" he says, and Cara blushes.

"Yeah, she does," Max replies. "She asked if she could, and while we're not gonna let her forget who her real mommy is, we didn't want her to feel different to Sapphire."

Chase nods his head, giving his brother a smile and I feel Jemima move a little closer to me. Neither of us says a word, but I know we're both thinking about the fact that Adam's been calling me 'Dada' for a while now. For several weeks, he continued calling everything and everyone 'Dada', which occasionally resulted in some embarrassing moments. But then he dropped it with everyone else, including Baxter, and now it's a name reserved just for me, and it still makes my heart burst every time he says it.

I glance over at Mason, who's sitting opposite, and he leans into Isabel and they whisper something, before he places his hand on her swollen bump and kisses her, and I have to smile.

"Where are Reagan and Ashley today?" I ask her, and she looks up at me.

"They're at home in Vermont," she says. "They've got exams this week, and they needed to revise."

"No." Mason shakes his head. "They've both got new boyfriends, who they're actually quite serious about, for once."

"That might have something to do with it," Isabel says, with a slight shake of her head. "Although I hope there's some revising going on, too. Reagan's got her finals coming up."

"We're gonna drive up there next weekend," Mason says.

"So you can find out whether they revised?" I ask.

"Yeah. But we're also going because Noah's just come out to his family, and while it wasn't the disaster he feared, it seems it could have gone better. So, we're gonna offer him some moral support… while Isabel checks out her sisters' new boyfriends."

"I'm not gonna check them out." She turns to face him.

"Aren't you?"

"No. My sisters are old enough to make their own decisions, and they'd only resent me if I interfered."

"Would they resent me?" Mason asks.

"If you interfered?" Isabel says, tilting her head and looking confused.

"Yeah. I wanna make sure these guys aren't doing anything they shouldn't."

Isabel purses her lips, trying not to giggle, and while she almost succeeds, I don't, and I burst out laughing. She joins me within moments, as does Jemima, and Mason shakes his head at us.

"If I remember rightly," I say to him, my arm firmly around Jemima's shoulder, "when we were in our early twenties, we were always doing things we shouldn't."

"Yeah, you were," Dad says, joining in our conversation.

"That's what your early twenties are for, isn't it?" Chase says.

"I always thought so," Ronan adds, and Mason looks at all of us. One at a time.

"I know. But I feel kinda responsible for Ash and Reagan."

"And I love you for it," Isabel says.

"What are you gonna be like if you have a daughter of your own?" I say, and Isabel blushes.

"That's not gonna happen," Mason replies. "Not this time around. We found out yesterday we're having a boy. We weren't gonna say anything yet, what with it being everyone's birthday, but…" The smile on his face is infectious and we all offer our congratulations before settling down again.

As the murmur of conversation picks up, I feel Jemima twist slightly and turn to see her looking up into my eyes.

"Can I ask you a question?" she says.

"Sure."

"Did you do a lot of things you shouldn't have done when you were in your early twenties?" Her eyes are alight and I know she's teasing, and I smile down at her.

"Oh, God… yeah."

She bites her bottom lip, just for a moment, and I raise my eyebrows, letting her know what I think of that move. "Well, I'm only in my early twenties, so do you wanna show me some of them later?"

"Show you? No. But I'll do some of them to you, if you ask me nicely."

"Oh…" she says, on a stuttered breath and I lean in, placing my lips beside her ear.

"Feel like getting down on your knees and begging?" I murmur, so only she will hear me. She nods her head and I smile, because I'm fairly sure she won't be the only one on her knees.

"He's finally gone to sleep," Jemima says, coming out into the living room and rolling her eyes. "He's had such a good day, though."

"He enjoyed playing with Thomas, didn't he?"

"Yeah. It's the first time he's really played with anyone his own age."

"Well, I'm sure we can get together with Chase and Eva again."

"Eva and Bree both mentioned something about us all meeting up again soon," she says, coming to sit beside me on the couch. "The kids all had so much fun."

"The grown-ups did too, didn't they?"

She leans against me but twists slightly so she can see me. "Yes, they did. I hadn't realized Cara and Eva were the same age as me."

I turn in my seat, so I can hold her better. "Does it bother you, being so much younger than me?"

She sits up, staring at me. "No. Why?"

I shake my head. "It's nothing."

"No, it's not. You've never brought up the age gap between us before, so why now?"

"It's just something your ex said when I went to get Adam from him."

"And you've kept quiet about it all this time?"

"Well, we've had more important things to think about."

She nods her head. "It obviously bothered you, though."

"It didn't bother me… not as much as when he said you weren't serious about us…"

"Which I've already explained wasn't true."

"I know." I pull her close to me again and kiss her.

"So, tell me, what did Donovan say?" she asks.

"He just wondered what you were doing with someone as old as me, that's all."

She snuggles into me. "I'm being happy, and safe, and loved. That's what I'm doing. They're all things Donavan wouldn't understand. So I wouldn't worry about anything he said."

"Okay. I won't then."

I shift forward and then stand, and although she nearly falls into the space I've created, she manages not to, and I hold out my hand.

"Come outside with me?"

"I'm not going swimming again," she says, shaking her head. "Not that we actually did any swimming. But aside from the fact that you dropped me in the water, and it was freezing cold, Adam might wake up."

"I'm not suggesting we go swimming. Although I didn't hear you complaining about us not swimming last night."

"No, but that's because I was too busy asking you to fuck me." She lowers her voice to a whisper as she says those last few words, and I have to smile at her.

"Hmm… and if I remember rightly, earlier on today, you said you felt like begging."

She smiles, biting her lip and says, "I do," and her choice of words makes me grin, as I take her hands in mine and pull her to her feet.

"C'mon then."

She giggles and lets me pull her outside and down the steps, although she hesitates slightly and tugs me back as I lead her over toward the lake.

"I said I didn't wanna…"

"We're not going swimming. I just wanna go over here." I nod in the direction of the lake and she relents, following me, until I stop, right on its edge. The sun is setting, casting orange and purple shadows over the still water, and I take her hands in mine, facing her, as she glances back at the cabin.

"Coming out here again… it's made me realize something," she says, as I open my mouth to propose.

"What's that?"

"The house. It's not big enough."

"For what?"

"For us to have a baby."

I chuckle. "You're not even pregnant yet… not as far as we know."

"Yes, but we've only got two bedrooms. Adam's and ours."

"Okay." I put my hands on her waist and pull her closer. "I'll speak to Chase, shall I?"

"Why Chase?"

"Because he's a construction engineer. I'm sure he can come over here and give us some advice about how to enlarge this place. It's not like we're short of space, and I don't know about you, but I don't really wanna move. I'd like to bring our kids up by the lake. It's beautiful, and peaceful and quiet. We can teach them to swim, and they can play with Baxter." I look back at the cabin myself. "We've got plenty of options.

We can extend out the back, or go up into the roof space. But before we do that, I guess you're gonna need to decide how many kids you want to have."

She seems surprised. "I—I don't know. It's not something I've thought about."

"Well, why don't we talk to Chase about adding three or four more rooms?"

"Three or four?" she says, startled.

"Yeah."

"You want us to have that many kids?"

"We can have as many as you want. I get that it's not something you can decide on right now. But, if we're gonna have construction work done, I'd rather do it all at once, rather than adding one room at a time. Why don't we build out as far as we can for now, and see what size family we end up with?"

"That sounds perfect." She leans up and kisses me, and because I can't help myself, I deepen the kiss, until we're both breathless, and I have to stop, before I forget why we came out here. "Is this the part where I'm supposed to beg?" Jemima says, sighing and gazing up at me, and rather than answering her, I drop to my knees. "A—Are you begging me?" she says, playfully.

Yes.

"C—Can I just say this?" I'm suddenly nervous, in case I've got this all wrong. What if she doesn't want the same things I do? What if marriage is the last thing on her mind? As she said just now, she's happy. She might not want to change things.

"Okay," she whispers, and I realize I have to say something.

I take a breath, letting it out slowly, to calm myself, and then I look up at her. "Every time I wake up with you, I fall a little more in love, and I wanna keep on falling in love with you for the rest of my life." I reach into my pocket and pull out the dark blue box I've had hidden there since we got back from the party. She gasps and covers her mouth with her hand, which I'm not sure is a good or a bad sign. But I've come this far, and I have to finish. "I want to be your lover. I want to be the father to our children… all of them. And I want to be your husband. And that means I need you to say yes."

She kneels in front of me. "Then ask the question."

"Please… please, will you marry me?"

"Yes," she says, throwing her arms around my neck. "God, yes."

I hold her close, kissing her hard, all my fears and nerves evaporating as I rock us back and forth, my heart bursting with joy.

We break the kiss eventually, and I lean back, opening the blue box and turning it so she can see the solitaire diamond ring inside and she glances up at me.

"I—It's beautiful," she murmurs, and I remove it, placing it on her finger and then raising her hand to my lips, and kissing the ring.

"You're sure? You like it?"

"I love it." She looks up at me. "I love you."

"I love you more."

I change position, sitting down and crossing my legs, before pulling her onto my lap, so she's leaning against me as we gaze across the lake.

"This is so perfect," she whispers.

"It is now."

"Were you nervous?" she asks, turning to look up at me.

"Terrified."

She giggles. "Why?"

"Because I wasn't sure you'd wanna get married. You might have been happy just to live together, rather than changing things."

"Are they gonna change because we're married?" she asks.

"No. I'm still gonna make you beg," I tease, and she shakes her head at me.

"Oh, are you now?"

"Yeah, starting right now."

I stand her up and get to my feet, taking her hand in mine as I lead her back toward the cabin. We gaze at each other the whole time, our eyes never wandering, but as we reach the steps, she stops and looks up at me.

"You know, you got that wrong, don't you?"

"What?"

"Your proposal. You're only supposed to go down on one knee, not two."

I shake my head, lifting her into my arms as I climb the steps. "One knee might be good enough for other people, but not for you."

"Why not?"

"You don't get it, do you?" I stop in the doorway.

"Get what?"

"That nothing is good enough for you. I'm certainly not."

"Yes, you are."

"No. You're my everything, Jem. You're my world. I will crawl over broken glass for you. I'll walk through fire. I'll do anything for you."

"Anything?" she says, with a sparkle in her eyes.

"Yes. Anything."

"Even get on your knees and beg?"

"Yes. Even get on my knees and beg."

"Wanna prove that?" she says, playfully.

"I thought I just did."

She shakes her head. "That wasn't begging. That was asking nicely."

I chuckle. "You want begging, babe. You've got it."

She laughs as I close the door and carry her through to the bedroom, where we both practice our begging skills... very, very quietly.

The End

Thank you for reading *Making your Peace*. I hope you enjoyed it, and if you did I hope you'll take the time to leave a short review.